"Thomas Greanias is a superb writer who knows how to tell a tale with style and substance."
—Nelson DeMille

HANG ON FOR THE PULSE-POUNDING SUSPENSE OF THOMAS GREANIAS'S NATIONAL BESTSELLING *ATLANTIS* THRILLERS!

The truth is down there . . .

RAISING ATLANTIS

A *New York Times* and *USA Today* bestseller
and #1 bestselling eBook

"A roller coaster that will captivate readers of Dan Brown and Michael Crichton, penetrating one of the biggest mysteries of our time."
—*The Washington Post*

"It's a lot like *The Da Vinci Code*, but I like the ending on this one better. . . . A gripping page-turner."
—Sandra Hughes, CBS News

RAISING ATLANTIS and _THE ATLANTIS PROPHECY_
are available from Simon & Schuster Audio and as eBooks

"An enchanting story with an incredible pace."

—*The Boston Globe*

"A wonderfully honed cliff-hanger—an outrageous adventure with a wild dose of the supernatural."

—*Clive Cussler*

"A gripping plot . . . colorful characters . . . and some clean, no-nonsense writing . . . adds to the reading speed and suspense."

—*Chicago Tribune*

"*The DaVinci Code* started the new genre of historical mysteries, but *Raising Atlantis* shines in its own light."

—*Publishers Weekly*

A centuries-old warning holds explosive implications for America's destiny. . . .

THE ATLANTIS PROPHECY

A *New York Times, USA Today*, and
Publishers Weekly bestseller

"Relentlessly action-packed, with tantalizing twists and twirls on every page."

—Steve Berry, *New York Times* bestselling author of
The Charlemagne Pursuit

"Greanias keeps the pace breakneck and the coincidences amazing, sweeping readers right into Conrad's struggle."

—*Publishers Weekly*

"A top-flight thriller."

—Blogcritics.org Books

"Finally, a hero worthy of our admiration! Conrad Yeats is patterned after the suave, debonair agents of the past—with enough emotion to make him lovable. An excellent, intelligent read."

—FreshFiction.com

"This addictively exciting book provides a satisfyingly good read."

—*I Love a Mystery*

THE ATLANTIS LEGACY

THOMAS GREANIAS

POCKET BOOKS
New York London Toronto Sydney

Pocket Books
A Division of Simon & Schuster, Inc.
1230 Avenue of the Americas
New York, NY 10020

This book is a work of fiction. Names, characters, places, and incidents either are products of the author's imagination or are used fictitiously. Any resemblance to actual events or locales or persons, living or dead, is entirely coincidental.

These titles were originally published individually by Pocket Books.

This Pocket Books trade paperback edition June 2009

Manufactured in the United States of America

10 9 8 7 6 5 4 3 2 1

ISBN 978-1-4391-4902-7
ISBN 978-1-4391-6404-4 (ebook)

For Alex & Jake

ACKNOWLEDGMENTS

Thanks to my editor, Emily Bestler, and to Judith Curr, Louise Burke, Sarah Branham, Laura Stern, and the rest of the family at Atria and Pocket. Truly you are publishing's best and brightest. Thank you, Simon Lipskar, for believing in me from the beginning, and thanks to all my friends and fans at @lantisTV and on the Web who first made *Raising Atlantis* a No. 1 bestselling eBook and audiobook.

To those world-class authorities on archaeology and affairs of state who lent me their ears during the research of *Raising Atlantis*—including Kent Weeks, Zahi Hawass, Thomas R. Pickering, and Bill Schniedewind—you all have my deepest respect and gratitude.

Many thanks to certain daughters of Freemasons and Air Force officers, certain syndicated Washington columnists, and certain Congressional and White House officials who made the making of *The Atlantis Prophecy* so much fun. Special thanks to the docents and staff at Mount Vernon, the Library of Congress, the U.S. Capitol, and the National Archives for their generous assistance and outstanding public service; you are a national treasure.

An extra-special thanks to my son, Alex, for his research on Benjamin Banneker and for the example he set during his year as student body president at his elementary school, looking out for the interests not just of his friends and little brother, Jake, but of everyone on the schoolyard. America needs more leaders like you.

Finally, I'd like to thank my wife, Laura. Though the earth give way and the mountains fall into the sea, I will always love you.

THE ATLANTIS LEGACY

RAISING
ATLANTIS

Nothing lasts long under the same form. I have seen what once was solid earth now changed into sea, and lands created out of what was ocean. Ancient anchors have been found on mountaintops.

—-Pythagoras of Samos,
Greek mathematician (c. 582–c. 507 B.C.)

In a polar region there is continual disposition of ice, which is not symmetrically distributed about the pole. The earth's rotation acts on these unsymmetrically deposited masses, and produces centrifugal momentum that is transmitted to the rigid crust of the earth. The constantly increasing centrifugal momentum produced this way will, when it reaches a certain point, produce a movement of the earth's crust over the rest of the earth's body, and this will displace the polar regions toward the equator.

—-Albert Einstein,
U.S. physicist (A.D. 1879–1955)

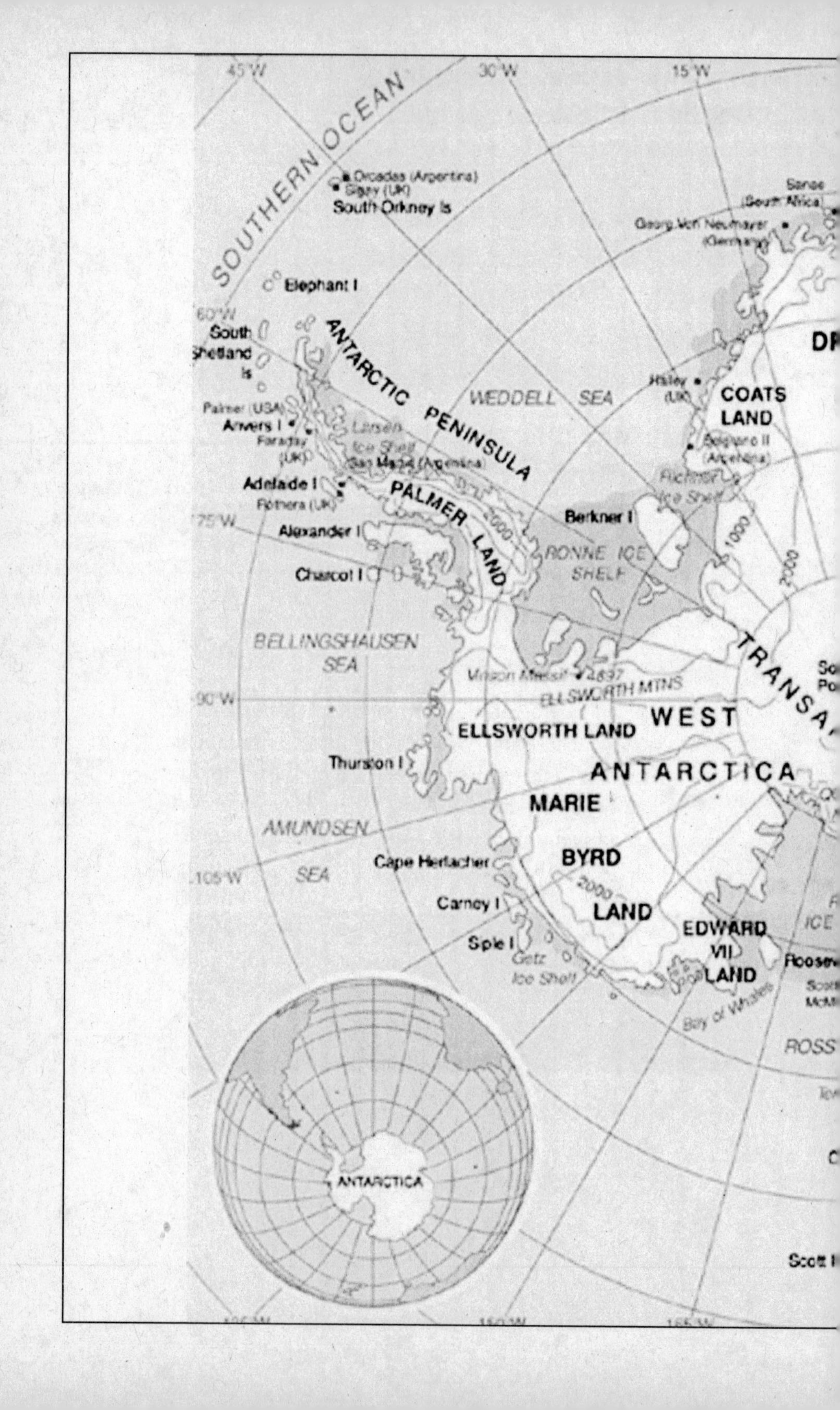

45°W
30°W
15°W
SOUTHERN OCEAN
Orcadas (Argentina)
Signy (UK)
South Orkney Is
Sanae
(South Africa)
Georg Von Neumayer
(Germany)
Elephant I
60°W
South
Shetland
Is
ANTARCTIC PENINSULA
WEDDELL SEA
Halley
(UK)
COATS
LAND
Palmer (USA)
Anvers I
Faraday
(UK)
Larsen
Ice Shelf
San Martin (Argentina)
Belgrano II
(Argentina)
Adelaide I
Rothera (UK)
PALMER LAND
Berkner I
75°W
Alexander I
2000
1000
2000
RONNE ICE
SHELF
Charcot I
BELLINGSHAUSEN
SEA
TRANSA
Vinson Massif 4897
ELLSWORTH MTNS
90°W
WEST
ELLSWORTH LAND
Thurston I
ANTARCTICA
MARIE
AMUNDSEN
BYRD
Cape Herlacher
105°W
SEA
2000
Carney I
LAND
EDWARD
VII
LAND
Siple I
Getz
Ice Shelf
Bay of Whales
ROSS
ANTARCTICA
Scott I

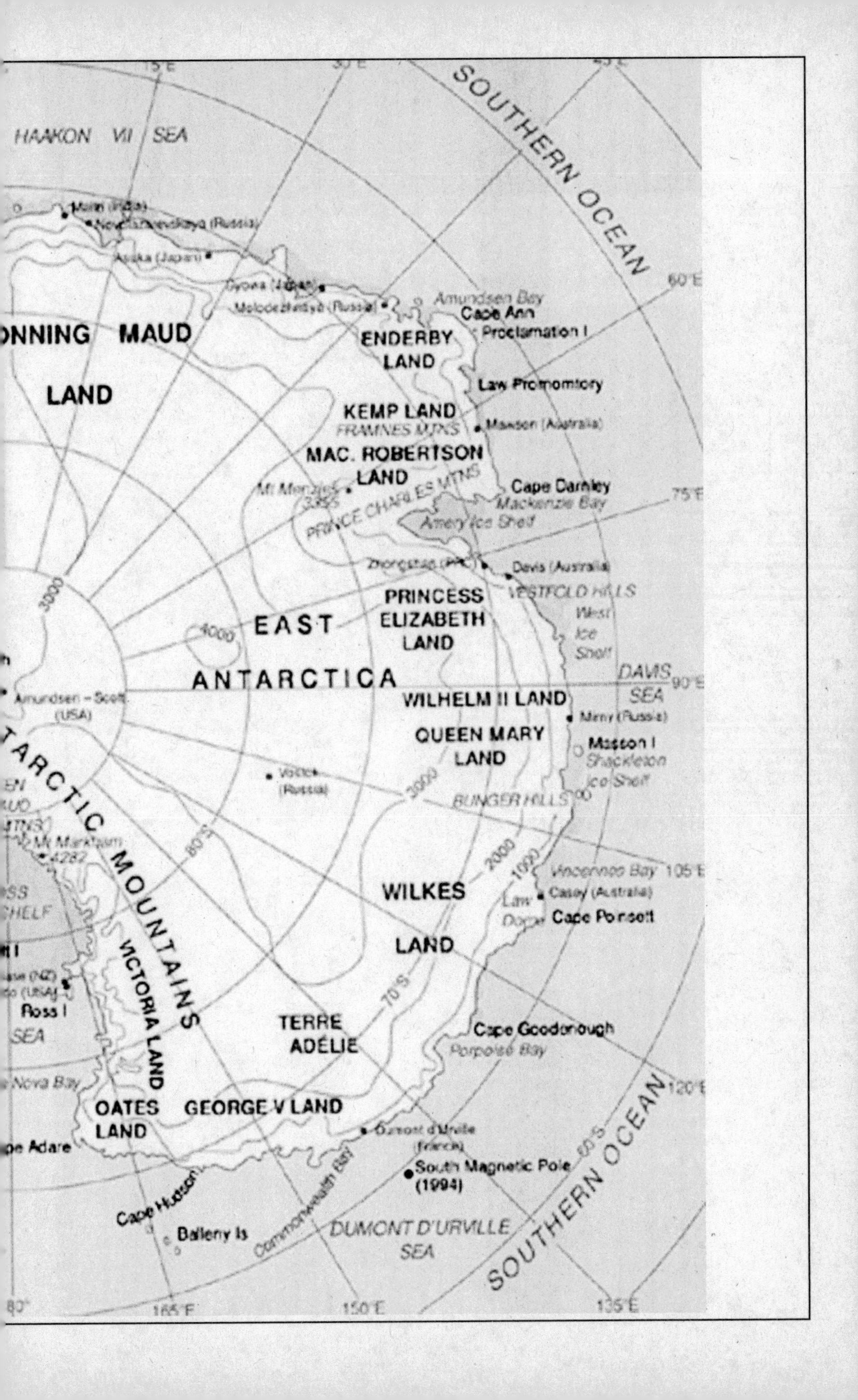

SOUTHERN OCEAN
HAAKON VII SEA
ONNING MAUD
LAND
ENDERBY LAND
Amundsen Bay
Cape Ann
Proclamation I
Law Promontory
KEMP LAND
Mawson (Australia)
MAC. ROBERTSON LAND
PRINCE CHARLES MTNS
Cape Darnley
Mackenzie Bay
Amery Ice Shelf
Davis (Australia)
VESTFOLD HILLS
PRINCESS ELIZABETH LAND
West Ice Shelf
EAST ANTARCTICA
Amundsen – Scott (USA)
DAVIS SEA
WILHELM II LAND
Mirny (Russia)
QUEEN MARY LAND
Masson I
Shackleton Ice Shelf
Vostok (Russia)
BUNGER HILLS
Mt Markham 4282
Vincennes Bay
Casey (Australia)
WILKES LAND
Cape Poinsett
Ross I
VICTORIA LAND
TERRE ADÉLIE
Cape Goodenough
Porpoise Bay
OATES LAND
GEORGE V LAND
Dumont d'Urville (France)
South Magnetic Pole (1994)
Cape Hudson
Balleny Is
Commonwealth Bay
DUMONT D'URVILLE SEA
SOUTHERN OCEAN
60°E
75°E
90°E
105°E
120°E
135°E
150°E
165°E

PART ONE
DISCOVERY

1

DISCOVERY MINUS SIX MINUTES

EAST ANTARCTICA

Lieutenant Commander Terrance Drake of the U.S. Naval Support Force, Antarctica, paced behind a snow dune as he waited for the icy gale to pass. He badly needed to take a leak. But that would mean breaking international law.

Drake shivered as a blast of polar air swept swirling sheets of snow across the stark, forsaken wasteland that seemed to stretch forever. Fantastic snow dunes called *sastrugi* rose into the darkness, casting shadows that looked like craters on an alien moonscape. Earth's "last wilderness" was a cold and forbidding netherworld, he thought, a world man was never meant to inhabit.

Drake moved briskly to keep himself warm. He felt the pressure building in his bladder. The Antarctic Treaty had stringent environmental protection protocols, summed up in the rule: "Nothing is put into the environment." That included pissing on the ice. He had been warned by the nature geeks at the National Science Foundation that the nitrogen shock to the environment could last for thousands of years. Instead he was expected to tear open his food rations and use a bag as a urinal. Unfortunately, he didn't pack rations for reconn patrols.

Drake glanced over his shoulder at several white-domed fiberglass huts in the distance. Officially, the mission of the American "research team" was to investigate unusual seismic activity deep beneath the ice pack. Three weeks earlier the vibes from one of those subglacial temblors had sliced an iceberg the size of Rhode Island off the coast of

East Antarctica. Floating off on ocean currents at about three miles a day, it would take ten years to drift into warmer waters and melt.

Ten years, thought Drake. That's how far away he was from nowhere. Which meant anything could happen out here and nobody would hear him scream. He pushed the thought out of his mind.

When Drake first signed up for duty in Antarctica back at Port Hueneme, California, an old one-armed civilian cook who slopped on the mystery meat in the officers' mess hall had suggested he read biographies of men like Ernest Shackleton, James Cook, John Franklin, and Robert Falcon Scott—Victorian and Edwardian explorers who had trekked to the South Pole for British glory. The cook told him to view this job as a test of endurance, a rite of passage into true manhood. He said a tour in Antarctica would be a love affair—exotic and intoxicating—and that Drake would be changed in some fundamental, almost spiritual way. And just when this hostile paradise had seduced him, he was going to have to leave and hate doing so.

Like hell he would.

From day one he couldn't wait to get off this ice cube. Especially after learning upon his arrival from his subordinates that it was in Antarctica that the old man back in Port Hueneme had lost his arm to frostbite. Everyone in his unit had been duped by the stupid cook.

Now it was too late for Drake to turn back. He couldn't even return to Port Hueneme if he wanted to. The navy had closed its Antarctica training center there shortly after he arrived in this frozen hell. As for the one-armed cook, he was probably spending his government-funded retirement on the beach, whistling at girls in bikinis. Drake, on the other hand, often woke up with blinding headaches and a dry mouth. Night after night the desertlike air sucked the moisture from his body. Each morning he awoke with all the baggage of a heavy night of binge drinking without the benefits of actually having been drunk.

Drake shoved a bulky glove into his pocket and felt the frozen rabbit's foot his fiancée, Loretta, had given him. Soon it would dangle from the rearview mirror of the red Ford Mustang convertible he was going to buy them for their honeymoon, courtesy of his furloughed pay. He was piling it up down here. There simply was no place to blow it. McMurdo Station, the main U.S. outpost in Antarctica, was

1,500 miles away and offered its two hundred winter denizens an ATM, a coffeehouse, two bars, and a male-female ratio of ten-to-one. Real civilization was 2,500 miles away at "Cheech"—Christchurch, New Zealand. It might as well be Mars.

So who on earth was going to see him paint the snow?

Drake paused. The gale had blown over. At the moment, the katabatic winds were dead calm, the silence awesome. But without warning the winds could come up again and gust to a deafening 200 mph. Such was the unpredictable nature of Antarctica's interior snow deserts.

Now was his chance.

Drake unzipped his freezer suit and relieved himself. The nip of the cold stung like an electric socket. Temperatures threatened to plunge to 130° below tonight, at which point exposed flesh would freeze in less than thirty seconds.

Drake counted down from thirty under his foggy breath. At T minus seven seconds he zipped up his pants, said a brief prayer of thanks, and looked up at the heavens. The three belt stars of the Orion constellation twinkled brightly over the barren, icy surface. The "kings of the East," as he called them, were the only witnesses to his dirty deed. Wise men indeed, he thought with a smile, when suddenly he felt the ice rumble faintly beneath his boots before fading away. Another shaker, he realized. Better get the readings.

Drake turned back toward the white domes of the base, his boots crunching in the snow. The domes should have been a regulation yellow or red or green to attract attention. But attention was not what Uncle Sam wanted. Not when the Antarctic Treaty barred military personnel or equipment on the Peace Continent, except for "research purposes."

Drake's unofficial orders were to take a team of NASA scientists deep into the interior of East Antarctica, charted by air but never on foot. They were to follow a course tracking, of all things, the meridian of Orion's Belt. Upon reaching the epicenter of recent quakes and building the base, the NASA team immediately began taking seismic and echo surveys. Then came the drilling. So the "research" had something to do with the subglacial topography of the ancient landmass two miles beneath the ice.

What NASA hoped to find buried down here Drake couldn't imagine, and General Yeats hadn't told him. Nor could he imagine why the team required weapons and regular reconn patrols. The only conceivable threat to the mission was the United Nations Antarctica Commission (UNACOM) team at Vostok Station, a previously abandoned Russian base that had been reactivated a few weeks earlier. But Vostok Station was almost four hundred miles away, ten hours by ground transport. Why NASA should be so concerned about UNACOM was as much a mystery to Drake as what was under the ice.

Whatever was down there had to be at least twelve thousand years old, Drake figured, because he'd read someplace that's how long ice had covered this frozen hell. And it had to be vital to the national security of the United States of America, or Washington wouldn't risk the cloak-and-dagger routine and the resulting international brouhaha if this illegal expedition were exposed.

The command center was a prefab fiberglass dome with various satellite dishes and antennae pointed to the stars. As he approached the dome, Drake set off loud cracking pops when he passed between several of dozens of metal poles placed around the base. The bone-dry Antarctic air turned a human being into a highly charged ball of static electricity.

The warmth generated by thermal heaters placed beneath the banks of high-tech equipment welcomed Drake as he stepped inside the command center. He had barely closed the thermal hatch when his radio officer waved him over.

Drake stomped over to the console, shaking off snow. He discharged his fingers on a grounded metal strip along the console edges. The sparks stung for a second, but it was less painful than inadvertently zapping the computers and frying their data. "What have you got?"

"Our radio-echo surveys may have triggered something." The radio officer tapped his headset. "It's too regular to be a natural phenomenon."

Drake frowned. "On speaker."

The radio officer flicked a switch. A regular, rhythmic rumble filled the room. Drake lowered his parka hood to reveal a tuft of dark hair standing on end. He tapped the console with a thick finger and cocked his ear. The sound was definitely mechanical in nature.

"It's the UNACOMers," Drake concluded. "They're on to us. That's probably their Hagglunds snow tractors we're picking up." Already Drake could picture the impending international flap. Yeats was going to go ballistic. "How far away, Lieutenant?"

"A mile below, sir," the bewildered radio officer replied.

"Below?" Drake glanced at his lieutenant. The humming grew louder.

One of the overhead lights began to swing. Then rumbling shook the ground beneath their feet, like a distant freight train closing in.

"That's not coming from the speaker," Drake yelled. "Lieutenant, raise Washington on the SAT-COM now!"

"I'm trying, sir." The lieutenant flicked a few switches. "They're not responding."

"Try the alternate frequency," Drake insisted.

"Nothing."

Drake heard a crack and looked up. A small chunk of ice from the ceiling was falling. He stepped out of the way. "And the VHF band?"

The lieutenant shook his head. "Radio blackout."

"Damn!" Drake hurried to the weapons rack, removed an insulated M-16 and moved to the door. "Get those satellite uplinks online!"

Drake opened the hatch and burst outside. The rumbling was deafening. Breathing hard, heaving with each long stride, he ran across the ice to the perimeter of the camp and stopped.

Drake raised his M-16 and scanned the horizon through the nightscope. Nothing, just an eerie green aura highlighted by the swirling polar mist. He kept looking, expecting to soon make out the profile of a dozen UNACOM Hagglunds transports. It felt like a hundred of them. Hell, maybe the Russians were moving in with their monster eighty-ton Kharkovchanka tractors.

The ground shook beneath his feet. He glanced down and saw a jagged shadow slither between his boots. He jumped back with a start. It was a crack in the ice, and it was getting bigger.

He swung his M-16 around and tried to outrun the crack back to the command center. There were shouts all around as the tremors brought panicked soldiers tumbling out of their fiberglass igloos. Then, suddenly, the shouts were silenced by a shriek of wind.

Freezing air rushed overhead like a wind tunnel. The katabatic blast knocked Drake off his feet. He slipped and fell flat onto the ice pack, the back of his head slamming the ground so hard and fast that he instantly lost consciousness.

When Drake came to, the winds had stopped. He lay there for several minutes, then lifted his aching, throbbing head and looked out from beneath his snow-dusted parka hood.

The command center was gone, devoured by a black abyss, a huge crescent chasm about a hundred yards wide. The cold was playing tricks on him, he hoped, because he could swear this abyss stretched out across the ice for almost a mile.

Slowly Drake dragged himself toward the scythelike gorge. He had to find out what happened, who had survived and needed medical attention. In the eerie silence he could hear his freezer suit scrape along the ice, his heart pounding as he reached the edge of the abyss.

Drake peered over and aimed a flashlight into the darkness. The beam bathed the glassy blue-white walls of ice with light and worked its way down.

My God, he thought, this hole has to be at least a mile deep.

Then he saw the bodies and what was left of the base. They were on an ice shelf a few hundred yards down. The navy support personnel in their white freezer suits were hard to distinguish from the broken fiberglass and twisted metal. But he could easily pick out the corpses of the civilian scientists clad in multicolored parkas. One of them was lying on a small ice ledge apart from the others. His head was bent at an obscene angle, framed in a halo of blood.

Drake's mind swirled as he took in the remnants of his first command. He had to check the other bodies to see if anyone was still breathing. He had to find some equipment and get help. He had to do something.

"Can anybody hear me?" Drake called out, his voice cracking in the dry air.

He listened and thought he heard chimes. But the sound turned out to be the frozen limbs of his radio officer, clinking like glass as they dangled over smashed equipment.

He shouted into the wind. "Can anybody hear me?"

There was no response, only a low howl whistling across the abyss.

Drake looked closer and saw some sort of structure protruding from the ice. It wasn't fiberglass or metal or anything from the base camp. It was something solid that almost seemed to glow.

What the hell is that? he thought.

An appalling silence fell across the wasteland. Drake knew then with chilling clarity that he was alone.

Desperately he searched for a satellite phone in the debris. If he could just get a message out, let Washington know what had happened. The hope that help was on the way from McMurdo Station or Amundsen-Scott might give him the strength to set up some sort of shelter, to make it through the night.

A sudden gust shrieked. Drake felt the ground give way beneath him, and he gasped as he plunged headlong into the darkness. He landed with a dull thud on his back and heard a sickening snap. He couldn't move his legs. He tried to call for help but could only hear a hard wheezing from his lungs.

Overhead in the heavens, the three belt stars of Orion hovered in indifferent silence. He noticed a peculiar odor, or rather a change in the quality of the air. Drake could feel his heart pumping in some unfamiliar but regular pattern, like he was losing control of his body. Still, he could move his hands.

His fingers crawled along the ice and grasped his flashlight, which was still on. He scanned the darkness, moving the beam across the translucent wall. It took a moment for his eyes to adjust. He couldn't quite make out what he was looking at. They looked like pieces of coal in the ice. Then he realized they were eyes, the eyes of a little girl staring straight at him out of the icy wall.

He stared back at the face for a moment, a low moan forming at the back of his throat when he finally turned his head away. All around him were hundreds of perfectly preserved human beings, frozen in time, their hands reaching out in desperation across the ages.

Drake opened his mouth to scream, but the rumbling started again and a glistening avalanche of ice shards crashed down upon him.

2

DISCOVERY PLUS TWENTY-ONE DAYS

NAZCA, PERU

CONRAD YEATS SCALED THE SIDE of the plateau under the blazing Peruvian sun and looked across the plains of Nazca. The empty, endless desert spread out hundreds of feet below him. He could pick out the gigantic figures of the Condor, Monkey, and Spider etched on the baked expanse that resembled the surface of Mars. The famous Nazca Lines, miles long and thousands of years old, were so enormous that they could be seen only from the air. So could the tiny dust cloud swirling in the distance along the Pan-American Highway. It settled near the van he had parked off to the side. Conrad pulled out his binoculars and focused below. Two military jeeps pulled up to the van and eight armed Peruvian soldiers jumped out to inspect it.

Damn, he thought, how did they know where to find me?

The woman on the opposite line adjusted her backpack and said in a flat French accent, "Trouble, Conrad?"

Conrad glanced at her cynical blue eyes framed by a twenty-four-year-old baby-smooth face. Mercedes, the daughter of a French TV mogul, was his producer on *Ancient Riddles of the Universe* and helped him scout locations.

"Not yet." He put the binoculars away. "And it's Doctor Yeats to you."

She pouted. Her ponytail swung out the back of her Diamondbacks baseball cap like an irritated thoroughbred's tail flicking flies. "Doctor Conrad Yeats, world's greatest expert on megalithic architecture," she intoned like the B-actor announcer for their show.

"Discarded by academia for his brilliant but unorthodox theories about the origins of human civilization." She paused. "Adored by women the world over."

"Just the lunatics," he told her.

Conrad eyed the last ledge beneath the plateau summit. He was stripped to the waist. Strong and muscular, his body had been toughened and tanned from tackling the hills of the world's geographical and political hot spots. His dark hair was too long, and he had it tied back with a strip of leather. His lean thirty-nine-year-old frame and chiseled features made him look tired and hungry, and he was. Tired of life's journey, hungry for answers.

It was his quest for the origins of human civilization—the "Mother Culture" which had birthed the world's most ancient societies—that drove him to the earth's remote corners. His obsession, a nun once told him, was really his quest for the biological parents who had vanished after his birth. Perhaps, he thought, but at least the ancient Nazcans left him more clues.

Conrad grabbed the ledge overhead and gracefully pulled himself onto the summit of the flat plateau. He reached down, took hold of Mercedes's dusty hand and pulled her up to the ledge. She fell on top of him, deliberately, and he sprawled on his back. Her playful eyes lingered on his for a moment before she looked over his shoulder and gasped.

The summit was sheered off and leveled with laserlike precision. It was like a giant runway in the sky over the Nazcan desert, and it afforded breathless views of some of the more famous carvings.

Conrad stood up and brushed off the dust while Mercedes relished the view. He hoped she was taking it all in, because her next vista would be from behind bars unless he figured out some way to elude the Peruvians below.

"You have to admit it, Conrad," she said. "This summit could have been a runway."

Conrad smiled. She was trying to get a rise out of him. Since the carvings could only be seen from the air, some of his wacky archaeologist rivals had suggested that the ancient Nazcans had machines that could fly, and that the particular mount on which he and Mercedes stood was once a landing strip for alien spaceships. He wouldn't mind one showing up about now to take him away from Mercedes and the Peruvians. But he needed her. The show was all he had left to fund his research, and she was his only line of credit.

Conrad said, "I suppose it's not enough for me to suggest that aliens who could travel across the stars probably didn't need airstrips?"

"No."

Conrad sighed. It was hard enough for him to contend with the sands of time, foreign governments, and goofball theories in his quest for the origins of human civilization without ancient astronauts eroding what little respect he had left in the academic community.

At one time Conrad was a groundbreaking, postmodern archaeologist. His deconstructionist philosophy was that ancient ruins weren't nearly so important as the information they conveyed about their builders. Such a stand ran against the self-righteous trend toward "preservation" in archaeology, which in Conrad's mind was code for "tourism" and the dollars it brought. He became a maverick in the press, a source of bitter jealousy among his peers, and a thorn in the side of Near East and South American countries who laid claims to the world's greatest archaeological treasures.

Then one day he unearthed dozens of Israelite dwellings from the thirteenth century B.C. near Luxor in Egypt that offered the first physical proof for the biblical account of the Exodus. But the official position of the Egyptian government was that their ancient forefathers never used Hebrew slaves to build the pyramids. Moreover, only the Egyptian government had the right to announce discoveries to the media. Conrad didn't discuss his find with them before talking to the press, thus violating a contract that every archaeologist working in Egypt had to sign before starting a dig. The head of Egypt's Supreme Council of Antiquities called him "a stupid, lazy jerk" and banned him forever from Egypt.

Suddenly, the tables had turned, and Conrad the iconoclast had become Conrad the preservationist, demanding international protection for his "slave city." By the time Egypt allowed camera crews to the site, however, the crumbling foundations of the Israelite dwellings had been bulldozed into oblivion to make way for a military installation. There was nothing left to preserve, only a story nobody believed and a reputation in tatters.

Now he was worse off than ever. Stripped of his stature. Strapped for cash. In the arms of Mercedes and her crazy reality TV show that peddled entertainment, not archaeology, to the masses. He couldn't go back to Egypt, and soon the same would be said of Peru and Bolivia and a growing number of other countries. Only the hard discovery of humanity's Mother Culture could rescue him from ancient astronauts and this purgatory of cheap documentaries and even cheaper flings.

Concern clouded Mercedes's face. "We could blow a whole day just getting a crew up here for your stand-up," she said, brooding for a moment before her face suddenly brightened. "Much better to stick with an aerial from the Cessna and a voice-over."

Conrad said, "That kind of defeats the purpose, Mercedes."

She shot him a quizzical glance. "What are you talking about?"

"I see it's time we perform a sacred ritual," he told her, taking her hand. "One that will unleash a revelation."

Conrad dropped to his knees, pulling her down next to him. Mercedes's eyes sparkled in expectation. "Do as I do, and behold a great mystery."

Mercedes leaned next to him.

"Dig your fingers into the dirt."

They slowly dug their fingers through the hot, black volcanic pebbles into the cool and moist yellow clay beneath.

"This in your script?" she asked. "It's good."

"Just rub the clay between your fingers."

She did, and then lifted a small clump to her nostrils and smelled it, as if to experience some cosmic epiphany.

"There you go," he told her.

A look of confusion crossed her face. "That's it?"

"Don't you see?" he asked. "This ground is too soft for the landing of wheeled aircraft." He smiled at her in triumph. "So much for your fantasies of ancient astronauts."

He should have known his simple, scientific test wouldn't go over well with her. Her eyes turned into steely blue slits of rage. He had seen the transformation before. That's how she got to where she was in TV, that and her father's money.

"The show needs you, Conrad," she said. "You think differently than others. And you've got credentials. Or had them anyway. You're a twenty-first-century astro-archaeologist, or whatever the hell you are. Don't piss it away. I want to keep you on. But I'm under pressure to deliver ratings. So if you don't play ball, I'll get some toothy celebrity who plays an archaeologist on TV to take your place."

"Meaning?"

"Give the freaks who are watching what they want."

"Ancient astronauts?"

A serene smile broke across her baby face as she adopted a fawning, adoring gaze. He groaned inwardly.

"Professor Yeats," she gushed, wrapping her arms around him and kissing him on the mouth.

Unable to extract himself, or come up for air, he kissed her back contemptuously, feeling her body respond to his own self-hatred. Obviously what the French dramatist Molière said about playwrights applied to archaeologists as well. He was the prostitute here. He started out doing it for himself, then for a few friends and universities. Hell, he might as well get paid for it.

Suddenly the wind picked up and Mercedes's ponytail slapped him across the face. A gleaming metallic object hovered in the sky. He shaded his eyes and recognized the shape of a Black Hawk military chopper fitted with side-mounted machine guns.

Mercedes followed his gaze and frowned. "What is it?"

"Trouble."

Conrad reached behind her and pulled out a Glock 9 mm automatic pistol from her backpack. Mercedes's eyes grew wide. "You sent me through customs with that?"

"Nah, I bought it in Lima the other day." He pulled out a loaded clip from his belt pack and rammed it into the butt of the pistol. He tucked the gun behind his belt. "I'll do the talking."

Mercedes, speechless, nodded.

The chopper descended, the wind from its blades kicking up red dust as it touched down. The door slid open, and six U.S. Special Forces soldiers in field uniforms stepped down onto the summit and secured the area before a lanky young officer in a blue USAF flight suit clanked down the metal steps to the ground and walked up to Conrad.

"Doctor Yeats?" the officer said.

Conrad looked him over. He appeared to be about his own age, a slim, easygoing man Conrad had seen somewhere before. He wore a single black leather glove on his left hand. "Who wants to know?"

"NASA, sir. I'm Commander Lundstrom. I work for your father, General Yeats."

Conrad stiffened. "What does he want?"

"The general needs your opinion on a matter of vital interest to the national security."

"I'm sure he does, Commander, but the national interest and my own are two different things."

"Not this time, Doctor Yeats. I understand you're persona non grata at the University of Arizona. And in case you hadn't noticed, an armed goon squad is climbing up that cliff. You can come with me, or you could spend a few weeks in a Peruvian jail cell."

"So you're saying I can either see my father or go to jail? I'll have to think about it."

"Think about this," Lundstrom said. "Your little friend there might not want to bail you out of jail when she discovers you've been using her to smuggle a stolen Egyptian artifact into the country so you can pawn it off to a wanted South American drug lord."

"Another lie coming out of Luxor. Where did I allegedly find this artifact?"

"The Egyptians say you looted it from the National Museum of Baghdad when the city fell to invading American forces during the Iraq war. They got the Iraqis to confirm it. At least that's what they're telling the Peruvians, Bolivians, and anybody else who will listen."

Conrad tried to muffle his rage at the Egyptians even as he calculated the chances of Mercedes letting him rot in prison. He concluded she'd probably let the guards have a few whacks at him before bailing him out.

"Very nice," Conrad told Lundstrom. "But all the same, I'm going to have to pass up this wonderful opportunity." Conrad offered his hand to wish Lundstrom a hearty good-bye.

But the commander didn't budge. "There's more, Doctor Yeats," he said. "We've found what you've spent your whole life looking for."

Conrad looked him in the eye. "My biological parents?"

"Next best thing. You'll be briefed when we get there."

" 'There' almost got me killed last time, Commander. Look, why don't you find somebody else?"

"We tried." Lundstrom paused, letting the reality sink in that Conrad wasn't at the top of anybody's list these days. "But if her disappearance is any indication, it appears that Dr. Serghetti has already been retained by another organization to investigate this matter."

"Serena?"

Lundstrom nodded.

Conrad's mind raced through a number of scenarios, all of them entirely unpleasant and utterly thrilling at the same time. Just hearing her name made him come alive. And the thought that he and Serena and his father and the distinct worlds each of them inhabited would for the first time collide made him wonder if the space-time continuum could handle it or if the universe itself would explode.

"This isn't going to end well, Commander, is it?"

"Probably not. But General Yeats is waiting."

"Give me a minute."

Conrad turned and walked back to Mercedes, who had been watching the exchange with a furrowed brow, and kissed her. "I'm sorry, baby. But I'm going to have to go."

"Go?" she said. "Go where?"

"To visit a real ancient astronaut."

Conrad reached into her pack again and took out a gold Nineteenth Dynasty Egyptian statuette of Ramses II, who was pharaoh during the alleged Exodus. He had found it in the slave city, and it was the one thing left in his life that proved he wasn't insane. He gave it to Mercedes.

"Now you never knew where this came from, just in case the nice gentlemen coming over the ledge ask you when they escort you back to Lima."

Mercedes's mouth dropped as Conrad and Lundstrom climbed into the Black Hawk. The door shut and the military chopper lifted up and away.

Conrad looked down at the shrinking plateau. By the time he remembered to wave good-bye to Mercedes, the militia men had reached the summit and the chopper was over the side of a mountain.

Conrad turned to Lundstrom. "So what on earth does my father want with me?"

"It's where on earth," said Lundstrom, throwing him a white polar "freezer" suit. "Catch."

3

DISCOVERY
PLUS TWENTY-TWO DAYS

ACEH, INDONESIA
ROME

Dr. Serena Serghetti skimmed across the emerald rice fields at two hundred feet, careful to keep the chopper steady. The sun had burst through the dark clouds, but thunder rumbled across the lush mountainside, and rain threatened.

She was nearing the town of Lhokseumawe in the war-torn corner of Indonesia that used to be known as the Dutch West Indies. There were twenty thousand orphans in the province, casualties of a decades-long struggle between Acehnese separatists and the Indonesian military. Now Al Qaeda terrorists had injected themselves into the mix on the Muslim side, making the situation even more combustible. She had to do something to help these children whom the rest of the world had forgotten.

As she passed over the wetlands, she glanced down and saw the sun glint off the oil slick. A discharge from an oil well in Exxon Mobil's Cluster II had contaminated the local paddy fields, orchards, and shrimp farms. It had happened before, but this leak looked far more threatening. The widows and orphans in the nearby villages of Pu'uk, Nibong Baroh, and Tanjung Krueng Pase would be devastated. They would have to move to another area for at least six months, maybe a year, their sustenance wiped out.

She was about to flick on the onboard remote camera when a voice spoke in her headphone in heavily accented English. "Welcome to Post Thirteen, Sister Serghetti."

She glanced starboard and saw an Indonesian military chopper with side-mounted machine guns keeping pace with her chopper. The voice spoke again. "You are going to land on the helipad in the center of the complex."

She banked to the right and started to climb when four bullets raked the side. "Land immediately," the voice said, "or we'll blow you out of the sky."

She gripped the joystick tightly and dropped lower toward the helipad. She lightly touched down on the platform as soldiers in field greens surrounded her chopper, fingers gripping their M-16s.

They were Kopassus units—Indonesian special forces—based at nearby Camp Rancong, she realized as she stepped out of the chopper with her hands up. Camp Rancong, the site of many reported tortures, was owned by PT Arun, the Indonesian oil giant, which was itself partially owned by Exxon Mobil, which facilitated Post Thirteen.

The wall of Kopassus forces parted as a jeep drove up. It braked to a halt and an officer, a colonel judging by his shoulder boards, stepped out and sauntered over. He was a slim young man in his twenties. Behind him straggled an older, bloated Caucasian civilian, whom by his lethargic and nervous demeanor Serena guessed to be the site's token American oil executive.

"What is the meaning of this?" she demanded.

"The infamous Sister Serghetti," the colonel said in English. "You speak Acehnese like a native but certainly do not look like one. Your pictures in the media don't do your beauty justice. Nor hint of your skills as a pilot."

"I learned on the job, Colonel," she said dryly in her native Australian accent.

"And which job would that be? You seem to have so many of them."

"Dropping food and medical supplies to the poorest of the poor in Africa and Asia because their governments are so corrupt that U.N. shipments rarely make it to their intended villages," she said. "They either disappear or rot on the docks because the roads are impossible to drive."

"Then you're in the wrong place, ma'am," said the American in a southern drawl. "I'm Lou Hackett, the chief executive for this here operation. You should be in East Timor helping the Catholics stand up to Muslims. What the hell are you doing here in a pure Muslim province like Aceh?"

"Documenting human rights abuses, Mr. Hackett," she said. "God loves Muslims and Acehnese separatists too. Maybe even as much as American businessmen."

"Rights abuses? Not here," Mr. Hackett said. He was keenly watching her chopper, now being stripped by a crew of Kopassus technicians.

Serena looked him in the eye. "You mean that's not your oil slick out there soaking the local shrimp farms, Mr. Hackett?"

"I would hardly call an innocent accident a human rights violation."

Mr. Hackett wiped the sweat from his brow with an old, worn handkerchief. Serena had to remind herself that he was an exception to big oil's remarkable progress in recent years.

"So your company didn't build the military barracks here at Post Thirteen where victims of human rights abuses claim to have been interrogated?" she went on, glancing at the Indonesian colonel. "Or provide heavy equipment so the military could dig mass graves for its victims at Sentang Hill and Tengkorak Hill?"

Mr. Hackett looked at her as if she were the problem and not his oil discharge. "What do you want, Sister Serghetti?"

The Indonesian colonel answered for her. "She wants to do to Exxon Mobil and PT Arun what she did to Denok Coffee in East Timor."

"You mean break the grip of a cartel controlled by the Indonesian military and let the people sell their goods at market prices?" she asked. "Hmm, now that's a thought."

Hackett had clearly had enough. "Hell, if the East Timorese want to be slaves for Starbucks, that's their business, Sister. But when you threw the military out of the coffee business, they took a special interest in mine."

"Here's another thought, Sister Serghetti," the colonel said, handing her a sheet of paper. It was a fax. "Leave."

She looked the fax over twice. It was from Bishop Carlos in Jakarta, winner of the 1996 Nobel Peace Prize. It said she was urgently needed in Rome. "The pope wants to see me?"

"The pope, the pontiff, the Holy See, whatever the hell you call him," said Mr. Hackett. "Just call yourself lucky to walk out of here."

She turned toward her chopper in time to see several soldiers carry away the dismantled cameras from its belly.

"And the people of Aceh?" she pressed Mr. Hackett as the colonel nudged her toward his jeep. He was apparently keeping her chopper. "You can't pretend this isn't happening."

"I don't have to pretend anything, Sister," Mr. Hackett said, waving her a smug good-bye. "If it ain't in the news, it ain't happening."

Twenty-four hours later, Serena leaned back in the rear of the unmarked black sedan as old Benito nudged it through the angry protesters and camera crews in Saint Peter's Square. That she could arouse such strong sentiments seemed impossible. And yet the demonstrations outside were meant for her.

She was only twenty-seven, but she had already made a lifetime's worth of enemies in the petroleum, timber, and biomedical industries or anyone who put profit ahead of people, animals, or the environment. But her efforts inadvertently left a few of the people she had hoped to save jobless. Well, maybe more than a few, judging by the mob outside.

Dressed in her trademark urban uniform of an Armani suit and high-top sneakers, she hardly looked the part of a former Carmelite nun. But that was the point. As "Mother Earth" she made headlines, and with recognition came influence. How else would the style-over-substance media, the secular world, and, ultimately, Rome take her seriously?

God was another matter. She wasn't sure what he thought of her, and she wasn't sure she wanted to know.

Serena stared through the rain-streaked window. Vatican police were pushing back the crowds and paparazzi. Then, out of nowhere, *whap!*—there was a loud crack, and she jumped. A protester had managed to slap his placard against the glass: FIND ANOTHER PLANET, MOTHER EARTH.

"I think they miss you, *signorina*," said the driver in his best English.

"They mean well, Benito," she replied, looking at the throngs with compassion. She could have addressed him in Italian, French, German, or a dozen other languages. But she recalled Benito wanted to work on his English. "They're scared. They have families to feed. They need someone to blame for their unemployment. It might as well be me."

"Only you, *signorina,* would bless your enemies."

"There are no enemies, Benito, just misunderstandings."

"Spoken like a true saint," he said as they left the mob at the gate and curved along a winding drive.

"So, Benito, do you know why His Holiness has summoned me to the Eternal City for a private audience?" she asked, casually smoothing her pants, trying to hide the anxiety building inside.

"With you it is always hard to say." Benito smiled in the mirror, revealing a gold tooth. "So much trouble to choose from."

Too true, she thought. When she was a nun, Serena was usually at odds with her superiors, an outcast within her own church. Even the pope, an ally, once told *Newsweek* magazine, "Sister Serghetti is doing what God would do if only he knew the facts." That made good copy, but she knew that no court of public opinion could protect her within these gates.

Born of an illicit affair between a Catholic priest and a housemaid outside Sydney, Serena Serghetti was filled with shame as a little girl. She grew up among sordid whispers and hated her father, who denied his patrimony to the end and died a drunken fraud. She silenced the whispers by pledging sexual purity at age twelve, excelling in her study of linguistics and, most shocking of all, joining a convent at sixteen. Within a few years she had become a living example of redemption to the Church and a walking, talking reminder to humanity of its ecological sins.

It was a good run while it lasted, which was almost seven years. Then, a few months after a personal crisis in South America, she returned to Rome for moral guidance and instead discovered that the Vatican was refusing to pay its water bills, hiding behind its status as a sovereign state and the obscure Lateran Treaty of 1929, which established that Italy must provide water for the 107-acre enclave for free but made no provision for sewage fees. "We neither render unto Caesar the taxes we owe Caesar, nor render unto God the honor we owe God as his stewards of Creation," she said when she publicly renounced her vows and embraced the environment.

It was then that the media dubbed her "Mother Earth." Ever since, she couldn't stop people from addressing her as such, or as "Sister Serghetti." She was probably the world's most famous former nun. Like the late Princess Diana before she died, Serena was no longer part of the church's royal family and yet somehow had become its "Queen of Hearts."

Swiss Guards in crimson uniforms snapped to attention as her sedan pulled up to the entrance of the Governorate. Before Benito could open the door for her and offer her an umbrella, she was already climbing the steps in the rain at a leisurely pace, her sneakers splashing in the puddles as she looked up to the sky and enjoyed feeling a few drops on her face. If her history with the Vatican was any guide, this was probably the last breath of fresh air she'd be enjoying for a while. A guard smiled as she passed through the open door.

It was warm and dry inside, and the young Jesuit waiting for her recognized her instantly. "Sister Serghetti," he said cordially. "This way."

There was the buzz of activity from various offices as she followed the Jesuit down a maze of bureaucratic corridors to an old service elevator. To think it all started with a poor Jewish carpenter, she thought as they stepped inside and the door closed.

She wondered if Jesus would find himself as much a stranger in his church as she did.

She frowned at her reflection in the metal doors of the elevator and smoothed out her lapels. So ironic she should care, she realized, knowing the silk and wool were spun by the sweat of some poor child in a Far East factory to feed the global consumer market. The clothes and the image they projected represented everything she hated, but she used them to raise money and consciousness in a media age more obsessed with a former nun's look than her charity. So be it.

But would Jesus wear Armani?

It was an insane world, and she often wondered why God had either made it that way or had simply allowed it to mutate into such an abomination. She certainly would have managed things differently.

The office she was looking for was on the fifth floor and belonged to the Vatican's intelligence chief, a cardinal named Tucci. It was Tucci who would brief her and escort her to the papal residence for her private audience with the pope. But the cardinal was nowhere to be found. Still, the young Jesuit ushered her inside.

The study seemed older and more elegant than befit Tucci's reputation. Medieval paintings and ancient maps graced the walls rather than the more modern, contemporary art that Tucci was reputed to favor.

Older and more elegant still was the man seated in a high-back leather chair with a pair of seventeenth-century Bleau globes on either side. The white regalia with the gold lace at the throat perfectly offset the silver hair. He looked every bit an urbane, handsome man of the faith, and the eyes, when he glanced up from the file he was reading, were clear and intelligent.

"Sister Serghetti," said her Jesuit escort, "His Holiness."

The pope, whom Serena instantly recognized, needed no introduction. "Your Holiness," she said as the Jesuit closed the door behind her.

The great man seemed neither stern nor beatific to her. Rather, he radiated the businesslike aura of a CEO. Except that this corporation was not traded daily on the exchanges of New York, London, and Tokyo. Nor did it forecast its future growth in terms of quarters, years, or even decades. This enterprise was in its third millennium and measured its progress in terms of eternity.

"Sister Serghetti." The pope's voice conveyed genuine affection as he gestured to a chair. "It's been too long."

Surprised and suspicious, she sank into a leather chair while he looked over her Vatican file.

"Ozone protests outside the United Nations headquarters in New York," he read aloud in a quiet yet resonant voice. "Global boycotts against biomedical companies. Even your Internet home page registers more hits than mine."

He looked up from the file in his lap with quick, bright eyes. "I sometimes wonder if your obsession to save Earth from the human race is motivated by some deeper, inner desire to redeem yourself."

She shifted in her leather seat. It felt hard and uncomfortable. "Redeem me from what, Your Holiness?"

"I was acquainted with your father, you know."

She knew.

"Indeed," the pope went on, "I was the bishop to whom he came for advice upon learning that your mother was pregnant."

This Serena did not know.

"He wanted your mother to have an abortion."

"That doesn't surprise me," she said, scarcely able to contain the bitterness in her voice. "So I take it you advised him not to?"

"I told him that God can make something beautiful even out of the ugliest of circumstances."

"I see."

Serena didn't know if the pope expected her to thank him for saving her life or was simply relating historical events. He was studying her, she could tell. Not with judgment, nor pity. He simply looked curious.

"There's something I've always wanted to ask you, Serena," the pope said, and Serena leaned forward. "Considering the circumstances of your birth, how can you love Jesus?"

"Because of the circumstances surrounding his birth," she replied. "If Jesus was not the one, true Son of God, then he was a bastard and his mother, Mary, a whore. He could have given in to hatred. Instead he chose love, and today the Church calls him Savior."

The pope nodded. "At least you agree the job is taken."

"Indeed, Your Holiness," she replied. "He gave you a pretty good job too."

He smiled. "A job which I'm told you once said you'd like to have someday."

Serena shrugged. "It's overrated."

"True," the pope replied and eyed her keenly, "and rather unattainable for former nuns who have repeated the sins of their fathers."

Suddenly her camera-ready facade crumbled and she felt naked. With this pope, a private audience was more like a therapy session than an inquisition, and she had run out of righteous indignation to prop herself up.

"I'm not sure I understand what His Holiness is getting at," she stammered, wondering just how much the pope knew. Then, remembering the fate of those who so often underestimated him, she decided it was best to come clean before she further embarrassed herself. "There was one close call, Your Holiness," she said. "But you forget I'm no longer a nun nor bound by my vows. You'll be happy to know, however, that I plan to remain celibate until I marry, which I suspect will be never."

The pope said, "But why then did—"

"Just because we did not physically consummate our relationship did not mean we did not emotionally," Serena explained. "And my feelings left me no room for doubt that I could not be a bride of Christ in this life and burn with passion for a man. Not without being a hypocrite like my father. So if you're thinking of using this issue to undermine my credibility—"

"Nonsense," said the pontiff. "Doctor Yeats's name came up in an intelligence report, that's all."

"Conrad?" she asked, awed by the Vatican's operatives.

"Yes," said the pope. "I understand you met him in Bolivia during your former life as our most promising linguist."

She leaned back in her chair. Perhaps a manuscript had turned up that required translation. Perhaps His Holiness had a job for her. She began to breathe easier. She was relieved to escape the subject of her celibacy, but the pope's reference to Conrad had aroused her curiosity.

"That's right. I was working with the Aymara tribe of the Andes."

"An understatement," the pope said. "You used the Aymara language to develop translation software for the Earth Summit at the United Nations. This you accomplished with a personal laptop computer after experts at a dozen European universities using supercomputers failed."

"I wasn't the first," she explained. "A Bolivian mathematician, Ivan Guzman de Rojas, did it in the 1980s. Aymara can be used as an intermediate language for simultaneously translating English into several other languages."

"Six languages only," the pope said. "But you've apparently unlocked a more universal application."

"The only secret to my system is the rigid, logical structure of Aymara itself," she said, her confidence returning in force. "It's ideal for transformation into computer algorithm. Its syntactical rules can be spelled out in the kind of algebraic shorthand that computers understand."

"I find this all quite fascinating," he told her. "As close to hearing the whisperings of God as man may likely get in this life. Whyever did you give it up?"

"I still make a contribution now and then, Your Holiness."

"Indeed, you are quite the freelancer. Not only are you Mother Earth and an official goodwill ambassador for the United Nations, but I see you worked on the *Latinatis Nova et Vetera,*" he said, referring to the Vatican's "new look" Latin dictionary designed by traditionalists to catapult the ancient tongue of Virgil into the new millennium.

"That's right, Your Holiness."

"So we have you to thank for coining the Latin terms for *disco* and *cover girl—caberna discothecaria* and *terioris paginae puello.*"

"Don't forget *pilamalleus super glaciem.*"

The pope had to pause to make the mental translation. "Ice hockey?"

"Very good, Your Holiness."

The pope smiled in spite of himself before growing very serious. "And what do you call a man like Doctor Yeats?"

"A *sordidissimi hominess,*" she said, not skipping a beat. "One of the dregs of society."

The pope nodded sadly. "Is this man the reason why you chose to suppress your gifts, leave the Church, and run off to become Mother Earth?"

"Conrad had nothing to do with my decision to devote my energies to protecting the environment," she said, sounding more defensive than she intended.

The pope nodded. "But you met him while working with the Aymara tribe in Bolivia, shortly before you left the Church. What do you know about him?"

She paused. There was so much she could say. But she would stick with the essentials. "He's a thief and a liar and the greatest, most dangerous archaeologist I've ever met."

"Dangerous?"

"He has no respect for antiquity," she said. "He believes the information gleaned from a discovery is more important than the discovery itself. Consequently, in his haste to uncover a virgin find he will often destroy the integrity of the site, future generations be damned."

The pope nodded. "That would explain why the Egyptian Supreme Council of Antiquities has forbidden him from ever setting foot in Luxor again."

"Actually, the council's director general lost some money to Conrad in a card game when they were consulting on the Luxor Casino in Las Vegas," Serena said. "The way I heard it was that he paid Conrad off with a Nineteenth Dynasty statuette and that Conrad's been trying to unload it on the black market ever since. He needs the money, badly I understand, in order to keep going. It would make a wonderful addition to our collection here if you're interested."

The pope frowned to show he did not appreciate her dry sense of humor. "And I take it the story is the same in Bolivia, where Doctor Yeats was barred a year after your encounter with him?"

Serena shrugged. "Let's just say that he found a certain *generalissimo*'s daughter to be more interesting than the ruins."

"Do I detect a note of jealousy?"

Serena laughed. "There will always be another woman for a schemer like Conrad. The treasures of antiquity, on the other hand, belong to all of us."

"I'm getting a clear picture. Whatever did you see in him, Sister Serghetti, if I may ask?"

"He's the most honest soul I've ever met."

"You said he was a liar."

"That's part of his honesty. What does he have to do with all this?"

"Nothing, really, beyond his effect on you," the pope said, but Serena felt there was more to it than that.

"But what am I to you, Your Holiness, if you'll forgive my asking? I'm no longer a Catholic nun or Vatican linguist or any other official appendage of the Church."

"Be it as a nun or lay specialist we contract with, Serena, you'll always be part of the Church and the Church will always be part of you. Whether you or I like it or not. Right now, our chief interest is in how the Aymara came up with their language. It's so pure that some of your colleagues suspect it didn't just evolve like other languages but was actually constructed from scratch."

She nodded. "An intellectual achievement you'd hardly expect from simple farmers."

"Exactly," said the pope. "Tell me, Sister Serghetti, where did the Aymara come from?"

"The earliest Aymara myth tells of strange events at Lake Titicaca after the Great Flood," she explained. "Strangers attempted to build a city on the lake."

"Tiahuanaco," said the pope, "with its great Temple of the Sun."

"Your Holiness is well informed," Serena said. "The abandoned city is said to have originally been populated by people from 'Aztlan,' the lost island paradise of the Aztecs."

"A lost island paradise. Interesting."

"A common pre-Flood myth, Your Holiness. Many myths speak of the lost island paradise and have a deluge motif. There's the ancient Greek philosopher Plato's account of Atlantis, of course. And the Haida and Sumerian, too, share a similar story of their origins."

The pope nodded. "And yet it's hard to imagine two more different cultures than the Haida and Sumerian, one in the rainy Pacific Northwest of America and the other in the arid desert of Iraq."

"That a common myth of some event is shared by disparate cultures isn't evidence that such an event took place," she said dryly, the academic in her taking over. "Fossil records and geology, for example, tell us there was a flood, an ice age, and the like. But whether there was a Noah who built an ark, and whether he was Asian, African, or Caucasian, is pure speculation. And there's certainly no proof of any island paradise."

"Then what do you make of these similar stories?"

"I've always considered them to be indicators of the universality of the human intellect."

"So to you Genesis is nothing more than a metaphor?"

She had forgotten the pope's habit of turning their every conversation back to her faith. She slowly nodded. "Yes, I suppose so."

"You don't seem so sure."

"Yes, definitely." There, she said it. He had forced her to say it.

"And the Church itself? Just a good idea gone bad?"

"Like all human institutions, the Church on earth is corrupt," she said. "But it's given us hospitals, orphanages, and hope for the human race. Without it civilization would sink into a moral abyss."

"I'm glad to hear you say that." There was tenderness in the pope's eyes and a tone of disbelief in his voice as he asked her, of all people: "Sister Serghetti, I want you to pause and consider whether the Spirit is prompting you in your heart to take on a holy mission that may truly make you worthy of your calling as Mother Earth."

The only thing the Spirit was telling her was that something wasn't right here. She had rebuked the Vatican and left the Church. Now the pope was asking her to be his official emissary. "What sort of mission?"

"I understand you are an official observer and adviser to the implementation of the international Antarctic Treaty."

"I'm an adviser for the Treaty's Committee for Environmental Protection," she explained. "But I represent Australia, Your Holiness, not the Church."

The pope nodded and tapped his fingers on his armrest. "You know those recent news reports about seismic activity in Antarctica?"

"Of course, Your Holiness. A glacier the size of Delaware was sliced off last month after the most recent temblor. And another one the size of Rhode Island broke away before that. In short order it may all add up to the equivalent of the entire eastern seaboard of the United States."

"What if I told you that our intelligence sources have located a secret and illegal American military expedition in Antarctica, in land claimed by your own homeland, Australia?"

"I'd say the Americans are violating the Madrid Protocol of 1991, which established Antarctica as a zone of peace reserved exclusively for scientific research purposes. All military activities are banned from the continent." Serena leaned forward. "How do you know this?"

"Three U.S. spy satellites recently disappeared from orbit," he explained.

She blinked. How long had the Vatican been in the business of tracking foreign spy satellites? "Perhaps they stopped working or were deliberately destroyed," she suggested.

"Dead U.S. satellites are usually left in orbit," the pope explained as easily as if he were discussing New Testament hermeneutics. "And if one satellite, let alone three, had died, congressional overseers would have made more noise than Vatican II. That did not happen."

"I'm afraid we've stepped beyond my area of expertise, Your Holiness," Serena said. "What are you suggesting happened?"

"The satellites were placed into orbits that would move more slowly across the skies than other high-altitude spy cameras, giving them more time to photograph targets."

"Targets?"

"Military strikes are usually mounted immediately before a spy satellite passes overhead, so they can record the damage before the enemy has time to cover it up. But after the latest seismic activity in Antarctica, no known spy satellites would have passed over the affected area. That suggests that one or more of the missing satellites may be watching."

"Are you suggesting the U.S. military is actually causing those seismic shock waves?" she asked.

"That's what I want you to find out."

She sat back in her chair. The pope had no reason to lie to her. But there must be more to this than what he was telling her. Why else would the Holy See take such profound interest in an empty continent populated by more penguins than Catholics?

"Is there something more you want to tell me?" she asked. "Does it involve Doctor Yeats?"

The pope nodded. "He apparently has joined the American expedition in Antarctica."

So it did involve Conrad, she realized, but in an altogether unexpected scenario. "Why would the American military need an archaeologist?"

The pope said nothing, and Serena knew in an instant that the Vatican was enlisting her help as a linguist and not as an environmentalist. All of which meant the Americans had found something in Antarctica. Something that would require the expertise of archaeologists and linguists. Something that had clearly rattled the Vatican. The only reason the pope was reaching out to her was because he had no other choice. The Americans obviously weren't consulting with him. But perhaps they should have, she suddenly realized.

"You have something to show me, don't you, Your Holiness?"

"I do." With gnarled fingers, the pope unfurled a copy of a medieval map across his desk. It was dated 1513. "This was discovered in the old Imperial Palace in Constantinople in 1929. It belonged to a Turkish admiral."

"Admiral Piri Reis," she said. "It's the Piri Reis World Map."

"You recognize it, then." The pope nodded. "So you've undoubtedly seen this too."

He passed across an old U.S. Air Force report. It was dated July 6, 1960, code-named Project Blue Book.

"No, I haven't," she said with interest, picking up the slim report. "Since when does the Vatican have access to classified American military intelligence?"

"This old report?" the pope said. "I'd hardly call it classified. But the addendum is."

She thumbed through the pages, written by the chief of the cartographic section of Westover Air Force Base in Massachusetts. The conclusion of Air Force officials was that the Antarctic portions of the Piri Reis World Map did accurately depict the Princess Martha Coast of Antarctica and the Palmer Peninsula.

Her eyes lingered on the last page, where Lieutenant Colonel Harold Z. Ohlmeyer of the Eighth Reconnaissance Technical Squadron wrote:

> The geographical detail shown in the lower part of the map agrees very remarkably with the results of the seismic profile made across the top of the ice cap by the Swedish-British-Norwegian Antarctic Expedition of 1949. This indicates *the coastline had been mapped before it was covered by the ice cap.* The ice cap in this region is now about a mile thick. We have no idea how the data on this map can be reconciled with the supposed state of geographic knowledge in 1513.

Then came the Pentagon addendum, dated 1970 and handwritten in bold strokes by USAF Colonel Griffin Yeats. She knew that this was

Conrad's father, and it made the hair on her neck stand on end. The note said:

> All future reports regarding Piri Reis World Map and Project Sonchis shall be passed through this office and classified accordingly.

"Sonchis," she repeated, closing the report.

"Any significance?"

"There was an Egyptian priest named Sonchis who allegedly provided Plato with his detailed account of Atlantis."

"Admiral Reis's map states it is based on even earlier source maps going back to the time of Alexander the Great."

"You're saying what exactly, Your Holiness?"

"Only an advanced, worldwide maritime culture that existed more than ten thousand years ago could have created these source maps."

Serena blinked. "You believe that Antarctica is Atlantis?"

"And its secrets are buried under two miles of ice," he said. "What we are dealing with is not just a lost ancient civilization, but the lost Mother Culture your friend Doctor Yeats has been searching for, one possessing scientific knowledge that we have yet to comprehend."

"If this turns out to be real it will throw many things into question," Serena replied, "including the Church's interpretation of the Genesis account in the Bible."

"Or uphold it," the pope said, although he didn't sound hopeful. "But should that be the case, we are all the worse for it."

"You've lost me, Your Holiness."

"God has shown me a prophecy about the end of time," he said. "But I have not revealed it to the Church because it is too terrible to contemplate."

Serena sat on the edge of her seat. Her usual concerns aside, this pope certainly seemed to have control of his senses and be of sound mind. "What did you see, Your Holiness?"

"I saw a beautiful rose frozen in ice," the pope said. "And then the ice cracked, and out of the crack came fire and a war waged by the sons of God against the Church and all mankind. In the end the ice melted and tears rolled off the petals of the rose."

Serena recalled the sixth chapter of Genesis, which said that the "sons of God"—fallen angels, according to church tradition—ruled the Earth in an ancient epoch of time. Their offspring, born of women, did so much evil that God destroyed them and the entire human race in the Great Flood, save for Noah and his family. But Serena also recalled that apocalyptic visions, whether from the Bible or from the mouths of young Portuguese shepherds, do not detail the future in high-definition clarity. Instead they synthesize it and set it against a unified, timeless backdrop of symbols that require interpretation.

"So Your Holiness feels that this vision, the myth of Atlantis, and the current American military activities in Antarctica are altogether one and the same?"

"Yes."

She tried to mask her doubt, but each element alone strained credulity. "I see."

"No, you don't," he said. "Look closer." The pope held a rolled-up parchment in his hand. "This is one of the source maps we believe Admiral Reis used. The map, really."

Serena slowly reached forward and took the map from the pope's hand. As soon as she clutched it in her own, she felt a jolt of anticipation surge through her veins.

"It has Sonchis's name on it," the pope said. "But the rest of the writing is pre-Minoan."

She said, "Give me a few weeks and—"

"I was hoping you could decode it on the way to Antarctica," the pope said. "I have a private jet fueling up on the runway for your journey."

"My journey?" Serena said. "You said it yourself, Your Holiness. This city, if it truly exists, is buried under two miles of ice. It might as well be on Mars."

"The Americans have found it," the pope insisted. "Now you must find them. Before it is too late."

The pope placed one hand on the terrestrial globe to his right and the other on the celestial globe to his left.

"These globes were painted by Dutch master cartographer Willem

Bleau in 1648," he said. "At the time they, too, displayed the 'modern world.' Unfortunately, they depict an entirely wrong version of the planet and the heavens. Look, California is an island."

She looked at the terrestrial globe and saw monsters in the sea. "I'm familiar with Bleau's work, Your Holiness."

"What everybody once thought was true is false," he replied. "A warning that the way we see the world today will probably look equally wrong a few centuries hence. Or a few days."

"A few days?" Serena repeated. "Your prophecy is to be fulfilled within a few days and you have not revealed it to the Church?"

"There are bitter spiritual, political, and military implications, Sister Serghetti," the pope said, continuing to address her as a nun, a member of the family, and not an outsider. "Just consider what would happen should moral anarchy reign on Earth because humanity has cast aside the Judeo-Christian tradition."

"I have, Your Holiness, and that day came a long time ago to the rest of the world outside Rome."

The pope said nothing for an uncomfortable minute. Finally, he cleared his throat and said, "Have you ever wondered why you chose to join such a secure and predictable surrogate family as the Church?"

Serena remained silent. It was a question she took pains to avoid asking herself. The truth was that despite her public differences with it, she believed the Church was the hope of humanity, the only institution that kept an amoral world from spinning out of control.

"Perhaps because as a nun you felt it would be easy for you to be right with God," the pope said. "Perhaps because you desperately needed to know beyond a shadow of a doubt that you were acceptable to him."

The pope was probing so close to the truth that it was almost too unbearable for Serena to remain in the room. She wanted to run away and hide.

"It's not by my good deeds but by God's mercy through Christ's atoning death on the cross that my immortal soul is saved, Your Holiness."

"My point exactly," the pope said. "What more do you hope to add?"

Serena could feel the emptiness inside her like a dull ache. She had no answer for the pope but wanted to say something, anything. "Banishing me to Antarctica to expose the Americans isn't going to—"

"Finally make you worthy of your calling as Mother Earth?" The pope looked at her like a father would his daughter. "Sister Serghetti, I want you to go to nature's 'last wilderness' and find God—away from all this." He gestured to the books and maps and works of art. "Just you and the Creator of the universe. And Doctor Yeats."

4

DISCOVERY PLUS TWENTY-THREE DAYS, SIX HOURS

ICE BASE ORION

THE COMMAND CENTER OF ICE BASE ORION was a low-ceilinged module crammed with consoles and crew members watching their flickering monitors in the shadows. But to Major General Griffin Yeats it was a triumph of Air Force logistics, erected in less than three weeks in the most alien terrain on planet Earth.

"Thirty seconds, General Yeats," said Colonel O'Dell, Yeats's neckless executive officer, from the shadows of his glowing console.

An image of Antarctica hovered on the main screen. The ice-covered continent was an eerie blue from the vantage point of space, a great island surrounded by a world ocean and an outer ring of land-mass, the navel of the Earth.

Yeats stared at the screen incredulously. He had seen that very picture of the Southern Hemisphere once before, from the window of an Apollo spacecraft. That was almost a lifetime ago. Still, some things never changed, and a sense of awe washed over him.

"Satellite in range in fifteen seconds, sir," O'Dell said.

The video image blurred for a moment. Then a gigantic storm cloud jumped into view. Yeats saw what looked like the legs of a spider swirling clockwise around Antarctica. There were twelve of these legs or "strings of pearls"—low-pressure fronts endemic to the region.

"That's one hell of a storm," Yeats said. "Give me the specs."

"Looks like we've got four separate storms merging into a double-low, sir," O'Dell reported. "Almost four thousand miles wide. Big enough to cover the entire United States."

Yeats nodded. "I want the runway cleared again."

The room got quiet, only the low hum and soft beeps of the computers and monitors. Yeats was aware of the stares of his officers.

O'Dell cleared his throat. "Sir, we should warn six-nine-six."

"Negative. I want radio blackout."

"But, sir, your—Doctor Yeats is on board."

"We've got forty men on that transport, Colonel. And a fine pilot in Commander Lundstrom. No transmissions. Buzz me on their approach."

"Yes, sir," said O'Dell with a salute as Yeats marched out of the command center.

The floor-to-ceiling window in General Yeats's quarters framed the yawning ice gorge outside, offering him a skybox seat of the excavation. Pillars of bluish, crystal plumes billowed out of the abyss. And at the bottom was everything he and Conrad had been searching for.

Yeats poured himself a Jack Daniel's and sat down behind his desk. He hurt like hell and wanted to howl like the katabatic winds outside. But he couldn't afford to let O'Dell or the others see him at less than his best.

He propped his right boot on the desk and pulled his pant leg back to reveal a scarred and disfigured limb, his parting gift from his first mission to this frozen hell more than thirty-five years ago. The pain throbbed a few inches below the knee. Goddamn tricks the cold played on him down here.

But damn if it didn't feel good to be in charge again, he thought, catching a dim reflection of himself in the reinforced plexiglass window. Even now, in his sixties, he still cut a commanding figure. Most of the baby faces on the base had no idea who he used to be way back when. Or, rather, who he was supposed to have been.

Griffin Yeats should have been the first man on Mars.

The *Gemini* and *Apollo* space veteran had been tapped for the job in 1968. The Mars shuttle, as originally formulated by rocket pioneer Wernher von Braun in 1953 and later revised by NASA planners, was scheduled to depart the American space station Freedom on November 12, 1981, reach the red planet on August 9, 1982, and return to Earth one year later.

If only politics were as predictable as the orbit of the planets.

By 1969 the war in Vietnam had sapped the federal budget, and the moon landing had temporarily satiated Americans' appetite for space exploration. With congressional opposition to the mission mounting, President Nixon rejected the Mars mission and space station program. Only the space shuttle would get the green light. It was a catastrophic decision that set the Mars program back for decades, left the space shuttle all dressed up with no place to go, and cast a rudderless NASA adrift in the political backwaters of Washington without a clear vision.

It also killed Yeats's dreams of greatness.

The desk console buzzed and broke Yeats's trance. It was O'Dell in the command center. "Sir, we think we've picked them up on radar. Twenty minutes to landing."

"Where are we with the runway?"

"Clearing it now, sir, but the storm—"

"No excuses, Colonel. I'll be there in a minute. You better have an update."

Yeats took another shot of whiskey and stared outside. At the time Nixon decided to scrap the Mars mission, Yeats was here in Antarctica, in the middle of a forty-day stay in a habitat specifically designed to simulate the first Martian landing. They were a crew of four supported by two Mars landing modules, a nuclear power plant, and a rover for exploring the surrounding territory.

Antarctica was as cold as Mars, and nearly as windy. Its snowstorms packed the same kind of punch as Martian dust storms. Most of all, the continent was almost as remote as the red planet, and in utter isolation a crew member's true character would reveal itself.

For Yeats it was an experience that would forever change his life, in ways he never imagined. Four men walked into that mission. Only one limped out alive. But to what? To roam the subbasement corridors of the Pentagon as a creaky relic of the old space program? To raise an orphaned boy? To lose his wife and daughters as a result? Everything had been taken away from him.

Today he was taking it back.

5
DISCOVERY PLUS TWENTY-THREE DAYS

IT WAS FREEZING IN THE FUSELAGE of the C-130 Hercules transport when Conrad woke with a start. Groggy and sore, he rubbed his eyes. He was strapped in with two dozen Special Forces commandos sporting polar freezer suits and insulated M-16s.

He felt another jolt. For most of the flight they had soared through clear skies and over endless white. But now they were floating in some murky soup, and the turbulence grew worse by the second. The giant cargo containers in the rear shifted, straining their creaky tie-downs with each shock.

Conrad glanced at his multisensor GPS watch, which used a network of twenty-seven satellites to pinpoint his location anywhere on the globe and was accurate to within a hundred feet. But the past sixteen hours aboard various military craft must have chewed up the lithium batteries, because the longitudinal and latitudinal display was blanked out. The built-in compass, however, spun wildly—NE, SE, SW, NW. They must be nearing a polar region, he realized, most likely the South Pole.

He turned to the stone-faced commando sitting next to him and shouted above the whine of the turboprop engines, "I thought military personnel were banned from Antarctica."

The commando checked his M-16, stared ahead, and replied, "What military personnel, sir?"

Conrad groaned. This was precisely the sort of bullshit he had to put up with his entire life as the son of Griffin Yeats, a washed-out

NASA astronaut who had somehow managed to march through the shadowy corridors of power at the Pentagon to become an Air Force general. Yeats firmly believed that truth should be divulged strictly on a "need to know" basis, starting with the circumstances surrounding Conrad's birth.

According to Yeats's official version of events, Conrad was allegedly the product of a one-night tryst between a Captain Rick Conrad and a nameless Daytona Beach stripper. When Captain Conrad died in Antarctica during a training mission, the woman dropped off their bastard child at the doorstep of the Cape Canaveral infirmary. A short time later she herself died of a drug overdose. NASA, eager to maintain the squeaky clean image of its astronauts, was only too eager to cut the red tape and let Captain Conrad's commanding officer and best friend, Major Griffin Yeats, adopt him.

Growing up, however, Conrad began to doubt the veracity of Yeats's story. His stepmother, Denise, certainly did. From the beginning she suspected that Yeats was Conrad's biological father and that he used Captain Conrad's death as a convenient cover to explain the birth of his own illegitimate son. No wonder she divorced Yeats when Conrad was eight and moved away with her daughters, ages eleven and nine, the only friends Conrad had.

Finally, after years of base hopping and misery, Conrad had become enough of a rebel to have been tossed out of several schools and to confront Yeats. Not only did Yeats deny everything, but he refused to use his government contacts to help Conrad decisively identify his biological parents. That alone gave Conrad all the reason he needed to hate the man.

But by then it was obvious that General Yeats didn't really seem to care what Conrad or anybody else thought of him. Despite his failed career as an astronaut, Yeats went from one promotion to another until he finally got his star, and with it command of the Pentagon's mysterious Defense Advanced Research Projects Agency, or DARPA. Thanks to the financial backing of the Reagan administration throughout the 1980s, Yeats and his team of extremist military planners invented the Internet, the global positioning system, stealth technology, and the computer mouse, among "other things."

This mission, Conrad concluded, no doubt fell into the latter category of "other things." But what, specifically? Conrad had long suspected that a fabulous discovery lay under the ice in Antarctica. After all, East Antarctica was an ancient continent and at one time tropical. Yeats had obviously found something and needed him. Or maybe this was merely a sorry attempt at some sort of father-son reconciliation.

Two big turbo jolts brought Conrad back to the freezing fuselage of the C-130. Without asking permission, he unbuckled his strap and stumbled toward the cockpit, grabbing an occasional strut in the fuselage for support.

The glass flight deck was deceptively bright and airy. Conrad could see nothing but white beyond the windshield. Lundstrom sat in the pilot's seat, barking at his copilot and navigator. But the engines were whining so loudly that Conrad couldn't catch what he said.

Conrad shouted, "Could I at least see this phenomenal discovery before you kill me?"

Lundstrom definitely looked annoyed when he glanced back at him over his shoulder. "Get back to your seat, Doctor Yeats. Everything's under control."

But the pilot's eyes betrayed his anxiety, and suddenly Conrad knew where he had seen him before. Until four years ago, Conrad recalled, Lundstrom had been a space shuttle commander. His leather glove, now tightly gripped around the steering column, disguised a hand that had been badly burned and disfigured along with a third of his body in an explosion on the launch pad before his aborted third mission.

Conrad said, "Come on, Lundstrom, riding the space shuttle couldn't have been this bumpy."

Lundstrom said nothing and returned his attention to the steering column.

Conrad scanned the weather radar and saw four swirling storms converging into a double-low.

"We're flying into that?"

"We're going to slip between the back side of one low and the front side of the other before they merge," Lundstrom said. "McMurdo advises us that back side winds of the first low won't exceed a hundred knots. Then we ride the front side of the other low, tailwinds of about a hundred and twenty knots pushing us downhill all the way to the ice."

"In one piece?" McMurdo, Conrad knew, was the largest American station on the continent. "I thought McMurdo had a big airstrip. Why can't we land there and try again here tomorrow? What's the rush?"

"Our window is closing fast." Lundstrom tapped the radar screen. "Tomorrow those two lows will have merged into one big nasty mother. Now get back to your seat."

Conrad took a seat behind the navigator. "I am."

Lundstrom glanced at his copilot. Conrad could see their reflections in the windshield. Apparently they had decided he might as well stay.

Lundstrom said, "Your file warned us that you were trouble. Like father, like son, I suppose."

"He's not my real father, I'm not his real son." At least at this moment Conrad hoped not. Like most Americans he had suspected the existence of a database with information about him somewhere in Washington. Now Lundstrom had confirmed it. "Or wasn't that information in my file?"

"That along with some psychiatric evaluations," Lundstrom said, obviously enjoying this exercise at Conrad's expense. "Nightmares about the end of the world. No memories before the age of five. You were one screwed-up kid."

"Guess you missed the joys of being breastfed milk tainted with LSD and other hallucinogens," Conrad said. "Or having full-blown flashbacks when you were six. Or kicking the asses of little Air Force brats who said you were a screwed-up kid."

Lundstrom grew quiet for a moment, busying himself with the controls.

But Conrad's interest was piqued. "What else does my file say?"

"Some shit you pulled the first time we went to war with Iraq in the 1990s."

Conrad was still in grad school back then. "Ancient history."

"That's what I heard," said Lundstrom. "Something about Soviet MiGs and the Ziggurat at Ur."

Conrad nodded. Four thousand years ago Ur was the capital of

Sumer in the land of Abraham. Today it was buried in the sands of modern-day Iraq. "Something like that."

"Like what?" Lundstrom seemed genuinely curious. Apparently Conrad's file didn't include everything.

"The Iraqis had a nasty habit of building military installations next to archaeological treasures as shields for protection," Conrad said. "So when U.S. satellites detected two Soviet MiG-21 attack jets next to the ruins of the ancient Ziggurat at Ur, the Pentagon concluded the Iraqis were parking the MiGs there to avoid bombing."

Lundstrom nodded. "I remember hearing that."

"Well, they also suspected Hussein himself was holed up inside the ziggurat," Conrad went on. "So I gave them the targeting information they needed to launch a Maverick missile at the site."

"A Maverick? That was first-generation bunker buster. You're shitting me."

"Only a Maverick could burrow its way beneath the pyramid and destroy it from the inside out and make the explosion look like an Iraqi mishap."

"So you'd wipe an eternal treasure from the face of the earth just to kill some *despot du jour*?" Lundstrom actually seemed shocked. "What the hell kind of archaeologist are you?"

"The kind you nice people apparently need," Conrad said. "So now why don't you tell me—"

Suddenly a throbbing whine alerted the crew. Lundstrom gripped the controls. The copilot checked his instruments.

The navigator shouted, "Side winds at two-fifty G have shifted around to eighty G!"

"Wind sheer," said Lundstrom, adjusting the yoke. "Damn, she's stiff. Looks like we found the jet stream."

Conrad braced himself against his seat as the plane hit heavy turbulence and the gyros began to wander and go wild.

"Gyro's tumbling," called the navigator.

Lundstrom shouted, "Give me a celestial fix."

The navigator swung to the overhead bubble sextant that protruded out the topside skin of the plane and tried to read their location from the stars. But he shook his head. "Soup's too thick to extrapolate a reading."

"Ever heard of GPS?" Conrad shouted over the din.

"Useless with the EMP."

Electromagnetic pulse? thought Conrad. Those kind of microwaves, generated by small explosions of the nuclear variety, had a tendency to knock out all sophisticated technological gear. That explained why they were flying in such an old crate. What the hell was Yeats doing down there on the ice?

Conrad said, "What about a goddamn Doppler navigation system?"

"Negative."

"Listen to me, Lundstrom. We have to radio the tower at McMurdo for help. How far away are we?"

"You don't get it, Conrad," said Lundstrom. "We're not landing at McMurdo. Our designated landing site is elsewhere."

"Wherever 'elsewhere' is, we're not going to make it, Lundstrom," he said. "You've got to change course for McMurdo."

"Too late," said Lundstrom. "We passed our point of safe return. We're committed."

"Or should be," said Conrad, "along with Yeats and your whole sorry bunch in Washington."

The navigator shouted, "Headwinds skyrocketing—a hundred knots! Ground speed dropping fast—a hundred fifty knots!"

The plane's four engines strained to push against the headwinds. Conrad could feel the resistance in the vibrations in the floor beneath his boots. The turbulence rose through his legs like coils of unbridled energy until his insides seemed to melt. For a dead man he felt very much alive and wanted to stay that way.

"Keep this up and we'll be flying backward," he grumbled.

"Headwinds a hundred seventy-five knots," the navigator shouted. "Two hundred! Two twenty-five!"

Lundstrom paused a moment and apparently considered a new strategy. "Cut and feather numbers one and four."

"Copy," said the engineer, shutting down two engines.

"Ground speed still dropping," said the navigator, sounding desperate. "Fuel's almost spent."

Conrad said, "What about an emergency landing on the ice pack?"

"Possible," said Lundstrom. "But this is a wheeled bird. Not a ski bird."

"Belly land her!" Conrad shouted.

"Negative," said Lundstrom. "In that stew downstairs we'd probably cream into the side of a berg."

Another side wind blast hit them so hard that Conrad thought the plane would tip over on its back and spiral down to the ice. Somehow Lundstrom managed to keep her level.

"You've got to do something," Conrad shouted. "Jettison the cargo!"

"General Yeats would sooner jettison us."

"Then we have to radio for help."

"Negative. We have radio blackout. Radio's useless."

Conrad didn't believe him. "Bullshit. This is a black ops mission. There's no goddamn radio blackout. Yeats just wants to keep this quiet." Conrad slipped behind the radio and tried to put on a headset. But the shaking made it difficult.

"What do you think you're doing?" Lundstrom demanded.

Conrad slipped the headset on. "Calling for help."

Conrad heard a click near his ear. But it wasn't the headset. It was the sliding of a sidearm receiver. He turned to see Lundstrom pointing a Glock 9 mm automatic pistol at his head. Conrad recognized it as his own, which he was relieved of upon boarding the chopper back in Peru. "Get your ass back in your seat, Doctor Conrad."

"I'm in my seat." Conrad flicked on the radio switch. A low hum crackled. "You can't kill me. You need me, Lundstrom. God knows why, but you do. And you better put my gun away. It's been known to go off accidentally. If this ride gets any bumpier you might miss my head and put a hole through the windshield."

Lundstrom looked outside at the raging skies. "Damn you, Conrad."

Conrad leaned over the radio microphone, aware of the barrel of the pistol wavering behind his head as he adjusted the frequency. "What's our call sign and frequency?"

Lundstrom hesitated. Then a huge jolt almost ejected him out of his seat. Lundstrom lowered the pistol as the turbulence rocked the cockpit. "We're six-nine-six, Conrad," Lundstrom shouted, reaching over to adjust the frequency.

Conrad clicked on the radio microphone. "This is six-nine-sixer. Requesting emergency assistance."

There was no response.

"This is six-nine-sixer," Conrad repeated. "Requesting emergency assistance."

Again, no response.

"Look!" shouted the navigator. "Ice Base Orion."

"Ice Base Orion?" Conrad repeated.

The mist parted for a moment, opening a window onto the wasteland below. A panorama of mountains poked up out of the ice, filling the entire horizon as far as Conrad could see. The flanks of jagged peaks dribbled whipped-cream snow into the bottom of a great valley marked by a black crescent-shaped crack in the ice. Perched on the concave side of the crack was a human settlement of domes, sheds, and towers. Conrad saw it flash by before they were swallowed up by the mist again.

"This is it?" Conrad asked.

Lundstrom nodded. "If only we can find the strip."

"The strip?" asked Conrad when a thunderous bolt of turbulence almost knocked him out of his chair. If he hadn't strapped himself in, he realized, his head would now be part of the instrument panel.

"The runway," Lundstrom explained. "Bulldozed out of the ice."

"We're making a white-on-white approach?" Conrad stared at the swirling snow outside the flight deck windshield. Strobe lights and boundary flares were useless against the glare of a whiteout. With the sky overcast, there were no shadows and no horizons. And flying over a uniformly white surface makes it impossible to judge height or distance. Even birds crash into the snow. "You guys are borderline lunatic."

The radio crackled.

"Six-nine-sixer, this is Tower." A gruff, monotone voice came in. "Repeat. This is Tower calling six-nine-sixer."

"This is six-nine-sixer," said Lundstrom, grabbing the microphone. "Go ahead, Tower."

The controller on the other end said, "Winds fifteen cross and gusting to forty knots, visibility zero-zero."

Conrad could tell Lundstrom was doing the math, wondering whether to go for it or go into holding and pray for a miracle.

"Winds shifting to dead cross, gusting to sixty knots, sir," shouted the navigator.

Conrad grabbed the microphone back. "Trying to land this tin crate on a giant ice cube is suicide and you know it."

"Search-and-rescue teams standing by," the controller said. "Over."

Conrad looked hard into the mist as Lundstrom brought them in. Visibility was nil in the fog and blowing snow. Suddenly the curtain parted again and a row of black steel drums appeared on approach dead ahead. The strip itself was marked in Day-Glo signboards.

"We're coming in too low," he said.

"Commence letdown," Lundstrom ordered.

The copilot gently throttled back, working to keep the props in sync.

The radio popped. "Begin your final descent at the word 'now,' " the controller instructed.

"Copy."

"You are right on the glide slope."

"Copy," said Lundstrom when a nerve-wracking dip shook the plane from front to back. Conrad tightened the straps of his seat harness and held his breath.

"You are now below the glide slope," the controller warned. "Decrease your rate of descent and steer two degrees left."

"Copy." Lundstrom gently tugged the steering column and Conrad could feel the C-130 level off.

"You are now back on the glide slope," the controller said. "Coming right down the pike at two miles to touchdown . . ."

Conrad could still see nothing out the windshield but a white wall.

". . . right on at one mile to touchdown . . .

". . . right on at one-half mile . . .

". . . one-quarter mile . . .

". . . touchdown."

Conrad and Lundstrom stared at each other. They were still floating.

"Tower?" repeated Lundstrom.

An eternity of silence followed, then a slamming crunch. The commandos toppled like dominos over one another and then dangled weightlessly from their weblike seats. The tie-downs in the rear snapped apart and the cargo shifted forward.

Conrad heard the crack and looked back to see several metal containers fly through the main cabin toward the cockpit. He ducked as something whizzed past his ear and struck Lundstrom in the head, driving the pilot's skull into the controls.

Conrad reached for the steering column just as the ice pack smashed through the windshield and everything collapsed into darkness.

6
DISCOVERY PLUS TWENTY-THREE DAYS, SEVEN HOURS

It was the bleeping sound of the C-130's homing beacon that finally brought Conrad back to consciousness. He blinked his eyes open to a flurry of snow. Slowly the picture came into focus. Through the broken fuselage he could see pieces of the transport scattered across the ice sheet.

He glanced at Lundstrom. The pilot's eyes were frozen open in terror, his mouth gaping in a fixed scream. Then Conrad saw a metal shard protruding from Lundstrom's skull. He must have died on impact.

Conrad swallowed hard and gasped for breath. The Antarctic air seemed to rush inside and freeze his lungs. He felt punchy, light-headed. This is no good, he told himself, no good at all. His internal, core temperature was dropping. Hypothermia was setting in. Soon he'd lose consciousness and his heart would stop unless he took action.

He fumbled for his seat buckle, but his fingers wouldn't move. He glanced down. His right hand was frozen to the seat. His fingertips were white with frostbite. He knew that meant the blood vessels had contracted and the tissue was slowly dying.

Conrad surveyed the cockpit, trying not to panic. Using his numb but gloved left hand, he grasped a thermos from behind Lundstrom's corpse. He worked it until the top popped open. Then he poured the hot coffee over his right hand, watching a cloud of steam rise over his sizzling hand as he peeled it away from the chair. He looked at his seared palm. It was bloody red and blistered, but he was too numb with cold to feel any pain.

He dragged himself over to the copilot and put an ear to his lips. He was breathing, just barely. So was the navigator. Conrad could hear a few low groans from the commandos in back.

Conrad reached for the transmitter. "This is six-nine-sixer," Conrad said breathlessly, leaning over the microphone. "Requesting emergency assistance."

There was no answer. He adjusted the frequency.

"This is six-nine-sixer, you bastards," he repeated.

But no matter which frequency he dialed, he was unable to break through. After several minutes of empty hissing, the transmitter finally went dead.

Nobody could hear him, he realized.

Conrad worked his way through the cockpit debris, searching for a backup radio. But he couldn't find one. Surely they had to have a beacon, an EPIRB signal at the least. But perhaps Lundstrom and his team didn't want to be found in a case like this.

The only thing he discovered was a single flare, and that from his own pack. A lot of good it would do him.

What a sorry way to die, he thought, staring at the flare in his gloved fist. You survive an airplane crash only to turn into a Popsicle. God, how he hated the cold. It was all he ever knew as a child, and to die in the snow was the last way he wanted to go. It would signify he had not traveled as far from home as he once dreamed. And he would never reconcile with his father.

How's that for irony? he thought as he scanned the temperature reading on his multisensor watch. The digital thermometer displayed −25° F. Then he took a closer look and realized he had missed a digit. −125° F.

Conrad slumped to the floor with the rest of the crew, his eyelids starting to get heavy. He fought to stay awake, but it was a losing battle, and he had begun to drift off into unconsciousness when suddenly the plane started to shake and he thought he heard a dog barking.

He opened his eyes, dragged himself over to his backpack on the floor, and managed to sling it over his shoulder. He then fumbled for his flare, his fingers working slowly, slid down through a hole in the fuselage, and fell onto the ice.

The thud sharpened his senses.

Conrad staggered to his feet and looked across the barren ice. But there was nothing to see. If anything, the snow was coming down even harder. Then, out of the mist, a huge tractorlike vehicle appeared.

It looked like one of those big Swedish Hagglunds. Its two fiberglass cabs were linked together and ran on rubber treads that left wide waffle tracks in the snow.

Conrad quickly broke his flare and started waving his hands. His arms felt heavy and he couldn't feel the flare in his fist.

The Hagglunds plowed to a stop in front of him. The forward cabin door opened. A white Alaskan husky jumped out and ran past Conrad to the wreckage. Conrad heard clanking and saw the white boots of a large figure emerge from the Hagglunds and descend the rungs of the small ladder to the ice pack.

Conrad could tell from the towering frame and crisp, spare movements that it was his father. Stiff in a white freezer suit with charcoal under his goggles to block the snow glare, Yeats marched toward him, his powerful strides crunching deeply into the snow.

"You broke my radio blackout orders, son." Yeats stood there like a statue, snow flying all around him. "You blew our twenty."

"It's good to see you, too, Dad."

Yeats took the flare from Conrad's hand, dropped it into the snow, and ground it under his boot. "You've attracted enough attention."

A geyser of anger suddenly erupted inside Conrad. Anger at Yeats and at himself for letting his father reach out across time and pull him back into this personal frozen hell.

"Lundstrom's dead along with half your men." Conrad gestured with his frostbitten hand toward the plane.

Yeats spoke into his radio. "S-and-R teams," Yeats barked. "See what you can salvage from the cargo hold before the storm buries us alive."

Conrad glanced back at the wreckage and men, which would soon be forgotten under the merciless snow. Then the husky trotted out with a wristwatch in his mouth. Its face was smeared with frozen blood. Conrad felt the husky brush past his leg and looked on as it ran for the Hagglunds.

"Nimrod!" Yeats called out after the dog. But the husky was already scratching at the door of the forward cab.

"Nimrod's the only one here with half a brain." Conrad marched toward the Hagglunds. But when he reached the forward cab and grasped the door handle, Yeats blocked it with a stiff arm.

"Where do you think you're going?" Yeats demanded.

Conrad cracked open the icy cab door, letting Nimrod jump into the warm cab first. "Don't piss in your pants, Dad. In this cold, something might fall off."

Conrad glanced at his bandaged hand as he followed Yeats down an insulated corridor inside the mysterious Ice Base Orion. A medic in the infirmary had dressed the hand as best he could. But now that it was thawing, it hurt like the living daylights.

Classical music was piped in through hidden speakers. Only the thin polystyrene walls separated them from the furious storm raging outside. Eight inches and what sounded like the faint strains of Symphony No. 25 in G Minor.

"Mozart," Yeats said. "Some bullshit experiments proved that classical music has a positive effect on the cardiovascular system. A decade from now it will be blues or rap or whatever turns on the geeks."

They passed through another air lock into a new module and Conrad felt a weird sensation of vertigo. The upper half of the module looked exactly like the bottom half. And the ceiling area was packed with instrument panels, circuit breakers, temperature dials, and dosimeter gauges. The panel clocks, like Yeats's wristwatch, were set on central time—Houston.

Then Conrad noted the NASA markings all around and suddenly realized that Ice Base Orion was never intended for use on Earth. It must have been designed to be an orbiting space station or a colony on one of the polar caps of Mars, where the ice would be tapped for water and life support.

"What the hell is this place you've built down here?" Conrad asked.

"Welcome to the most inaccessible human settlement on the planet, son."

They turned a corner, and Conrad followed Yeats down another long corridor. Conrad could hear a low hum beneath the music as they walked. And every now and then, a shudder seemed to pass through the entire base like a train had just rumbled by.

"We've got a command center, biodome, mobile servicing center, an astrophysics lab, an observatory, and modules for materials processing, remote sensing, and medical research," Yeats said.

"You forgot the drill rig," Conrad said. "That would explain the shaking."

Yeats pretended he hadn't heard him and pointed in the opposite direction. "The brig is that way."

This whole base is a brig, thought Conrad as he looked down a tunnel toward a sealed-off air lock. "Where is anybody going to go that you need to lock him up?"

"The harsh conditions here are known to send men over the edge," Yeats said.

Conrad looked at his father. "Is that what happened to you?"

Yeats stopped and turned around abruptly in front of a door marked AUTHORIZED PERSONNEL ONLY. As if anybody else was around to violate security procedures.

"Follow me through this door, son," said Yeats, his hand resting on the release bar, "and you just might go over the edge yourself."

Standing on a platform inside the cavernous laboratory was a pyramid about ten feet tall. A solid piece of rock with an almost reddish glow, it was marked by four grooves or rings around its sides. The rings began halfway up the slopes and grew closer together toward the top.

Conrad let out a low whistle.

"Pentagon satellites picked up a dark anomaly beneath the ice shortly after the last big quake some weeks ago," Yeats said. "We put a survey team on the ground, but they couldn't pick up anything solid. The anomaly appeared to be invisible to radio-echo surveys. That's when we started drilling. We hit the stone a mile beneath the ice cap. Clearly it's not a natural rock formation."

No it wasn't, Conrad thought with growing excitement as he studied the stone. The U.S. State Department's official position was that no human had set foot on Antarctica before the nineteenth century. Yet this rock was at least as old as the ice that covered it—twelve thousand years. That strongly suggested the remains of a civilization twice as old as Sumer, the oldest known on Earth.

Conrad ran his hand across the smooth face of the stone and inserted a finger into one of the strange grooves. This find could be it, he thought, nearly trembling now, the first evidence of the Mother Culture he had been seeking his entire life.

"So where's the rest of it?" he asked.

Yeats seemed to be holding back. "Rest of what?"

"The pyramid," Conrad said. "This is a benben stone."

"Benben?"

Now Yeats was just playing dumb, clearly eager to see if his investment in him was worth the cost. Conrad didn't mind singing for his supper, but he wasn't going to settle for crumbs.

"An ancient Egyptian symbol of the bennu bird—the phoenix," Conrad said. "It represents rebirth and immortality. It's the capstone or pyramidion placed on top of a pyramid."

"So you've seen it before?"

"No," Conrad said. "They're missing from all the great pyramids of the world. We know them mostly through ancient texts. They were replicas of the long-lost original benben stone, which was said to have fallen from heaven."

"Like a meteorite," finished Yeats, staring at the rock.

Conrad nodded. "But a benben this size means the pyramid beneath it would have to be enormous."

"A mile high and almost two miles wide."

Conrad stared at Yeats. "That's more than ten times the size of the Great Pyramid in Giza."

"Eleven point one times exactly," said Yeats. So his father had indeed done his homework. "Bigger than the Pentagon. And more advanced. Its exterior is smoother than a stealth bomber, which may explain why it's been invisible to radio-echo surveys. These grooves on this capstone are P4's only distinguishing exterior characteristic. Beyond its sheer size, of course."

Conrad touched the benben stone again, still incredulous that civilization existed on Earth at an earlier date and at a more advanced level than even he previously imagined.

"P4," Conrad repeated. So that's what they were calling it. Shorthand for the Pyramid of the Four Rings. It made sense. "And it's at least twelve thousand years old."

Yeats said, "If it's as old as this benben stone, then P4 is at least six billion years old, son."

"Six billion?" Conrad repeated. "That's impossible. Earth is only four and a half billion years old. You're telling me that P4 could be older than the planet?"

"That's correct," Yeats said. "And it's right under our feet."

7

DISCOVERY
PLUS TWENTY-FOUR DAYS, FIFTEEN HOURS

YEATS COULD HEAR THE FAINT STRAINS of Mozart beneath the drone of two ventilation fans pumping air inside his compartment as he watched Conrad analyze the data from P4 on his laptop.

Cupping a mug of hot coffee in his bandaged hand, Conrad shook his head. "Nothing ever changes with you, Dad, does it?"

Yeats stiffened. "Meaning?"

"You never taught me how to fly a kite or how to throw a split-fingered fastball when I was growing up," Conrad said. "No, I had to learn that kind of stuff on my own. With you it was always, 'What do you think of this weapons system design, son?' or 'How'd you like to watch the launch of my new spy satellite?' And whenever I see you on this stinking planet, the scenery is always the same. It's always some military base. Always dark. Always cold. Always snowing."

Yeats glanced out the picture window at the storm raging outside. The whiteout was so bad he couldn't even see the ice gorge anymore. What was left of the C-130 was long buried by now. He was relieved Conrad had survived the crash, and he was happy to see him. But it was clear Conrad didn't feel the same way, and that hurt.

"Maybe I bring it with me." Yeats poured himself a third shot of whiskey and nodded to the laptop data. "Anyway, the analysis dating appears conclusive."

"For the benben stone only," Conrad began as another wave of those trainlike shudders passed through the room.

"That was ours," Yeats said, referring to the drilling being done to clear the ice around the top of P4 at the bottom of the abyss. "You'll know the real jolt when you feel it."

"And you think P4 is causing the earthquakes?"

"You're the genius, son. You tell me."

Conrad sipped his coffee and grimaced. "What the hell is this? Diesel sludge?"

"It's the water. The station's supply comes from melted snow. The soy-based food is even worse."

Conrad pushed the coffee away. "Just because P4's benben stone is allegedly six billion years old doesn't mean the rest of the pyramid is that old or that aliens built it."

"Who said anything about aliens?" Yeats tried to maintain a blank expression, but Conrad was way ahead of him.

"Meteorites have been bombarding the earth since the planet was first formed—like that four-and-a-half-billion-year-old Martian rock they found here in Antarctica a few years back," Conrad said. "Humans could have found a meteorite billions of years later and carved it into a benben stone."

Yeats downed his Jack Daniel's. "If that makes you feel better."

"Well, *somebody* built P4," Conrad said. "And they built it long before ice covered Antarctica or any human civilization was thought to exist. Whatever else the builders of P4 were, they were advanced, possibly more advanced than present-day human civilization."

Yeats nodded. "Which means whoever gains access to their technology theoretically could alter the world's balance of power."

"Still paranoid about asymmetrical force?" Conrad said. "No wonder you're willing to risk lives and break international law by fielding a military presence in Antarctica."

Yeats paused. "You mean Atlantis."

"Atlantis? You think there's a city down there?"

Yeats nodded. "For all we know P4 is only the tip of the iceberg, so to speak."

"Atlantis is just a name, a myth," Conrad said. "Maybe that myth is based on what you think you've found. Maybe not. Maybe it's our long-lost Mother Culture. Maybe not. A proper excavation of P4 alone would require decades of research."

That was just like Conrad, Yeats thought. It wasn't enough to find the greatest discovery since the New World. No, Conrad had to be "right" about it, lest he be another Columbus who had discovered what had always been there.

"We don't have decades, son," Yeats explained. "We have days. I saw one of your TV specials and you said flat out that Antarctica was Atlantis."

Yeats clicked on his computer and an *Ancient Riddles* promo popped up. Yeats glanced at Conrad, who grimaced in embarrassment.

"Atlantis," boomed the baritone announcer. "The ancient city of fantastic wealth and military power described by the ancient Greek philosopher Plato in his *Dialogues* in the fourth century B.C. An entire civilization swallowed up by the sea in a single day. Its survivors sought refuge all over the world and built the pyramids of Egypt, the ziggurats of South America, and other ruins of unexplained origins. Come explore the unexplained with astro-archaeologist Doctor Conrad Yeats."

Yeats turned it off. "Well?"

"What I said is that Antarctica is the only place on Earth that *literally* fits Plato's description of Atlantis," Conrad explained. "I never said I actually believed Plato's account was true. Remember, it's a publish-or-perish world in academia, Dad, and only the wildest ideas garner attention."

Yeats frowned. "You're saying Plato is a liar?"

Conrad shrugged. "Plato was simply an idealist who dreamed up a perfect paradise, Atlantis, to express his yearnings."

Yeats was disappointed in Conrad's flippant response and narrowed his eyes. "Whereas you have no ideals."

"Every archaeologist has his favorite address for Atlantis," Conrad said. "Most think it's the island of Thíra in the Mediterranean, which sank into the sea after its volcano exploded. That was nine hundred years before Plato penned his account of Atlantis. Others favor the North Atlantic or Troy in Turkey, a city which itself was considered a myth until its ruins were recently discovered. Still others suggest that Atlantis was really the Americas and that the lost city could well lie beneath Lake Titicaca, or Los Angeles for that matter."

Yeats said, "But none of these were anything like the high-tech civilization Plato insisted was destroyed almost twelve thousand years ago."

"True."

"So this could be Atlantis."

"It could be." Conrad shrugged. "Look, all I'm saying is that if you throw a dart at a world map you'll find somebody's idea of Atlantis," Conrad said. "Or, if you're like my show's producer, you could throw darts at solar systems on celestial charts. The possibilities are infinite. I can't draw any conclusions until I get inside P4."

"I can't promise you'll get inside, son," Yeats said. "Not yet. This is a military operation. So if you've got a theory about P4, put up or shut up."

"Fine. Then I'll take my frequent flier miles and go home."

"Goddamn it, Conrad." Yeats smashed his fist into the tabletop. "You're not going anywhere. And if you want to get inside P4, you better tell me something I don't already know."

Conrad stood up and walked over to the window. For a wild moment Yeats worried that Conrad would pick up a metal chair and try to shatter the reinforced glass. But he simply stared outside as the wind howled. The man had learned to master the rage that had consumed him as a boy.

"OK then," Conrad finally said without turning around. "My best guess is that P4 may well be the original on which the Great Pyramid in Giza was modeled, except on a much grander scale. In other words, P4 is the real deal and the Great Pyramid that Khufu built is an inferior clay replica."

"Your best guess?" Yeats repeated. "I can't work off hunches, son."

"It's more than that," Conrad said. "Your own data says the base is aligned at the cardinal points—north, south, east, and west. It's also sloped at an angle of fifty-one degrees, fifty-two minutes—just like the Great Pyramid. And knowing what I do about the Great Pyramid, up close and personal, I can make some educated guesses about P4."

Yeats exhaled. "Like what?"

"Like the probability that P4 is a representation of the Southern Hemisphere of Earth."

"Whereas the Great Pyramid in Egypt is a representation of the Northern Hemisphere of Earth," Yeats said. "I get it. So what?"

Conrad crossed the floor to the desk and tapped a few keys on his laptop. "The hemisphere is projected on flat surfaces as is done in mapmaking." He turned his laptop around so Yeats could see the graphic on his screen. It looked like a German cross. "This is the pyramid if we flattened it out. The apex represents the South Pole, and the perimeter represents the equator."

"Go on."

"This is the reason why the perimeter is in relation two pi to the height," Conrad explained. "P4 thus represents the Southern Hemisphere on a scale of one to forty-three thousand two hundred."

"Represents the Southern Hemisphere in relationship to what?" Yeats asked.

"The heavens," said Conrad. "The ancients associated certain meanings with various constellations. Once I determine this pyramid's celestial counterpart in the skies we'll have a better idea of its function."

"Function?" Yeats repeated. "It's a tomb, right?"

"Pyramids themselves were never designed to serve as burial places, although they were used that way in some cases," Conrad said. "Their higher purpose was connected to the ancient king's quest for eternal life. To attain it he would have to participate in the discovery of a revelation that would unveil the mystery of 'First Time.'"

"First Time?" Yeats stared hard at him. "What's that?"

"It's the secret of Creation," Conrad said. "How the universe was formed, how we got here, where we're going."

"Where we're going? Now how the hell would the builders of P4 know that?"

"The ancients believed that the cosmic calendar resets itself every twenty-six thousand years or so," Conrad said. "Each epoch of time ends in some cataclysm leading to a new creation or age. Survivors of such global extinction events would naturally want to warn future generations."

"So this secret goes all the way back to Genesis?"

"Earlier than that," Conrad said. "According to Aztec and Mayan myths, there have been at least five Suns or Creations. This is allegedly the Fifth Sun we're living in."

"What happened to the Fourth Sun?" Yeats demanded.

"Well, according to the ancients, it was destroyed by the Great

Flood," Conrad said. "Based on the four rings we found on the benben stone, my guess is that P4 was built at the very dawn of the Fourth Sun, just after the destruction of the Third Sun, right around the time the biblical story of Genesis says God created the heavens and the earth."

"You just told me P4 goes further back than that."

"That's because inside the pyramid I expect to find a repository of knowledge from the previous three Suns," Conrad said. "It might even contain the secret of First Time itself, something older than the known universe."

Yeats started pacing back and forth, unable to contain his excitement. His bum leg was killing him, but he didn't care. "You sure about all this?"

"Won't be until I get inside." Conrad's face darkened. "But it's fair to assume that, whatever else is down there, P4 holds a legacy of knowledge at least as great as our own."

"Which is why we have to get inside first," Yeats concluded. "Because it won't be long before we have company."

Conrad asked, "You find the entrance yet?"

"I've got a drill crew working out of a rig we've set up on P4's summit," Yeats said. "The top of the pyramid, about fifty feet of it, sticks out of the bottom of the abyss like the tip of an iceberg. The crew has been drilling a hole down the east face toward the base. That's where the computer models say we'll find the entrance. We're about halfway there."

Conrad said, "You're drilling in the wrong place."

Yeats took a deep breath. "OK, then. Where should I be drilling?"

"The north or south face, although with P4 I'd favor the north face," Conrad said. "Less than a half mile down the drill crew will most likely find the entrance to a large shaft that will take us into the heart of P4."

"Most likely?" Yeats huffed. "You want me to pull my team off mission just to follow your instinct?"

"Look, if P4 is indeed the original on which the Great Pyramid was modeled, then I suspect we'll find two shafts radiating from the center of the pyramid out the south and north faces of the exterior.

If the similarities I'm seeing continue to play out, then we can use these shafts to get inside P4 in half the time it's going to take you right now."

"And what exactly is the function of these shafts? If they exist."

"I have an idea," Conrad said. "But I'd have to get inside P4 to be certain."

"Naturally," Yeats grumbled.

"I thought the price of admission to P4 was to tell you something you didn't already know," said Conrad when the intercom buzzed. "I just did."

"What you told me means nothing if we can't find this shaft you allege exists," Yeats said.

"You will," Conrad insisted when the com beeped again.

Irritated, Yeats flicked on his screen. It was O'Dell in the command center. "What is it?"

"One of our long-range patrols just reported in," O'Dell said. "Looks like Doctor Yeats's little distress call attracted some attention. We've got company."

8

DISCOVERY PLUS TWENTY-FOUR DAYS, SIXTEEN HOURS

THE AIR LOCK DOOR SLID OPEN and a blast of polar air blew in with a flurry of snow. An ethereal figure emerged from the cloud in a green Gore-Tex parka. And even before the fur-lined hood dropped and the ultraviolet glasses came off, Conrad instinctively knew who it was.

"Serena," he said.

Every man has his own Atlantis, Conrad knew, a part of his past or himself that seems submerged and gone forever. Serena Serghetti was his Atlantis, and now she had suddenly resurfaced.

Serena said nothing for a minute, simply smiled at him and looked around. Then Nimrod trotted up to her and licked her wool mitten. She scratched the appreciative husky's ear.

Conrad glanced at Yeats, who was standing silently next to him, and at the two armed MPs in freezer suits behind Serena. All seemed to be waiting for some sort of utterance.

Finally, Serena spoke her first words to Conrad in four years. "You have a permit for her?" she asked, petting Nimrod.

Conrad blinked, incredulous. Perhaps he was so lost in the moment he hadn't heard her correctly. "For the dog?"

Serena nodded. "Huskies have been banned from the continent since 1993, as have any species not indigenous to Antarctica. I think that includes you, Conrad, along with your friends here."

Yeats stared, jaw open. "You two know each other?"

"Don't you recognize her?" Conrad said. "This is Serena Serghetti, aka Mother Earth, formerly the Vatican's top linguist and now an environmentalist and official pain in the ass."

"Only if you're an ass," Serena said brightly and extended a mitten toward Yeats. "General Yeats, you look warm-blooded in person. Not at all like Conrad described you."

Conrad looked at Yeats, who let the dig slide. "The Vatican?"

"Actually, I'm here as a representative of the Australian Antarctic Preservation Society and an adviser to the environmental committee of the United Nations Antarctica Commission. This land belongs to Australia, you see, according to Article Four of the Antarctic Treaty, of which the United States is a member. All members are required to give notice of expeditions, stations, and military personnel and equipment active in Antarctica. You haven't stated your business on our territory, General Yeats."

Conrad's mind was reeling, trying to take in her mysterious appearance in this frozen hell, let alone this bizarre exchange with his father about arcane minutiae in international law.

Yeats cleared his throat. "Article Four, while recognizing that some nations lay claim to territory, expressly states that those claims do not have to be honored by other nations," Yeats said evenly. "In other words, seventy nations instead of seven could have territorial claims here, Sister Serghetti, but the United States does not recognize their validity."

"Maybe so," Serena replied. "But there's no ambiguity to Article One, which clearly and forcefully bans any measure of a military nature, which is tough luck for you."

"Unless such measures are for scientific purposes."

"And what purpose is that, Conrad?"

Conrad realized she was addressing him. And he said the first thing that popped into his head. "We're mounting a salvage operation."

He studied her reaction as she looked around and took in the command center doors down the corridor and soldiers with polar-protected M-16s.

"You mean for that C-130 that crashed?" she asked. "I saw the wreckage when I landed on your runway."

Conrad glanced at Yeats, who seemed impressed. Not only was

she Mother Earth. She was also the Flying Nun. No wonder Yeats's jaw was on the floor. "You landed a plane?" Yeats asked.

"Your base is hard to miss with a fissure as wide as the Colorado River snaking around it. Did you cause that crack?"

"It was already there," Yeats said defensively.

"Then you won't mind if I have a look," she said. "The Antarctic Treaty provides for the right of access and inspection to all bases. Consider us official inspectors."

She stepped aside and Conrad saw behind her four well-built young men with dark, deep-set eyes. Video and sound equipment rested heavily on their broad shoulders.

Conrad said, "Who are they?"

"My camera crew. As long as we're making an inspection, I assume we can take pictures?"

"Sure," said Yeats, who motioned to the MPs to relieve the men of their equipment. "You can inspect everything from the brig."

Conrad watched Serena and her crew in their respective cells on two monitors in the command center. The men were sitting quietly on the floor like caged foxes. Serena, meanwhile, was stretched across her bunk like Sleeping Beauty.

"You can't just lock up Mother Earth," he told Yeats. "The world's going to find out."

But Yeats was focused on the other monitors that showed various grainy images of the P4 Habitat and a drill rig atop the flat summit of P4, where a work crew was tunneling down the north face of the pyramid as Conrad had instructed.

"You better pray your hunch about a shaft pays off, son. Or I just might lock you up too. And, frankly, in your case, the world won't give a shit."

Conrad opened his mouth to say something when Colonel O'Dell walked up with a file. Conrad caught his disapproving glance and realized he was the only civilian running loose on the base. O'Dell looked itchy to toss him into the brig with the rest of them.

"Here's that NSA report on Sister Serghetti, sir."

"Thank you, Colonel."

Conrad watched as Yeats scanned the file. "The NSA keeps files on nuns?"

"Nuns who develop a universal translator based on the Aymara language," Yeats said. "The NSA has been trying to get its hands on Sister Serghetti's system ever since. The Aymara language is so pure that the NSA suspects it didn't just evolve like other languages but was constructed from scratch."

"Explain that to us, Doctor Yeats," O'Dell blurted out.

Yeats shot O'Dell a nasty glare, but Conrad didn't flinch.

"The earliest Aymara myth says that after the Great Flood, strangers attempted to build a city on Lake Titicaca," Conrad said. "We know what's left of it as Tiahuanaco, with its great Temple of the Sun. But the builders abandoned it and disappeared."

"And just where on earth did these builders come from?" Yeats asked him in earnest.

"According to legend, they came from the lost island paradise of Aztlan. The Aztec version of Atlantis," Conrad said, staring at his father. "So what are you saying?"

Yeats closed the file. "The Good Sister might know the language of the people who built P4."

Serena had always pictured Antarctica as a symbol of peace and harmony, a model for how humans could live with one another and all species with which they shared the planet. She had also held similar such illusions about her relationship with Conrad. But now as she looked around her cell inside Ice Base Orion, her dream had melted away to reveal four cold walls, a tiny sink, and a urinal.

There was a hidden camera somewhere, she was sure, and General Yeats and that tosser Conrad no doubt were watching her every move. But they couldn't read her mind. So she sat on her bunk and pretended to be alone with her thoughts.

As an Australian she felt more kinship with Antarctica than the Americans. So often as a little girl she would look across the sea and know that the great white continent was on the other side. Australia was the closest of the world's nations to Antarctica and claimed

42 percent of it, including most of East Antarctica and the very ground—or ice over the ground—on which the Americans had constructed this secret facility.

But for all her work in Antarctica—mostly saving leopard seals or minke whales—her experience had been confined to the spectacular landscapes on the fringes of the continent. There the wildlife was wonderful and the auroras glorious. But this mission into the interior snow deserts had proven Antarctica to be an empty continent indeed. Even now within the warmth of this American base, she could sense the barrenness.

Serena also thought she could hear crackling noises from the shell's expansion joints. Stations built on ice tend to sink under their own weight as the heat they generate melts the surrounding ice. This station, probably days old, was just settling in.

She remembered her capture at the secret airstrip carved out of the ice and her subsequent escort to Ice Base Orion. The Hagglunds tractor in which the Americans transported her had passed a power plant along the way. It was buried a hundred yards away from the living quarters behind a protective snow dune. Too far away to service diesel engines in this cold, she thought. That's when she realized it was probably a compact nuclear plant. Probably a 100-kilowatt system.

At first she was outraged. How dare the Americans bring nuclear materials onto the continent! she thought. Ninety percent of all the ice in the world was here. Any meltdown could cause global catastrophe. This alone was more than enough to bust the Americans with the U.N.

But now her fury at the Americans for breaking every international law on the books had turned to fascination. However cool she played it with Conrad and General Yeats back at the air lock, she was in fact burning with excitement. There was Conrad, of course. But clearly her mission here involved much more than protecting the unspoiled Antarctic environment from the Americans.

Something momentous had been found down here, she realized, just like the pope said. Something that could turn history—and the Judeo-Christian tradition—on its head. In spite of all this, however, she felt exhilarated. Of all the candidates His Holiness could have chosen to be his eyes for this historic event, he had chosen her.

She heard the door unlock with a buzz and turned.

When the MP opened the door of the brig and ushered Conrad in, Serena was sitting on the edge of her bunk, sipping diesel tea from a Styrofoam cup. Conrad noted the silver bride of Christ band on her left ring finger that signified her spiritual union to the one and only Son of God. That would be Jesus to her, unfortunately, and not some disreputable scoundrel like Conrad Yeats. He wondered why she was still wearing it. Probably to keep his likes at bay.

"Conrad." Serena managed a smile. "I figured they'd send you. You always did have odd ideas for a secret rendezvous."

Conrad saw she was down to her wool sweater now, her black hair falling softly over her shoulders. Underneath she was probably wearing polypropylene inner liners to move sweat away from her skin, or acrylic thermal underwear. As for what was wrapped under that, Conrad didn't have to imagine, and he realized he was the one sweating.

"What's so odd?" He reached over and touched her face. "You're still cold."

"I'm fine. What happened to you?"

He looked at his bandaged hand. "Occupational hazard."

"Like Yeats? I would have put you and me together before I ever thought I'd see you with your father."

"Like you and your *GQ* boys in the next—"

"Cell?" She smiled. "Worried about some competition, Conrad?" she asked. "Don't be. If I were the last woman on earth and you were the last man, I'd become a nun again."

Conrad stared into her soft brown eyes. It was the first time they had been alone, face-to-face, in four years, and Conrad secretly felt she looked more beautiful than ever. He, on the other hand, felt old and worn down. "What are you doing here, Serena?"

"I thought I might ask you the same question, Conrad."

He was itching to tell her about the ruins beneath the ice, that his theories were true. But he couldn't. After all, they had never dealt with the ruins of their own lives on the surface.

"You're not just here to save the environment," Conrad stated. "When you came through that air lock, you weren't surprised to see me."

"You're right, Conrad," she said softly and put a warm hand to his face. "I missed you and had to see you."

Conrad pulled back. "You are so full of it, and you know it."

"Oh, and you're not?" The floor began to rumble. Serena sat back in her bunk and glanced at her watch. She's timing the shakers, he thought to himself. Suddenly she said, "When were you going to inform the rest of the world about your discovery?"

Conrad swallowed hard. "What discovery?"

"The pyramid under the ice."

Conrad blinked in disbelief but said nothing. Still, there was no use fighting the fact that somehow she knew as much as or more than he did about this expedition.

"So what else did God tell you?"

"I'd say the team has been drilling exploratory tunnels in the ice around the pyramid," she said. "And I'd bet that by now your cowboy father has probably found a door."

There was a minute of silence. They were no longer locked in their typical give-and-take banter but were fellow truth-seekers. Conrad was glad she was there and angry at the same time. He was worried about her safety and yet felt threatened by her presence, as if somehow she was standing in his way.

"Serena," he said softly. "This isn't some oil platform that you can chain yourself to in order to protest the production of fossil fuels. A few dozen soldiers have already died on this expedition, and it's practically a miracle you and I are even talking."

A cloud of sober reflection passed over Serena's face. She was processing her own thoughts. "I can take care of myself, Conrad," she said. "It's you I'm worried about."

"Me?"

"Your father hasn't told you everything."

"What else is new?" Conrad shrugged. "Passing along a piece of information for him is like passing a kidney stone. So he's hiding something. So are you, Serena. A lot more. Look, neither the United States nor the Vatican is going to be able to keep a lid on something this big."

Her eyes narrowed. "Conrad, I know you're not this naive, so it must be denial," she said. "Tell me, how did Yeats lure you down here? Did he promise you credit for the find of the ages? Maybe more help in finding your true parents?"

"Maybe."

"Trust me, Conrad," she said, the pain of personal experience in her eyes, "there are some answers you don't want to know."

"Speak for yourself, Serena."

"Conrad, this isn't about you and this isn't about me. It's about the world at large and the greater good. You have to consider other people."

"I am considering them. This is an unprecedented development in human history. And I want to share it with the world."

"No, you want to magnify the great name of Doctor Conrad Yeats," she said. "To hell with the rest of the world. But why should you care? It's the information about Earth that's more important than the planet or its people. Isn't that how it goes with you? You haven't changed a bit."

"If you're referring to our relationship, you knew exactly what you were doing then, Miss High and Mighty. You just didn't want to take responsibility for your actions."

"I was pure as the driven snow, Conrad. But you pissed on me. Just like you're going to piss on this planet."

"Hey, it's not like we actually did anything."

"My point exactly," she said. "But you didn't do much to contradict the rumors, did you?"

"I am not the bad guy here."

"Aren't you?" she asked. "You're nothing but a pawn of the United States, willing to betray everything you believe in about international cooperation and the brotherhood and sisterhood of humanity to satisfy your selfish curiosity."

"I don't want to change the world," he told her. "I just want to understand it. And this is our best shot yet to make sense of who we are and where we came from. You make it sound like the fruit of forbidden knowledge. One bite and we'll all be cursed."

"Maybe we already are, Conrad. Isn't that what attracted you to me in the first place? I was your forbidden fruit. Just like these ruins you've found under the ice."

"Try the other way around, Serena," he said. "And my mind is made up."

Serena nodded. "Then you might as well take me down with you."

Conrad stared at her incredulously. The only reason he was here was because he was the world's leading authority on megalithic architecture and the son of the general leading the expedition. Serena didn't have a prayer. "You've got to be kidding."

"What happens when you come across some inscription down there?" she asked simply. "Who's going to figure it out? You?"

Not only had he failed to extract any meaningful information from her, Conrad thought with a sinking feeling, but she also had directed their conversation to precisely this point. The point that Yeats had just predicted this would all come to. And somehow, Serena knew as much.

"Granted, I'm no linguist, but here and there I've picked up a thing or two."

"Like a venereal disease?" she shot back. "For all you know, Conrad, the only reason you're here is because they thought they couldn't get me."

The thing that bothered Conrad the most was that she said it with absolute humility. It wasn't a boast, but a plausible probability. Then Conrad realized she was playing to the security camera near the ceiling. She had been talking to Yeats all along.

"You're unbelievable, you know that?" he told her. "Absolutely unbelievable."

She flashed him a warm smile that could melt the ice caps. "Would you have me any other way?"

9

DISCOVERY PLUS TWENTY-FOUR DAYS, SIXTEEN HOURS

U.S.S. *CONSTELLATION*, SOUTHERN OCEAN

"DAMN YEATS," cursed Admiral Hank Warren.

The short, powerfully built Warren scanned the blacked-out silhouettes of his carrier group's battle formation with his binoculars from the bridge of the aircraft carrier U.S.S. *Constellation*. They were twenty miles off the coast of East Antarctica, and Warren's mission was to keep his battle group undetected until further orders.

To that end, all radars and satellite sets were turned off. Only line-of-sight radios capable of millisecond-burst transmissions were allowed. Extra lookouts with binoculars were posted on deck to sweep the dawn's horizon for enemy surface ship silhouettes and submarine periscope feathers.

The idea was to get the battle force in close to the coast without betraying their position and then strike at the enemy without warning. A diesel-powered carrier was good at that. But who the hell was the enemy down here? He and his battle force were freezing their asses trying to avoid detection, and the only enemy they were intimidating was the penguins.

Meanwhile, an unidentified aircraft using a U.S. Navy military frequency had placed a distress call before disappearing from radar. And if the crew of the *Constellation* heard it, then others had heard it too.

All he knew was that this had something to do with that crazy bastard Griffin Yeats, and that made him even more uneasy.

Way back when, Warren had done some time with the U.S. Naval

Support Task Force, Antarctica. It was his rescue team that found Yeats wandering in a stupor back in '69 after forty-three days in the snow deserts, the sole survivor of a training mission for a Mars launch that never happened. The nut insisted on dragging three NASA supply containers with him even though the navy had its own. Not a care about the three bodies he left behind. Only later did Warren's team learn that the containers Yeats dragged out with him were radioactive. But that's the kind of man Yeats was, unconcerned with the havoc he wreaked in other people's lives if they got in the way of his own agenda. When Warren filed a complaint, all he got was the "classified" and "need to know" bullshit.

Now, more than thirty-five years later and bearing the rank of admiral, Warren was still in the dark when it came to Yeats. And it frustrated him to no end. His crew had just picked up a short-burst distress call from what appeared to be some black ops flight calling itself 696, which apparently crashed on approach to some phantom landing strip. Yeats's fingerprints were all over this debacle, and Warren was personally going to see to it that the man got the early retirement he deserved.

"Conn, Sonar," shouted the sonar chief from his console.

"Conn, aye." Warren had the conn for the morning watch. It was important for the crew to see him in command and even more important for him to feel in command.

"Lookouts report unknown surface vessel inbound at two-zero-six," the sonar chief reported. "Range is under a thousand yards."

"What!" the admiral blurted. "How the hell did we miss it?"

Warren lifted his binoculars and turned to the southwest. There. A ship. The letters across the bow said MV *Arctic Sunrise.* It was a Greenpeace ship, and on board was a guy pointing a video camera with a zoom lens at the *Constellation.*

"Helmsman, get us out of here!"

"Too late, sir," said a signalman. "They've marked us."

The signalman pointed to a TV monitor.

"This is CNN, live from the *Arctic Sunrise.*" The reporter was broadcasting from the bow of the Greenpeace ship. "As you can see behind me, the U.S.S. *Constellation,* one of the mightiest warships ever made, is cruising off the coast of Antarctica, its mission shrouded in secrecy. But first, CNN has captured on video large cracks in this Antarctic ice shelf, which suggest that the collapse of the shelf is imminent."

A scruffy college type, the kind who wouldn't last a week at Annapolis, came on-screen to say, "Scientists consider the rapid disintegration of this and other ice shelves around Antarctica a sign that dangerous warming is continuing."

Footage appeared of an iceberg that had split off the coast a few weeks ago. The reporter's voice-over noted that the towering ice cube covered two thousand square miles, with sheer walls rising almost two hundred feet above the waterline, and had an estimated depth of one thousand feet.

"And now a bizarre new twist to the global warming phenomenon has surfaced regarding accusations of unauthorized nuclear tests by the United States in the interior snow deserts of Antarctica."

The CNN report concluded with a long shot of the *Constellation*'s ominous profile on the ocean horizon at dawn.

"Aw, hell," said Warren. MSNBC and the other network news shows would soon give out the same information. It couldn't get any worse. "Damn you, Griffin Yeats."

10

DISCOVERY
PLUS TWENTY-FOUR DAYS,
SIXTEEN HOURS

SERENA SAT ON HER BUNK, listening to the whirring of the two fans pumping air and God knew what else into the cold brig. She shivered. Images she had trained herself to suppress had resurfaced after seeing Conrad. Now, as she hugged her body to keep warm, the memory of their last time together came flooding back.

It had been March, six months after they first met at the symposium of Meso-American archaeologists in La Paz, Bolivia's capital. She was still a nun then, and they were seeing each other almost daily, working side by side on a research project in the lost city of Tiahuanaco high in the Andes.

Conrad Yeats was intelligent, attractive, witty, and sensitive. He was almost more spiritual than her colleagues from Rome, and what attracted her to him most was the purity of his calling. Some found his unorthodox theory of a Mother Culture threatening, but to her it made a wild kind of sense, based on her own studies of world mythologies. She and Conrad were approaching the same conclusion from different ends, he from archaeology and she from linguistics.

On the last night of their field studies program he invited her to join him for a "revelation" on Lake Titicaca, about twelve miles away from Tiahuanaco.

It was a curious place for good-byes, she thought as she strolled the shore. Locals and tourists alike were bustling about and drinking beers at the lakeside taverns as the sun began to set.

Then a tanned and handsome Conrad showed up in an elegant reed boat, like some Tiahuanacan visage come to life. The boat came from the lake's island of Suriqi. It was a fifteen-footer made from bundled totora rushes, wide amidships and narrow at either end with a high curving prow and stern. Tight cords held the bundles of reeds in place.

"Look familiar?" he asked as he beckoned her aboard. "Just like the boats made from papyrus reeds that the pharaohs used to sail the Nile during the Age of the Pyramids."

"And I suppose, Doctor Yeats, that you can explain how these strikingly similar designs could arise in two such widely separated places?" she asked, playing along.

It was just one of the many mysteries of Lake Titicaca, he said in his best tour guide twang and offered to take her to the middle of the lake to show her his "revelation."

She had a pretty good idea what that revelation was and smiled. "There's nothing you can show me in the middle of the lake that you can't show me here."

"I wouldn't go that far," he told her.

She shouldn't have gone with him. The sisters had a policy of traveling in pairs and never being alone with a man in a room with the door closed. It wasn't out of fear or paranoia but for appearances' sake. There must not be a hint of impropriety that would harm the cause of Christ.

But Conrad, as usual, was too persuasive to resist.

He paddled with long, powerful strokes and they glided across the silvery surface. At 12,500 feet above sea level, Lake Titicaca was the highest lake in the world, and it felt like it. Serena thought she could almost touch the heavens.

"Now the odd thing about this lake is that it's located hundreds of miles from the Pacific, yet it contains ocean-variety fish, seahorses, crustacea, and marine fauna," Conrad lectured with a wink.

"And you think it's seawater from the Genesis flood?" Serena asked.

Conrad shrugged. "When the waters receded, some got dammed up here in the Andes."

"I guess that explains the docks in Tiahuanaco."

Conrad smiled. "Right. Why else would the ruins of a city twelve miles away have docks?"

"Unless it was once a port and the south end of this lake extended twelve miles and more than a hundred feet higher," Serena concluded. "Which means civilization flourished here before the flood and Tiahuanaco is at least fifteen thousand years old."

"Imagine that."

She could. She wanted to. A world before the dawn of recorded history. What was it like? Were people really that much different from us today? she wondered. There must have been women like me back then, she thought, and men like Conrad. He had dropped his skeptical pose and opened up so beautifully out here. So different from his posture before the academics.

The night air was chilly, and Serena was huddled in the bow. Conrad paddled slowly. The twilight sky above was a magnificent turquoise blue, and the lake stretched on like glass for eternity.

For the longest time they were silent, gliding along the reeds with only the dip of Conrad's paddle making soft lapping sounds like an ancient metronome. Then, when they were in the middle of the glistening waters, he pulled up his paddle and let them drift beneath the stars.

"What's wrong?" she asked.

"Nothing." He produced a basket of food and wine. "Absolutely nothing at all."

"Conrad," she began, "I really should be getting back. The sisters will worry."

"As well they should."

He sat beside her and kissed her, then pushed her gently backward until she was lying down. He stroked her face and kissed her on the lips, and she shivered.

"Conrad, please."

Their eyes locked, and she thought of his childhood pain, their connection, thought that if there was ever any man to do this with, any time of her life and any place on the planet, this was it.

"Tomorrow I go back to Arizona and you go back to Rome," he whispered in her ear. "And we can remember our last night in Bolivia as the night that never happened."

"You got that right," she said, and pushed him overboard to a satisfying splash.

Inside his compartment, as he packed his gear for the impending descent to P4, Conrad, too, was thinking about that night with Serena on the reed boat.

He had always been in awe of her determination and courage. And her beauty was unmatched. Yet she wore it so effortlessly, as if she didn't care whether she was seventeen or seventy. She was charming and self-effacing, even funny. But that night it had been her glimmering eyes, almost glowing under her dark hair, that had mesmerized him.

She told him she had always admired his purity and single-mindedness. He was what he was, she said, and not like herself—someone able to pretend to be what she was not. He wondered what dark secret she was about to confess but soon realized she had none. Her only sin was being an unwanted child.

It was then, for a fleeting moment, that he came closest to knowing her. For the first time he grasped her holy death wish and understood her drive to be a martyr, a saint, a woman who counted. If anything, he realized, her works of compassion were her way of avoiding intimacy. She feared being "found out" and thus not measuring up to her standards, much less God's. She would do anything to avoid those feelings of not being needed, of feeling worthless, a "mistake" like her birth. But she didn't fear that rejection from him. She knew he loved her.

And that's how he knew she truly loved him.

He felt he had come to the end of his lifelong quest, had found the Temple of God. That he was a thief in the sacred shrine, taking what did not belong to him, only made the experience more exciting, dangerous, and satisfying than any relic or ancient artifact he had ever taken, before or since.

But he knew it was over when she pushed him off the reed boat and into the freezing waters of Lake Titicaca. When he climbed back on board, she wasn't laughing. It hadn't been a prank. Instead the fear had returned to her eyes.

Suddenly Conrad realized she was the one who had stolen something from him. "Where do you think you're going?" he asked.

"Back to Tiahuanaco," she said, "before anybody realizes I'm missing at breakfast."

"Be a risk taker. Let's enjoy what time we have."

"I'm disappointed in you, Doctor Yeats," she said, handing him the paddle. "I didn't think you were the kind of man who took advantage of nuns."

Conrad, a man with no small ego, was disappointed that she had spurned his advances. Worse, she was denying her own complicity. "And I didn't think you were the kind of nun who cares what other people think."

"I'm not," she shot back.

She was right, of course. That much was obvious to anybody. But Conrad also sensed that what she was truly afraid of was her feelings for him, of losing control. And if Serena Serghetti could be defined as any kind of nun, she was most definitely the kind who made damn well sure she was always in control.

Their parting was not happy. She acted as if she had made a huge mistake and had potentially blown her whole future with their night together. In truth, however, she didn't regret it for a minute. At least that's what Conrad eventually concluded. What Serena feared was further intimacy. Like she had something to hide. Then he understood. It was herself. She had disappointed herself and as a result felt unworthy of him.

She was wrong, he knew, and he vowed to prove to her that she was worth something without the title of Sister and that he was worth the price of her sacrifice. But she would have none of it.

The last memory he had of her was standing at the shore, trying to kiss her good-bye, and watching her run to hail a cab. He waved to her, but she never looked back. He tried to reach her in Rome by phone a week later, and after months of unreturned calls, he even showed up at one of her conferences unannounced. Now she had become famous, throwing herself so fully into her work that he wondered if it was the unwanted child in her she wanted to forget, or him.

In any case, a private audience with Mother Earth, he soon

discovered, was about as probable as his discovering his beloved lost Mother Culture.

Until now.

The nun's got titanium balls, Yeats thought as he reviewed Serghetti's exchange with Conrad on a video monitor in the command center. *I have to give her that. The pope knew exactly what he was doing when he sent her.*

"How does she know so much, sir?" asked O'Dell, who was standing next to him.

"Moot point now," said Yeats. "I doubt the Vatican wants her to talk. But for all we know, she's right. Her presence may even be necessary for what's ahead."

"And your son, sir?"

Yeats looked at O'Dell. "What about him?"

"I've seen the DOD report." O'Dell looked concerned. "Your boy's been in therapy since kindergarten. Nightmares of cataclysmic doom. Visions of the end of the world. With all due respect, sir, he's a lunatic."

"So he had a traumatic childhood," Yeats said, wishing O'Dell would put a lid on it. "Didn't we all? Besides, the DOD doesn't have his complete file. Trust me, I wrote it."

Yeats was about to turn his attention back to the monitor when Lieutenant Lopez, one of his communications officers, walked up. Besides Sister Serghetti, young Lopez was the only other woman at Ice Base Orion.

"General Yeats," she reported. "I think you better see this."

Yeats followed her to the big screen and saw the U.S.S. *Constellation* on TV with a CNN logo in the lower right corner.

"Warren," Yeats cursed under his breath. He stared at the intrepid Greenpeace vessel juxtaposed on-screen with the mighty *Constellation*. *Goddamn that sausage in a sailor suit!*

O'Dell said, "How did they know, sir?"

"Take a wild guess, Colonel." Yeats pointed to Sister Serghetti in her cell on the little monitor. "She's been stalling the whole time, waiting for the cavalry to arrive. It's only a matter of time before an army of U.N. weapons inspectors comes knocking at our door."

Which meant the insertion team had to be in and out of P4 before then, Yeats concluded, and he mentally began to make the calculations. P4 would have to be wiped clean of significant technology or data before any internationals reached the site.

"It gets worse, sir," Lopez said. "McMurdo reports that Vostok Station intercepted our communications with Flight six-nine-six. They've already dispatched a UNACOM team."

Yeats groaned. "I knew it. Who's leading the team?"

"An Egyptian air force officer," she said, handing him a report. "Colonel Ali Zawas."

"Zawas?" Yeats looked at the photo of a handsome man in uniform with dark, thoughtful eyes and black wavy hair. "Holy shit."

O'Dell said, "He wouldn't be related to—"

"He's the secretary-general's nephew," Yeats said. "And he's a graduate of the United States Air Force Academy. Flew with the Allies during the first Gulf War and downed two Iraqi jets for us. Damned fine officer and gentleman." Yeats handed the report back to Lopez. "What kind of backup does Zawas have, Lieutenant?"

"Well, there are the Russians at Vostok under the command of a Colonel Ivan Kovich. And the Aussies are offering support from Mawson Station." She paused. "So are some of our own American scientists from Amundsen-Scott who have been kept out of the loop."

"Damn it!" Yeats growled. "The whole world's going to be here in a few hours."

"Not with this storm kicking up again, sir," O'Dell said. "ETA six hours. WX Ops says this thing is going to slam us hard. Might pin everybody down for three weeks."

Yeats looked out the window. The skies had darkened. Snow pelted the glass like bullets. "The storm might stop the Aussies, but it will only slow down Zawas and his UNACOM team." Yeats turned to O'Dell. "You hold off the barbarians here on the surface while I take the insertion team down to P4."

O'Dell said, "And how am I going to explain holding Mother Earth against her will?"

"You won't have to," Yeats said. "I'm taking her with us. Now."

PART TWO

DESCENT

11

DESCENT HOUR ONE

THE ABYSS

The sky over the chasm turned an ominous deep black, and Serena felt the wind pick up with a sudden chill. If this was supposed to be a lull in the polar storm, she didn't want to stick around for the real deal. Mist boiled up from the abyss below, where the nearest shelter, the so-called P4 Habitat, was a one-mile drop.

"You sure you're up for this, Sister?"

It was Yeats, sliding down the icy wall above her in his white freezer suit, grinning like the devil under the blinding light of his headtorch. Back on the surface, he had detailed the risks to her about coming down with the insertion team. But what other choice did she have? To wait back at the base with the rest of the world until the team resurfaced would be to remain in the dark.

"Technically, it's Doctor Serghetti, General," she said, digging the crampon attached to her plastic boot into a toehold. "And I climbed Everest with my first Mother Superior."

"She give you the garter?"

Yeats was pointing to Serena's harness. It actually did look like a red garter belt with two loops around her thighs. In case of a fall it would spread the shock evenly throughout her lower body.

"No, just this." Serena pulled out her ice ax and hammered an ice screw into the frozen wall before attaching a new line with a carabiner. She wanted to show Yeats she was more than up to the challenge. But in fact she was feeling strange. Her heart was pounding and she was breathing rapidly. "Do you smell something?"

"Yeah," said Yeats. "Your story."

She had never met the infamous Griffin Yeats until Ice Base Orion, only heard about him from Conrad. But she didn't trust him. Like Emerson said: "Who you are speaks so loudly I can't hear what you're saying." The guy was a rogue at heart, just like this expedition. He simply did a better job of hiding it than Conrad, who was refreshingly honest and even charming about his shortcomings. She also concluded that Yeats hadn't agreed to let her join the team out of the kindness of his heart or even because he valued her for her expertise as a linguist.

"Tell me again why you changed your mind and let me tag along?"

"If anything, I learned from NASA that women are always a pleasant addition to astronaut crews."

She had expected something sexist like that coming from him. "Gee, I thought it was because women are actually better with precision tasks, more meticulous, and more flexible at multitasking than men."

"Whenever they're not too emotional or easily upset," Yeats replied and dropped out of sight just as Conrad rappeled alongside her.

"Anything wrong?" Conrad asked.

Serena sighed and shook her head. "Your father never stops, does he?"

"It's not in his nature," Conrad answered without feeling. "Once he's programmed, he keeps going and going until he finishes the job."

"And leaves a trail of bodies behind him."

"Then we better not let him get too far ahead of us," Conrad said, rappeling down.

She went after him. He was an expert climber in tropical climates. But overconfidence could be fatal in icy conditions like this. And she was worried for him. For his soul. For her own too. Because in trying to save him once before she felt she had condemned them both.

Conrad was within reach now, and she dropped down a few feet and found a hold. The color of the ice was a beautiful blue and almost seemed to glow. "Pretty," she said.

"Don't stop, Serena. Keep going." Conrad spoke rapidly.

Serena continued to ease up on her line. But Conrad's physiology concerned her. Was he hyperventilating? Serena didn't know and could feel her own breathing quicken to an unnaturally fast pace. Her heart too. The pounding was regular but fast.

She eased up a bit more when Conrad motioned with a gloved hand. "Down there," he said. "See it?"

Serena peered into the mist below. A hole parted and she could see a grid of lights, like a landing pad. "I see."

"No, do you see it?"

Suddenly Serena could see that the landing pad was in fact the flattened summit of a gleaming white pyramid rising sharply through the floor of the abyss. She had to shade her eyes from the glare of the lights off the pyramid's surface.

"P4," she heard herself saying under her breath.

"Don't ask me how it got here," Conrad said, now sporting his sunglasses. "I can't explain it yet. But I will."

The conviction in his voice inspired confidence. His excitement was pure, unadulterated, and moving. Not a trace of fear, she thought with envy, just genuine curiosity and enthusiasm. She had almost forgotten what that felt like.

She slipped on her sunglasses. The flat summit, brighter than the whitest snow, was blinding. So this was why the pope had sent her down, she realized. She had suspected something spectacular, but she was completely unprepared for the sight or dimension of this monument. It was gigantic.

She was staring at it in wonder when she heard her line creak.

"Just some slack," Conrad assured her. "No worries."

She heard a sharp crack and the ping of metal. The piton holding her line in the ice popped out, and she thought she was falling.

"Conrad!" she shouted as she buried her ice ax into the wall and hung on.

But Conrad said nothing. She looked to her side. He was gone. It was his piton that had popped out.

She looked down in time to see Conrad fall into the mist.

"Conrad!" she screamed.

Yeats rappeled down beside her.

"You couldn't wait until afterward to bury him?" he asked, scanning the billowing mist below. Yeats flicked Conrad's line with the back of a gloved finger. "He's still floating."

She heard a crack and looked up to see the ice screw on her own line start to slip. She instinctively pulled out her ice ax and swung it at Yeats, who put up a defensive arm. "Hold this," she said and suddenly felt herself plunging into space.

She fell through the cloud a few seconds later, hurtling toward the lights below when her line snapped tight and she stopped with a jolt. For a moment she feared she had shattered her pelvis. But her harness had done its job.

She caught her breath and could hear her windproof parka squeaking against the nylon rope as she swung back and forth.

"Conrad?" she called.

"Over here," he replied. "I found something."

She swung her head in the direction of his voice, and her headtorch found him swinging ten feet from the wall, unable to get a hold.

"Hang on," she said as she swung over.

It took three tries before her arc was wide enough to reach him. As she swung toward him, she held out her hand, and he gripped it tight, holding her next to him. They swung together in space for a few seconds, clinging to each other.

"Finished bungee jumping, Conrad?" she asked, trying to mask her anxiety with sarcasm.

"Look!" he said.

She turned in the darkness and her headtorch bathed the wall with light. There was something in the ice. Then her eyes focused and Serena found herself face-to-face with a little girl, frozen in time.

"Dear Jesus," she whispered.

"Remember when you told me the only way we'd get together again was when hell freezes over?" he told her. "Well, here we are."

The mist lifted and the light from below flooded the entire wall. In an instant Serena could see hundreds of human beings, their faces frozen in fear. All of them seemed to shout out at once. Serena covered her ears, only to realize that she was the one screaming.

12

DESCENT HOUR THREE

HABITAT MODULE

An hour later, inside the warm P4 habitat module, Conrad was concerned as he looked at Serena on the fold-out surgical table. Her eyes blinked rapidly beneath the high-intensity lights, an oxygen mask over her mouth and several EKG electrodes attached to her chest. Her hair was brushed back from her face and the belt around her cargo pants loosened.

Conrad pointed out the fogged-up porthole at the American flag Yeats had planted atop the pyramid summit.

"Focus on the flag and breathe deeply," he told her as he administered the oxygen from a heavy white canister.

Her parka and outerwear were gone, and he tried not to gaze at her full breasts rising and falling beneath her wool undershirt. She had been hyperventilating since they reached the bottom of the ice gorge, spooked, it seemed, by the frozen graveyard that entombed them. Conrad glanced at the EKG monitor. Only now was her heart rate returning to the upper register of the normal range.

"Better?" he asked her after a minute.

She looked at him like he was a lunatic for asking.

Conrad looked around the cramped habitat perched atop P4's flat summit at the bottom of the gorge. It was a single module, fifty-five feet long and fourteen feet in diameter. Yeats was huddled with the three technicians by the monitors. One was Lopez, a female officer Conrad recognized from Ice Base Orion. The other two were fair-haired steroid freaks who answered to the names of Kreigel and Marcus. They were clearly Yeats's muscle down here.

Conrad turned to Yeats. "Was there any particular reason why you forgot to mention the frozen bodies?"

"Yeah," said Yeats. "I wanted to see your reaction."

Conrad gestured at Serena and glared at Yeats. "Satisfied?"

"Quit whining." Yeats stood up, a hypodermic in hand. He flicked the syringe with his finger, and a clear liquid squirted into the air. Serena squirmed.

Conrad watched in alarm as Yeats grabbed hold of Serena's arm. "What are you doing to her?" he demanded.

"Giving her a shot of the stimulant eleutherococcus," said Yeats, injecting it into Serena's arm before Conrad could stop him. "It's a plant extract of the ginseng family. Deep-sea divers, mountain rescuers, and cosmonauts take it to resist stress while working under inhospitable conditions. About the only damn usable thing the Russians ever contributed to our space program."

The drug seemed to be working. Conrad looked at Serena, who was breathing more evenly now, although there was anger in her eyes. Clearly this wasn't a woman who was used to being taken care of.

"She'll be fine," said Yeats. "Now, if you don't mind, I've got to check my drill team's search for that mythical shaft of yours."

"As mythical as P4," Conrad called out as Yeats opened the hatch and stepped outside. Subzero polar air whooshed inside.

"You seem to be holding up just fine, Conrad," Serena said, catching him off guard. She had removed her oxygen mask. "I take it this isn't the first time you've seen frozen bodies at least twelve thousand years old?"

He looked down at her, barely able to contain his excitement. It wasn't every day he found evidence for his theories, or proof that he wasn't crazy. "Those bodies explain how the pyramid got here."

"Got here?" She managed to sit up, the color returning to her high cheekbones. "What are you talking about? Did it move?"

Conrad dug into his pack and produced a frozen orange. "I chipped this out of the wall," he said. "This proves Antarctica was once a temperate climate."

Serena looked at the orange. "Until it suddenly froze over one day, I suppose?"

Conrad nodded. "Hapgood's theory of earth-crust displacement."

"Charles Hapgood?" Serena asked.

"That's right. Dead for years. So you've heard of him?"

"The university professor, yes, but not this displacement theory."

Conrad always relished an opportunity to tell Mother Earth something she didn't know. Holding up the orange, he said, "Pretend this is Planet Earth."

"OK." She seemed willing to humor him.

He snapped open a pocket knife and carved an outline of the seven continents on the thawing peel. "Hapgood's theory says the ice age was not a meteorological phenomenon. Rather, it was the result of a geological catastrophe about twelve thousand years ago." Conrad rotated the orange upward so that the United States was in the Arctic Circle and Antarctica was closer to the equator. "This was the world back then."

Serena lifted an eyebrow. "And what happened?"

"The entire outer shell of Earth's surface shifted, like the skin of this orange." Conrad rotated the orange downward until it resembled Earth as they knew it. "Antarctica is engulfed by the polar zone while North America is released from the Arctic Circle and becomes temperate. Ice melts in North America while it forms in Antarctica."

Serena frowned. "What caused this cataclysmic shift?"

"Nobody really knows," said Conrad. "But Hapgood thought it was an imbalance of ice in the polar caps. As ice built up, they became so heavy they shifted, dragging the outer crust of the continents in one piece to new positions."

Serena eyed him. "And you'd be willing to stake what's left of your reputation on this earth-crust displacement theory?"

Conrad shrugged. "Albert Einstein liked the idea. He believed significant shifts in Earth's crust have probably taken place repeatedly and within a short time. That could explain weird things, like mammoths frozen in the Arctic Circle with tropical vegetation in their stomachs. Or people and pyramids buried a mile beneath the ice in Antarctica."

Serena put a soft hand on Conrad's shoulder. "If that helps you make sense of the world, then good for you."

Conrad stiffened. He thought she'd be as excited as he was by the evidence. That they were two of a kind. Instead she was attacking the conclusion he had drawn. More than that, she was attacking him personally. He resented this cavalier dismissal—by a woman of religious faith, no less—of a plausible scientific hypothesis from one of the greatest minds in human history. "Does the Vatican have a better theory?"

Serena nodded. "The Flood."

"Same difference," Conrad said. "Both fall under the God-Is-a-Genocidal-Maniac Theory." But as soon as the words were out, he was sorry he had said them to her.

"Hey, mister, you watch your mouth," said a female voice from behind.

Conrad turned to see Lopez looking cross at him. Another Catholic, he realized. Lopez looked at Serena and asked, "You want me to kick his ass for you?"

Serena smiled. "Thanks, but he gets it kicked enough already."

"Well, the offer stands," Lopez said before returning to her work. The Aryan twins, Kreigel and Marcus, looked disappointed. Conrad figured they must be Lutheran, agnostics, or simply of good German stock who in another time and place might have distinguished themselves as poster boys for Hitler's SS.

Serena reached for her parka and slipped her arms through the sleeves. "What are you suggesting, Conrad?" She was trying to zip her parka, but the EKG wires were in the way. "That God is to blame for humanity's every famine, war, or lustful leer?"

He realized she was looking straight at him now, her warm, brown eyes both accusing him and forgiving him at the same time. It irritated the hell out of him. So maybe he had been watching her breasts a little longer than he should have, he thought. He was only human. So was she, if she'd only admit it.

"I saw the way you looked at the little girl in the ice," Conrad said softly. "It was like you were looking at yourself. Hardly the wicked sort the Genesis flood was intended to punish."

"The rain falls on the just and the unjust," she said absently. "Or in this case the ice."

Conrad could tell her thoughts were someplace else. She couldn't see her EKG numbers jumping again.

Conrad pointed to the monitors. "Look, maybe we should take you back up and bring down an able-bodied replacement." He reached over to help her with the EKG wires. "I don't want you to get hurt."

She angrily knocked him away with her shoulder and ripped off the EKG leads. "Speak for yourself, Doctor Yeats."

Conrad rubbed his head and stared at her in disbelief. "Could you send signals that are possibly more mixed?"

She zipped up her parka and jumped to her feet. "Who's mixed up here, Doctor Yeats?"

Conrad stood still, aware of Lopez staring at him with interest. So were Kreigel and Marcus. The soldiers looked like they were just itching for the good nun to give the evil archaeologist a hard knee to the groin.

Then the hatch door opened and another blast of cold shot into the module with Yeats.

"You're right, Yeats," Conrad said coolly. "She's fine."

"Good. Now gear up. We're going into P4," Yeats said. "The drill team just found your shaft."

13

DESCENT HOUR FOUR

UPPER CHAMBER

THE SHAFT WAS ABOUT SEVEN FEET WIDE and seven feet high, Serena guessed, and sloped into total darkness. A coin toss had won her the bragging rights of being the first inside, this after the drill team had sent a twenty-two-pound, six-wheeled modified Mars Sojourner down the shaft with a blowtorch and camera. The remote robot confirmed what Conrad had suspected: the shaft led directly to a chamber in the heart of P4.

As Serena stood on the landing the Americans had erected along the north face of P4 and looked into the mouth of the shaft, she could feel her heart racing. She was still disturbed by the little girl frozen in the ice, she realized, not to mention the sudden, cataclysmic end to an entire society. If only the child hadn't looked so terrified.

She had always taken comfort in the theory that Genesis was a myth and the flood a theological metaphor. Yes, fossil evidence suggested a natural cataclysm. And no, she harbored little doubt that there was some sort of global deluge. But as divine retribution for humanity's wickedness? That was simply Moses's opinion. Unfortunately, she found the alternative worldview, that impersonal cycles of nature wiped out entire species in random fashion, even more distressing, if only because it sapped any meaning from her righteous indignation.

Perhaps it had something to do with her own childhood, she could hear the Holy Father telling her. She had seen herself as a child, an innocent victim, encased in ice, frozen in time like parts of her own personality. Or maybe it was simply the failure of her faith to provide any genuine comfort regarding the inexplicable evil and suffering in this world. It was as if Satan had his own guardian angel—God. But then that would make God the Devil, a thought too terrible for Serena to dwell on.

Her trance was broken by Conrad's voice behind her.

"If you'd like, Serena, I could always take the lead."

She glanced over her shoulder at Conrad and frowned. He was cocky now that he had found a back door into the pyramid. The implication in his eyes was that once again he was right, as always. Not just about P4 but about everything else, including her. As if in time he could figure her out like any other archaeological riddle.

Infuriated, she said, "So you can translate ancient alien inscriptions too?"

"The written word is but one form of communication, Sister Serghetti, as you well know," Conrad replied.

She hated this sort of academic posturing, probably because she was so often guilty of it herself. Or maybe because, like their exchange in the habitat module, it denied the intimacy she felt they had established during the descent down the ice chasm.

"Besides," Conrad added, "I don't think we'll find any inscriptions inside."

"How would you know that?"

"Just a hunch." Conrad ran his hand across the shiny white surface of the pyramid. "Now notice the interlocking casing stones that sheath the whole structure."

If there were any fine grooves, she couldn't see them because of the brilliant reflection. "So how come our pyramids don't shine white like this?"

"The sheathings were stripped for mosques during the Middle Ages," Conrad explained. "The pyramids became cheap quarries. Feel it."

Serena ran her glove across the surface. There was a glassy feel to the stone. "A different ore?"

Conrad smiled. "You noticed. No wonder radio-echo surveys never detected the pyramid. You were right, Yeats. This stuff is slicker than a stealth bomber."

"And harder than diamonds," Yeats added impatiently from somewhere behind Conrad. "Broke all our drills trying to bore holes before we found the shaft. We don't have a name for it yet. Now if we could move ahead and—"

"Oreichalkos," Conrad answered.

Conrad's voice seemed to bounce up and down the shaft walls. Serena asked, "What did you say?"

"*Oreichalkos* is the name of the enigmatic ore or 'shining metal' Plato said the people of Atlantis used," Conrad said. "It was a pure alloy they mined, an almost supernatural 'mountain-copper.' It sparkled like fire and was used to cover walls—and for inscriptions. I'm betting the outer six feet of the pyramid is made of this stuff."

He seemed way too sure of himself. She said, "You think you have all the answers, don't you?"

"We won't know until we get inside, will we?"

"And what if the builders laid a trap?" she said.

"The Atlanteans are the ones who got trapped, remember?" Conrad said. "Besides, the builders never intended entrants to penetrate from the sky, through this shaft. The only booby traps, if any, are scattered around P4's base and any tunnels leading up to key chambers."

She looked over Conrad's shoulder at Yeats, whose brow was furrowed with either concern or, more likely, impatience. Lopez, Kreigel, and Marcus, standing next to him, were as stone-faced as ever.

"Let's find out," she said and stepped into the shaft.

Conrad was right about the *oreichalkos,* she soon discovered. About seven or eight feet into the shaft, the surface of the walls changed to a rougher, darker kind of stone or metal. It scraped lightly on her Gore-Tex parka, but she found that she could creep down the shaft with both feet by leaning back and holding her line taut. The light from her headtorch could only pierce about fifty feet of the darkness ahead.

"How are we doing down there?" called Yeats. His voice sounded flat and tinny in the shaft.

"Fine," she replied.

But she didn't feel fine. The air was heavy and suffocating. The wet, dense walls seemed to close in on her the farther they descended down the thirty-eight-degree grade. As she crept along the shaft, a tingling sensation started in the small of her back and slowly rose up her spine.

Twenty minutes later they emerged from the shaft into a massive, somber reddish room that seemed to radiate tremendous heat and power. It was completely empty.

"There's nothing here, Conrad," she said, her voice echoing. "No inscriptions. Nothing."

"Don't be so certain."

She turned and watched Conrad rappel off the wall from which the shaft emptied, followed by Yeats and his three officers.

Conrad swept the room with his floodlight, revealing walls made of massive granitelike blocks. The floor and ceiling were likewise spanned by gigantic blocks. The chamber was longer than a football field and Serena guessed more than two hundred feet high. Yet it felt like the walls were pressing down on her.

"Talk about megalithic architecture," Conrad said as he ran his light beam across the ceiling. "The engineering logistics alone for this are amazing."

Conrad was right about the architecture, she thought. It revealed much about its builders. That's what made linguistics so intriguing to her. Language often tried to hide or manipulate meaning. In so doing it revealed the true nature of the civilization behind the artifacts.

But there were no inscriptions here. There was nothing. Even in the sparest of digs she could usually find an object that connected her in some way to the people of those times. A shard of pottery, a figurine. They were more than artifacts. They belonged to thinking, feeling human beings. It was like looking through her father the priest's personal items after he died and finding the most trivial yet telling clues about her past.

She felt no connection here. Nothing. Just absolute emptiness, and it was chilling. Not even a sarcophagus—a burial coffin, which if her memory of Egyptian pyramids served her, should have been at the western end of this chamber, but wasn't. At least a tomb was built for someone. But this place was cold, utilitarian, aloof.

"I don't see any other shafts," she said. "You said we'd find another one. And there are no doors. We're stuck."

"There it is." Conrad's beam caught the shaft in the southern wall. It looked just like the one they had emerged from.

Serena said, "All we're going to find at the end of it is the ice pack."

Conrad took a closer look and nodded. "In the Great Pyramid in Giza, the southern shaft led the deceased pharaoh to his reed boats to sail his earthly kingdom. The northern shaft was for him to join the stars in the celestial kingdom."

"That's nice," she said. "But I don't see the burial coffin of a deceased pharaoh in here."

Serena watched as Conrad walked to the center of the room. His footsteps seemed to reverberate more loudly the closer to the center he went.

"What are you doing?" she asked.

"If there's nothing inside the room, then we have to look at the room itself." Conrad walked over to the western wall and turned to face east. He took out what looked like a pen and bounced a thin laser beam off the walls. Then he checked his readings. "This chamber forms a perfect one-by-two rectangle," he announced. "And the height of this room is exactly half the length of its floor diagonal."

"So?"

"Since the chamber forms a perfect one-by-two rectangle, the builders have expressed a golden section, phi."

"Phi?" asked Yeats.

"Phi is an irrational number like pi that can't be worked out arithmetically," Conrad explained. "Its value is the square root of five plus one divided by two, equal to 1.61803. Or, the limiting value of the ratio between successive numbers in the Fibonacci series—the series of numbers beginning 0, 1, 1, 2, 3, 5, 8, 13—"

"In which each term is the sum of the two previous terms," said Serena, completing his lecture. "What's your point?"

"The builders left nothing to chance here. Every stone, every angle, every chamber has been systematically and mathematically designed for some grand purpose. This isn't only the oldest and largest structure on the planet. It's the most perfect too."

She swallowed hard. "Meaning?"

"Meaning it's humanly impossible."

Serena studied him carefully and concluded that he believed what he was saying. She didn't yet, but she was impressed with his brilliance. It was rare she met a man smarter than she was. Only Conrad was perhaps too brilliant for his own good, like the geniuses used by the Americans to build the atomic bomb during World War II. And too sure of himself. He obviously somehow fancied he was going to take something out of P4 and stake his claim in history.

But Yeats would never allow it, she knew, glancing at the American general. His cold, stone-faced expression told her that once Conrad had served his usefulness he would be disposable. Not as his son, but certainly as an archaeologist. Conrad, however, was too smart to be disposable. Which is why she wasn't worried so much by what Conrad was saying as by what he wasn't saying.

"So now you're concluding that P4 is alien?" She shook her head. "The bodies we found in the ice are human. Yeats said the lab autopsies proved as much."

"That doesn't mean those people built P4," Conrad said. "This thing might have been here long before they arrived."

The way he referred to "this thing" bothered her. P4 wasn't a thing. It was a pyramid. Or was it? Without any inscriptions, she was powerless to find any meaning for this monument or argue with Conrad, except to say, "You don't know that for sure."

"Have some faith." Conrad crossed the room and walked over to the opposite shaft. He then pulled out a handheld device from his belt.

"What are you doing?" she said.

"Launching my astronomical simulator." Conrad pushed a button to call up a graphic on the display. "The northern shaft we came through is angled at thirty-eight degrees twenty-two minutes. This southern shaft is angled at fifteen degrees thirty minutes."

Serena walked over. "You lost me."

"You're forgetting this pyramid may be a meridian instrument to track the stars," Conrad said as he glanced at the palm display. "The shafts in the king's chamber of the Great Pyramid, for example, target Orion and Sirius. My hunch is that they were modeled after this. All we have to do is match the shafts with various celestial coordinates throughout history and we can date P4 to the precise—" Conrad stopped short. He was staring at his display.

"Go on," Serena said.

"Wait." Conrad frowned. "This can't be right."

"What is it?"

"Something wrong, Conrad?" asked Yeats, who was still looking up the southern shaft with his flashlight.

"The angle of the shafts targets certain stars in a certain epoch," Conrad said. "This shaft targets Alpha Canis Major in the constellation of the Great Dog. It was known as Sirius to the ancients, who associated it with the goddess Isis, the cosmic mother of the kings of Egypt."

"As opposed to the cosmic king Osiris," Serena said.

Conrad's eyes lit up. "Whose constellation Orion is rising in the east right now."

"You told me all this back at Ice Base Orion." Yeats was now impatiently looking over Conrad's shoulder.

"You don't understand," Conrad explained, and Serena herself was trying to catch up. "This shaft targets Alpha Canis Major right now, on the cusp of the Age of Aquarius, as seen from the South Pole at sunrise on the spring equinox."

Yeats said, "It's September, Conrad."

"For you northerners," Serena reminded Yeats. "It's spring here and in the rest of the Southern Hemisphere." She turned to Conrad. "So what's the meaning?"

"Well, from a fixed point on the ground, the skies are like the odometer on a car. The heavens change over one complete cycle every twenty-six thousand years," he explained. "Meaning either this pyramid was built twenty-six thousand years ago, during the last Age of Aquarius. Or—"

"Or what?" she demanded.

"Or it was built to align with the stars at a date in the future." He looked her in the eye, and she felt her spine tingle. "For this present moment, right now."

14

DESCENT HOUR FIVE

ICE BASE ORION

Inside Ice Base Orion on the surface, O'Dell was lying on his bunk, listening to Chopin, waiting for some word from Yeats and the team below, when suddenly the walls began to shake and the Klaxon sounded.

Every so often the daily monotony of the base was broken by a "sim," or simulation. A Klaxon would sound, and the crew would rush to their posts in the command center, where warning light panels and the diagnostic computers were located. A flashing SIM light on the panel was the crew's notification that the emergency was not real.

But since O'Dell was the man who ordered sims, and he didn't order this event, he knew no SIM light would be flashing. He could feel his pulse quicken and his adrenaline spike as he darted out of his wardroom and headed for the command center module, where the crew was already gathered around the main monitor screen.

"We've got a breach at the outer perimeter, sir," said the lieutenant on duty. "Sector Four."

O'Dell looked at the grainy picture of swirling snow. And then a large gray object emerged through the mist. "It's the Russians," he cursed as he recognized the Kharkovchanka tractor.

"Breach in Sector Three," shouted another officer, followed by several others.

"Sector Two breach, sir!" another said.

"Sector One!"

"Sector Three!"

O'Dell looked around the room at the monitors: Kharkovchanka tractors everywhere. The Russians had surrounded the base. He stood very still, the gravity of the situation slowly sinking in. Then he felt a tap on his shoulder. "Sir?"

O'Dell turned to see his communications officer. He blinked. The officer's lips were moving, but O'Dell couldn't hear anything. "What?"

"I said the Russians are hailing us, sir. Do you want to respond?"

O'Dell took a breath. "Can we reach General Yeats?"

"We lost contact with his party as soon as they penetrated P4."

Before O'Dell could reply, a call came over the intercom from the east air lock. "Ivans at the gate!" O'Dell heard the Russians banging against the door with what sounded like the butts of their AK-47s. He exhaled and turned to his communications officer. "Inform the Russians that a reception committee will greet them at the east air lock."

"Yes, sir."

"Meanwhile, let's hide everything we can."

O'Dell marched out of the command center and into a maze of polystyrene corridors lined with bright, reinforced glass windows. A glance outside at the village of cylindrical modules and geodesic domes told him it would be impossible for him to hide what his team was doing here.

He passed through an air lock into a module where the strains of a Mozart symphony grew louder. He passed a cleanup crew outside the lab containing the benben stone. The double doors with the AUTHORIZED PERSONNEL ONLY sign had disappeared behind a fake glass window that was conveniently fogged up. He just hoped the Russians wouldn't look too closely. But it was probably too much to ask for, much like his prayer that they would miraculously be blinded to the dosimeters located in various panels to measure radiation from the base's nuclear reactor. That alone qualified as a smoking gun that would effectively end his career, O'Dell realized. Yeats would then end his life.

Two unarmed MPs were waiting for him by the air lock. O'Dell nodded, and slowly the heavy inside door opened. The icy air took his breath away as two figures—one large and squat, the other tall and slim—came in and stomped their boots. The squat man lifted his hood and O'Dell saw the ugliest red swollen face of his life.

"I am Colonel Ivan Kovich," he said triumphantly in English but with a thick Russian accent. "And you are in very big trouble. Very big."

Before O'Dell could reply that Ice Base Orion was simply a humble research station, Kovich began to cough uncontrollably. His tall, lanky aide pounded his commanding officer on the back until Kovich waved him off.

"Read it to him, Vlad," Kovich said, and by way of introduction added, "This is Vladimir Lenin, great-great-grandson of Lenin himself."

O'Dell watched with interest as the young officer produced a crumpled piece of paper from his parka and smoothed it out. Apparently this Lenin hadn't risen quite so high in the ranks as his ancestor. In halting English he said, "You are in violation of Article One of international Antarctic Treaty. No military allowed. Treaty gives us right to inspect base."

The young Lenin glanced at Kovich, who nodded, and then put the piece of paper away.

"Any questions?" Kovich asked O'Dell.

O'Dell said, "How many of you will be joining us?"

"As many Russians as there are Americans here on this base and at the bottom of that gorge outside," Kovich said.

"What about Colonel Zawas and his team?"

"We hope you tell us," Kovich said. "We have not heard from his patrol. They have vanished into thin air."

15

DESCENT HOUR FIVE

THERE WAS SILENCE inside the chamber. Yeats looked at Conrad and could tell from his expression that something had gone horribly wrong with his calculations. The nun could tell too, he thought.

Yeats said, "Any chance you—"

"No mistake," Conrad said. "The southern shaft, which we know was built at least twelve thousand years ago, is designed to align with the star Sirius as it appears in our skies present day. The northern shaft likewise targets Al Nitak, the middle star in Orion's Belt."

There was more, Yeats could tell, but Conrad wasn't talking, and Yeats knew why. Serena was also studying Conrad closely.

"Even if you're right about the astronomical alignments, why now?" she asked Conrad. "Do you think P4 has anything to do with the recent earthquakes?"

To Yeats's relief, Conrad said nothing.

"I think we ought to call Ice Base Orion before we proceed any farther." Yeats pulled out his radio and adjusted the frequency. "Ice Base Orion, this is Team Phoenix."

There was no response, just hissing and popping.

"Ice Base Orion," Yeats tried again. "Do you copy?"

Again, no answer.

"Damn," Yeats said. "These walls must be interfering."

"They didn't interfere with the video that the probe sent," Serena said. "Maybe your base isn't there anymore. Maybe it's been buried by the snowstorm."

"Look, Sister Serghetti—" Yeats snapped.

"Doctor Serghetti," she corrected.

"Look, Doctor Serghetti, we've got a case of radio blackout probably caused by this polar storm. That's all. Considering the weather on the surface, I say we wait it out down here. And as long as we're here, we do what we're supposed to do. Lopez, Marcus, Kreigel!"

The three officers snapped to attention. "Sir!"

"Set up a new command and logistics post inside this chamber. The habitat is probably unstable. Bring whatever you need down here." Yeats put a hand on Conrad's shoulder. "You said something back on the surface about four shafts in the pyramid."

"Yes," said Conrad. "I suspect the other two shafts, if they exist, are in a lower chamber. We'll need to find it to be sure."

"To be sure of what?" Serena pressed.

Conrad said, "I'll know when we get there."

"And just how are you going to get there?" she asked.

"Through that door."

"What door?" Yeats asked.

"That door."

Yeats watched Conrad turn toward the shaft they had emerged from and scan the wall to the right with his flashlight. There in the corner, to Yeats's amazement, was an open passageway. It had been behind them.

"That wasn't there before," Serena said hoarsely.

"Yes, it was," Conrad said. "It's always been there."

Once again Conrad's sense of space and dimension awed Yeats. He wouldn't be surprised if Conrad already had mapped out the entire interior of P4 in his head.

"I'm telling you it wasn't," Serena insisted.

"And I'm telling you that you missed it," Conrad said. "Chill out, OK?"

"Fine." She took a step toward the open door. "Then what are we waiting for?"

Yeats blocked her with his arm. "You stay here while Conrad and I search for those two other shafts."

Yeats could see a flash of fury in Serena's eyes. She clearly had trouble taking orders. No wonder she was such a pain in the ass for the Vatican. She pressed against his arm toward the doorway, but Conrad gripped her shoulder and pulled her back.

"It's all right, Serena," Conrad said. "When we find the other shafts, we'll come back for you."

That'll be the day, Yeats thought. "Of course we'll come back for you," he told her. "As soon as we find something."

"Promise," added Conrad earnestly, which bothered Yeats. Conrad didn't have the right to promise anybody anything.

The look on Serena's face told Yeats that she didn't believe Conrad for a second. "Fine," she said. "Go."

Yeats nodded to Marcus and Kreigel, who took up positions at the doorway, and then he followed Conrad out of the chamber and down a low, square tunnel.

As they proceeded through the dark, Yeats worried that he had badly miscalculated in allowing Mother Earth to join the team. Not because there was anything wrong with her, but because something clearly was wrong with Conrad whenever she was around.

A little space, Yeats hoped, would clear the kid's head.

The strategy paid off several minutes later when they reached a solid horizontal platform. It looked like some kind of altar. Conrad suddenly stopped.

"What is it?" Yeats asked.

"This lies exactly along the east-west axis of the pyramid," Conrad explained. "It marks the point of transition between the northern and southern halves of the monument."

"So?" Yeats was about to take another step when Conrad braced him with his arm. It was stronger than Yeats expected.

"Look." Conrad aimed his flashlight into the darkness, revealing what looked like a gigantic subway tunnel plunging toward the center of the earth. Running down the middle of the shiny floor was a sunken channel about forty feet wide and twenty feet deep. It mirrored precisely the design of the vaulted ceiling at its apex three hundred feet overhead. "This is the main corridor or Great Gallery."

"Goddamn it, son." Yeats stepped back from the ledge. "You

certainly know your way around this place. You sure you've never been here before?"

"Only in my dreams."

"Looks like a nightmare to me," Yeats said as he peered over the ledge. "Where does it go?"

"Only one way to find out." Conrad unraveled rope from his pack. "The slope is about twenty-six degrees and the floors are slick. We'll need to use lines. Just stick to the ramparts and try not to slide into the channel."

They had descended about a thousand feet when Yeats suddenly lost all sense of direction. It was the same sort of vertigo he sometimes felt back at Ice Base Orion on the surface. He couldn't tell which end of the tunnel was up or which was the floor or ceiling. Yeats rubbed his eyes, which stung from the salt of his cold sweat, and continued down the Great Gallery.

Conrad said, "You didn't really bring Serena as an observer, did you?"

Yeats sensed that Conrad actually missed the nun. Good grief, he thought, they had only just left her. "Hell, no," Yeats said. "I want to see how much she knows about this thing. It's more than she's letting on."

Conrad asked, "What makes you so suspicious?"

"My job description."

"Then maybe Serena shouldn't be alone."

"I've got three good officers standing guard."

"I just don't think we needed to leave her behind."

"Yes, we did. And now you can tell me whatever you couldn't tell the good sister. Namely, what you're really thinking."

"It's probably nothing," Conrad said. "Pure coincidence."

"No such thing in this place," Yeats replied. "Talk."

"Look around." Conrad gestured across the vast, gleaming gallery. "No inscriptions, religious iconography, or any discernible symbolism in this gallery or the pyramid."

"So?"

"So this isn't a tomb. It's not even a puzzle for initiates to wander through and solve like I proposed earlier."

"Then what the hell is it?"

"It feels like we're inside some enormous machine."

Yeats felt a deep and disturbing jolt inside his bowels. The news was like some sort of prophecy, both expected and alarming. "Machine?"

"I think it's supposed to do something."

There was a heaviness in the air. Yeats cleared his throat. "Do what?"

"I don't know. Maybe disaster struck the builders before they ever got a chance to turn it on."

"Maybe."

"Or maybe," Conrad went on, "this machine caused the disaster."

Yeats nodded slowly as the words sunk in. Somehow he had felt it all along. He wanted to tell Conrad more. But now was not the time. Conrad would hopefully figure it out on his own anyway.

Descending to the Great Gallery, Conrad was sorry he had left Serena behind in the upper chamber. And not just because he wanted her to see for herself how right he was about P4. He could tell from her eyes how put out and excluded she felt. He knew the sensation well and felt a twinge of guilt for not sticking up for her with Yeats. But he wasn't about to blow his own chance to explore the lower levels and lead the way to the greatest archaeological discovery in human history.

As soon as he reached the bottom of the gallery, however, Conrad's mental map of the pyramid's interior began to unravel. He faced a fork branching off into two smaller tunnels. There should have been three.

He could hear Yeats's heavy breathing behind him. "Well?" Yeats demanded impatiently. "Which way?"

Conrad studied the two "smaller" tunnels. Each was more than thirty feet high. One continued along the twenty-six-degree slope of the gallery. The other dropped ninety degrees into a vertical shaft. Neither satisfied him.

Conrad instinctively turned around and began to search for a third tunnel that would double back beneath the gallery. But he couldn't find it.

"What are you doing?" Yeats asked.

Conrad patted the cold wall and said nothing. He was positive the central chamber he was looking for was on this level. And if the Great Pyramid in Giza was indeed modeled after P4, then the corridor leading to that central chamber should have been there at the bottom of the gallery.

But it wasn't.

Perhaps he was assuming too much to think the ancient Egyptians got it right from the Atlanteans. Even if his initial hypothesis was correct, that didn't mean the Egyptians had the knowledge or means to fashion an accurate copy of P4.

"The chamber we're looking for is on this level," he said. "But we'll have to access it from below."

"Fine," Yeats said. "Which tunnel?"

"Theoretically, both corridors should lead to the burial chamber," Conrad said, hesitating.

Yeats said, "As long as it isn't ours."

"You don't understand," Conrad said. "The burial chamber at the bottom of the pyramid serves as a kind of cosmic dressing chamber where the king can dance and celebrate the completion of life. At the top of the pyramid is the phoenix or benben stone, symbolizing resurrection. There's an ascension to all this."

"I get it," said Yeats. "And somewhere in between, the hocus-pocus happens."

"At the central chamber," Conrad said. "That's where we can expect to find a repository of texts or technology to unlock the meaning of P4." Conrad took another look around. "Since the access corridor isn't here, I suspect the burial chamber will point the way."

"So which tunnel leads to the burial chamber?"

Conrad could feel Yeats's brooding stare. The reality was that he was still getting used to attacking this pyramid from the top down, when every previous experience in his life was from the bottom up.

Conrad looked down the first tunnel. It would be natural to continue along the slope of the gallery they had just passed through. But he suspected that tunnel led to the main entrance of P4. It was probably blocked at some point to keep outsiders from entering P4 at the ground level.

"Make up my mind, son."

"Door number two," Conrad said. "We'll take the vertical shaft."

"OK." Yeats leaned over the shaft and dropped a new line.

Conrad emerged from the bottom of the vertical shaft a half hour later, dropping into a lower north-south corridor. This, too, was more than thirty feet high. Yeats had just landed behind him when the alarm on Conrad's watch started beeping.

"You've got an appointment somewhere?" Yeats asked.

"We're under the base of P4." Conrad pulled back his left glove and tilted his wrist to reveal the blue electroluminescent backlight of his multisensor watch face. In addition to a built-in digital compass, barometer, thermometer, and GPS, it included an altimeter graph. "We've descended almost a mile and a half. I set the alarm for my target altitude."

Yeats pulled out his own USAF standard-issue altimeter. "You were off by more than a quarter mile," Yeats said. "We're barely a mile down."

Conrad looked at his altimeter doubtfully. His father wasn't cutting him any slack now. Not an inch. Much less a quarter mile. This might as well be the first human landing on Mars as far as Yeats was concerned, Conrad realized, and NASA allowed no margin for error. As Conrad rolled it over in his head, he concluded Yeats was right. If anything, P4 was more significant to humanity than Mars. It was certainly closer. Palpably so.

"So which way now?" Yeats pressed. "North or south?"

Conrad cut his line and instinctively turned to the north. "This way."

After about 1,200 feet, the floor sloped suddenly and almost doubled the height of the ceiling. Fifty yards ahead was the entrance Conrad was looking for. He could feel his blood starting to really pump.

"This is it," he said.

They entered a vastly larger space. The beams of their head-torches disintegrated into nothingness as the floor beneath their boots sloped at a slight grade. Engulfed in darkness, and feeling very cold,

Conrad sensed that this cavity was in some ways many times larger than the upper chamber they had left at the top of the Great Gallery. Yet the emptiness beyond the torchlight beams also felt compressed in some way. This was definitely uncharted territory, he realized, and could feel the tension in his gut.

"I'm tossing out a flare—thirty-second delay," Yeats said. "Three, two, one."

Conrad could hear Yeats heave the stick into the dark. Mentally he counted down as he pulled out his digital camera to capture whatever image would burst forth. A few seconds later the chamber exploded with light.

Conrad shielded his eyes as he panned what fleetingly resembled a stone crater with his camera. As his eyes adjusted to the light, he began to see that's exactly what they were standing in. They were on the rim of a titanic crater almost a mile in diameter. But it was only two hundred feet high.

The flare sputtered and died. Once again Conrad and Yeats were in darkness.

Yeats said, "Show me what you've got."

"Right here."

Conrad replayed the footage on the flat display screen on the back of his camera. It glowed bright in the darkness.

"Stop," said Yeats.

Conrad paused the screen. There was something in the center of the crater. A circle or hub of some sort.

"Can you zoom?"

"A little."

Conrad, fingers tingling with adrenaline, magnified the image until it filled the display. But the picture was still too blurred to make it out clearly.

"Let's go," he said.

Conrad and Yeats marched in unison toward the center, careful not to lose their balance on the sloping floor. Conrad could feel his heart pounding. He'd never experienced any sort of chamber like this in Egypt or the Americas, nothing even remotely similar in size or configuration.

At the half-mile mark Yeats called a halt.

Conrad lowered his flashlight beam to the floor and found something about ten yards in front of them. Carved across the polished stone floor were four rings radiating from an oval cartouche in the center, like some magnificent seal.

Yeats let out a low whistle. "Finally, inscriptions for Mother Earth."

"Not quite," said Conrad, breathing hard. Part of him wanted to run back and get her. Another part refused to admit he couldn't figure this out by himself. "It's an icon or symbol."

"Then even you should be able to decipher it."

Conrad walked to the center of the floor, where a familiar-looking hieroglyphic was inscribed inside the oval cartouche. It was of a god or king seated inside some sort of mechanical device. He resembled a bearded Caucasian and wore what looked like an elaborate head ornament known as an Atef crown. And he held some sort of scepter in his hand. It looked like a small obelisk.

"This figure looks familiar," Conrad heard himself saying, "but I can't put my finger on why."

Conrad looked again at the cartouche on the floor. The image inscribed inside was similar to the symbols he had seen depicting the gods of Viracocha in the Andes and Quetzalcoatl in Central America. But this otherworldly symbol awakened something primeval and terrifying inside him, and suddenly he knew why.

"This pyramid is dedicated to Osiris." Conrad's voice wavered.

"So what?" said Yeats. "I thought most of these pyramids were dedicated to some god."

"You don't understand," Conrad said excitedly. "This seal suggests P4 was built by the King of Eternity himself, the Lord of First Time."

"First Time?"

"The Genesis epoch I told you about back at Ice Base Orion, the time when humanity emerged from the primordial darkness and was offered the gifts of civilization from the gods," Conrad said. "Ancient Egyptian texts say these gifts or technologies were introduced through intermediaries or lesser divinities known as 'The Watchers' or *Urshu*."

Yeats paused. "So you think the *Urshu* were the Atlanteans who built P4?"

"Maybe," Conrad said. "I'm sure Serena has her own interpretation. But there's no denying that we've found the mother lode." Conrad could hear the triumph in his voice. "The Mother Culture."

"First Time," Yeats said.

"First Time," Conrad echoed and spoke the phrase in his best Ancient Egyptian: *"Zep Tepi."*

As soon as the words fell out of his mouth, they seemed to swirl around the chamber, spinning out from the center of the crater floor like some centrifugal force. The floor started to shake.

Suddenly the cartouche split open and Conrad stumbled backward as a pillar of fire shot up from the floor and through a circular shaft in the ceiling.

"Whoa!" he shouted and slipped flat on his back. He started to slide across the bottom of the crater floor toward the fiery hole.

Yeats grabbed his arm and held him back. "Easy, easy, easy."

Then the fire burst disappeared and the rumbling stopped. All that remained was a craterlike shaft where the cartouche had split open.

Conrad felt a tug as Yeats pulled him up on his feet. "Now where on earth do you think that goes, son?"

Conrad leaned over and peered down the fiery shaft. For a flickering second he glimpsed a glowing tunnel that seemed to descend to the very bowels of the earth. But the residual heat from the blast burned his forehead and he quickly pulled away.

"From the looks of it," Conrad said, gingerly touching his forehead to see if it was still there, "I'd say the pit of hell."

16

DESCENT HOUR SIX

IT WAS THE VODKA.

It had to be the vodka, Colonel Ivan Kovich swore, when he first beheld the pyramid at the bottom of the ice chasm. That or some experimental hallucinogenics the Americans had slipped into his drink at their base on the surface.

Whatever it was, he decided, it was part of an American plot to drive the Russian people insane. It had started with the imperialist capitalist bankrolling of the Communist revolution in 1917. It had moved into full gear with the installation of Stalin and the gulags, and then the slaughter of twenty million during World War II. It culminated in the humiliating disintegration of the Soviet Union in 1991 and rise of the golden arches of American hamburger stands in Moscow.

Now that the United States was the world's undisputed superpower, Kovich was convinced, the Americans were simply keeping the Russians alive for their own cruel pleasure, starving their bodies of nutrients with Big Macs and their souls with TV shows like *Baywatch.*

It was from this hell that Kovich had sought refuge in the spare, unspoiled beauty of Antarctica, only to stumble across a veritable Four Seasons Resort in the snow in the form of Ice Base Orion. With state-of-the-art computers, plush sleeping quarters, toilets that flushed, and a stockpile of food, the only thing lacking was a swimming pool and health spa.

The concierge of Hotel Orion, Colonel O'Dell, was pleasant enough during the inspection. But the American grew increasingly nervous when Russian dosimeters detected radiation, and Kovich suggested a survey of the gigantic ice chasm over which the base was perched.

Kovich was convinced he was on the verge of discovering a rogue nuclear testing facility, mostly because Russia itself had one at the other end of the planet in the Arctic Circle.

Only after reaching the bottom of the abyss and beholding the protruding summit of a pyramid did Kovich realize that the Americans had pushed him and his twenty Russian comrades over the brink. And how could he ever forget the horror on his men's faces when they saw the hundreds of human bodies frozen in the walls of this ice tomb?

Truly their commanding officer had finally led them down to hell.

The shiny white exterior of the pyramid didn't even show up on their radio-echo scans from a few feet away. It was obvious the Americans had developed a supersecret, indestructible stealth material that could render their fleets and bombers both invisible and invincible.

As if that were not enough, a message played in Kovich's head over and over again: "Wait, there's more!" the voice repeated, like some terrible American infomercial. "Much, much more!" As a special bonus at the bottom of hell, the Americans had left what looked like an RV parked atop the pyramid summit along with another hole that beckoned them farther.

Here at this "habitat" Kovich left the two American observers who had accompanied them down, along with five of his men. He and the rest of his team proceeded down the seven-foot-tall shaft and didn't reach the other end for a good half hour.

They emerged inside what seemed to be a massive stone oven the size of an Olympic stadium. And inside this chamber were four American soldiers—two men and two women—who surrendered their weapons but refused to say a word.

As a final bonus, there seemed to be no way out of this tomb. When attempts to reach Vlad and the rest of the crew at Ice Base Orion on the surface failed, Kovich feared the worst.

He had been duped, he concluded. This was a trap. They had

been lured into this mass grave so they could be killed. Meanwhile, the Americans would monitor their slow descent into madness with hidden cameras and use the results in their training videos for new recruits.

Finally, one of his men found an open passageway.

Kovich left a few men to guard the Americans and took the rest down a low, square tunnel to a plateau overlooking what looked like a gigantic Moscow metro tunnel plunging toward the center of the earth. It was at least one hundred meters tall, he guessed, and could swallow Russia's GUM retail mall, the biggest in the world. Running along its shiny walls and floor and ceiling were sunken channels about forty feet wide and twenty feet deep.

"Look, sir!" shouted one of his soldiers, pointing into the abyss. "There's more!"

Peering over the ledge, Kovich could only rub his disbelieving eyes. For inside one of the channels were two lines daring him to descend even farther.

Something rose up inside Kovich's bubbling psyche, bursting through the swirling images of fast food, bikinis, Ginsu knives, and self-improvement CDs. That something was the stark realization that he and his men were going to die. They would never make it back to the surface again.

With chilling clarity, Kovich made the last strategic decision of his life: if they weren't leaving this tomb, then neither were the Americans.

17
DESCENT HOUR SEVEN

Inside the subterranean boiler room beneath P4, Conrad applied a cold canteen to his scalded forehead as a dull glow from the shaft crept across the crater floor. Still smarting from the burn, he removed the canteen and noticed some singed eyebrow hairs clinging to the condensation on the outside.

"Things are certainly heating up," Yeats was telling him. "We better move out before another blast fries both of us. Between frostbite on your hand and second-degree burns on your face, you've already got two strikes against you."

"Let's at least get a reading," Conrad said. "You've got a remote heat sensor, don't you?"

Yeats produced a small ball from his backpack. "The shell is made of the same stuff NASA uses on the outer tiles of the space shuttle," Yeats said. "Stand back."

Conrad watched Yeats toss it into the shaft. A minute later the numbers showed up on Yeats's handheld computer. Conrad looked it over.

"Before your little heat-shielded sensor melted during its descent," Conrad said, "it plunged four miles and recorded a temperature of almost nine thousand degrees Fahrenheit."

"Mother of God," Yeats said. "That's as hot as the surface of the sun."

"Or the molten core of the earth," Conrad said. "I think this is a geothermal vent."

"A geothermal vent?" Yeats narrowed his eyes. "Like the kind found in oceans?"

Conrad nodded. "One of my old professors discovered a hot spot like this west of Ecuador, about five hundred miles out in the water and eight thousand feet down," he said. "There's very little life at the bottom of the ocean because there's no light and the temperatures are below freezing. But where there are cracks in the earth's crust, the heat from the core escapes to warm the water. That's how some forms of ocean life—earth-heated crabs, clams, ten-foot-long worms—survive down there."

Conrad looked around. This geothermal chamber had to be the same kind of thing. The only question was whether the Atlanteans built P4 over an existing vent to harness its heat or possessed such advanced technology that they could tap Earth's core—or any planet's, for that matter—for unlimited power.

"According to Plato, Atlantis was destroyed by a great volcanic explosion," Yeats said. "Maybe this was the cause of it."

"Or maybe this is the legendary power source of Atlantis," said Conrad. "The Atlanteans allegedly had harnessed the power of the sun. Most scientists naturally assumed this meant solar power. But this geothermal vent taps into Earth's core—which is as hot as the surface of the sun. So this could be the so-called power of the sun that Atlantis possessed."

"Could be," said Yeats.

But Conrad could tell Yeats had another purpose in mind for P4, and it probably had little to do with its archaeological or even technological value. "You have another theory?"

Yeats nodded. "What you're really saying is that P4 is essentially a giant geothermal machine that can channel heat from Earth's core to melt the ice over Antarctica."

Conrad grew very still. He hadn't thought about it in terms quite so catastrophic. In his mind that kind of thinking was the domain of environmental alarmists like Serena. But a slow-growing angst crept over him as he remembered the bodies in the ice chasm above P4 and Hapgood's earth-crust displacement theory. He hadn't entertained the possibility that a natural disaster on the scale of a global shift of the earth's crust—the culmination of a forty-one-thousand-year-old geological cycle—could be triggered by design. Yeats, on the other hand, seemed to have given this scenario some serious thought. At the very least, Conrad had to agree that there was enough heat bottled up beneath P4 to melt so much ice that rising sea levels would certainly wipe out coastal cities on every continent.

"Yes, I suppose this machinery could warm Antarctica," Conrad said slowly. "But to what end?"

"Maybe to make the continent or planet more habitable for their species," Yeats went on. "Who the hell cares? The point is that there must be a control room somewhere, and we've got to find it. Before anybody else does."

"Right," Conrad said, wondering why he should be so surprised that Yeats was as practical a man as he was. "That would be the central chamber we've been looking for, the one with the two hidden celestial shafts."

"Then let's get the hell out of here and go for it," Yeats said. "Before this thing goes off again—for real."

As they made their way back up to the gallery, Conrad was haunted by fear that he had just done what he denied ever doing—destroyed the integrity of a find. Worse, he may have destroyed himself and others with it. He could almost hear the whispers that had haunted him his entire career now chasing him up the tunnel: "Tomb Raider" . . . "Raper of Virgin Digs" . . . "Conrad the Destroyer." Now, more than ever, they had to get back to Serena, find P4's secret chamber, and make sure this cosmic heat valve was shut off.

Upon reaching the fork at the bottom of the Great Gallery, Conrad wasn't surprised to find three tunnels now instead of two.

"Now don't tell me you saw that one before too," Yeats said.

"No, it definitely wasn't there before," Conrad said. "Maybe something we did in the lower chamber opened a door."

Conrad looked up the gallery toward the upper chamber and saw several figures rappeling down.

Yeats saw them too and gripped his arm. "Fall back," he whispered. "That's an order."

They cut their headtorches and retreated to the new access tunnel, where they took cover on either side of the entry. Pressing his back against the wall, Conrad looked across at Yeats. His father's silhouette was blackened by the dim glow radiating out from the bottom of the gallery.

"Team Phoenix, copy," Yeats spoke into his radio microphone. But there was no response. "Copy me, Team Phoenix." Again, nothing. "Goddamn it."

Conrad pulled out his nightscope and peered around the corner. Two figures dropped down onto the landing at the bottom of the gallery. Their green eyes—night-vision goggles—bobbed up and down in the dark. Conrad pulled back and looked at his father.

"Who are they?" Conrad whispered.

"Can't say," Yeats said. "But they sure as hell aren't mine. Move."

They started down the long, dark access tunnel. This corridor was thirty-five feet tall, but it felt much smaller after the grandeur of the Great Gallery they had descended. After about 1,200 feet due south, the floor sloped sharply into a larger tunnel with a ceiling twice as high.

"Over there." Yeats pointed his flashlight beam to the floor.

About a hundred yards ahead was either a doorway or the end of the tunnel. It was hard to tell. But then Conrad felt a blast of air. He looked up and found a shaft in the ceiling of the tunnel. There was another one in the floor, angled at the same slope.

"That could be one of those two extra star shafts that lead into the secret chamber," he said. "I think it cuts through this corridor. I'll have to drop a line down to be sure."

Yeats said, "I'm going to follow this corridor for another hundred yards or so to see what's at the end. Then I'll come back and you can tell me what you found."

Conrad watched Yeats disappear while he uncoiled a line down the shaft. He was peering over the edge cautiously when he heard the scrape of a boot behind him and he swung around to see a pair of green eyes glowing in the passageway.

"And who the hell are you?" Conrad asked.

The figure in the night-vision goggles raised an AK-47 machine gun. "Your worst nightmare," he said with a thick Russian accent and fingered his radio. "This is Leonid calling Colonel Kovich. I've captured an American."

"The hell you have." Conrad kicked the AK-47 out of Leonid's hands and picked up the broken laser sight from the floor. Leonid whipped out a Yarygin PY 9 mm Grach pistol just as Conrad painted his forehead with a red dot from the laser sight. Conrad hoped Leonid couldn't see there was no gun attached to it. "Drop it. Now."

The Russian dropped his gun and Conrad exhaled.

"Very good."

A bone-handled hunter's knife slid out of the Russian's right sleeve and dropped into the palm of his hand. There was a click as his thumb found the button, and his arm swept up, the blade streaking for the soft flesh beneath Conrad's chin.

Conrad, anticipating such a move the second he heard the click of the knife, blocked the arm and grabbed for the wrist with both hands, twisting it so that the Russian dropped the knife and cried out in pain. Conrad wrenched the arm around and up, still keeping that excruciating hold in place. This time the Russian screamed as muscles tore, and Conrad ran him headfirst into the wall and then plunged him into the floor shaft.

Conrad was peering into the darkness below when he heard footsteps. He grabbed the Russian's AK-47 from the floor and looked up to see Yeats running toward him.

"Dead end," Yeats said. "What the hell happened here?"

Conrad was about to tell him when he felt a yank at his ankle. He looked down and saw his nylon line tightening like a noose around his boot, realizing a second too late that the Russian had somehow snagged it on his way down and was taking Conrad with him.

"Hold this!" Conrad tossed Yeats the other end of the line as he plunged down the shaft in the tunnel floor. "Don't let go!"

Tumbling through the darkness, Conrad struggled to clip his line to his harness. He could sense himself falling through one level after another, with no end in sight. He tensed up as he braced himself for something to break his fall.

Soon the line around his boot slacked off while the line around his harness stiffened. Finally, he burst into some large space. His line snapped tight and caught him in midair. He dangled helplessly.

"Dad!" he called. "Can you hear me?"

There was nothing at first, then the faintest, "Barely!"

Conrad fingered his belt for a flashlight and switched it on. The shock of what he saw took a few seconds to sink in.

He was swinging like a pendulum inside a magnificent chamber in the shape of a geodesic dome. His fingers tingled with adrenaline as he scanned the ceiling with his beam. The apex of the dome was about two hundred feet above him. Scattered across the four merging walls were numerous constellations. It looked like some kind of cosmic observatory.

He lowered his beam. Some kind of altar with a two-foot-tall obelisk in the center rose from the stone floor. And impaled on it was the Russian.

"Dad!" Conrad shouted. "I found it!"

18
DESCENT HOUR EIGHT

CONRAD CUT HIS LINE and dropped twenty feet to the floor of the geodesic chamber. He looked up at the star carvings scattered across the domed ceiling almost two hundred feet above him. There was no other entrance into this chamber that he could see. Only the overhead shaft. This was a virgin find. His find. He was the first human to set foot in this chamber in more than twelve thousand years. For all he knew, he was the first human ever.

Except, that is, for the Russian impaled on the obelisk in the center of the chamber. Conrad had to push hard to lift the corpse off the obelisk and onto the floor, so that he could drag it off to the side.

Conrad wiped the Russian's blood off his hands and slowly circled the altar with the obelisk while he waited for Yeats to find his own way into the chamber. Tingling with anticipation, he pointed his torch beam at the four rings radiating out from the altar. Then he lifted the beam until it splashed the obelisk with light.

It looked like a classical obelisk. Its height was ten times its width. Except for its rotundalike base, it resembled a two-foot-tall scale model of the Washington Monument. On every side were technical inscriptions, the only inscriptions so far inside the entire pyramid.

He'd eventually need Serena's help to crack their meaning, he realized as he pulled out his digital camera and took pictures. For now he took special note of a series of six rings on one of the obelisk's four sides and a sequence of four constellations—Scorpio, Sagittarius, Capricorn, and Aquarius—on another.

Most important, the obelisk looked exactly like the scepter held by Osiris in that royal seal he had seen on the floor of the geothermal chamber. Historically the king's scepter connoted awesome power, the very power his father the general was looking for and afraid somebody else would capture.

This is the Scepter of Osiris, he thought. *This is the key to P4, the geothermal vent and everything else.*

Conrad leaned forward to take the obelisk when a hidden door began to rumble open—a series of doors, really. Four great granite slabs began to part from the bottom up.

Conrad stepped back as the last door opened to reveal a lone figure standing in a corridor that seemed to lead to the Great Gallery.

"Conrad."

He knew it was Serena before she stepped into the chamber. Behind her emerged a big Russian, holding an AK-47, its laser sight glowing.

"Doctor Yeats, I presume?" The voice carried a thick Russian accent. "My name is Colonel Kovich. Where is Leonid?"

Kovich shoved Serena toward him, and Conrad caught her in his arms.

"Thank God you're OK," he breathed as he pulled her close.

But her business-only stare froze him. Then she glanced at the obelisk. She also took in the corpse on the floor and, much to his horror, connected it with the blood on his hands.

"Eureka, Conrad," she told him. "You've found it. I hope it was worth the price."

He said, "I can explain."

"You killed Leonid," Kovich said.

"Actually, he tried to kill me," Conrad said. "That was just before he fell down a shaft without a line. In case you hadn't noticed, your officers aren't the best-equipped in the world."

At that moment a gruff voice from behind the Russian said, "You can say that again."

Conrad turned to see Yeats march into the chamber pointing an AK-47 at Kovich. "Damn piece of shit jammed on me twice. Now drop your rod, Kovich."

Kovich frowned and placed his AK-47 on the floor next to

Leonid's corpse. "Please, General Yeats," Kovich chided. "We are soldiers."

Yeats walked over to Kovich and gave him a good swift knee to the groin. The Russian doubled over in agony. "Put your ass on the floor," Yeats ordered. "Then cross your legs. Don't screw up unless you want to look like your comrade here."

Kovich stared at the massive hole in Leonid's chest, then slid down the wall like Humpty-Dumpty. Yeats whipped the butt of his gun against the Russian's skull. Conrad heard a crack and Kovich crumpled to the floor, moaning in pain.

"He'll live," Yeats said. "But we've got dozens of armed Ivans crawling all over this place, so we don't have much time. What have you found?"

"This obelisk," Conrad said. "It's the key to the pyramid."

Yeats looked at the inscriptions on the sides of the obelisk. "You know what these mean, Doctor Serghetti?"

"They say that Osiris built this thing," Serena said, surprising Conrad by how easily she could translate the writings. "The obelisk is his scepter. It belongs in the Shrine of the First Sun."

"What's that?" Yeats demanded.

"The 'Place of First Time' I was telling you about back at Ice Base Orion," Conrad said excitedly. All of which made sense to Conrad, because the figure of Osiris he had seen in the geothermal chamber was sitting on some kind of seat or throne. The Seat of Osiris was obviously located in this Shrine of the First Sun—along with the Secret of First Time itself.

"So then we'll grab this Scepter of Osiris and put it where it belongs, in this so-called Shrine of the First Sun," Yeats said.

"Not a good idea, General." Serena pointed to the markings on the south face of the obelisk, which included a series of six rings. "The inscriptions under the six rings say the machinery controlled by the pyramid was set in motion by Osiris in order to keep a check on humanity—a sort of cosmic 'reset' mechanism designed to wipe the slate clean six times before the end of time."

"A check on humanity?" Yeats said. "What's that supposed to mean?"

"It means the Atlanteans built this thing to prevent us from getting too advanced," Serena said. "Kind of like the Tower of Babel in Genesis. The idea is that technological advancement is meaningless without moral advancement. So humanity is constantly tested to prove its goodness or nobility."

"Six times," Conrad said. "You said humanity gets six chances before the end of history. Where did you get that?"

"The six Suns, Conrad." She read the inscriptions within each ring on the south face of the obelisk. "The First Sun was destroyed by water. The Second Sun ended when the terrestrial globe toppled from its axis and everything was covered with ice. The Third Sun was destroyed as a punishment for human misdemeanors by an all-consuming fire that came from above and below. This pyramid was built at the dawn of the Fourth Sun, which ended in a universal flood."

"So we're the children of the Fifth Sun, just like the Mayan and Aztec myths?" Conrad asked. "Is that what you're saying? That we're condemned to repeat the sins of the ancients?"

"No, that's what your precious obelisk says," Serena said. "And as for repeating the sins of the ancients, if the past century of human history is any guide, then we already have—in spades."

Conrad was quiet for a moment. She had a point. Finally, he said, "And just when exactly does the Fifth Sun end and the Sixth Sun begin?"

"Just as soon as you remove the Scepter of Osiris from its stand."

"Seriously?" Conrad said.

"Seriously."

"She's lying," Yeats said.

"No, I'm not." She glared at Yeats. "It says here that only 'he who stands before the Shining Ones in the time and place of the most worthy can remove the Scepter of Osiris without tearing Heaven and Earth apart.' Anybody other than the most worthy will trigger unimaginable consequences."

"Shining Ones?" Yeats said. "Who the hell are they?"

"Stars," Conrad said. "The Shining Ones are stars. The builders could read the stars, which foretell a specific moment in the space-time continuum, a 'most noble' moment. This is humanity's 'escape clause,' so to speak, the secret that breaks the curse of the ancients once and for all."

"How convenient for you, Conrad," Serena said. "The answer is written in the stars, and you can interpret those however you want."

"You mean like the wise men and the birth of Christ?"

Serena wasn't biting. "That's completely different."

Conrad pressed her. "Or the fish symbol of the early Christians, which just happened to coincide with the dawn of the Age of Pisces and which, coincidentally, is about to end with the dawn of a new Age of Aquarius."

"Meaning what, Conrad?" Serena demanded.

"Meaning the age of the Church is over, and that's what's got you and your friends at the Vatican in a tizzy."

"You're wrong, Conrad."

"The stars say I'm right."

Yeats pointed to one side of the obelisk. "You mean stars like those four constellations on the scepter?"

"No, the ones up there." Conrad pointed up at the engravings on the domed ceiling. "This chamber is a kind of celestial clock. Watch."

He put his hand to the obelisk and heard Serena gasp as he twisted it like a joystick, moving it one way and then another. As he did, a dull rumble began and the geodesic dome overhead began to move in sync.

"If we want to set the skies for a certain time, we begin with the cosmic 'hour hand' or age, which corresponds to the zodiac," he said. "We're at the dawn of Aquarius, so that constellation is locked over there to the east."

As he spoke it, the dome reverted to its original position.

"The 'minute hand' of the clock comes from a location, such as the Southern or Northern hemispheres."

Here Conrad moved the obelisk, and an entirely new pattern of stars rotated up from beneath the chamber floor. He rotated the dome farther, however, until he could lock the original pattern overhead.

"A third, more precise setting comes with the various equinoxes of the year."

Conrad made his final adjustment and completed his demonstration by locking everything as it was before he started. The rumbling ceased.

"So you see, Serena, the obelisk and altar around which we stand represent the earth at a fixed location. The constellations on the dome above us are the heavens. Together they 'lock' at a fixed point in time."

Serena, apparently still shaken by what she obviously perceived to be his reckless meddling with an artifact, said, "And how are the stars in the chamber aligned right now?"

"They're aligned to the obelisk like the heavens over Antarctica in the present day," he said conclusively, as if there could be no debate.

"Which I suppose must surely be the most worthy moment in human history," she said, "because the great Conrad Yeats is alive and he discovered it."

Conrad smiled. "Finally, we agree on something."

Serena looked at him with scorn. "Has it dawned on you that maybe you're the biggest jackass of all time and that this is humanity's most ignoble moment if you remove that obelisk?"

It had indeed dawned on Conrad, and now he was getting annoyed with her.

"Think about it, Serena," he told her. "If what you're saying is true, then P4's builders knew that only an advanced civilization with sophisticated technology could even locate this pyramid, much less penetrate it. It's our advancement that makes us noble. So this moment simply must be the most worthy time, and this obelisk is the key to the knowledge of the origins of human civilization."

"Or maybe it's a Trojan horse," she said. "Maybe that obelisk is like the hour hand of a clock, the pin in a grenade. You remove it and our day is over, Conrad."

"Or maybe you're afraid the Church is going to lose its place as the arbiter of Genesis," he said, having heard enough of her hysterics. "Maybe it's time to let go of ignorance and fear and make way for a new day of enlightenment."

Conrad looked at Yeats, who gestured to the obelisk.

"Just pick up the goddamn scepter, son. Because if you don't, there are dozens of armed Russians outside this chamber who might, and God knows how many more UNACOMers on the ice."

Conrad glanced at Serena and approached the Scepter of Osiris.

He could feel her fear as he placed his hands on the obelisk. It felt smooth, as if the inscriptions were beneath its surface.

"You're dreaming, Conrad, if you think your father is going to let you walk out of P4 with that scepter," she said. "At least within the context of the United Nations, there's a chance the rest of the world will know about your find."

Conrad hesitated. He felt a weird floating sensation inside, something he couldn't explain. Reaching for the obelisk, he could feel tiny vibrations radiating from it. But then he pulled back.

"What in God's name are you waiting for?" Yeats demanded.

Conrad wasn't sure. This was a once-in-a-millennium chance to make his mark in the sands of time and turn history on its head with a spectacular discovery. It was his one shot at immortality.

"I'm telling you, Conrad, don't rush into this," Serena urged him. "You might unleash something you can't undo."

"You don't know what you're talking about, Sister," Yeats said. "Somebody is going to remove this obelisk, and it had better be Conrad. Because he's the only one who can do it. If anybody is worthy, it's him."

"Allow me to be a character witness and tell you that you're completely wrong," Serena said. "Just because he's your son doesn't mean—"

"Conrad's not my son."

Conrad stopped cold. So did Serena. Even the Russian held his breath. A heavy silence filled the chamber.

"Fine, you're his adoptive father," Serena said quietly, apparently sympathetic to Conrad's sensitivity to the subject.

"Not even that." Yeats shed his supply pack and started to rummage through it.

Conrad stared at his father, wondering what sort of revelation he was about to produce. Why now, of all times? Conrad thought. Why here, of all places?

"He is." Yeats held up a digital camera.

"You have his picture?" Conrad looked at the digital image in the viewing screen. It was a picture of the Seal of Osiris from the floor of the geothermal chamber.

"This is your father," Yeats said.

Conrad stared at the figure of the bearded man inside the mechanical-looking throne and felt something stir deep inside him, from a place he never knew existed.

"What are you saying?"

"I found you in a capsule buried in the ice more than thirty-five years ago," Yeats said in a grim voice that rattled Conrad to the bone. "You couldn't have been more than four."

Conrad was silent. Then he heard a giggle. It was Serena.

"My God, Yeats," she said. "How dumb do you think we are?"

But Yeats wasn't laughing, and Conrad had never seen the look in his father's eyes that he did right now.

"You don't need anyone to tell you what's true, son," Yeats said. "You know it."

Conrad's mind was racing. Yeats had to be lying. After all, Conrad had his DNA tested in search of his parentage, and there was nothing that would suggest he wasn't a red-blooded American male. On the other hand, setting aside its utter implausibility, it explained everything about his lost early years.

"If this is a lie, then you're one sick son of a bitch," Conrad told Yeats. "But if it's the truth, then everything else is a lie, and I've never been anything more to you than a science project. I'm damned either way."

"Then save yourself now, Conrad," Yeats said. "I was the same age you are when Uncle Sam scrubbed the Mars mission and took my dream away from me. I never had a choice. You do. Don't be like me and regret losing this opportunity for the rest of your life."

The dirty trick worked. As Conrad stared at Yeats, he could behold a cracked reflection of his future self should he fail now. It was a visage that made him shudder.

Serena seemed to sense she had lost the battle. "Conrad, please," she begged.

"I'm sorry, Serena," he said slowly as he began to twist the obelisk in its socket. As he did, the curved walls of the geodesic chamber began to spin and the constellations above them changed. With a dull rumble, the floor itself began to rotate.

"We need more time to figure this out," Serena screamed, lunging for him. "You just can't make a decision for the rest of the world. You've got to wait."

But Yeats stopped her cold with the barrel of a Glock in her face. "Like Eisenhower stopping on the banks of the Elbe when he should have beat the Russians to Berlin in 1945?" he said. "Or Nixon pulling the plug on the Mars mission in 1969? I don't think so. Decisive force was required then, and it is now. I'm not stopping anywhere short of my mission's objective."

Conrad glanced at Serena trying to squirm out of Yeats's arms. "Don't do it, Conrad. I swear—"

"Stop swearing, Serena," he told her. "You'll only break another vow."

Reaching for the obelisk with both hands, he told himself that this opportunity was simply too irresistible to pass up. And if he let this moment go, then he might as well count his life as over.

"Please, Conrad . . ."

Conrad could feel the obelisk easing away from the altar as he lifted it free and clear. He smiled in triumph at Serena.

"There," he said with a trace of relief. "That wasn't so—"

But the rest of his sentence was cut off by an ear-splitting crack.

"Oh, my God," Serena breathed as a great rumbling overhead grew deafening.

The domed walls of the chamber spun at fantastic speeds like some cosmic coil ready to snap. Then, suddenly, the spinning stopped. The constellations locked, and an explosive shock wave rocked the pyramid.

19

DESCENT HOUR NINE

ICE BASE ORION

Inside Ice Base Orion on the surface, Colonel O'Dell was playing poker with Vlad Lenin and two other Russians in the mess hall module when their plastic cups of vodka began to shake and the Klaxon sounded.

O'Dell looked at the puzzled Vlad. Whatever it was, it wasn't the Russians. He darted out of the mess module, Vlad right behind him.

A group of Americans and Russians were already huddled around the main monitor screen inside the command center when O'Dell ran in. The display was blinking SOLAR EVENT.

"That can't be right," said O'Dell, stepping into the circle of concerned faces.

A lieutenant called up the computer display for CELSS, the Controlled Environmental Life Support System that kept the crew alive in space and in Antarctica. He located the sensor that was giving the abnormal reading.

"The readings are coming from below, sir," he said, holding on to the console as the shaking intensified. "The only other explanation I can think of is the SP-100."

O'Dell cast an involuntary, nervous glance at Vlad, who did not seem to comprehend what the lieutenant had said. The SP-100 was Ice Base Orion's compact nuclear power plant, a hundred-kilowatt system buried a hundred yards away behind a snow dune.

"My God." O'Dell took a deep breath. "Dosimeter readings?"

"I've got penetration of the outer wardrooms at two hundred

seventy rems, sir. I'm recording sixty-five rems here in the command center, with each of the crew absorbing fifteen rems. We're still below the safety threshold."

But it was the shaking that was scaring the daylights out of O'Dell and the Russians. "Now what?"

"No choice, sir," the lieutenant said. "We've got to retreat to the doghouse."

The doghouse was an Earth capture vehicle under the command center and supply tanks, shielded from the SP-100's high-energy protons by the command center's aeroshell.

"Get as many of the crew inside as possible," he ordered.

The American crew quickly obeyed and ditched the command center in orderly fashion. The Russians, however, looked around the empty command center, then dashed in the opposite direction to the outer air lock and their Kharkovchankas.

"Wait!" O'Dell called as he ran after them.

But they had cracked open the inner and outer doors and escaped by the time he reached the air lock. A blast of snow slapped O'Dell's face as he grabbed a freezer suit, goggles, and gloves from the nearest storage compartment and ran outside.

The Russians were starting up their Kharkovchankas. O'Dell raced toward the row of Hagglunds transports and grabbed the door of the nearest forward cab.

"Where the hell do they think they're going?" he said out loud, intending to hail them from the Hagglunds. The last thing he needed was Yeats or Kovich or the U.N. blaming him for more Russian deaths.

He was about to scramble aboard his Hagglunds when he felt a jolt. He looked down as a crack in the ice shot past his feet. His mouth opened in horror, and then he felt something sharp clamp down on his glove. It was Nimrod, Yeats's dog, frantically pulling him with his teeth.

"Get out of here!" he yelled as he opened the door, but Nimrod jumped into the cab.

O'Dell heard what sounded like a series of thunderous explosions and looked back to see the base break away like an iceberg. Then he felt a rumble and watched in horror as the ice beneath him began to spiderweb.

The ice was melting!

He jumped into the cab with Nimrod. As soon as he closed the door, the Hagglunds lurched forward and back. Cracks radiated out on the ice below. My life is over, he thought, when the fiberglass cab dropped into the swirling, freezing water and was washed away. Then, feeling the transport bob up and down, he nearly choked with elation. "Goddamn, it does float!" he screamed to Nimrod, who was leaping from seat to seat in a frenzy.

The Russian Kharkovchankas, however, were dropping like stones beneath the bubbling surface of the icy waters.

O'Dell frantically switched on the windshield wipers. As the sheets of water were temporarily whisked away, he glimpsed a churning landscape. There was no Ice Base Orion, only what looked like a mushroom cloud forming in the air. For a wild moment he thought the reactor had blown, but the SP-100 didn't possess the destructive power he was witnessing.

Another shock wave sent his head to the floor beneath the dashboard. He heard his skull crack against something sharp as the cab spun wildly away, Nimrod barking incessantly.

20

DESCENT HOUR NINE

The rumbling inside P4's obelisk chamber grew so loud that Serena could barely hear herself shouting at Conrad, who stood frozen like a statue, the Scepter of Osiris tightly gripped in his hand.

"Put it back!" she screamed.

Conrad stepped toward the altar when suddenly the floor beneath his feet split open and a blazing pillar of fire shot up and turned Colonel Kovich into embers.

Conrad leapt back from the gaping hole as the altar disappeared down a fiery shaft. What was left of the Russian exploded in a cloud of dust. The obelisk fell to the floor.

Serena reached down to grab it but lunged too far and teetered over the edge. For a horrific few seconds she hovered above the hell hole and could feel its searing heat burning her cheeks. Then Conrad, coming up from behind, yanked her back from the brink.

For a moment she was safe in his arms, looking up into his concerned eyes with gratitude. But before she could catch her breath a shock wave rocked the chamber and threw them off their feet. The obelisk slid across the floor.

"The scepter!" she shouted.

Yeats dashed to retrieve it. But as the vibrations grew more violent, his right leg gave way, and he tumbled back into the floor shaft. He managed to catch the ledge at the last second. Serena could see his fingers sticking up above the shaft, clawing at the stone floor.

Conrad picked up the obelisk from the floor and grabbed Serena. "See if you can reach him!"

With Conrad firmly clasping her hand, she peered over the edge of the shaft and was surprised to see Yeats swinging above the infernal abyss.

She knew she didn't have the strength to pull him up, but she shouted to Conrad, "I think I can give him a tug and he can climb out himself."

She stretched out her hand when another jolt hit, sending Leonid's corpse sliding into the shaft. The corpse struck Yeats on the way down. Yeats's fingers disappeared and Serena heard Conrad cry out.

"Dad!" Conrad shouted.

Then she felt Conrad pulling her away so he could look down into the shaft. He stood there, paralyzed, trying to comprehend that his father was really gone.

Serena looked around the chamber as everything shook. She didn't want to leave. But she didn't want to stay behind and melt either. So she put her hand on Conrad's shoulder and said, "There's no time to mourn for those we're about to follow."

Her words were enough to bring Conrad back.

"This chamber is going to turn into a furnace in a few seconds," he said, picking up the pack Yeats had left behind and slinging it over his shoulder. "Back to the gallery!"

They ran to the outer corridor. The rumbling wasn't so loud here, she thought, following Conrad down the long tunnel. But when they emerged into the Great Gallery, Conrad stopped and looked up.

"Now might be a good time for you to say a brief prayer," he said.

"Conrad, what's happening?"

"I think P4 is releasing a burst of heat through the shafts, melting the ice outside," he said. "And the water is being processed through this machinery."

She followed Conrad's gaze up the gallery and squinted her eyes. There was a shadow swirling in the distance at the top. Then she felt the first droplets of water splash against her cheek and realized what was coming.

"Oh, my God!" she screamed as the cascades of a gigantic

waterfall began to tumble down the gallery behind them. "We've got to take cover!"

Now she was pulling him back to the chamber.

"Not yet," he told her, "or we'll fry."

Already the water was knee-deep in the tunnel. By the time they were halfway back to the chamber, it was up to their waists. In seconds the current swelled to a torrent and swept them off their feet.

Serena reached for Conrad but couldn't feel him anymore. She panicked and splashed desperately, taking in water, gasping for breath. She was going to drown, she realized. They were going to be flushed away and drown. Surely this is not what God intended for her life, she thought. But then she remembered the little girl in the ice and realized she had seen too many faces just like hers around the world to know for sure what God intended for her. All she knew was that she wanted to live, and she wanted Conrad to live too.

Oh, God, she prayed, help us.

A shadow fell across her, and she looked up to see Conrad standing in the entry of the tunnel to the star chamber, water swirling around his knees. He held the obelisk in one hand.

"Grab the other end!" he yelled above the rushing waters.

She reached up and clasped the obelisk and let Conrad pull her up. But she felt a tug at her ankle and looked down to see a bloody face emerge from the water.

It screamed something unintelligible, and she tried to shake it off. But it pulled still harder. Suddenly she recognized the disfigured face of one of Kovich's men from the upper chamber.

"Hold on!" Serena yelled and let Conrad pull her up.

Once over the ledge, she turned to help the Russian. The soldier's burned legs had barely cleared the ledge when Serena heard Conrad's shout.

"Hurry!"

Then she saw the door to the star chamber closing down behind Conrad, a great granite slab dropping from the ceiling. Conrad, obelisk in hand, ducked into the chamber, which had apparently cooled back down, and started waving them in.

Serena was still dragging the Russian across the entrance to the chamber when a massive crash behind her rocked the tunnel. She glanced back to see that the door had closed, sealing off the water. Pausing to catch her breath, she heard Conrad cry out her name. He was pointing to the ceiling. Three more great doors were dropping, the second one right over her head.

She lurched forward, her soaked parka weighing her down like a cement tomb as she struggled to drag the Russian, whose limbs had stopped moving.

"Serena!" Conrad shouted.

The third door was dropping.

She fell to her hands and knees and dragged the Russian across the floor. Then she felt Conrad's hands clasp her ankles like leg irons and start to pull. Her knees slipped and she fell flat on her stomach.

"Let him go!" he shouted.

"No!" Serena gripped the Russian's cold hands tightly, even as Conrad towed her inside.

The Russian was halfway through when the slab door sliced him in two. Suddenly Serena realized she was dragging only half a body. And still she found it hard to let go, to accept that there was nobody left for her to save.

With a massive scraping sound, the fourth and final door started to drop. She struggled to free herself from the cold grip of the legless corpse. Finally, the hand fell away, and at the last moment something whisked her inside as the final granite slab sank with a sickening thud.

Serena turned to thank Conrad but saw him sprawled on the floor, his hair matted with blood. He must have struck the back of his head against the falling door when he pulled her in.

"Conrad!" she called. "Conrad!"

She scrambled to his limp body. But there was no movement. And the chamber was shaking too violently for her to take a pulse. She saw the obelisk on the floor next to his pack—Yeats's pack—and picked it up.

Another temblor hit, and she backed herself up against the shaking walls until they began to burn with tremendous heat. She moved away, stumbling across the floor, her body shaking uncontrollably as she tried to keep her balance.

She was alone now, she realized, and fell to her knees with the obelisk cradled in her arms, praying to God that the quaking would stop, all the while trying not to think about the little girl in the ice. There was a loud blast and she looked up as the whole chamber seemed to turn upside down.

21
DESCENT HOUR NINE
U.S.S. *CONSTELLATION*

The boom of the huge glacier collapsing into the water was like a bomb blast, knocking Admiral Warren off his feet and shattering the glass of the bridge on the U.S.S. *Constellation*.

Another boom followed seconds later, and then he heard more still as the massive waves crashed over the bow. Glass fragments were scattered across the flight deck, where seventy-six attack jets were straining at their chains.

"Admiral?"

Warren turned. It was a signalman.

"FLASH traffic." The petty officer handed over the clipboard and held a red-covered flashlight over the dispatch so Warren could read it.

"God Almighty," said Warren as he started reading. "U.S. Geological Survey sensors at McMurdo just registered an eleven-point-one shock wave."

"Admiral!" shouted a lieutenant.

Warren looked up in time to glimpse a towering, muddy green wall of water descend on the bow and wash over the flight deck, scattering the attack jets like toys and crashing into the superstructure where he stood. A deafening crack split his ears as the crush of water demolished the bridge. Desperately he searched for something to hang on to.

Water filled the compartment. Warren held the bar of a console and braced his back against the wall to stay upright. On calm waters, the 86,000-ton carrier rose 201 feet above the waterline. But these swells were lifting the aircraft carrier like an empty Cuban cigar box.

Warren coughed up some water and yelled to anyone who could hear him. "Turn us into the wave or we'll capsize!"

He strained to hear his command received with an "Aye, sir!" from a helmsman, but there was no sound beside the crash of water.

When the wave broke, he looked around the bridge and saw two floating bodies. The rest had been swept to sea. He ran down the stairs to the wheelhouse, gripping the rail tightly. The wheelhouse was empty.

He turned toward the coast to see another towering gray mass, a cliff-size wave. He grabbed a chain reserved for one of his 55,000-pound planes and hoisted it on his broad shoulders and headed down to the flight deck.

Men and planes were thrashing about the tilting deck. Then a new wave lifted the carrier toward the sky. As he fell through the air, still clutching the chain, Warren saw a rail. Water crashed over the deck again, knocking him to his knees. But he saw his salvation. If he could just reach the rail in between waves, he could chain himself down.

The next wave split the twin-finned JSF attack jet in front of him, and Warren ducked to avoid being sliced in half by a broken wing. He willed himself to stand, his numb legs wobbling beneath him, and broke into a run, splashing through the shallows toward the rail.

Part of him wanted to slip and fall so he could just stop fighting and die, but he stayed on his feet until he rammed into the rail. He reached up and grabbed the heavy chain on his shoulders with both hands and lashed himself to the rail before the next wave crashed.

The winds and spray swept the deck as he clung for his life. The wave broke over the bow, and just as Warren could feel the force lift his body off the deck and sweep him aside, his chain caught and held.

For more than a minute he stayed that way, sure his arm would be torn off and he would be washed away like the remaining planes on deck. But God help him, he swore, he was going to survive this cataclysm if only to pay back Yeats. Then, slowly, he felt the carrier shifting and heard the creak of the massive steel buckling. He looked up and saw that the entire ship was on the verge of capsizing before the giant swell had passed.

"Goddamn you, Yeats!"

PART THREE

DAWN

22

DAWN MINUS FIFTEEN HOURS

INSIDE P4'S STAR CHAMBER, Conrad coughed as the whiskey stung the back of his throat. He looked up at Serena sitting next to him. Her wet hair was wiped back, her face pale.

"Jack Daniel's?" he asked hoarsely.

"Found it in Yeats's pack." She reached over and touched his face. The feeling of her hand on his face brought him back to life. "You're warm."

"This whole place feels warm." Conrad sat up and felt a terrific pain at the base of his skull. He groaned. "Where's the obelisk?"

"I don't know," Serena said.

"It was right here." Conrad quickly scanned the star chamber. He saw the empty altar standing in the middle of the cartouche. Something in his gut churned and he remembered a nightmare about the floor splitting open. "Where's Yeats?"

"Disappeared down the floor shaft."

Conrad looked for the shaft, but it had closed up again beneath the altar. He's dead, thought Conrad. He felt himself shake, his heart beating rapidly.

"I'm so sorry about your father, Conrad."

He looked into her eyes. She was indeed sorry, he thought. But there was something peculiar about the way she looked at him now. Something different. He wouldn't call it fear, but there was something else in her eyes that put distance between them. Surely she didn't believe Yeats's bizarre revelation about his origins, did she? It was obviously a psychological ploy.

"You don't actually believe—"

"Whatever else you may be, Conrad, you're clearly not on anybody's 'most worthy' list—not God's, not the Atlanteans' and not mine," she said. "You're still going to die for your sins. Only this time it looks like you're going to take the rest of us with you straight to hell. That's what I believe."

Conrad could only stare at her. "You never stop, do you? You always have to have the last word."

"Yes."

Then Conrad saw something gleaming on the floor. He reached out to touch it. Was it sunlight? He looked up at the ceiling and blinked his eyes. The two concealed shafts he suspected had been there all along were now wide open, and a beam of sunlight strained through the southern shaft and touched the center of the floor where the obelisk had been.

Had the ice chasm overhead collapsed? he wondered with alarm. What about Ice Base Orion? The horrific thought that P4's geothermal vent might have melted the ice or even shifted the earth's crust briefly drifted across his consciousness, but he quickly suppressed it. Had something so catastrophic happened, he and Serena would be dead.

"What time is it?" Conrad asked Serena.

"Three in the afternoon," she said. "Antarctica has equal hours of daylight and darkness in September. So we only have a few hours until dusk."

Conrad craned his neck at the shafts on the sloping north and south walls of the chamber. He could crawl out one to check. It was the only way out. But the angles of the shafts looked steep, and it was at least a thousand feet up to God knows what.

"I'll need to have a look outside," he told her.

She nodded slowly, as if she had reached the same conclusion long before he had regained consciousness. "You'll need these to climb up the shaft."

She was holding pressurized suction-cup pads for the knees and hands.

"Where did you get those?" he asked.

"Your father's pack," she said. "He seemed to have prepared for everything."

Conrad looked at the altar in the center of the room covering the shaft that had swallowed his father. "Not quite everything."

Conrad rose to his feet, took the suction gear from Serena, and crossed the floor to the southern shaft. He stared up at the sun and blinked. "Looks like the polar storm cleared."

"That's what it looks like." Serena didn't sound so sure. She didn't even look like she wanted to know.

"If there are any search parties looking for us, we need to send a signal or flare," he told her, strapping the suction pads on. "I'll have to crawl up through the shaft. And I'll carry up a line with me, just in case it's our only way out and you'll need to join me. Meanwhile, you try to raise Ice Base Orion on Yeats's radio and tell them what happened."

He could feel her searching his eyes for clues. "What did happen, Conrad?"

He wanted to hold her in his arms, if she'd let him, and tell her everything was going to be OK. But they both knew that would be a lie. "I'm going to find out," he told her. "I promise."

The square of light overhead grew larger as Conrad neared the top of the shaft. It had been a steeper climb than he expected, slowed by the suction pads he needed for traction, and he was out of breath. The wind whistled as he gripped the outer edge of the shaft and pulled himself up to the light of day.

The brightness was harsh and he blinked rapidly, allowing several seconds for his eyes to adjust. When they did, he blinked again in disbelief.

Spread out a mile below him were the ruins of an ancient city. Temples, ziggurats, and broken obelisks lay strewn amid what had been—could be—a tropical paradise. He noticed a series of concentric, circular waterways radiating out from the base of the pyramid complex, which he deduced was the center of town. It was an advanced, otherworldly city grid hidden for twelve thousand years under two miles of ice.

Until now.

Conrad shaded his eyes. The subglacial terrain stretched out in a six-mile radius from the pyramid—a tropical island in a sea of ice. In the distance he could see the snowcapped Transantarctic Mountains.

The air smelled crisp and fresh, and he could hear the distant rumble of waterfalls. Somehow his fears and doubts and petty ambitions were swept away by the majesty of it all. But as he gazed out across the new world, he suddenly wondered what had happened to the old.

23

DAWN MINUS FIFTEEN HOURS

U.S.S. *CONSTELLATION*

Admiral Warren splashed across the inside hangar deck of the U.S.S. *Constellation,* surveying the damage. The ship hadn't capsized after all, but the deck had taken on enough water to sink the *Titanic* twice. And yet the old girl was still afloat, limping along on emergency power.

Initial reports coming in from the U.S. Geological Survey in Golden, Colorado, and some earthquake-forecasting agency in Japan blamed the tidal wave on a major quake in East Antarctica—11.1 on the Richter scale. But Warren couldn't confirm it with McMurdo or Amundsen-Scott. All communications with American bases on the continent had been cut off by a burst of EMP.

All of which seemed to validate reports coming out of Moscow and Beijing that the "seismic event" in Antarctica was really a secret U.S.-sponsored nuclear explosion—a flagrant violation of the international Antarctic Treaty.

The electromagnetic pulse, or EMP, had also blinded spy satellites overhead. Warren was told that if he couldn't get a bird up in the air to fly reconn over the epicenter, it was going to take at least sixteen hours before any U.S. forces could reach the target to either prove the nuke accusations false or cover up Yeats's dirty work.

"Goddamn you, Yeats," Warren muttered as he stepped around the floating pieces of a broken wing. Looked like one of their F/A-18 Hornets. The rest was mangled with what used to be an S-3B Viking.

Warren shook his head. Twenty-six wounded, three in critical condition and nine missing. And that was just the *Constellation*. News reports said one-third of the island of Male, the Maldives's capital, was underwater. Even a small rise in sea levels at this point could wipe out the island nation—all 1,180 islands. The entire population of 263,000 inhabitants was at risk.

The only positive news Warren could report back to Washington was that his crew had managed to rescue the Greenpeace protesters from their now-sunken ship. The meddlers were helping out with the wounded and serving up some of the best damned coffee Warren had ever tasted.

He was on his fourth cup when one of his radio officers splashed over. "EAM coming over Milstar, sir."

Warren watched a sock float past him on the hangar deck. Milstar was the president's communications link to senior military commanders. The $17-billion Military Commanders' Voice Conference Network was designed to enable commanders to discuss whether a ballistic-missile launch threatened North America and, if so, to determine the appropriate response.

"Priority one, sir."

"I'm coming."

Warren took a final gulp as he eyed the rad-hardened Black Hawk chopper that several of his maintenance crew were working on in the corner—at his orders. He then crumpled the Styrofoam coffee cup and tossed it on the hangar floor, where it floated away.

Inside the *Constellation*'s war suite, the water was only ankle deep. Warren walked in to find his senior officer, McBride, seated at the conference table. Next to McBride, to Warren's surprise and dismay, was the scruffy Greenpeace geek from the *Arctic Sunrise* whom CNN had featured. He was fiddling with some candy-colored laptop computer that looked like a toy.

Warren frowned. "What's this civilian doing here, McBride?"

"This is Thornton Larson, a Ph.D. in geophysics from MIT," McBride said. "He reviewed the Milstar downloads and has a presentation for you."

"Couldn't your officers figure it out, McBride?"

McBride said, "The data is so off the charts, sir, we felt we needed a second opinion. Dr. Larson has some valuable insights."

Warren sat down and studied the disheveled Larson. The smart-ass hasn't even discovered the razor blade, he thought to himself, and McBride was sharing national security secrets with him. "Enlighten me, Larson."

"I was able to retrieve one final image from a satellite overhead before its innards were fried by that EMP," Larson said excitedly. "I cleaned it up and here it is."

Warren looked up at the large wall screen. A blue-tinted image of Antarctica, all too familiar to Warren these days, came into view. But in the middle of it, or rather just off center in East Antarctica, was a brown-yellow dot.

"Is that awesome, dude, or what?" Larson could only marvel at his work.

"God almighty, tell me that's some storm and not ground zero," Warren said.

Larson addressed the image on the wall screen. "Well, hello Mr. Ground Zero, are you ready for your close-up?"

The brown-yellow dot on-screen started to magnify, frame by frame, until Warren found himself looking at a crater in the ice, and at the bottom of it was a complex of pyramids, temples, and waterways. The kid was obviously playing them all for fools, Warren decided.

"You think you're pretty funny, Larson, don't you?" Warren said, starting to get up. "Let's see how hilarious the brig can be."

"Please, sir," McBride said. "We checked it out and this guy hasn't doctored anything."

Warren slowly sat down, his thoughts immediately turning to Yeats. The SOB must have known all along. "So you're telling me what I'm seeing on that screen is for real?"

"What you're seeing is a localized event, like a garage band on the verge of stardom," Larson said. "This is just the first single off an album I'll call *Mother Nature's Cacophony in Doomsday Major.*"

Warren gave McBride his "your ass is on the line here" stare, which his executive officer acknowledged.

Larson said, "Your attention, class."

Warren looked up at the large wall screen. The image of an ancient city surrounded by ice was gone. In its place, spinning in the center, flickering with each power drain of the carrier's electrical system, was what looked like a thermal image of the sun in space.

"Tell me what I'm looking at on the screen, Larson."

"Earth's core, baby," Larson said. "The *core!* A new technique similar to a medical sonogram enables us to generate an image of the inner planet. I've used the latest version of PowerPoint on my G5 to generate—"

Warren waved his hand impatiently. "Get to the point."

"Earth is an onion, man, made up of layers," Larson said. "And it's a rotating onion too, churning up hurricanes and storms in the atmosphere. But the core spins independently, and changes there can trigger significant consequences near and at the planet's surface. I'm talking *consequences.*"

"You mean earthquakes and tidal waves?" Warren said.

"Big time," Larson said. "Albert Einstein, Dr. Relativity himself, even theorized that the outer crust, the lithosphere, periodically shifts over the asthenosphere due to ice buildup in the polar regions."

"What are you saying?"

"What I'm saying, baby, is that we seem to be witnessing what is known as an earth-crust displacement. You dudes in the military-industrial complex prefer the perverse little acronym ECD."

Warren didn't know what this kid was smoking, but he had to know where this theory was going. "And what's this ECD going to do?"

"Well, here's where it gets really nasty," Larson said. "Antarctica is going to get pushed toward the equator and North America into the Arctic Circle."

Another computer image appeared on-screen, this one of Earth. Warren felt his own temperature rise as Antarctica moved up toward the center of the globe, ice free, and North America was pushed to the top of the globe.

Warren said, "So you're saying we're better off staying here and sunning on the beaches of Antarctica rather than freezing our asses off in the USA, which is going to get buried under two miles of ice."

"Bingo!" Larson said. "Bingo! An ECD would cause extinctions to occur on different continents at different rates, based on varying changes in the world's latitudes. I've mapped the projected lines of destruction. We'll call them PLDs. Hey, I made up a new acronym! Well, these PLDs are pretty damn awesome, I've got to tell you."

On-screen Larson drew a circle around the globe, through the North and South poles. "The line of greatest displacement runs through North America, west of South America, bisects Antarctica, travels through Southeast Asia, goes on to Siberia, and then back to North America. All the continents along the line of greatest displacement—or LGD—are about to experience mass extinctions."

"Nobody knows the future," Warren said, uncomfortable with this green alarmist's certainty. "If you ever read old five-year budget projections from the Pentagon, you'd know that. How long will it take for this alleged ring of death to make us all extinct?"

"It's only an estimate, but my models project an ECD taking place over the next couple of days and running itself out within a week."

Warren was stunned. "All that destruction in a few days?"

"Dude, it took God only six days to create the universe, according to Genesis," Larson said. "Why should an ECD take any longer to destroy it? It's like a coil that can unwind with unstoppable, devastating speed once it reaches threshold."

Warren leaned forward. "This has happened before?"

"Several times."

"And I suppose you were there to measure them all?"

"I wish," Larson said. "The last one was roughly eleven thousand six hundred years ago, about 9600 B.C. That's when the geological record says vast climatic changes swept the planet. Massive ice sheets melted, ocean levels rose. Huge mammals perished in great numbers. A sudden influx of people flowed into the Americas. It was *party* time, you know?"

"And this happens every twelve thousand years or so?"

"No, every forty-one thousand years," Larson said, who had suddenly hit his own threshold and run out of gas. He plopped down on a seat. "We aren't due for an ECD for another thirty thousand years. Somehow the cycle has been accelerated. I don't know how."

Neither did Warren. But he was pretty damn sure who was responsible. "And how soon until we reach threshold?" Warren demanded. "What kind of countdown are we talking about here?"

"The ECD should reach threshold by dawn tomorrow morning."

Larson started counting on his fingers with a glazed look in his eyes. "Damn, that's less than fifteen hours. One last night to get lucky before it all goes poof."

Admiral Warren could only stare at the kid in the hope that his Ph.D. stood for Piled Higher and Deeper. Otherwise, they were all out of luck.

24

DAWN MINUS FOURTEEN HOURS

SERENA PACED BACK AND FORTH across the floor of the geodesic star chamber while she waited for Conrad to return.

Something had gone horribly wrong. She could smell it in the air and feel it in her bones. Something on a large scale, something very profound, had occurred. Her stomach felt terribly unsettled, like it did when she didn't eat or drink anything for hours except one cup of espresso after another. If only she had acted on her doubts earlier, or been more persuasive with Conrad, or stalled Yeats longer.

As she paced and pondered, she eyed the empty altar in the center of the room uneasily. In one terrifying moment it had opened up like the pit of hell and incinerated Kovich and swallowed Yeats.

Perhaps it was a geothermal vent of sorts, something that could tap the heat of Earth's interior and harness its power. After all, the most advanced fuel cells ever devised by human engineers generated the by-products of heat and water. P4 certainly had plenty of both.

In any case, she concluded, P4 was following the preprogrammed instructions of its builders, whoever they were. And it was clearly intended to create some kind of global extinction event unless humanity could come up with some kind of "most noble" moment to justify its existence.

Looking to her left and her right, she reached into her pack and pulled out the Scepter of Osiris. She held the gleaming obelisk in her hands. For some intuitive reason she had lied and failed to tell Conrad she had it.

She moved over to the empty altar and eased the scepter into its rotundalike base. There was a rumbling as the geodesic star ceiling whirled. She tried to reset the heavens as they appeared before Conrad removed the obelisk. The whirling stopped and she waited. Nothing happened. Whatever Conrad did could not be reversed. So much for her virginity. Clearly she was no more "worthy" than he was.

She removed the obelisk from the altar and felt a shudder from the wall behind her. She turned to see the four chamber doors open in a row.

For a long minute she stood there, frozen, wondering what to do. Then she looked at the obelisk in her hands. Something about it seemed different. The side with the four suns had changed. Now there were six, the sixth sun being the largest. Her worst fears had been realized: a new age was dawning, which could only spell the end for the old age.

What had not changed was the inscription that said the Scepter of Osiris belonged in the Shrine of the First Sun. Somewhere nearby, she realized, was a structure like P4, a monument to an epoch in time. If P4 was the Pyramid of the Fourth Sun, then the Shrine of the First Sun must have been built during the First Time or Genesis. If Conrad was right, then Genesis simply had to be the "most worthy time," since in the beginning God looked upon creation and said it was "good."

She had to find this Shrine of the First Sun and its secret, she resolved. Then she could reset the star chamber to the most worthy time and stop whatever was happening.

But where was this shrine and how would she even recognize it?

Conrad would know. She walked over to the square patch of sunlight beneath the southern shaft and with her eyes followed Conrad's line up the shaft. There was a flicker of daylight at the other end. What was taking him so long?

Serena turned from the shaft and surveyed the empty chamber. There on the floor was Yeats's backpack. She had already rummaged through it once, but now she noticed that the lining in back didn't look right. Upon closer inspection she realized there was something flat sewn inside.

She pulled out a military knife from the same pack and used it to slash through the lining. Inside she found a folded blueprint of some sort. It appeared to be a technical schematic of some kind of pillar. Then, all of a sudden, she recognized the "pillar" as the obelisk in her hand, complete with the rotunda at its base.

As she suspected, the Americans knew far more about this place than Yeats admitted. Clearly Yeats had this blueprint before they even entered P4, much less found the obelisk. Somehow Yeats knew the Scepter of Osiris was down here before he ever saw it.

Surely Yeats's crazy story about finding Conrad in the ice wasn't true, she told herself. It was simply a ploy to play on Conrad's emotions during a crisis situation. Even Conrad thought as much.

But there was something Conrad had mumbled before he woke up, something she had been pondering ever since. It had sounded like a moan made in pain. But there was something about the structure and syntax and accent of the sound that rang familiar. And now as she thought about it, she realized Conrad had been repeating the word *Mama* in some kind of pre-Aymaran form. But there was no way Conrad could know that.

A chill shot up her spine. Maybe Conrad was an Atlantean after all. Or maybe she was crazy. She picked up the obelisk and compared it to the blueprint. They looked identical, except for the markings, which, as she had just seen, possessed the ability to change.

Serena opened her pack and removed her coffee thermos. She twisted the outer shell until it unlocked and then slid it off like a sheath. She then rolled the blueprint around the outside of the inner tube and slid the outer shell back on, twisting it until it locked. It was a hiding place she had learned to rely on more than once in her journeys. Then she placed the thermos back into her pack.

She looked up at the southern shaft, thinking she shouldn't leave without Conrad. But he had been gone too long, she told herself as she glanced at the open doorway. She couldn't wait forever. And who knew where Conrad's path of self-discovery would take his loyalties? She, on the other hand, knew exactly what she had to do. She had to take the Scepter to the Shrine of the First Sun. There she would find, she hoped, the so-called Secret of First Time that would somehow enable her to stop whatever was happening.

As for Conrad, it was clear she could not trust him, just like she could not trust Yeats. For all she knew she couldn't trust the pope or even God. How could he let this happen—again? She thought of the girl in the ice. She couldn't get the expression on her face out of her mind. This had happened once before, so clearly God could let it happen again. But she couldn't.

She put the obelisk back in her pack, slung the pack over her shoulder, and stepped out of the chamber through the open door. The tunnel led her to a fork at the bottom of the Great Gallery, and she took the middle tunnel down and out through P4's entrance.

When Serena emerged from the dark interior of P4 into the light of day, it seemed to her that the sun was more brilliant than ever. It was hot, but it was the dry kind of heat that she liked. Antarctica was a desert climate with or without the ice, she thought as she shaded her eyes. More likely, however, the heat originated from the vast geothermal machinery underground.

A minute later, after her eyes had adjusted, she realized that she was standing in the center of a city at the bottom of some great crater. Walls of ice lifted up in the distance, forming a spectacular backdrop for this desert landscape of pyramids, obelisks, temples, and waterways. She could hear the roar of a distant waterfall.

She closed her eyes and took a deep breath. The rush of fresh, oxygen-rich air overwhelmed her senses. So did the realization that there were probably centuries of research down here, and if she lived a thousand lifetimes she still would just be getting started at unraveling the city's mysteries.

Whatever else, she realized, this discovery changed everything about human history.

Eyes still closed, she thought she heard a dog barking. Ridiculous, she thought, and realized she should be praying, listening for some inner prompting from the Holy Spirit or direction from God. But all she heard was that barking, and it was getting louder and more annoying. Then she blinked her eyes open to see Yeats's husky, Nimrod, trotting toward her.

She was surprised by the joy she felt and called out to him, "Here, boy!"

Nimrod ran into her arms and started licking her face.

"Are you OK?" she asked him. "Is everybody else OK?"

Nimrod immediately turned and started running in the other direction, pausing to look back.

"You want me to follow, boy?"

Nimrod barked and kept running and this time did not look back.

Serena followed the canine for a half hour along what appeared to be the main waterway of the empty city. But the longer they walked, the less it felt like a city. There was nothing to suggest anybody ever actually lived here on the plateau. No streets, just waterways. Some coursing with glistening water, others dry. And the ground between the pavilions was barren. No plant life, nothing. Maybe that would change in a few days.

Perhaps the dwellings were on the outskirts, she wondered, still buried under ice. But these monuments, however coldly magnificent, reminded her of a city of abandoned oil rigs she once toured along the Caspian Sea in the former Soviet Union: miles of rusted pipes you could drive a truck through and ghostly refineries that stretched like heaps of filth across the horizon.

She also had the uneasy feeling of being watched, although she knew that was absurd. There was nobody around to watch her. Then again, Nimrod was here. Maybe there were others. She occasionally lost sight of the dog but always remained within earshot of his barks. Then the barks grew louder, and she realized he was waiting to show her something.

From a distance she could see the object glisten in the sun. Soon she came upon a smashed Hagglunds tractor on the banks of the water channel. The rear cab was crushed to bits, fragments of fiberglass gleaming across the ground. But the front cab seemed intact.

Serena walked over to the driver's side door, which was ajar, and opened it. She gasped as the body of Colonel O'Dell crumpled to the ground at her feet, his head a bloody mess with bits of the dashboard matted in his hair. Nimrod sniffed the corpse with a whimper.

Poor O'Dell, she thought, realizing she would have to bury his body. It would be only proper. But first she had to see if the tractor's transmitter was working and if there was any food or water. She hated to admit it, with O'Dell lying there on the ground, but she was famished.

She climbed inside the cab and searched methodically for any SAT phones, weapons, food packs, anything. But the cab had been stripped of everything save for a single meal-ready-to-eat and a shortwave radio.

She tore open the MRE. Nimrod made it clear that he expected a share of the food, nuzzling his way into the cab.

"Oh, OK," she said. "Come on in."

Together they split the meal. But the longer she chewed, the more she realized what she was really hungry for was news. She eyed the shortwave radio, wondering if it worked, but perversely almost hoping it didn't.

Unable to bear it any longer, she turned the radio on. It worked. The static grew louder as she turned up the volume and then searched the band of frequencies to find the BBC. When she did, the announcer's voice was filled with tension.

"Mass evacuations of U.S. coastal cities are under way," the announcer said. "The federal government reports that it is opening up the nearly six hundred fifty million acres of public land it owns—almost thirty percent of the United States—for refugees."

Bit by bit, the details began to fill in: the massive "seismic event" in Antarctica that split off a glacier the size of Texas, the swamping of the Maldives and other Pacific Islands, the meetings of the U.N. Security Council in New York, and accusations of secret American nuclear weapons tests in Antarctica.

Dear Lord, she thought. What have we done? Serena looked at her food and suddenly lost her appetite. She didn't stop Nimrod from finishing the meal.

Various commentators, analysts, and scientists of the international sort soon weighed in, some expressing fears that the ice cap was breaking up, others that rising sea levels would wipe out coastal cities and sink low-lying lands such as Florida. Those with access to the corridors of power confessed to hearing whispers of a potential shift in Earth's crust and global geological catastrophe.

She turned off the radio and removed the Scepter of Osiris from her backpack. Staring at it, thinking about all that it had wrought thus far, she felt her stomach churn.

She opened the passenger door of the cab. Nimrod jumped out and ran to the river's edge and began lapping up water. She walked over and squatted next to him and looked across to the other side. It was about five hundred feet away.

Seeing that Nimrod was no worse for his drink, she removed an empty water bottle from her pack and dipped it into the water. The current was so strong it ripped the bottle away in an instant, so she cupped a hand into the water and sipped. She was splashing some water on her oily, dusty face when she heard a yelp.

She looked over to see Nimrod lying on his side, panting heavily, eyes in shock. She spit the water out of her mouth and looked him over.

"What's wrong, boy?" she asked, suddenly worried as she stroked his ear. "Please don't tell me it's the water."

It wasn't. There was blood coming from Nimrod's thigh. She looked closer. It looked like a bullet hole.

"Oh, God," she began to say when a bright red dot appeared on Nimrod's furry chest. A second later blood spurted out. She jumped back and screamed.

A dozen soldiers in UNACOM uniforms emerged from the horizon and closed in around her with their AK-47s at the ready. Their commanding officer stepped forward from the circle around her and spoke into his radio.

"This is Jamil," the man said in Arabic. "We have one survivor, sir. A woman."

The accent sounded Egyptian to Serena, and this was confirmed when she heard the reply on the radio: "Bring her to me."

"Yes, sir."

Before Serena could move, Jamil motioned to one of his men, and the grunt flung her across the ground, holding her down with one hand and considerable strength. He ripped open her fatigues, slipped a hand inside, and felt her up and down.

"What is this?" the soldier said with a Saudi accent, yanking away a switchblade knife.

The Saudi held up the knife and sprang the blade, eliciting howls of laughter from his comrades. Then he flipped the knife across the air to bury itself in the dirt. His eyes sparked fire as he stood over Serena, hands on his hips.

Serena had had enough. The Saudi was about to step away when she kicked him in the groin. As he doubled over in pain she jumped up and prepared to knee his bowed face. But suddenly a half-dozen red dots painted her chest and she looked up to see the barrels of a dozen AK-47s pointed at her.

Serena put her hands up in surrender and looked at the Saudi she had kicked. He was groveling in the dirt. Another Arab came behind her, this one an Afghan by the sound of his accent, and marched her outside the circle to stand before the commanding officer, Jamil.

Jamil seemed delighted by her performance. "Ah, what have we here?"

"I'll show you," said Serena in Arabic, and with her elbow spiked the face of the Afghan behind her. He let out a cry and dropped his AK-47. Serena took it and pointed it at the wounded soldier.

"Let me go," Serena ordered Jamil, digging the AK-47 into the back of the Afghan. "Or I'll kill your man here."

"You couldn't hurt a butterfly, mademoiselle."

Jamil took out a pearl-handled Colt, aimed it at Serena's hostage, and shot him dead himself. Serena watched in stunned silence as the Afghan fell to the ground, leaving her standing alone and exposed to Jamil's pistol.

"Hand over the Scepter of Osiris, mademoiselle, or I'll kill you too."

"You know about the scepter?"

"Shoot her," another soldier told Jamil.

Jamil smiled. "Not before she tells me what she knows."

The wind picked up and Serena looked up to see a chopper flying in. It was one of those French jobs she had flown a couple of times herself, a Z-9A, and it apparently belonged to the UNACOMers, because Jamil wasn't terribly concerned with its arrival.

"The scepter, I said."

"I've hidden it in a safe place," she said. "Let me go and I'll show you."

But one of Jamil's men, who was ransacking Serena's pack, suddenly called out and produced the obelisk.

Jamil took the obelisk in his hands, examined it for a moment, and then looked at her and laughed. "Tell Colonel Zawas we have found the Scepter of Osiris."

25

DAWN MINUS THIRTEEN HOURS

From his perch near the summit of P4, Conrad had a bird's-eye view of the lost city in the late afternoon. If only Dad could see this, he thought, gazing out from the mouth of the exterior shaft.

The city was comprised of concentric waterways laid over a grid. Wide avenues flanked by temples and pavilions radiated outward from the central P4 compound. This layout reminded him of the Avenue of the Dead in Teotihuacán, Mexico, and even the National Mall in Washington, D.C.

About a mile long, the necropolis was anchored by P4 in the center, a Sphinx-like structure at the east end, and at the west end a step-pyramid with working waterfalls that churned brightly in the sunlight. The dimensions were spectacular.

Most astounding of all, Conrad could see the various rings of pavilions slowly shifting and locking into place. Or was it P4 that was slowly rotating? He couldn't tell. At any rate, the builders did more than construct a city aligned to the stars before an ancient earth-crust displacement shifted the continent. They constructed a city in which the monuments could somehow realign themselves, perhaps through the hydraulic pressure of the water that coursed through its very veins.

Conrad tried to let this otherworldly landscape sink in, to burn this image into his memory so he'd never forget it. The magnitude of its scale, however, defied comprehension. There were probably ten square miles of city to explore inside a crater of ice whose walls rose two miles into the sky along the city outskirts. And that was only the part of the city that was visible. Conrad could only assume what he saw was part of a bigger metropolis.

He was tempted to slide back down the shaft that instant to tell Serena what he had found, if only to convince himself. But he knew he must first capture a picture. He pulled out his pocket digital camera and panned the valley below. Whatever else he took away from this city, he could at least have this, proof that he was the first person in twelve thousand years to glimpse humanity's earliest epoch. Perhaps he was the first human to glimpse an entirely alien civilization. Maybe even his own, if Yeats was to be believed.

Yeats's revelation raised more questions than it answered. It certainly raised a wall between him and Serena. He had seen the uncertainty in her eyes as she studied him back in the star chamber. He couldn't tell if it was for who he was or what he had done. But the pangs of guilt for an obsession that cost the life of the only man who might have answers for them—Yeats—refused to subside.

The reality was that the only father he had ever known was dead.

He loved me, Conrad thought. He did the best he could. He even tried to tell me that in his own way. Now Yeats was gone, and they'd never have the father-son reconciliation Yeats deserved.

Conrad suddenly felt nauseated. But he took a deep breath of fresh Antarctic air and asked himself what Yeats would say. And the answer that came to mind was clear.

Yeats would no doubt quote some military figure like Admiral Mahan of the American Navy during the Revolution and say: "Whenever you set out to accomplish anything, make up your mind at the outset about your ultimate objective. Once you have decided on it, take care never to lose sight of it."

For Conrad, the objective was clear: he had to map the city and find its Shrine of the First Sun, which was clearly a memorial to the epoch of First Time. Inside the shrine would be the Seat of Osiris, just like the one on the royal seal he had seen. If he could bring the scepter from the star chamber into the shrine and sit in the Seat of Osiris he would unlock the Secret of First Time—surely the "time and place of the most worthy."

Holding his camera up, Conrad panned to his right and to his left, up to the sky and down to the ground. Then he zoomed in on various structures, starting with the Sphinx-like landmark in the east and working his way toward the step-pyramid with the waterfalls in the west.

Satisfied he had captured everything he could, he replayed some of the images on the viewfinder screen to make sure once again that he wasn't dreaming. As he did, however, he saw a dot moving across the ground. It was over by the great waterway that cut through the heart of the city.

Heart surging with fear and excitement, Conrad pointed the camera in the dot's direction, slowly boosting the magnification. There it was, a blurry image, definitely moving. No, there were two blurry figures. He focused further. Suddenly the first one jumped into view.

It was Nimrod, the husky from Ice Base Orion. And walking beside him was Serena. A few moments later the dog dropped in his tracks and a dozen figures surrounded Serena before a chopper landed next to the group. The encounter did not look friendly.

Conrad lowered his camera only to see a swarm of military choppers buzz overhead. Before he could wave, a burst of machine gun fire came his way, raking the side of the pyramid.

He slid down the shaft as fast as he could to the star chamber, which was completely empty. Serena was gone, Yeats's pack was gone, and the sequence of doors leading out to the gallery was wide open.

Something rattled overhead, and as Conrad looked up the shaft he had just slid down, a smoking canister dropped to the floor. Conrad's eyes started to burn and he realized it was tear gas. He ran out of the chamber.

Once at the fork at the bottom of the gallery, he looked down the tunnel Serena must have taken to P4's entrance. A dozen pairs of glowing green eyes were coming his way. His only choice was to drop down the shaft toward the boiler room. He landed in a torrent of water washing down the subterranean channel away from P4.

He was racing down the channel now, caught in a current of such power that there was nothing he could do except keep his head above water. What the hell had he gotten himself into now? he wondered. Then he saw the mouth of a tunnel closing in on him, and a second later he was swallowed up by the darkness.

Deep beneath the ancient city, Conrad splashed in the darkness, gasping for air as he was swept through the underground canals. The freezing water disoriented him, and all he could hear were furious sucking sounds all around.

He bounced off a wall and spun in circles as the canal merged with another, larger tunnel. The overwhelming push of the new stream churned the raging river into a whirlpool. He glanced over his shoulder as a white curl of foam bore down on him in the darkness. He thought it would kill him, but instead the wave lifted him over a stone bank to a walkway.

Out of the water, he paused to catch his breath when another wave flooded in, the water grasping at his knees, trying to suck him back in. But it receded quickly and he was up on his feet, moving down the walkway. A cursory glance told him this tunnel was at least twice as high as those inside P4.

As he made his way through the labyrinth that crisscrossed beneath the city, Conrad was both awed and angered by the extent of the builders' subterranean infrastructure. He could spend an eternity studying this city, he thought, and if he didn't find a way out of here very soon he just might.

He also was angry at Serena, another one of life's mysteries he'd felt he would never understand. She obviously didn't trust him. Why else would she have left him back at P4 to venture off on her own? She had gone into her survivor mode and for all he knew considered him the enemy. And yet he was anxious about her safety after witnessing her capture.

A few minutes later he came to a fork in the tunnel and stopped. Two smaller aqueducts, each about forty feet high and twenty feet wide, presented themselves. Then he heard a faint rumble coming from the right aqueduct. He stared into the darkness and saw a glimmer of light. It was growing larger as the rumble grew louder. It was another surge of water coming down the pike, and in a few seconds the force would slam him against the tunnel walls and kill him.

His only way out, he realized, was to run into the left aqueduct. He dove in before a wall of water from the right pipe flooded the larger tunnel. From inside the left aqueduct, knee-deep in water, he watched the deluge roar for a full three minutes before it emptied itself out.

When it was over, he realized he was shaking. Too close, he thought as he rose to his feet. He took his first step down the aqueduct when he heard a distant splash. For a second he expected another torrent of water to wipe him out. But none came. He cocked his ear. This splashing had a rhythm to it.

He peered into the darkness. Someone in the distance was walking toward him. More than one, actually, because now he could hear the coarse murmur of conversation growing louder. They were speaking Arabic.

Conrad took a step back toward the large tunnel. The splash of his boot was louder than he intended. He froze. For a second he heard nothing. Then the sound of splashing footsteps picked up its pace.

"Stop!" called one of the figures in English.

Conrad glanced over his shoulder to see two pairs of glowing green eyes bobbing in the blackness. He ran back into the large tunnel. Then a shot rang out and he ducked as a bullet ricocheted off a wall. He froze at the fork before the two aqueducts. Slowly he turned around and saw the red dot on his chest. No, two dots.

Conrad grew very still as the pair emerged from the left aqueduct in night-vision goggles. They were wearing UNACOM uniforms, their AK-47s still trained on his chest. But these didn't look like U.N. weapons inspectors to him.

"Radio Zawas, Abdul," said the one on the right.

The one called Abdul tried to make the call but only got static. "We have to surface," he said, sounding frustrated. "These walls are blocking the signal."

Abdul's partner started toward Conrad when another rumble began in the distance. Conrad edged toward the right aqueduct.

"Stop!" Abdul demanded. "Where do you think you are going?"

"To the surface like you said," Conrad replied without looking back. As he approached the mouth of the right aqueduct he could feel a cool wet breeze on his face. The distant roar grew louder. Then a bullet whizzed past his ear and he stopped and turned around.

Abdul and his companion were almost twenty yards away in the large tunnel, staring beyond him with growing curiosity. They were saying something, but the rumble from behind was too loud for Conrad to hear them. Then, just as Conrad could feel the first drops of water spraying his back, he saw them lower their weapons and start running away.

Conrad dove into the left tunnel as a wall of water blasted out of the aqueduct behind him and flushed the soldiers away. And then the mighty flow thinned into a tiny stream, as if some automatic timer had turned off the faucet. They were gone.

Conrad stood still, listening to the trickle of water and his heavy breathing, when he heard a splash from behind. He spun around and saw a hulking figure walking toward him in the dark, growing larger and more menacing until he emerged from the shadows and ripped off his night goggles.

"I've been looking for you," said Yeats.

"Dad!" Conrad wanted to throw his arms around his father.

But Yeats instead bent down and picked up something shiny floating in the water. Conrad could see it was an Egyptian ankh from the neck of one of the soldiers. The crosslike necklace with a circle at the top was a symbol of life, but it meant little to the dead soldier now. Yeats held the ankh up to the light of his headtorch.

"At least you're starting to screw things up for somebody else now, Conrad," he said.

26

DAWN MINUS TWELVE HOURS

SERENA FELT HOT AND UNCOMFORTABLE inside the Z-9A jet helicopter as it jerked haphazardly across the plateau. The Egyptian pilot was having some trouble keeping the overloaded chopper steady, and each dip brought spews of profanity from the UNACOM soldiers in back. Meanwhile, Jamil's stench was offensive in the cramped space. She could feel his cruel eyes fixed on her breasts with each lurch of the chopper.

"You are enjoying the ride, no?" he asked in Arabic.

"Not so much as you," she said. "Maybe if your pilot lets me take the stick."

Jamil looked at her, eyes burning with rage. "You dare talk back to me?"

She said nothing. She focused on the spectacular views of the city and waterways below, wondering what had happened to Conrad and who these UNACOM soldiers really were and what they wanted.

She had known that Colonel Ali Zawas was in Antarctica on behalf of the United Nations, and these men clearly reported to him and were no doubt taking her to him now. Perhaps their UNACOM assignments were merely covers to position themselves. Perhaps these soldiers had been lying in wait all along to relieve the Americans of whatever they found beneath the ice. Jamil seemed to know about the Scepter of Osiris. How?

The few answers she had gleaned thus far were grim: the Americans at Ice Base Orion were dead, along with the Russian weapons inspectors, and now Zawas and his arsenal controlled the city, until American reinforcements arrived. By then, however, it would be too late to stop Zawas from accomplishing his mission, whatever that might be, much less the impending worldwide geological cataclysm.

The chopper banked right, and in a flash she saw the great water channel below and beyond it, at the end of an acropolis, a gigantic step-pyramid looming like a dark fortress. The Temple of the Water Bearer is how Jamil referred to it as he spoke to the pilot, and indeed it lived up to its name. Two Niagara-like waterfalls tumbled down its sides, and some sort of encampment was set up in the promontory in between.

They descended along the temple's flattened eastern face between the two huge waterfalls and touched down on a landing pad on the promontory below. Those waterfalls, Serena realized as the door slid open and the soldiers emptied out, had been responsible for the low rumble she had been hearing ever since she emerged from P4 into the city. It was the power of those vibrations that made her feel uneasy and provided a constant sense of foreboding.

She climbed out and surveyed her surroundings. Two ramparts of narrow steps wound to the ground on either side. In the center sat crates of equipment. In back was an iron gate, before some sort of entrance to the temple. Meanwhile, a tower and antiaircraft gun stood atop the summit overhead. There must have been a second helipad up there, because she could make out the blades of another chopper hanging over the side. She looked over the ledge. Down below were dune buggies, and even a Navy SEAL–type of rubber raft with an outboard motor tied at the base of the falls. Whoever these people were, they were well financed and well prepared.

The makeshift iron gate opened, and a man sauntered across the promontory. Like the other soldiers, he wore a camouflaged United Nations uniform. The only difference was that he was bareheaded and wore no badges or rank, yet she recognized him immediately.

He was Colonel Ali Zawas, an Egyptian air force colonel and scion of Egypt's most prominent family of diplomats. He was born and raised in New York City until he graduated from the U.S. Air Force Academy and moved back to Cairo. More American than Egyptian. She had seen him several times before at the United

Nations, once at the American University in Cairo. But he was always in dress uniform at formal functions, not in the menacing field fatigues he now sported. He also normally had dark, wavy hair, which was now shaved off.

Zawas paused in the center of the promontory before the group of soldiers. Jamil moved in smartly and saluted. Zawas waved it off. He was a handsome man with deep-set eyes. There was a brief exchange in Arabic. Serena couldn't quite catch all of it, but the contempt on Zawas's face was enough.

His eyes traveled over the men casually, and fixed on her. He stood there staring at her in the silence, then said something to Jamil, who walked over, grabbed Serena by the arm, and propelled her in front of him. She fought to control the panic that surged inside her, for fear would not help her now, and schooled herself to play it cool.

She kept her head down, but Zawas lifted her chin, and she looked into the dark eyes. "If you're an Atlantean," he said in English, "then this is indeed paradise. But I take it you are an American."

She shook her head and said in a low voice, "No, Colonel, I'm from Rome."

It took a moment for her Australian accent to register, and then she saw the shock of recognition. Then a broad, genuine smile crossed his face. "Sister Serghetti, it is you," he said. "What on earth are you doing here?"

"It's Doctor Serghetti, Colonel, and I was going to ask you the same question," she said, looking around at his troops. "You don't really expect me to believe you are acting on behalf of the United Nations?"

Zawas smiled. She realized he was amused that she was the one demanding answers. "Consider us representatives of certain Arab oil producers who have the most to lose from the discovery of alternative energy sources." He took her arm and said casually over his shoulder, "Get to work, Jamil."

Jamil gave them enough time to get clear then shouted something unintelligible that was drowned out in the immediate uproar as the soldiers began to break out equipment. Drills, seismic meters, metal detectors, explosives.

They reached the steps leading up to the iron gate and the

entrance to the temple, and Zawas paused, turning to look at her, a slightly quizzical frown on his face.

"I didn't recognize you at first," he told her. "It's been so long, and you're usually not so dirty on those magazine covers."

"Sorry to have disappointed you."

"Not at all. I find it quite becoming."

She studied him closely. Handsome, shrewd, even gentle if he wanted to be, she was sure of that.

"And why is that?"

"It brings you down to earth." He smiled faintly, opened the front gate, and led her inside.

The chamber was sparsely furnished. Table, chairs, computers, a cot. As he closed the door, he took her backpack from her and dropped it on a chair.

"Please, sit down."

He politely pulled out a chair for her, and she sat down. He seated himself on the opposite side of the table.

She wasted no time. "So that's what you think you'll find down here?" she asked him. "An alternative energy source?"

"Not just any source, Doctor Serghetti, but *the* source," he told her. "The legendary power of the sun itself that the Atlanteans are said to have harnessed. What else did you think General Yeats and Doctor Yeats were after?"

Serena couldn't say, her eyes involuntarily glancing at her pack on the chair. She considered the blueprints of the obelisk that she had hidden inside her thermos. What she really wanted to know was why Zawas seemed to believe Antarctica was Atlantis, let alone that there was some all-powerful "source" behind its power.

"So you're here because you're just as power hungry as the rest of them," she said. "That's not your reputation at the United Nations."

"On the contrary," he said. "I'm concerned that faltering economies in the Middle East will permit increasingly influential mullahs to sow unrest and seize power. That I must use animals like Jamil to stop the rest of his kind is but one of geopolitics' many ironies."

"I've got it all wrong then," she said. "You're not a terrorist. You're really a patriot who's simply been misunderstood."

"You worry too much about the souls of men like me and Doctor

Yeats," he said. "Oh, yes, I know all about him. More than you even, perhaps. If he's still alive, we'll find him. You, however, should be asking yourself why you're down here. Clearly, it's not to protect the environment, which as you can see has altered significantly since your arrival."

"All right then," she said, folding her arms. "Tell me why I'm here."

"You're here because I sent for you."

Her mouth went dry. "You sent for me?"

"Well, maybe not you exactly, but somebody like you," Zawas said. "I knew I would need a translator to help me find the Shrine of the First Sun. Why else do you think I tipped off the Vatican about Yeats's expedition?"

Serena's heart skipped a beat. What was Zawas implying? What did he know that she didn't? "Just what exactly do you want me to translate?"

"A map."

Zawas unrolled an old parchment across the table.

Serena looked at it and realized it was a map of the city. The inscriptions were some sort of pre-Egyptian hieroglyphics. She could see the Temple of the Water Bearer clearly marked, along with other pavilions. It was a terrestrial map that mirrored the celestial map Conrad recognized from the Scepter.

"We found it some years ago in a secret chamber beneath the Great Sphinx at Giza," Zawas said. "Drawn by the ancient Egyptian priest Sonchis, the primary source for Plato's story of Atlantis. Of course, we had no way of knowing whether the map depicted a real place, let alone its location, until the American discovery of P4 in Antarctica."

She said, "So how did the Americans know the location of P4?"

"They didn't, as far as I know," Zawas said. "It was the seismic activity that brought them to East Antarctica. Only after they found something under the ice was the Vatican brought on board."

"The Vatican?" Serena arched an eyebrow. "I don't think so."

"The Vatican has its own map of Atlantis," Zawas said. "It originally had been stored in the Library of Alexandria during the time of Alexander the Great. Then the Romans stole it during their occupation of Egypt. Later, after the fall of the Roman Empire, it was moved to Constantinople. When Constantinople was sacked during the Fourth Crusade, the map was smuggled to Venice. There it was rediscovered in the seventeenth century by a Jesuit priest."

Serena felt shaky, the fury building inside her. But was she angry at Zawas for telling her this, or at the pope for telling her nothing? "I don't believe you."

"Why else would Rome be so eager to send you?" Zawas asked. "You didn't really think it was to save the virginal ecosystem of Antarctica?"

"Then what for?" she asked.

"Surely it was to protect itself, its power. The Church is no more noble than the secular, imperialist American republic. It fears any sort of real divine revelation that might undermine its influence in the course of human events. And that's what this is, Doctor Serghetti. Something older than Islam, Christianity, and even Judaism. Your superiors have every reason to be scared. And you have no reason to trust them or anybody else—only the man who bothered to tell you the truth. So come now, you will help me find the Shrine of the First Sun which contains the source."

"And if I don't?"

"Suffer like the rest of the world," he replied.

"The rest?"

"Ah, you haven't heard the news," he told her. "McMurdo Station has lost its ice runway. And the U.S. carrier group off the continent is recovering from that tidal wave and is running at half power. My intelligence tells me American forces are at least sixteen hours away. Until they get here, I am the ultimate power in Atlantis."

"And when they do get here?"

"It will be too late." Zawas's dark eyes flashed with determination. "I will have captured the technology housed in the Shrine of the First Sun, and the world's balance of power will be shifted. The United States will be wiped out, a victim of the earth-crust displacement it unleashed itself. Atlantis, on the other hand, will be ours."

"You're a fortune-teller too?"

"It's our destiny." He leaned forward and smiled. "You see, Doctor Serghetti, this is my people's Promised Land."

27
DAWN MINUS ELEVEN HOURS

Conrad zipped up a UNACOM weapons inspector's uniform and grimly noted the CAPT. HASSEIN tag over his left breast pocket. Yeats had a couple of these uniforms, sans bodies. Conrad could only guess how he had obtained them. He looked around the chamber Yeats had brought them to. It was stockpiled with computer equipment, M-16s, and explosives.

Conrad asked, "What is this place?"

"A weapons cache I found." Yeats was busy stashing bricks of C-4 plastique into a backpack. "I ended up down here after you flushed me down that shaft in P4 like a piece of shit. Crawled out, got my bearings, and got to work hauling whatever I could find."

"And this cache wasn't guarded by those goons outside?"

"No goons," Yeats said. "Not anymore."

Yeats's survival instincts were astounding even to Conrad, who had already fought hard to stay alive himself in the last several hours. How in the world did he survive that fall? Conrad wondered. He didn't know whether to give his father a medal or a kick in the groin. The man had yet to express relief at seeing his only son alive, nor had he uttered another word about his origins.

"How do you know all this won't get flushed away again?"

"I don't." Yeats checked the timers for the C-4. "But this alcove is separated from the corridors below. Anyway, we won't be sticking around much longer."

"So I see." Conrad eyed the bulging pack of C-4 that Yeats slung over his shoulder. "So you know who these guys are?"

"I trained their leader, Colonel Zawas."

Conrad stared at Yeats. "You trained him?"

"At the U.S. Air Force Academy in Colorado Springs under a U.S.-Egyptian military exchange program in the late eighties," Yeats said. "Came in handy a few years later during the Allied bombing of Iraq in the Persian Gulf War. An Arab pilot taking out two Iraqi jets proved to be priceless PR and legitimized the bombing campaign as a multinational effort."

"So that's what you taught him to do—kill other Arabs?"

"In my dreams," Yeats said. "No, I trained him in the Decisive Force school of warfare. The idea is to use overwhelming force to either annihilate an enemy or intimidate him into surrender."

"So the U.N. weapons inspection team was only a cover?" Conrad asked.

Yeats nodded. "Obviously, Zawas stacked the team with his own men. Probably offed the other internationals and plans to say we did it. I wouldn't be surprised if he put the Russians on us back at P4 and was just waiting for us to do all the hard work."

Conrad said, "So you're saying Zawas came with friends."

"And firepower," Yeats said. "In the real world, a few terrorists are no match against the world's lone superpower. But Antarctica is a different theater of war. It doesn't take much to overwhelm a small team of Americans on an otherwise empty continent."

"Well, his lieutenant killed your dog and abducted Serena."

Conrad could see the veins in Yeats's neck bulge. "So where's the obelisk?"

Conrad said nothing.

Yeats shot him one of those rare, withering glares that used to make Conrad crumble as a boy. "Goddamn it. Are you telling me that Zawas not only shot my dog but also has the Scepter of Osiris?"

"No, I said he has Serena."

"Same difference. Open your eyes. You heard Ms. Save-the-Earth back at P4. The Scepter of Osiris belongs in the Shrine of the First Sun. That's where she's going to lead Zawas."

"You're selling her short."

"You're thinking with the wrong head," Yeats said. "Our mission is to deny Zawas any advanced weapon or alien technology that could shift the world's balance of power. Asymmetrical force. Got that? Burn it into your brain."

"Gee, and I thought we were going to settle who I am and where I really came from, Dad," Conrad shot back.

Yeats paused, and Conrad could practically hear the whir of the hard drive behind Yeats's eyes as his father searched for an appropriate response.

"We do that by beating Zawas to the Shrine of the First Sun and setting a trap for him if and when Serena finally leads him there." Yeats patted his pack full of C-4 and moved on as if he had disclosed everything. "The problem, of course, is going to be finding it without them finding us first. Which is about the time between now and when Zawas discovers that several of his men are missing. They control the skies and everything on the surface. We're going to have to stay underground until dark."

"We'll need the stars, anyway," Conrad said, pulling out his handheld device with the images of the obelisk he had captured. "Because the scepter instructs the would-be sun king to put heaven and earth together. Only then will the 'Shining One' reveal the location of the Shrine of the First Sun."

"Serena never said that."

"I know," Conrad said. "The scepter did."

"I thought you couldn't read the inscriptions."

"Let's just say some things are feeling a little more familiar."

"So you believe me now?" Yeats asked. "About finding you in the capsule and everything?"

"I'll never believe everything you tell me," Conrad said. "And I reserve judgment on some things. But this inscription beneath the four constellations on one side of the obelisk is almost identical to the inscription Serena read for us."

"What's the difference?"

"The inscription Serena read to us warns against removing the scepter unless you're the most worthy, according to the Shining Ones, or else you'll tear Heaven and Earth apart," Conrad said.

"Which seems to be happening right now," Yeats said.

"So it seems," Conrad said. "But this inscription under the four zodiac signs tells the would-be Sun King how to find the Shrine of the First Sun with the help of a Shining One and bring Heaven and Earth together again."

"And what on earth is the Shining One?" Yeats asked.

"It's not of this earth. It's probably some kind of astronomical phenomenon. I'll know it when I see it."

"Hot damn, Conrad, looks like you really are the Sun King." Yeats slapped him on the back for the first time in years, and Conrad couldn't deny it felt good. "But where exactly are we supposed to consult this Shining One? There are millions of stars out there."

Conrad said, "We'll follow the map on the scepter."

"What map?"

"The four constellations." Conrad showed Yeats the 360-degree digital scan he had taken of the obelisk. "See? The zodiac signs of Scorpio, Sagittarius, Capricorn, and Aquarius."

Yeats looked at the image. "So?"

Conrad tapped his device. "So if this city is astronomically aligned, then maybe these celestial coordinates might have terrestrial counterparts."

"Maybe?" Yeats said. "You'll have to do better than that."

"We already know P4 is aligned with the middle belt star of Orion, Al Nitak," Conrad said, and Yeats nodded. "In the same way we might find strategically positioned shrines in the city that are aligned to Scorpio, Sagittarius, Capricorn, and Aquarius."

Yeats furrowed his brow. "Meaning we follow the pavilions or temples that correspond to these signs like some kind of heavenly treasure trail?"

"Exactly."

"So these celestial markers will lead us to Aquarius," Yeats said. "And then we find its terrestrial double."

"That's right," said Conrad. "It's dusk outside now. Soon the stars will be out. They'll serve as our map and lead us to some kind of monument dedicated to the Water Bearer. That's where the Shining One will be, to lead us to the Shrine of the First Sun."

Yeats nodded. "And everything we've spent our lives searching for."

28

DAWN MINUS SIX HOURS

Inside the Temple of the Water Bearer, starlight seeped into the chamber where Serena stood tied to a post. It was her punishment for refusing to help Colonel Zawas translate his map of Atlantis. To help Zawas locate the Shrine of the First Sun would be to betray Conrad, she reasoned, having concluded that Conrad, for all his faults, was still her best hope for stopping a global cataclysm. But even if Conrad could reach the shrine first, Zawas still had the scepter. Somehow she had to hold on long enough to figure out a way to steal it.

She could hear voices outside, and three dark silhouettes filled the doorway, blotting out the heavens. It was Jamil, flanked by two Egyptians. Serena stiffened as he unfurled a towel with assorted knives and needles across a small table.

"Colonel Zawas was disappointed he couldn't persuade you to cooperate, Doctor Serghetti," he said. "Now it's my turn."

"So I see," she said, staring at the cruel instruments on the table. "Isn't this a bit over the top? I already told Zawas that I don't know where the shrine is. Honest. If I did, I'd tell you."

"A brave front, Doctor Serghetti, really." Jamil looked over his wares, stocked mostly with syringes, knives of various shapes, and shock rods. "Ah, the tricks your Inquisition taught us."

He picked up a two-foot-long black club. Suddenly it came to life like lightning. It was an electric shock baton.

"This is my favorite," he said, waving it in front of her. A bolt of blue electricity sizzled between two metal prongs. "Each jolt delivers seventy-five thousand volts. A few pokes would leave you unconscious. A few more, dead."

"Is this what you intended your life to become, Jamil?"

Jamil cursed and tried to force her jaw open. She turned away. But he shoved the baton into her mouth. She choked on the metal rod as he dug it deeper.

"The Chinese like to shove this down a prisoner's throat and charge it up," he said as she gagged. "The current that races through your body will leave you crumpled on the floor in a pool of blood and excrement and in extreme pain."

She could feel the hot metal prongs at the back of her throat and moaned. But Jamil pulled it away and pushed the button again so she could see the blue electric charges flash between the prongs.

"There are other places I could ram this," he told her, and she unconsciously squeezed her thighs together. "Good," he said with a smile and set the shock rod down on the table. "I see you understand." He then picked up a syringe and with the back of his finger flicked the hypodermic needle. A yellowish fluid spurted out. "Now we can begin."

A few hours later, Serena regained consciousness and found herself in the dark, staring at a makeshift lantern Jamil had hung from the ceiling—his shock rod swinging on a rope, making grotesque zapping sounds as it flashed. She tried closing her eyes, but the zap-zap of the shock rod only seemed to grow louder. Or maybe it was the drugs injected into her bloodstream that made her feel so sloshed.

Somehow she sensed another presence in the chamber and opened her eyes to see a long shadow on the wall. Her eyes drifted to the doorway, where a fuzzy figure stepped inside.

"Conrad?" she said.

"It's nice to have dreams, Doctor Serghetti."

It was Zawas. Serena hung her head again as he walked over to the small table where Jamil had left his tools of torture.

"I'm told you haven't been terribly cooperative," Zawas said, examining Jamil's toys. "It was all I could do to keep Jamil from permanently erasing your memory with those chemicals of his. But he is an animal. He gives Arabs everywhere a bad name. You know that most of us are not at all like him. You must understand this. Your Church has priests who molest children. Yet you aren't about to abandon your mission. Neither am I."

She said nothing as he looked around the chamber. Her pack on the floor caught his eye. He circled round it and watched her face. Then he lifted it to the table and unzipped it. He began to rifle through its contents, examining her personal belongings—water purification tablets, hot water bottles, a flare, and the like.

Then he came to her green thermos. Her chest constricted as he began to unscrew the top. She prayed he wouldn't find the blueprint inside the secret shell. For all she knew, that blueprint contained enough information for him to find or deploy this unlimited power source he was searching for in the Shrine of the First Sun.

"You remind me of Pharaoh, Zawas," Serena said. "You know, from the Bible."

He seemed amused and put the thermos down on the table. "Then you know my authority comes from the gods themselves and you must answer to me."

"The gods of Egypt were defeated once before," she said. "They can be defeated again."

"History is about to be rewritten, Doctor Serghetti. But first I must find the Shrine of the First Sun. So far, its location has eluded me. As has Doctor Yeats. Oh, yes, he's alive. I know this because several of my men are missing," he said. "He killed them, just like he's killed so many others in Atlantis thus far in his selfish quest for the origins of human civilization. I know all about this man. He cares little for the consequences of his actions on governments, people, even the very sites he excavates. It's a good thing I saved you and the Scepter of Osiris from him."

Serena said nothing, because there was no defense against Zawas's accusations. They were true.

"Unlike the reckless Doctor Yeats, however," Zawas went on, "I appreciate and want to preserve natural beauty in all its forms, especially the feminine. I would hate to see a monster like Jamil mar you in any way."

That was a lie, she knew. "So you're a gentleman among the barbarians."

He looked at her carefully. "I see we understand each other well. It's not as if the Catholic Church hasn't wrapped itself up in nobility and social mercy only to make pacts with the devil at convenient points in history."

"Then you're a hero, really," she told him. "You just happen to be on the wrong side of history."

"Exactly," Zawas said. "Like Pharaoh during the Exodus. It was his bad luck that the eruption of the volcano at Thíra in the Mediterranean should produce the plagues you eagerly attribute to the God of Moses. There was no parting of the Red Sea. The Israelites crossed at the Sea of Reeds in only six inches of water. But it was enough to bog down the wheels of Pharaoh's chariots."

"Then it was a greater miracle than I thought," Serena said. "That all of Pharaoh's soldiers and horses should drown in six inches of water."

Zawas was not amused by her argument, she could see, and his face grew more stern in the flashing light. "History is written by the victor," he told her. "How else can you explain Judeo-Christian exaltation of an allegedly merciful and loving God who goes around killing the firstborn of the ancient Egyptians?"

"He could have killed them all," she said.

Zawas was put out. "So it was Pharaoh's fault?"

She tried to focus. Even in her somewhat shaky state she recognized this could be a pivotal moment in persuading Zawas. "You know that at certain points of history, everything rests on one man or one woman," she told him. "Noah and the ark. Pharaoh and the Israelites. God offered Pharaoh the divine opportunity to be the greatest emancipator in history. But his heart was stubborn and arrogant. Now is such a time. You may be such a man."

"Or you that woman," he said. "Where is the Shrine of the First Sun?"

"I honestly don't know."

"Then I honestly must give you to Jamil to finish the job," he said. "It's out of my control now. I wash my hands clean of this."

"Says Pontius Pilate."

"And I thought I was Pharaoh." He shook his head and threw up his hands. "Am I to be compared to every villain in your Scriptures? Have you ever considered the possibility that these leaders are history's true heroes and your saints the revisionist authors of fiction?"

He was about to turn and leave when his eyes once again drifted to the coffee thermos on the table.

"Why are you still carrying around your thermos?"

Serena said nothing, pretending not to hear.

But he was already untwisting the outer shell. He smelled the coffee and made a face. "I prefer tea myself."

He emptied the coffee onto the stone floor and then tried to screw the lid back on. As he did, the blueprint fell to the floor.

Serena caught her breath.

Zawas picked up the blueprint and let out a hearty laugh. Then he showed it to her and said, "Do you know what these schematics are?"

She hung her shoulders in defeat. "The blueprint to the Scepter of Osiris."

"No," he told her. "This is the blueprint to the Shrine of the First Sun."

She just stared at him, head rushing with dizziness.

"Yes," Zawas said. "Now I have three things Doctor Yeats wants. And if he won't lead me to the Shrine of the First Sun, then you will. I'll tell Jamil he has more work to do."

29

DAWN MINUS TWO HOURS

SCORPIO. SAGITTARIUS. CAPRICORN. For several hours Conrad led Yeats across the dark city, following each celestial coordinate to its terrestrial counterpart, and then moving on from one astronomically aligned monument to another. Each temple, pavilion, or landmark would in itself be the archaeological prize of the ages, but time and the buzz of choppers and searchlights overhead kept them marching forward. Finally, the heavenly treasure trail ended at the terrestrial counterpart to the constellation Aquarius, a spectacular temple dedicated to the Water Bearer.

The Sphinx-like pavilion loomed like a skull against the heavens, its silvery waterfalls glistening in the moonlight. Beyond it lurked the dark, towering peak of P4.

"That's it," Conrad said as he handed the nightscope to Yeats. They were crouched along the banks of the city's largest water channel, which flowed directly from the monument. "The Temple of the Water Bearer."

Yeats took a look. "That's not all you found. Look again."

Conrad scanned the Temple of the Water Bearer and suddenly saw lights around the base and promontory. "Zawas?"

"Looks like he's turned it into his base camp."

Conrad lowered the nightscope. "How the hell did they know?"

Yeats shrugged. "Maybe Mother Earth is helping him."

"Or maybe they have some sort of map."

"Doubtful," Yeats said. "You said yourself that the map is in the stars." Yeats paused. "Now you're absolutely sure you need to get in there? Because it's both our asses if Zawas catches us."

Conrad nodded. "Only by standing in the right place at the right time will the Shining One pinpoint the location of the Shrine of the First Sun," he said.

Yeats narrowed his eyes. "And where exactly are we supposed to consult this 'Shining One'?"

Conrad hesitated to break the bad news. "I suspect it's between the waterfalls at the Temple of the Water Bearer. In the middle of Zawas's base."

Yeats flipped his wrist and glanced at the luminous dial of his watch. "It's already zero four hundred hours. Almost dawn. The sun is going to be coming up. We don't have much time."

Conrad spent the next half hour surveying the temple from a distance while Yeats drew up a plan.

"You'll see the promontory on the east face is about a hundred and fifty feet high," Yeats told him. "Two narrow stairways on either side go to the base of the falls. Because of that, I doubt Zawas posts more than one guard at the bottom of each flight of steps. That and the fact he needs as many warm bodies as possible looking for the Shrine of the First Sun."

Conrad scanned the east face down the falls to the ground. Suddenly the sentries at the north end of the east face came into sharp focus. So did an inflatable attack boat moored beneath the falls. The upturned bow and stern cones told him it was a Zodiac Futura Commando, a favorite of special forces around the world.

"I see the guards," he said. "They've got a Zodiac inflatable tied up."

"Just one?"

"The others are probably patrolling the waterways, looking for us."

"Let me see." Yeats took the nightscope. "Zawas rotates his guards every three hours. At least that's the way he used to do things during U.N. peacekeeping jobs. This shift looks about done by the body language." Yeats handed the nightscope back to Conrad. "So we simply relieve the present shift a few minutes early. Then, after I make sure you're covered, we split."

"And just how do we do that?"

Yeats flicked on an old cigarette lighter to illuminate the drawing he had made in the dark.

"You find this so-called Shining One who's going to lead us to the Shrine of the First Sun," Yeats said, tracing a line toward the promontory with his finger. "I'll go to the summit where Zawas keeps his choppers and secure one for the getaway. You'll have six minutes to get from the promontory to the summit. Then we fly away."

"Just like that?" Conrad said.

"Just like that," Yeats said. "I'll rig the other choppers to blow so Zawas can't tail us in the air. It will buy us the time we need to beat him to the shrine."

Conrad stared at the lighter Yeats was using to illuminate his drawing. It was an old Zippo with a NASA emblem and an engraving to Yeats from Captain Rick Conrad, one of the crew who died in Antarctica in 1969 and the man Conrad was told was his biological father. That was back in the days when astronauts smoked. He had often snuck into Yeats's study to play with it. Once he almost burned down the house. He had hoped Yeats would finally figure out how badly he wanted something of his father's and just give the damn thing to him. But Yeats never did.

"I thought you quit smoking."

"I never quit anything in my life, son." Yeats flicked off the lighter and gave it to Conrad.

Surprised, Conrad felt the old, familiar weight of the Zippo in his hand for a moment and then flicked it on and off.

"What about Serena?" Conrad asked. "What about the obelisk?"

"If Zawas finds either one missing before you find the location of the Shrine of the First Sun, he'll be on to us and our mission is over," Yeats said. "And after we take off without the obelisk or the sister, he'll figure we failed. By the time he figures out we got what we really wanted, we'll already be inside the Shrine of the First Sun, have taken what we needed, and set a trap for him. Zawas will then bring us both the obelisk and Serena."

"If he doesn't kill her first."

"Will you listen to me for once," Yeats said angrily. "She's the one who's going to lead him to us. Trust me, Zawas is counting on her. He's not going to kill her until she's lost her usefulness."

"That's reassuring." Conrad offered the lighter back to Yeats, but to his amazement Yeats refused. "Let's go."

There were lights up above, the roar of churning water drifting from the falls all around. As he turned the final corner, Conrad could see the black cutout of a sentry at the base of the steps, and beyond him the Zodiac attack boat bobbing in the water. The Egyptian was smoking a cigarette. Conrad was about to step forward when his boot scraped the stone.

The sentry spun around. "Yasser?"

Conrad nodded and tapped his watch.

The sentry spat out a rebuke in Arabic and turned and left.

Conrad watched him march up the steps and took a quick look around. It would only be a few minutes before the sentry went back and found the real Yasser. Satisfied nobody was near, Conrad ascended the stone steps to the promontory.

The steps were narrow and water-slicked from the falls, but he reached the top quickly. Stepping onto the promontory, Conrad looked across to see another figure walk toward him.

"Yeats, is that you?" he whispered into his radio.

"I'm making a circle with my hand," Yeats said.

Conrad could barely hear him over the roar of the falls. But he could see the figure on the other side making a circle. "OK," Conrad said.

"Get to work," Yeats said. "And no matter what happens, stick to the plan and rendezvous in six minutes." Then he disappeared into the darkness.

Conrad walked up to the edge of the promontory between the falls and positioned himself. The tremendous vibrations of the falls rumbled beneath his feet, and he had to steady himself.

He gazed out and found what he was looking for. There, in the predawn of the spring equinox, the constellation of Aquarius was rising in the east. It was a perfect lock with the monument he was standing on. The Water Bearer on earth was staring at the Water Bearer in heaven. And the predawn sun—the Shining One—marked the spot.

He quickly pulled out the digital surveyor Yeats had packed for him and made his calculations. From what he could make out, the Shrine of the First Sun was buried ninety degrees to the south. That placed the X directly under the river, at a depth he guessed to be about a thousand feet. He scanned the horizon with his digital camera to mark it.

Conrad looked again at the skies. The first stain of dawn was glimmering. Soon Aquarius would be fully risen, a water bearer in the sky with its jar resting on the horizon. At the same moment, the sun—marking the vernal point—would lie somewhere beneath the last star pouring out from the jar.

Conrad glanced at his watch. It was almost 5 A.M. He had to move quickly, he thought, when he turned to see an Egyptian emerge from the temple and walk toward him.

"Why aren't you at your post, Yasser?" he barked.

"Why aren't you at yours?" Conrad grumbled back in passable Arabic. His Arabic was a jumble of odds and ends he had picked up over the years.

The man calmed down. "Taking a break," he said, or at least that's what Conrad thought he said. "These nuns, they do not break easily. They are trained to be martyrs. I have to be careful where I hurt this one. She can still be of use to me after she's dead."

Conrad noticed something in his hand. It was a fistful of hair. Serena's hair. Conrad wanted to kill him then and there and rescue Serena. But he knew he couldn't let the soldier see his face. So he simply laughed at his sick joke and turned around and looked ahead over the falls. Then he felt the barrel of an AK-47 digging into his back.

"So you've found the shrine, Doctor Yeats?"

He turned to him and looked into his smoldering eyes.

He smiled in triumph. "No need for the nun now," he said. "Where is it?"

"Over there," Conrad said, playing along. "See the constellation of Aquarius?"

He pointed with his left hand and the soldier couldn't help but follow. In that instant Conrad's right hand swept across his neck with the bone-handled knife he had lifted from the Russian back at P4 and had held in his sleeve. The blade left a thin red line.

He tried to call out but could only gurgle in shock as he staggered back over the promontory edge and disappeared into darkness. Conrad watched the body take two bounces off the monument and splash into the river.

Conrad turned to find the steps leading to the upper promontory and the flight deck, where he was supposed to rendezvous with Yeats. But then another Egyptian emerged from inside the temple and started walking toward him, and Conrad froze. The way the man carried himself told Conrad it was Colonel Zawas. And this time, he knew, there would be no escape.

30
DAWN MINUS ONE HOUR

It was a few minutes past five in the morning when Zawas stepped out of his chambers to have a smoke on the promontory and take another look at the blueprints of the Shrine of the First Sun he had obtained from Serena. Now that he knew what he was looking for, he only needed to know where to look.

Sucking on his unlit Havana under the stars, he noticed the skies were lightening. Soon the sun would be up and his window of opportunity to find the Shrine of the First Sun gone. He then saw one of his guards—it looked like Yasser—by one of the falls and walked over. Yasser stiffened to attention in the dim light as he approached.

"At ease, Lieutenant," Zawas said, and Yasser relaxed. "We don't see a sunrise like that often, do we?"

Yasser grumbled something that Zawas took to be a no. He realized most of his men were showing the effects of exhaustion and stress.

Zawas sighed and patted his pockets in search of some matches when Yasser's hand came up with an old-fashioned Zippo lighter. Zawas touched the tip of his Cuban cigar to the flame and inhaled. It felt wonderful.

"Carry on," Zawas said and walked back to his command quarters.

Halfway back, however, he realized there was something familiar about his hand-rolled cigar. No, it wasn't the cigar. It was the old silver Zippo lighter Yasser flashed. It was just like the one his grandfather had. Only Zawas wasn't aware of Yasser or any of his other men possessing such an artifact. He would have to ask Yasser where he found it.

But when Zawas turned to find Yasser, the guard was missing from his post. Zawas swore softly to himself and walked back to the promontory. Peering over the ledge down the falls, he could see nothing. It was as if Yasser had disappeared into thin air. Could he have actually fallen? Yasser was no such fool.

Zawas grabbed his radio from his belt. "Jamil!" he barked. "Round up your men. Conrad is here!"

But Jamil wasn't answering.

"Jamil," Zawas repeated when he heard a blast behind him.

Debris rained down, and Zawas looked up to see flashes of light from the top of the step-pyramid. Suddenly the flaming shell of a Z-9A chopper came tumbling down the east face, steel scraping against stone in an ear-splitting scream. Zawas dove back inside as it crashed onto the promontory and exploded in a ball of fire.

"The scepter!" he cursed.

He ran inside to the chamber where the obelisk was kept under guard. But the two guards were on the floor, dead, and the scepter was gone.

Conrad hit the water at the base of the Temple of the Water Bearer with such force that he thought he died. But a minute later he surfaced for air with a gasp and realized his splash from space went unnoticed by the guards below, thanks to the roar of the falls.

He swam over through the dark to the Zodiac inflatable, cut it loose, climbed on board and hit the motor. By the time the guards saw what was happening and started shooting, he was a hundred yards down the channel and racing away.

He glanced back over his shoulder to see the distant explosions coming from the top of the Temple of the Water Bearer. He also saw a big shadow coming down on him fast—one of Zawas's choppers. Its lights were out and it was flying low, practically on top of him, blocking out the stars. Conrad kicked the onboard motor into high gear but couldn't shake it.

The chopper then moved overhead and passed him by, landing a few hundred yards ahead on the banks of the water channel. As Conrad neared the bank, he could see a figure waving him down.

It was Yeats. And in his hand was the Scepter of Osiris.

"How did you get here?" Conrad asked as he pulled up to the bank.

"Followed the gunfire," Yeats said, stepping into the Zodiac. "You find the location of the shrine?"

Conrad looked in amazement at the helicopter. "Whatever happened to slipping in and out undetected?"

"I had to create a diversion and leave Zawas a clue at the same time."

Conrad felt the familiar pang of betrayal from his childhood. "You took the scepter and left Serena behind?"

"I didn't have much of a choice once I saw you and that goon, son," Yeats said matter-of-factly, in clipped military speed. "I knew the plan was blown. I grabbed what I could and took off. Now did you find the shrine or not? Zawas is pissed as hell and coming after us."

Conrad wiped a wet flop of hair from his forehead. "I found it. It's just ahead."

"That's my boy," Yeats said with an approving nod. "Let's go."

They followed the waterway into a tunnel. Conrad's GPS marker took them to a small dark corridor that branched off the subterranean waterway. At the end of it was some kind of stone grating.

"That's the door to the Shrine of the First Sun," Conrad said. "It's down there. About a thousand feet."

They ditched the Zodiac, sending it on its way down the tunnel as a decoy.

Conrad watched the boat disappear into the dark and then checked his GPS watch. They were running out of time. It was almost 5:15 A.M., and the first faint hint of dawn was falling across the city above.

They dug out the grating to find a manhole-size shaft. They slid down into another labyrinth of subterranean corridors, going deeper and deeper into the earth. A half hour later they reached a long dark tunnel that ended in a blue light.

"That's it," Conrad said.

Yeats pulled out his flashlight. Its beam revealed a door. As soon as they passed under the blue light, the door slid open, and they stepped inside a dark cavern. This chamber felt like the largest they had stood in yet.

"I'm sending out a flare," Yeats said. "Thirty-second delay."

Conrad shielded his eyes as Yeats flung the little cylinder into the chamber. He counted down to two seconds when everything exploded with light. For an instant he saw the unbelievable spectacle of a towering obelisk much like the one from P4. Only this one was cradled in some fantastic cylinder and stood at least five hundred feet tall. And at its base was some sort of great rotunda that had to be its entrance.

All around them, the terraced slopes of the cylinder rose up until they merged into a domelike ceiling. And Conrad realized they stood only halfway down this cavity by the time the light went out.

"Incredible!" he said, his voice echoing loudly.

They descended the steps that spiraled alongside the interior of the cylinder to the bottom and stood at the base of the giant obelisk and looked up. He could see no more than twenty feet overhead, except the blinking of red lights around the cylinder—the remote switches to the C-4 bricks Yeats had set on the way down.

"What the hell are you doing?" Conrad said.

"Setting a trap for Zawas," Yeats said.

"Who's got Serena, remember?"

"Don't worry, they're not on timers. I've got the detonator right here."

If that was supposed to comfort Conrad, it didn't. But he was too engrossed with their discovery to be distracted by an argument he couldn't win. Instead he followed Yeats through the rotunda to what appeared to be a doorway at the base of the giant obelisk.

Conrad wondered if it was even possible to enter at this point. Then he noticed a square shaft next to the door. It looked about the size of the base of the Scepter of Osiris.

"We might need the scepter to open this."

"Here you go, son," Yeats said, handing it over.

Conrad inserted the scepter into the square display and felt a small vibration. The door opened, and they stepped inside the giant obelisk.

Zawas clenched his jaw as he surveyed the wreckage outside. He cursed the name of Conrad Yeats, a man whose face he'd never even seen but who had managed to steal the Scepter of Osiris from under his nose.

Zawas shook his head as he looked down the waterfall to the burned-out shell of the Z-9A jammed into the basin, breaking off into bits as the water carried it down the river. With the other one gone too, he now had only one bird left to fly.

Zawas followed a chunk of windshield as it floated down the canal out toward the horizon, where the first rays of dawn were breaking as the stars began to fade. Something about the pattern of those stars caught his eye. And then he jumped back as he found himself staring at the constellation of Aquarius. Suddenly everything about the map made sense.

He ran into his quarters and looked at the Sonchis map. He stared at the Temple of the Water Bearer, his present location. Then he looked at the "key" symbols in the corner—the constellations of Aquarius, Capricorn, and Sagittarius. He was sweating slightly as he picked up the Sonchis map with shaking hands and stared at it as if for the first time.

He then rushed over to Serena's chamber and began to untie her.

"Things going awry, Zawas?"

"*Au contraire,* Doctor Serghetti," he said and pushed her outside to the promontory.

As they neared the ledge, she resisted, fearing he would throw her over. But instead he told her to follow the water canal with her eyes to the horizon with its first glint of dawn. And then she found herself staring face-to-face with the constellation of Aquarius.

"I've found the Shrine of the First Sun," he told her, "and that means I've found Conrad Yeats."

PART FOUR

DOOMSDAY

31

DAWN MINUS FORTY-FIVE MINUTES

INSIDE THE GREAT OBELISK, Conrad and Yeats stood on a circular platform five feet wide suspended in darkness. Conrad heard a low hum and could feel a greasy draft against his cheek. He flicked on his halogen flashlight. The beam shot out fifty feet before it struck a towering column and in less than a second ricocheted off three other metallic columns that surrounded them. Each bounce intensified the blinding light. Conrad closed his eyes.

"Shut it off!" Yeats shouted, his voice echoing in the darkness.

Conrad, eyes pressed shut, felt for a switch and turned off the halogen lamp. After a minute he blinked but couldn't shake the blinding afterglow. "Those columns of light," Yeats said, still rubbing his eyes. "What are they?"

"They're not made of light," Conrad said. "They just reflect and magnify any light that hits them. Hold on." Conrad reached into his pocket and pulled out the Zippo lighter. "This is low wattage. Ready?"

"For you to blind us?"

"It won't be so bad this time," Conrad said. "Put your shades on and relax."

Conrad put on his sunglasses and waited for Yeats to do likewise before Conrad flicked on the lighter. The effect was like a single candle burning in a cavernous cathedral. Surrounding them in the dim light were four glowing, translucent pillars, each about twenty feet in diameter, rising two hundred feet into the darkness above and two hundred feet into the abyss below.

"So here's your so-called Shrine of the First Sun," Yeats said, staring straight up.

"It's like being inside a bronze coffee filter," Conrad said, looking around and feeling very small. A halo of mist clung to the glowing pillars, which seemed to come together like a funnel at their apex high above. And the air definitely smelled greasy. Conrad looked down and wondered just how deep into the earth this Shrine of the First Sun descended, and how much farther must they go to discover the Secret of First Time. He was in awe of how much there was for him to absorb and painfully aware of the limited time.

"Look at this." Yeats guided the lighter close to a smooth, shiny pillar. The mirrorlike surface not only seemed to magnify the brightness a hundredfold but also seemed to tremble. "I bet this surface has a reflectance of greater than a hundred percent."

"That's significant?"

"The best we've been able to come up with is eighty-eight percent using aluminum."

"These columns aren't made of aluminum."

"No." Yeats ran his hand over the surface of the column. "They're made of something much lighter."

"Lighter?" Conrad touched the column. The surface was slick, almost liquid. Yet he could sense some kind of indefinable texture to it. "It feels as soft as a cobweb and as strong as steel. Like some sort of lighter-than-air silk."

"That's because the fabric is perforated with holes smaller than the wavelength of light." Yeats sounded almost excited. "I'd say somewhere between one micron or four hundredths of a mil thick. So what now? Do we go up or down this thing?"

Fabric. That's just the word he was looking for, Conrad realized. The surprise was that it was Yeats who came up with it. But he was right. These columns were like giant rolls of some thin, lightweight, and mirrorlike fabric so shiny they could be mistaken for the light they so brilliantly reflected.

"Up or down, son?" Yeats repeated.

"Up," Conrad said, surprising himself. Because in reality he didn't know. He had never come across anything like this shrine in the ancient pyramid texts of the Egyptians or in the tales of Meso-American lore. And he couldn't recall it from any childhood nightmares or memories. Its sole significance, so far as he could tell, was to serve as a live-scale projection of the obelisk he had taken from P4. But somewhere in this obelisk was the so-called Seat of Osiris, the final resting place of the scepter and the Secret of First Time. The only question was whether he would recognize it when he saw it, much less know what to do. "We're going up."

And so they were. The platform they were standing on began to lift like an elevator, carrying them up between the columns of light. Conrad looked up to see the columns funnel toward an apex.

"Hang tight," he said, tense but determined. He realized he had never been more excited about anything in his life.

They must have passed through several levels of compartments, Conrad figured, when he looked up to see a pinprick of light at the end. A minute later they emerged into a cool chamber. Suddenly the platform locked with a thud. Conrad stumbled backward toward the edge of the platform. Yeats caught his arm with a viselike grip.

"End of the line," he said.

Conrad paused to get his bearings. It felt cramped up here compared to the soaring spaces below. Their voices had stopped echoing, and the air felt cooler. Conrad removed his sunglasses and switched on his halogen lamp. This time there was no blinding reflection. The beam stabbed out and bathed the nearest wall in light.

A quick survey revealed one corridor on either side of them. Conrad entered the corridor to their right.

"This way," he said, his impatience hanging thick in the air, pushing them forward.

"Now how would you know?"

"According to you, I'm an Atlantean, remember?"

Conrad led him along the dark tunnel for a minute. At the end was a cryptlike door, about six feet tall. Next to it was a square pad much like the one at the outside entrance. Conrad focused his light on the door. Carved into its metallic surface were unusual engravings that at first defied comprehension. Only when Conrad ran his fingers across them did their meaning register.

"It's a constellation," he said flatly.

Yeats nodded. "That star right there is Sirius."

"The goddess Isis in her astral form." Conrad placed his hand on the cold metallic door, overcome with awe. His throat constricted and his heart beat faster. He could barely manage a whisper. "We found the queen's crypt."

"I was looking for the king's." Yeats sounded detached, business-like. "How much you want to bet we'll find that bastard Osiris down the opposite corridor?"

And the Seat of Osiris and the Secret of First Time, Conrad thought, when he saw a red dot on the back of his hand and spun around. Yeats was pointing his AK-47 at the door, the laser-sighting on.

Conrad jumped back. "What the hell are you doing?"

"You're going to open this door so we can see if the bitch is still in there."

Conrad, his pulse pounding, put his hand on the square pad, and he could feel a surge of energy. He pulled his hand back and the door slid open. A cool mist escaped from the chamber.

"You didn't even need the obelisk for that," Yeats said, almost in awe.

"Maybe once you use it, the system remembers," Conrad said.

"Or maybe your ID is already in the system."

They stepped through the cloud and into the small chamber. The red beam from Yeats's laser sight crisscrossed the cell and locked onto an intricate alcove of some kind. It was contoured for a human being no taller than two meters. Based on the shape, it was clearly a woman. She had two arms, two legs, ten fingers and ten toes, and an hourglass figure.

"Mama." Conrad looked at the display and let out a whistle. "Are you happy now, Yeats? You've met the enemy and she looks like us. Maybe it's not just me. Maybe we're all Atlanteans."

"Let's hope not. Not unless you want us to suffer the same fate. Now let's check out Papa."

Down the hall, the door to the Osiris crypt bore the markings of the Orion constellation on its surface. And this time Conrad didn't hesitate. He put his hand on the door and it split open. Again, a fine cool mist escaped. Yeats climbed through with his AK-47 with Conrad close behind. Conrad shined his light up on the far wall and caught his breath.

"Say hello to Daddy, Conrad," said Yeats.

This crypt was clearly contoured for a vertically standing creature that stood much taller than a human. Inside was an impressive harness or exoskeleton that appeared as mysteriously complex as the being it was designed for. A translucent bandolier crisscrossed the center ring and boasted an awesome array of instruments, gear, and, perhaps, weapons.

"Holy God," Conrad murmured.

"Not so holy if Mother Earth is right," Yeats said. "This one's about three meters high."

Conrad flicked on the Zippo and held it close to the edge of the harness. Whatever it was made of was fireproof and perhaps even indestructible for all intents and purposes. But it clearly supplied its bearer with only partial protection. Judging by the size of it, Conrad could only assume the rest of such a creature required little else.

Creature, he thought. Is that what his true father was? Is that what he was? He had more in common with the man next to him than whatever creature used that harness.

"There is no way in hell I'm related to the thing that belongs here," Conrad told Yeats. "It would have shown up in my DNA tests or something."

"If Serena is right and the Atlanteans are the so-called sons of God from Genesis," Yeats said, "then your biological father was a generation or two removed from the first coupling and more or less human."

"More or less human?" Conrad repeated. "That sounds even more—"

"Show me the goddamn Seat of Osiris, son. We're running out of time."

Conrad nodded. "It's got to be somewhere in here, closer than we think," he said. "If we split up, we'll double our coverage in half the time."

"Then you can hold on to this."

Yeats tossed over the Scepter of Osiris, which Conrad caught in one hand. The thing was practically vibrating with raw energy.

"Now switch your headset to our backup frequency," Yeats said. "It's marked with that little blue tape on the back. Blue is for backup."

"I get it. I get it." Conrad switched to frequency B. "Check."

"Check."

For a minute or two Conrad could hear Yeats's gravelly voice in his right ear as they continued exploring. But it didn't take long for Yeats to move out of range. By the time Conrad was satisfied he had explored every surface of the top story of the obelisk and returned to the central platform, Yeats had disappeared. Conrad was alone and disappointed. He had found nothing and wondered where Yeats went and what he had found.

Conrad stood there on the platform, inside the top chamber of the obelisk, and pondered the alien nature of the obelisk's interior. For all its strangeness there was something about this place that persuaded him to believe he had been here before. Or somewhere like here. An inner urge prompted him to look up at the ceiling. Something about it had bothered him. Now as he flashed his light on it he could see what he had missed before: a small square pad, just like the earlier one.

There was one more, hidden chamber above him, he realized with a surge of excitement.

It was also two meters beyond his reach.

Conrad managed to use the control lever to nudge the platform up half a level, careful not to squash himself against the ceiling, and placed his hand on the square pad. Suddenly the outer ring of some sort of hatch appeared before it split open to reveal another chamber above him with a cathedral ceiling—clearly the very top chamber of the shrine.

Conrad rode the platform up to the top level. His light scanned the chamber, revealing a large high-backed seat that lay horizontally on a kind of altar and pointed to the apex of the cathedral ceiling overhead.

Eureka, Conrad thought. The Seat of Osiris.

"Yes!" Conrad exclaimed out loud. He fumbled anxiously for his radio. "Yeats, I found it."

But there was no response. Where the hell was he?

"Yeats." The silence was eerie, unsettling.

He cranked his ear full of static until it hurt and still he heard nothing. So he switched it off. He wondered what Yeats could be up to, if he was OK. He felt a sick knot forming in his stomach. Well, he couldn't wait.

Slowly he circled the empty chair and surveyed the scene. His flashlight showed nothing else in the chamber. No artifacts, markings, or any evidence this room had ever been used before. But it all felt very familiar.

It was as if he had stepped into an ancient hieroglyph come to life. Ancient Egyptian reliefs of Osiris often showed the Lord of Eternity sitting in his chair and wearing his Atef crown, like the one inside the Seti I Temple at Abydos. Conrad also recalled the Man in the Serpent sculpture from the ancient Olmec site of La Venta, Mexico, which depicted a man seated inside a mechanical-looking device much like the chair before him. Then there was the sarcophagus lid inside the Temple of the Inscriptions at the Mayan site of Palenque in Chiapas, Mexico. That, too, revealed a mechanical design involving a man who appeared to be seated inside some kind of device.

Yes, he had been here before, he thought, feeling sweat begin to bead on his forehead. His hands felt heavy and clammy. Only this time the chair was real, the very Seat of Osiris. And so was the small altarlike base next to it, clearly the receptacle for the Scepter of Osiris. The only thing left to the imagination was for him to take the scepter, sit in that seat, and behold the Secret of First Time.

Conrad ran his hand over the smooth contours of the chair. It was like an empty eggshell. Conrad pressed the surface, felt it bend to his touch. He wanted to sit in it. But he remembered what had happened with the scepter in P4 and paused.

This time was different, he rationalized. The first time was a mistake. He knew that all too well. This time he was trying to correct that mistake, and if he didn't try, billions of lives could perish. Yes, he concluded, whatever his own shortcomings, however unworthy, he had to sit in the chair, if not for himself, then for humanity.

Conrad slipped into the Seat of Osiris, inserted the Scepter of Osiris into its receptacle, and looked straight up at the pyramidlike ceiling. This is interesting, he thought, feeling like one of his students on the Nazca Lines tour, waiting for some great revelation to materialize that never does.

"Sure, Conrad," he said out loud, just to hear the sound of

his voice. "You've finally made something of yourself. You've self-actualized yourself and become your astral projection. You are the Sun King."

He laughed nervously. If Mercedes could see him now, she'd be taping everything. He could picture the ads on TV: "Live from the Shrine of the First Sun! The Secrets of Atlantis Revealed! Witness the End of the World!" The way things were going, unfortunately, he soon would.

A wave of depression suddenly washed over Conrad as he sat in the Seat of Osiris. Had he traveled so far, and would humanity have to suffer so much, only to discover this was all some cosmic joke? What if the Secret of First Time was that there was no secret?

No, Conrad decided. Somebody went to too much trouble to build all this. And there were clearly some astronomical correlations he was missing. There must be a way to stop the earth-crust displacement. Perhaps he was simply the wrong man to find that way. He felt overwhelmed by a sense of helplessness. He had failed Serena. He had failed humanity. He had failed himself, period. What more could he do? This was indeed the end of the line.

Conrad leaned back in the seat, closed his eyes, and prayed: God of Noah, Moses, Jesus, and Serena. If you're there, if you care at all for Serena and all she cares for, then help me figure this thing out before Osiris and his kind screw your kind over for good.

Conrad opened his eyes. Nothing happened.

Again Conrad leaned back in the seat, and as soon as he did, he realized it had settled into a pocket and locked in with a click. Conrad tried to lean forward to look. But the egglike capsule, while comfortable, held him back.

He felt a sequence of vibrations shoot up his spine.

The chair was squeezing him, tightening around his waist and pushing down on his shoulders, devouring him. A metallic console telescoped itself beyond his forehead.

"Yeats!"

Suddenly the console overhead came to life with a beep. It glowed an eerie blue and a panel of instruments lit up. A tremendous shudder reverberated throughout the obelisk and Conrad could feel vibrations building in the back of his chair.

"Yeats!"

A single shaft of intense white light from above blinded him.

"Yeats!"

Then another flash shot up from below, imbuing the entire chamber in light. Conrad realized it was sunlight through two shafts above and below his reclined seat. Just like the star shaft in P4. Sunlight? Where did that come from?

Conrad managed to put on his sunglasses and gaze out the shafts. They were windows and framed a lightening sky. He had opened the doors of the silo.

Another shudder, and suddenly all became clear.

This obelisk isn't a shrine, he thought. It's a ship. A starship.

"Dad!"

Conrad tried to pull himself out of the seat. It wouldn't give. He tried twisting to the right. No. To the left. Yes. Now he hurled himself forward with everything he had and came out with a spark like an electrical cord from a socket. The console went dead and disappeared into the chair, the vibrations stopped, and the chair snapped forward and released its grip on him. Conrad, breathing heavily, collected himself.

For several moments he sat there on the floor, numb. But his mind was racing. He had no references for this experience in his past. Or did he? Ancient Egyptian funeral texts referred to a number of cosmic vessels intended to take the dead on celestial voyages to heaven. There was the "bark of Osiris," for example, and the "boat of millions of years." Egyptologists dubbed them "solar boats." There was also Kamal el-Mallakh's 1954 discovery of a 143-foot cedarwood boat buried in a pit on the south side of the Great Pyramid. Subsequent digging turned up similar boats in the same area—symbolic of the solar boats in which the souls of deceased kings could sail into the afterlife.

This silo, he realized, was on the south face of P4.

He remembered the markings of the three zodiac signs on the obelisk. He recalled the pyramid texts in Giza said the Sun King would ride his "Solar Bark" across the Milky Way toward First Time. To astro-archaeologists such as Conrad, the "solar bark" was a metaphor for the sun, specifically its ecliptic path through the twelve constellations of the zodiac in the course of a year. But what if it was more than a metaphor?

This is the actual Solar Bark, Conrad thought, the celestial ship built to take the would-be Sun King across the stars to First Time. He felt a shock wave of euphoria exploding within him.

But then the stark reality of his discovery suddenly sapped his hope: the Secret of First Time lay waiting at the end of the Solar Bark's intended destination. Yet the earth-crust displacement was only hours if not minutes away. There was no way to reset the star chamber in P4 to the date of First Time without completing the journey. The best he could do was guess the date of First Time based on the estimated light-years it would take to get to the Solar Bark's destination. And that information was beyond his grasp.

His radio headset squawked. Conrad said, "Yeats. Where the hell have you been?"

The voice that came over was Serena's. "Conrad."

"Serena?" he said. "Where are you?"

"Look out your cockpit window."

Conrad looked up and saw the silhouettes of Egyptian soldiers circled along the rim of the silo, guns and SAMs pointed in his direction. But what caught his eye was the outstretched arm of Zawas holding a gun to Serena's head.

Serena said, "Colonel Zawas wants you to know that unless you meet us at the base of the shrine in ten minutes and hand over the scepter, he's going to kill me. I told him you wouldn't do it. I'm not worth it and you're not that stupid."

Conrad spoke into the radio. "Tell Zawas I'm coming down."

32

DAWN MINUS TWENTY-FIVE MINUTES

CONRAD HEADED DOWN through the vast ship to the rotunda base. Along the way, it all made sense—the crypts were some sort of cryogenic chambers for the long interstellar flight, the towers of light some sort of propulsion system.

Conrad emerged from the Solar Bark to find the entire silo imbued with the first rays of dawn. Then he looked up and noted that the dome had split open. He shaded his eyes and felt a sharp poke at his back.

"Move it," said a voice from behind with an Arab accent.

Conrad, still blinking in the brightness, craned his neck to take a look. His curiosity was rewarded by a knock on the side of his head with the butt of an AK-47.

"Idiot!"

His head throbbing, Conrad stumbled forward beyond the rotunda.

Serena and Zawas were waiting for him. As Zawas took the scepter from his hands, Conrad looked over at Serena and swallowed hard. There was sadness in her eyes, but everything else about her was cool as ice.

"Tell me what these bastards did to you," Conrad said.

Serena said, "Not much compared to what the world is going to suffer, thanks to you."

"Doctor Yeats." Zawas studied him carefully. "Your reputation is well deserved. You've led us to the Shrine of the First Sun."

"A lot of good it will do you."

"I will be the judge of that." Zawas then held up the Scepter of Osiris before his men like some idol. There were no oohs and aahhs. These were professional soldiers Zawas had brought along for backup, Conrad thought, not mere fanatics. To them the obelisk might as well have been the head of an assassinated enemy, or a torched American flag, or a nuclear warhead. Their possession of such a symbol only confirmed their power in their own eyes.

Zawas then looked at him and said, "Now you will tell me the Secret of First Time, Doctor Yeats."

"I don't know. It's not there. And it may be impossible for us to discover."

Zawas narrowed his eyes. "Why is that?"

"The shrine, as you call it, is really a starship, intended to take the seeker to the place of First Time—the actual First Sun, as far as the Atlanteans are concerned."

"A starship?" Zawas repeated.

"Which is why we'll probably never know the Secret of First Time." He stole a glance at Serena, whose sad eyes told him she had concluded as much. "The existence of the Solar Bark implies the secret is not of this earth but at its intended destination, which from what I've gathered is somewhere beyond the constellation of Orion."

Serena's voice was scarcely stronger than a whisper. "So there's no way to stop the earth-crust displacement."

Conrad shook his head but fixed his eyes on hers. "Nothing I can come up with."

Zawas stepped up to Conrad and put his face within an inch of his. "You say this shrine is a starship, Doctor Yeats. You say there is no hope for the world. Then why didn't you take off?"

Conrad looked over Zawas's shoulder at Serena.

Serena could only shake her head in disbelief. "You're such a fool, Conrad."

A voice said, "Well, we finally agree on something, Sister."

Conrad turned around as Yeats emerged from behind a pillar in the rotunda, as grim as Conrad had ever seen him.

"Give me the obelisk, and the girl, Zawas," Yeats demanded. "And we'll be on our way."

Conrad, dumbfounded, stared at Yeats. "On our way where? You're just going to hop on a spaceship and go?"

"Damn straight I am."

Conrad realized that Yeats didn't necessarily care where he was going so long as he went somewhere. He was hell-bent on completing the space mission he had been denied in his youth.

"Look, if we don't go, son, then we'll just perish with the rest of them," Yeats said.

"You can rationalize it all you want, but I'm not biting."

Zawas tightened his grip on the scepter and gave a cool nod to his men, who circled Yeats with their AK-47s.

"You destroyed much of my base and cost me many good men," Zawas said. "Now you insult my intelligence."

Conrad shifted his gaze back and forth between Yeats and Zawas, their eyes locked on each other.

"You were never interested in finding a weapon or disabling some alien booby trap, Yeats, were you?" Conrad said, incensed at Yeats's desertion. "And you weren't interested in helping me find my destiny. You pulled that Captain Ahab routine all these years because you knew this thing was down here."

"I suspected it, son," Yeats said. "Now we know. This is the happy ending we've been working for ever since I found you. You're going home."

Home? Conrad thought. It was the first time in years he had ever even considered that he had a real home anywhere, much less not of this Earth.

Zawas cut in, "Surely you don't expect me to let you take off with the Solar Bark, do you?"

"As a matter of fact, I do," Yeats said.

Yeats's left arm swung up, holding a small remote control. He looked at Zawas with the coldest pair of pale blue eyes Conrad had ever seen. "I go or we all go," Yeats said. "I've got enough C-4 in here to blow us all to First Time without any starship."

Zawas's eyes darkened. "You're bluffing."

"Oh?" Yeats flicked one of the buttons, and a stereophonic beeping filled the silo as a circle of red lights in the shadows began to blink. "Go ahead, take a closer look."

Conrad watched as Zawas walked over to the nearest blinking box, bent over, and froze. Slowly he straightened and returned to his men. "Let Doctor Serghetti go."

"And the scepter, Colonel. Give it to her."

Conrad watched Zawas hand her the Scepter of Osiris and nudge her toward Yeats. "I'm sorry, my flower," Zawas said.

Yeats immediately grabbed her and pulled her toward the rotunda at the base of the Solar Bark. "Come on, Conrad."

But Conrad didn't move. He looked at Yeats and Serena and said, "I think I've just figured out the way to stop the earth-crust displacement. But the answer is back at the star chamber. Not there." He was pointing at the Solar Bark.

A bewildered look crossed Yeats's face. "It's too late. Let's go."

"No. I'm staying." He looked at Serena. "But I need the scepter and Serena."

Yeats shook his head. "I'm sorry, son. We need the scepter to take off."

Conrad could feel the fury building inside. "And what the hell do you want Serena for?"

"An incentive for you to reconsider," Yeats said, dragging her away toward the Solar Bark. "You want her, then come get her."

Conrad, desperate to run after her, looked on as she shot a quick glance back at him, her eyes filled with uncertainty. Then she disappeared inside the giant starship.

A moment later the ground started to rumble as the launch sequence began. Zawas could only watch in furious admiration at his former teacher before shouting to his soldiers to evacuate the silo.

"What about you?" Conrad shouted to Zawas. "Where are you going?"

"For cover," Zawas said. "If this alleged disaster should strike the planet, we are in the safest place of all. We can find survivors and rule a new world. If nothing happens, we have captured an unlimited energy source and will rule the world anyway."

"What about me?" Conrad asked.

"You can go to hell, Doctor Yeats," Zawas told him as two Egyptians tied Conrad to a pillar near the Solar Bark base. "Either the prospect of your death will force your father to abort his plans, or you'll depart this life in a blaze of glory when this Solar Bark of yours lifts off and its fires consume you."

Conrad watched as Zawas led his men out of the silo, leaving him alone. He strained at the ties that bound his hands. And he burned with desperation as he watched the Solar Bark rumble to life and prepare to lift off with Serena and the obelisk.

Inside the Solar Bark, Serena found herself with Yeats on a circular platform surrounded by four magnificent golden columns of light. Each column throbbed with energy. Yeats, still holding the remote to the C-4 in one hand, set the scepter down with the other. Suddenly the platform began to take them up.

"Yeats, if we don't reset the star chamber the whole earth will shift," she said, her voice spiked with anger and desperation. "Billions will die. You can't just take off."

"It's futile to go back," he said dismissively. His gaze was locked on the chamber above them. "You heard Conrad. Whatever the Secret of First Time is, it sure as hell ain't on earth. The survival of the human race dictates that we launch."

She looked at him. He wore the expression of a cocky warrior, pleased with himself and sure that nobody could stop him. His jaw was set and his eyes glinted in the dim glow of four light-filled columns. It made her furious—his complete unconcern for people who were about to lose their lives.

She said, "How do you know we'll even get off the ground?"

"What you see all around you is some kind of heliogyro system," Yeats said. "Those massive columns are an array of four unbelievably long heliogyro blades, like a helicopter's but on a massive scale. As soon as we leave Earth's orbit on an escape trajectory into space, they'll fan out and unfurl the solar sail."

Clearly she was in Yeats's world now, and however crazy the former astronaut was, he was the native in this terrain and she was the alien.

"Once deployed," Yeats went on, "the sail will function like a highly reflective mirror. When photons hit the surface, they impart pressure on it, creating a force to push the sail. The bigger the sail, the greater the force. And by tilting the mirror in different directions, we can direct the force wherever we choose."

"Don't tell me you actually think you can fly this thing."

"Like Columbus sailed the *Pinta,*" he said. "I'm sure all measurements, orbit determinations, equations of motion, and velocity corrections have been factored into the ship's navigation system."

She said nothing as the platform locked. Yeats shoved her with the tip of the obelisk down a long corridor that ended in a metallic door with strange carvings.

"Why would they build the ship like this?" she heard herself asking. She had to keep him talking, had to buy time so she could figure out a way to stop him.

"You'll have to ask them when we get there," Yeats said. "But I'm assuming this ship was built as a lifeboat and designed to travel long distances with minimal power. That's the beauty of this baby: it may be low thrust, but it has infinite exhaust velocity, since it uses no propellant. The solar sail is the perfect vehicle for interstellar travel."

"Except that it requires sunlight," Serena observed, "which we'll run out of as soon as we leave the solar system. Just like a sailboat on a windless ocean."

Yeats stopped at the door and said, "Gravity assist."

"Excuse me?"

"That's how we'll coast without light," he explained. He spoke so calmly and rationally it both frightened and infuriated her. "We'll fly around Jupiter close enough to use its gravity to boost ourselves into a faster trajectory toward the sun. Then we'll slingshot around the sun and pick up even more speed as we exit the solar system. At any rate, I'm sure this thing is packing an array of masers and lasers whose microwaves can generate huge accelerations and speeds in the sails."

"You seem to have convinced yourself, Yeats," she said. "How long will it take?"

Yeats paused. "At conventional speed, probably a year."

A year? Serena thought. "At that speed we wouldn't reach the next star for . . ."

"Anywhere between two hundred fifty to six thousand six hundred years."

Serena didn't even want to think how long it would be until they reached the target star. Or who would be there to greet them. "Any plans on staying alive in the meantime?"

"Yes."

Yeats stabbed the scepter into the wall and the door split open to reveal a chamber filled with cool mist. Serena stared inside and could make out what looked like an open coffin in the rear. The mold was of a shapely woman about Serena's size.

"Seems the builders thought of everything," Yeats said. "Welcome to your cryocrypt."

An alarm went off inside Serena's head as it dawned on her that Yeats expected her to lie inside that machine. She stiffened at the door and refused to go in. Then she felt a clammy hand on her neck. There was no way in hell she was stepping into that chamber.

"You first," she said, stomping the heel of her boot onto Yeats's toe and jabbing him in the stomach with her elbow.

He groaned and she spun around and kneed him in the groin and clasped her hands together to deliver a crashing blow to his hunched-over back. She rose to catch her breath, but then Yeats whipped his head up, nabbing her in the jaw and splitting her lip. She staggered back into the chamber as he straightened up. He lifted his head to reveal cold, dead eyes in the dim light. His arm came up pointing his gun at her.

"Say your bedtime prayers, Sister."

Yeats raised his boot and slammed it full force into her chest, driving her back into the crypt, which molded around her like clay. She felt a cold tingling inside her. It began in the small of her back, raced up her spine, and exploded throughout her entire body.

Suddenly everything began to go numb. She became very still, almost lifeless in the dark, but she could feel her heart pounding. Soon that started to fade. Then the crypt door shut and she felt nothing at all.

33
DAWN MINUS TWENTY MINUTES

CONRAD, STILL LASHED TO THE COLUMN, could feel the walls of the silo throb as the powerful thrusters of the Solar Bark began to hum. The greasy air from inside the ship now seeped out and smothered Conrad. He could also feel it heating up. The sunken shrine's open roof revealed the sky had turned overcast. Then the silo doors parted wider and loose rocks and debris began to fall.

Conrad closed his eyes as the dust came down. Blinking them open, he gazed out over the cavernous launch bay. For a moment, with all the smoke and confusion, Conrad couldn't see the starship and feared she was gone. Then a curtain of smoke parted and he glimpsed the unreal image of the Solar Bark shimmering behind the smoke. He could also see an AK-47 lying on the ground, apparently dropped by one of Zawas's soldiers in the panic of their retreat. But the machine gun was more than ten yards away, useless to him in his present predicament.

The air started to taste smoky. His eyes began to burn, his nose tingled in the grimy air. He struggled against the column, coughing on the smoke. With or without the Secret of First Time, he realized, the Scepter of Osiris was his only shot to reset the star chamber in P4 and stop the earth-crust displacement. And it was on board the starship. Somehow he had to break free and retrieve the scepter before the Solar Bark took off and fried him alive.

The thought of fire reminded him of the Zippo lighter Yeats had given him. He still had it in his breast pocket. If only he could figure out a way to get it into his hand, he could burn off the ropes. Conrad dropped his chin to his chest and pulled out his sunglasses with his teeth. He then slowly dug into his breast pocket with the glasses and attempted to lift the lighter. After a couple of minutes he gave up, his neck aching, but another jolt from the Solar Bark's engines drove him to give it one more try.

This time it worked. He was able to scoop the lighter into one of the glasses' lenses. Now with the glasses hanging from his mouth, the lighter balanced precariously, he decided to turn his head to the left and slip the extended goggle under the collar of his jacket and over his shoulder. If he could just reach the armpit of his sleeve . . .

The lighter slipped down his sleeve and with a few shakes landed in the palm of his hand. With some dexterity he flicked it on. The flame burned his hand and he cursed, almost dropping the lighter on the spot.

For a moment he froze, trying to figure out some way of burning the ropes off without inflicting third-degree burns on his wrists and hands. Finally, he concluded there was no way around it. He took a deep breath, clenched his teeth, and flicked the lighter. The flame stabbed his wrist as he worked on the ropes. Everything inside him wanted to drop the lighter but he forced himself to grip it tighter. Soon tears were streaming from his eyes. But he focused on the Solar Bark and the goal at hand.

The smell of his own charred flesh on the back of his hand—like burnt rubber—made him reel with nausea. Unable to bear it any longer, he felt the lighter slip from his fingers and heard it clank on the stone floor. The understanding sank in that he had lost his best chance for escape. Worse, he realized the smell of rubber had been the band of his wristwatch, which he had burned off.

Conrad groaned. With nothing left to lose, he attempted to pull his wrists apart. He felt the charred rope give a little before the sensation of it sliding across his wrists reached his brain and he shouted in agony.

One last time he pulled his hands apart, giving it all he had. His scorched, tender wrists strained at the ends of the rough ropes until finally the toasted strands began to shred, and suddenly his hands broke free.

Conrad lurched forward and stared at the rings around his trembling hands. He then tore two strips of cloth from his uniform and tied them around his wrists. He grabbed the AK-47 off the ground and ran wildly through the dust toward the Solar Bark.

He entered the rotunda and reached the outer door to the ship that he had found with Yeats earlier. It was closed tight, throbbing with energy that encompassed the entire giant obelisk. He placed his hand on the square pad.

The platform carrying Conrad emerged into the cool cryogenics level a minute later. Directly overhead he could see the hatch that led into the ship's command module. The circle of lights told him that Yeats was up there with the obelisk.

He looked to his left down the corridor that led to the Osiris chamber and to his right down the corridor that ended with the Isis chamber. He turned right.

At the end of the dark tunnel was an eerie blue light. As he approached the cryocrypt door, Conrad could see that it was closed and that the grooves carved into its metallic surface were glowing. In an instant he knew "Isis" was inside. Yeats had frozen Serena.

"Damn you, Yeats," he growled and struck the door with the butt of the AK-47.

He examined the square pad next to the door. He placed his hand on it and heard a high-pitched hum. The lights behind the grooves suddenly grew brighter, glowing with such intensity he had to shade his eyes and step back in the corridor. Then just as quickly the brightness faded to a dull glow, flickered like the last embers of a fire burning out, and finally went black.

Oh, God, Conrad thought. *What have I done?*

He struck the thick door, colder than ever, with his hands. He tried in vain to move it. But he knew it was futile. He gave up and let his body slide down the door to the floor when he felt it vibrate. The door was moving! He jumped to his feet and watched as the cryocrypt cracked open, an icy mist flowing out into the corridor. He didn't wait for it to clear before he plunged in to search for Serena.

She was in the crypt, her translucent skin almost blue when he grabbed her and carried her out over his shoulder into the corridor. He set her on the floor and began to massage her arms and legs. She was barely breathing.

Oh, God, he prayed under his breath. Don't let her die. "Come on, baby, come on," he repeated. "You can do it."

Slowly the color came back to her cheeks and her breathing became deeper and more rhythmic. When she opened her eyes, Conrad was shocked by their empty, lifeless quality.

"Serena, it's me, Conrad," he said. "Do you know where you are?"

She moaned. He brought his ears to her lips. "If you're Conrad Yeats, then this must be hell."

"Thank God." He breathed a huge sigh of relief. "You're OK."

She struggled to sit up and get her bearings. "Yeats?"

"Up in the capsule," he told her. "But he's going to come down before the launch to put himself into the Osiris cryocrypt. When he does, I'll be waiting for him."

"And me?"

"While he's with me, you go up into the capsule and get the scepter. Whatever happens to me, you've got to stop this ship from launching and get back to P4. Understood?"

She rubbed her temples. "So you really think we can stop the displacement?"

"I don't know, but we have to try," he said when the circle of lights above the central platform flashed.

"He's coming down," Conrad said. "I've got to take my position. You wait until he's well along the other corridor before you go up."

She nodded.

Conrad ran down the corridor toward the Osiris cryocrypt. By the time he got to the central shaft, the platform was on its way down with Yeats. Conrad ran through the mist into the open Osiris crypt and waited for Yeats.

Breathing hard, back against the wall, he felt something along his shoulder and turned to see the alien harness. The last thing he needed was to accidentally lock himself in the cryocrypt for the better part of eternity. Then he heard the chamber door open.

Conrad blinked his eyes and saw Yeats's figure in the mist. Conrad raised his AK-47 and stepped forward. "Mission aborted, Yeats."

"Is that you, son?" he said. "I'm impressed. I knew you'd join us."

"Give me the obelisk and Serena."

Conrad could see Yeats's eyes quickly take in the bandages on his wrists and note his unsteady grip on the AK-47. He couldn't believe he was pointing a gun at his father. Even if Yeats wasn't his biological father, and even if he hated him more often than not, Yeats was the only father Conrad had ever known.

"You're not going to use that on me, son."

"I'm not?"

"Kill me and you kill any chance of fulfilling your lifelong quest," Yeats said. "Only by lifting off in this new obelisk—the starship—and taking it to its intended journey will you ever discover your true origins."

"And what about my fellow man?"

"You're not a man, and it's too late to save Earth. The human race hasn't proved itself worthy, and the Secret of First Time can only be found at the end of the Solar Bark's celestial journey. You want to know it as much as I do. Hell, it's probably been programmed into your genetic code."

"Don't bet on it." Conrad pointed the AK-47 at him. "Remove your sidearm. Slowly. Two fingers."

Yeats unfastened the leather strap on his belt and carefully removed the Glock 9 mm pistol from its holster.

"On the floor."

Yeats placed the gun on the floor and lifted his hands up.

"Step back."

Yeats managed a smile as Conrad kicked the Glock away. "You and I are more alike than you care to admit."

"You're dreaming, Yeats." Conrad could tell Yeats was stalling for time, hoping to let the Solar Bark launch into its self-directed trajectory. But Conrad was waiting for Serena, hoping she'd hurry down with the Scepter of Osiris.

"I too am curious about a lot of things," Yeats said. "Not just the origins of human civilization but the universe itself. Ever wonder just why I wanted to go to Mars in the first place?"

"To plant your flag on the planet and be the first man to piss in red dirt."

"Comparative planetology, the scientists call it." Yeats seemed to grow more confident as he assessed that Conrad wasn't really going to shoot him. "They'd like to study the history of the solar system and the evolution of the planets by comparing evidence found on Earth, the Moon, and Mars. When we explore other worlds, we really explore ourselves and learn more accurately how we fit in."

Conrad said nothing, only watched in fascination as Yeats's worn face lit up with an almost spiritual inner light.

"For centuries we were guided by the ideas of the Egyptian astronomer Ptolemy, who taught that Earth was the center of everything," Yeats went on. "Then Galileo set us straight and we learned the sun is the local center about which we and the other planets revolve. But psychologically we still cling to the Ptolemaic view. Why not? As long as we stay here on Earth, we're the de facto center of everything that matters. You don't have to go to the Moon to understand this matter of watching Earth from afar. Space isn't about some technological achievement but about the human spirit and our contribution to universal purpose. Space is a metaphor for expansiveness, opportunity, and freedom."

Conrad raised his weapon again at Yeats's chest. "I must have missed the pancake breakfast with the Boy Scouts where you delivered that bullshit speech."

Yeats held his gaze, undeterred. "You want to know where this ends as much as I do."

A voice from behind Yeats said, "It ends right here, General."

Yeats spun around to see Serena, who was holding the Scepter of Osiris in her hand. Conrad could see Yeats's back stiffen in rage.

Conrad said, "Now you know the cryocrypts work, Yeats. So you won't mind stepping into this one for the time being." Conrad gestured toward the Osiris chamber.

"I think you should drop your weapon, son."

Conrad did a double take. Yeats had slipped his hand behind his back and produced a small pistol. Conrad never saw it coming. Neither did Serena.

Yeats smiled. "Be prepared, the Boy Scouts say."

Serena said, "Shoot him, Conrad."

Conrad took a step forward, but Yeats dug the snubby barrel of the pistol into Serena's temple. "Stay right where you are."

Conrad took another step closer.

Yeats yanked Serena's long black hair until she cried out in pain. "Now or never, son."

Conrad took a third step.

"I said drop it!" Yeats yanked Serena's hair even harder. Conrad knew he could snap her neck in a second if he wanted to.

"Don't listen to him, Conrad," Serena strained to say. "You know he's going to kill you."

But all it took for Conrad was another look into her frightened eyes to convince him that he could take no chances. He lowered his weapon.

"Good boy," Yeats said. "Now drop it."

Conrad dropped his AK-47 on the floor of the fore-aft passageway, where it clanked. He could see tears roll down Serena's face as their eyes locked.

"You're hopeless, Conrad," she whispered.

34

DAWN MINUS FIFTEEN MINUTES

Conrad watched Yeats pick up the AK-47 from the floor. They were only a few feet apart now and Conrad could see a manic look in Yeats's eyes that he hadn't detected from a distance. The man looked like an animal trapped in a snare, willing to bite his own leg off to get free.

"I knew you couldn't kill me," he said, keeping a tight hold on Serena, who struggled in his grip. "And I sure as hell don't want to kill you. But I will if I have to."

"Get your claws off her, Yeats."

"As soon as you're good and frozen, son. Maybe when we get to wherever we're going and thaw out, you'll come to your senses."

Conrad said, "You're going to have to kill me before you freeze me, Dad."

Conrad dove for the gun, and it exploded, the bullet plowing into his shoulder and spinning him to the floor. Dazed, he clutched his shoulder and saw blood pumping out between his fingers. He then looked up to see Yeats step forward to finish him off.

"I'll say hello to Osiris for you."

Yeats was about to knock him out with the butt of his gun when Conrad rolled back on his other shoulder and kicked Yeats in the chest with both feet.

The blow drove Yeats back into the pointed end of the Scepter of Osiris Serena was holding and she screamed. Yeats hit it with such force that he cried out in agony.

Dropping his gun, Yeats staggered for a few seconds before Conrad body slammed him into the cryogenic chamber. He shut the door as a blast of subzero mist blew out.

Suddenly all was quiet, save for the low hum of the ship's power surging through the consoles, walls, and floors.

Conrad struggled to stand in the shaft of light when Serena ran over and embraced him. Then she must have felt the warmth of his shoulder.

"You're a bloody mess," she told him.

"You just figured that out?"

She ripped off a strip of cloth from his sleeve and wrapped it around his upper arm and tied it tight, aware of his stare. "And now you've got everything you ever wanted. Maybe we really should walk off into the sunset together."

Conrad saw the bloody Scepter of Osiris on the floor. Picking up the scepter, Conrad realized she was right. All he had to do was let the Solar Bark take them to its preprogrammed destination and he'd finally discover the Secret of First Time.

He stared at her in disbelief. "Do you hear what you're saying?"

"I'm saying we don't know if this ECD is a global extinction event," she said. "Maybe humanity survives, or maybe we go the way of the dinosaur. But the only way to ensure the survival of our species is for you and me to proceed on course."

Conrad looked into her pleading eyes. She didn't want to go along for him, he realized, but rather for humanity. And she was willing to give up everything she held dear to do so.

"You'd have us condemn the world to hell?" he said.

"No, Conrad. We could create a new Eden on another world."

As he considered this insane idea, the ship started to rumble. He put a finger to her cheek and wiped away a tear. "You know we have to go back."

She knew, and she didn't resist as they silently rode the platform down to the base of the Solar Bark.

When they finally surfaced several hundred yards from the silo, the ground rumbled more violently than ever. He had barely pulled Serena out of the tunnel when a geyser of fire shot into the air, hurling them across the ground.

When he looked up he saw a dozen other geysers erupt in a ring around the silo as the Solar Bark lifted out of its crater and climbed into the sky. Conrad watched the starship carrying his father, dead or alive, disappear into the heavens.

"I hope to God you know what you're doing, Conrad." Serena ripped a torn lace from her boot and tied the burnt ends of her hair back. "Because that was the last flight off this rock."

35

DAWN MINUS TWO MINUTES

STANDING IN P4'S STAR CHAMBER, tears flowing down her cheeks, Serena watched the geodesic ceiling spin. The noise of the grinding, whirling dome was deafening, and she couldn't hear what Conrad was saying. He was standing by the altar, motioning her to come over.

"Put the scepter in the stand," he shouted.

She looked at the Scepter of Osiris in her hands and once again read the inscription to herself: *Only he who stands before the Shining Ones in the time and place of the most worthy can remove the Scepter of Osiris without tearing Heaven and Earth apart.* Was there ever such a "most worthy" moment in human history? Or was the Hebrew prophet Isaiah right when he said human acts of righteousness were like "filthy rags" before the holiness of God?

"Yeats was right, Conrad," she said as she felt her heart sinking. "The Atlanteans were too advanced for our level of thinking. We can't win."

"I thought we agreed that the gods of Egypt were defeated once before," Conrad said. He started talking faster, his voice rising. "Well, just when was that?"

Serena paused. "During the Exodus, when Moses led the Israelites out of Egypt."

"Exactly," Conrad said. "It was one of those cosmic events that changes cultural history, like a colliding meteorite changes natural history. If no Exodus, then no epiphany at Sinai. And if no Sinai, then no Moses, Jesus Christ, or Mohammed. Osiris and Isis would reign supreme, pyramids would dot Manhattan's skyline, and we'd be drinking fermented barley water instead of cafe lattes."

Serena felt her blood pumping. Conrad was onto something.

"The question is," Conrad continued, eyes gleaming as if on the verge of a great discovery, "what was the straw that broke Pharaoh's back and led him to release the Israelites?"

"Passover," Serena said. "When the God of the Israelites struck down the firstborn of every Egyptian but 'passed over' the houses of those Israelite slaves who coated their doorposts with the blood of a lamb."

"OK," said Conrad. "Now if only there was a way to be more inclusive and extend the Passover to all races."

But there was, she suddenly realized, and blurted out, "The Lamb of God!"

"Jesus Christ, you're right!"

Conrad's hands flew as he began to reset the stars on the dome of the chamber to re-create the skies over Jerusalem.

Suddenly the entire chamber seemed to turn upside down. But it was an optical illusion, she realized, as the heavens of the Northern Hemisphere suddenly flipped places with the Southern Hemisphere.

"OK, we've got a place on earth," Conrad said. "We need a year."

That was harder, Serena thought. "Tradition says Jesus died when he was about thirty-three, which would place the crucifixion between A.D. 30 and 33."

"You've got to do better than that." Conrad looked impatient. "Give me a year."

Serena fought the panic inside. The Christian calendar was based on faulty calculations made by a sixth-century monk—Dionysius Exiguus. Latin for "Dennis the Short." Appropriate, considering that Dionysius's estimates for the date of Christ's birth fell short by several years. Church scholars now placed the Nativity no later than the year King Herod died—4 B.C.

"A.D. 29," she finally said. "Try A.D. 29."

Conrad adjusted the scepter in its altar, and the dome overhead spun around. The rumble was deafening. "I need a date," he shouted. "And I need it now."

Serena nodded. The Catholic Church celebrated Easter at a different time each spring. But the Eastern Orthodox Church kept the historical date with astronomical precision. The Council of Nicaea in A.D. 325 decreed Easter must be celebrated on the Sunday after the first full moon of the vernal equinox, but always after the Jewish Passover, in order to maintain the biblical sequence of events of the Crucifixion and Resurrection.

She shouted, "Friday after the first full moon of the vernal equinox."

"Friday?" There was doubt in his eyes. "Not Sunday?"

"Friday." She was firm. "The resurrection was a demonstration of victory over death. But the most noble time had to be when Jesus was dying on the cross for the sins of humanity and forgave his enemies."

"OK," he said. "I need the hour."

"Scripture says it was the ninth hour," she said.

He looked at her funny. "Huh?"

"Three o'clock."

Conrad nodded, made the final setting and stepped back. "Say a prayer, Sister Serghetti."

The geodesic dome spun round and locked into place, re-creating the skies over Jerusalem circa A.D. 29 at the ninth hour of daylight on the fifth day after the first full moon of the vernal equinox.

"But now a righteousness from heaven, apart from the law, is revealed," she prayed under her breath, repeating the words of St. Paul to the Romans.

A sharp jolt rocked the chamber and she jumped back as the floor split open and the altar containing the scepter dropped down a shaft and disappeared. Before she could peer over the ledge, the shaft closed up into a cartouche bearing the symbol of Osiris. And she could hear something like the peal of thunder rumble below.

Suddenly it was eerily quiet. Serena could hear someone sobbing. It sounded like a young girl. She felt a tear roll down her cheek and realized it was her. For some reason she felt clean inside, as if all her worries and fears and guilt had been washed away.

"You did it," she said, embracing Conrad. "Thank God."

"How about when we get out of here?" he said when a deep, disturbing rumble echoed all around, inside and out.

Serena grew very still. "What's happening, Conrad?"

"I think we're about to be buried under two miles of ice."

36

DAWN

Zawas and his men were watching the Solar Bark disappear into the sky from their camp on the promontory of the Temple of the Water Bearer when the first big shock wave hit. Tents began to collapse, and Zawas panicked as he watched his only working Z-9A jet helicopter skid across the helipad to the ledge.

"Secure the chopper!" he shouted, and five Egyptians raced to tie it down.

No matter what may befall the rest of the world, Zawas told himself, no matter how many coastline cities should be swallowed up by the sea, there was no safer place on earth than where his team was established at that very moment. For should it take a day or a week, once the earth-crust displacement had run its violent course, the ground on which they were standing would be the center of the new world.

This is what he kept telling himself as his thoughts drifted to his extended family back in Cairo, most living in substandard "luxury" high-rise apartments that were bound to crumble in any major quake.

The air suddenly felt very warm, and the shocks grew more violent.

They were becoming so jarring, in fact, that he began to reconsider his strategy of encamping inside the Temple of the Water Bearer and wondered if an open area away from any monuments or shrines would be more prudent.

Zawas stepped inside his chamber off the promontory, found the Sonchis map on his desk, and rolled it up inside the nun's green thermos along with the American blueprints to the Solar Bark.

Another shock nearly threw Zawas from his chair. He gripped his desk to steady himself. But it too began to move. He screwed the outer shell of the thermos into place and threw it in his pack before the shouts of his men brought him outside. What he saw made him shrink back in terror.

The sky seemed to be falling.

Zawas grabbed a pair of binoculars and scanned the mountains of ice that formed a ring around the city. And then it hit him: the sky wasn't falling. Rather, it was the cliffs of ice surrounding the city that were falling.

An avalanche of ice from all sides was about to bury them all.

"Into the chopper!" Zawas shouted, waving his men in as he climbed inside the Z-9A and started the motor in a frantic bid to get airborne before impact. The blades started to move but then sputtered. The chopper was designed by the French but built under special license by the Chinese, who had supplied the Egyptians with several models. "Damn those infidels in Beijing!"

He tried to get the blades moving again while a dozen Egyptians piled inside. As the pilot took the controls, Zawas adjusted his binoculars to make a quick estimate of how much time they had until impact.

A wall of ice jumped into focus, and it was on course to slam the chopper and crumple them all into a bloody pulp of twisted metal and flesh. Zawas felt his heart stop beating as the foaming avalanche swept under the temple and began to rise toward the promontory. Then he could feel the chopper being lifted up toward the sky.

Inside P4's star chamber, Serena felt hot as she climbed up the southern shaft using the line Conrad had taken with him when he first surveyed the city. But when she looked back, Conrad was still in the chamber below, trying to pull himself up with one hand, the other dangling uselessly to the side in the bloody tourniquet. She could see water bubbling around his ankles and began to panic.

"Conrad!" she shouted.

She braced her boots against the sides of the shaft and stretched out her hand to grasp his right arm. She pulled with a grunt but felt his hand slip away and heard a splash.

"Use this," he shouted, waving what looked like a long scarlet bandanna. It was his tourniquet. He had untied it.

She wrapped one corner around her wrist and lowered her arm so Conrad could wrap the other around his wrist. She pulled so hard she could feel her back spasm in pain, and she cried out as she pulled harder until he finally climbed up in the shaft.

"Thanks," he said, breathing hard. "Now let's go."

Serena looked up the shaft at the square of blue sky. "Why bother?" she said, out of breath. "There's nothing out there. No radio, no way to signal anybody."

"It's our only shot," he said. "The subterranean geothermal vent is powering down. The last blast of heat it's giving off is probably melting everything around us, pumping the water through its hydraulic system. But the water is about to turn to ice. Everything's going to freeze."

Serena understood. "The girl in the ice. That's going to be us."

"Not if I can help it. Take this." He gave her the bloody tourniquet strip. "Use it like a flag. Now move! I'll be right behind you."

Reluctantly, she took the bloody rag and made her way up the shaft, aware of Conrad falling behind. Occasionally she'd call back and hear him reply, but each time the echo grew fainter.

Finally, she reached the square of the shaft, her fingers turning cold as they clawed the edge. The wind was howling, and the temperature was dropping just as suddenly as it had risen. She pulled herself up to look out and beheld a fantastic sight that took her breath away.

The entire bowl of ice surrounding the city was crumbling, the melting snow turning into a huge lake that was drowning the city a mile below. Already only the tops of the taller temples and obelisks were visible. And the waterline was rising against the pyramid below. It would be only minutes before it reached her.

"No, God, please," she said and looked back to Conrad.

But he was gone.

Filled with panic, she screamed, "Conrad!"

There was no answer.

She peered down the darkened shaft and saw something flicker. It was water, rising her way. And there was no sign of Conrad.

Conrad, unable to hold on any longer, slipped down the shaft into P4's star chamber, which was filled to the ceiling with water. Desperate for air, he clawed at the stone ceiling in the dark to find a shaft opening again. But all he felt was the water closing in on him.

Then a powerful suction from below grabbed his legs and pulled him down the pyramid's Great Gallery into some sort of pipe. Unable to hold his breath any longer, he let go and felt the water fill his lungs.

He was sinking into blackness when his body slammed against a stone grating. The water suddenly washed over him and receded down the drain.

Soaked and gasping for breath, he put his hands on the grating and pushed himself up. Then he ran wildly down the tunnel, trying to get his bearings, knowing he was totally lost. He was confused and more than a little worried about Serena. His body ached all over as he slogged through the water, which was ankle deep and getting deeper. Then he heard a rumble from behind.

He didn't need to turn around to know what was coming. He simply braced his body and took a deep breath. A wall of water slammed into him and swept him down a smaller tunnel. He gulped in some water as he was sucked in, tumbling over and over beneath the current.

Conrad held on as long as he could but felt his consciousness slowly slipping away. Unable to cling to anything, he let go. A blackness overwhelmed him and he felt himself whooshing through a tunnel.

Suddenly he was pushed into daylight and thrown almost fifty feet into the air by a geyser of water blasting out of the drain. He landed with a heavy thud on the trembling ground, the wind and water knocked out of him.

Unable to move for a few minutes, he was shaken by the earth tremors and deafening rumble of the ice mountains tumbling down into the city valley.

A trickle of water ran past his ear, and he realized there was no place to hide: above or below ground, anything under an altitude of two miles from the subglacial surface was about to be deluged and frozen. With dread he recalled the people in the ice he had seen during the descent to P4 and decided he did not want to be one of them.

Somehow he managed to get on all fours and crawl through the rising water. Within a few paces he could feel the temperature dropping as the winds whipped. He shivered in the cold, damp air.

He slowed down for a second when he saw a body floating his way, bloated and blue. As it passed by, Conrad recognized the face of Colonel O'Dell from Ice Base Orion. The expression of horror on the corpse's face motivated Conrad to pick up his pace.

The water was up to his knees now, and the bowl of mountains around the city was beginning to collapse like a tin can under the tremendous pressure. His shoulder hurt more than ever, the stabs of pain unbearable. He applied more pressure with his other hand as he rose to his feet and staggered. Then he saw a flash of color through the water.

It was a smashed red Hagglunds, a relic from Ice Base Orion. It was useless for travel, but the forward cab might provide a cocoon of shelter and life support.

Suddenly the ground pitched violently and Conrad was thrown facedown. He looked up to see a fifty-foot wall of water and ice thundering down on him. His jaw dropped in surrender at the spectacle. There was simply no place to hide from such a force of nature, and he knew then it was time for him to die. But he thought of Serena and with one last push reached up to the door of the Hagglunds and twisted the black handle until the hatch opened.

Then the water came. First a few droplets on his head. Then a spray.

He hoisted himself inside and barely managed to snap the seat belt in place and shut the door before the wall slammed into the Hagglunds and it was lost in a cauldron of churning water and ice.

37

DAWN PLUS ONE HOUR

SERENA LOOKED OUT ACROSS the stormy skies from inside the mouth of the southern star shaft near the top of P4. Whiteout conditions threatened, the clouds over the ice deserts in the distance were heavy with snow, and bolts of lightning flashed on the distant horizon.

Then she heard a familiar whirring noise overhead and looked up in stunned disbelief to see a U.S. military Black Hawk helicopter drifting across the stormy sky. She waved frantically.

A rope ladder dropped down like something out of a dream, and she took a firm hold. She glanced back down the dark shaft and saw something shiny. She hesitated and looked closer. It was water, coming up like a geyser. She tugged the rope ladder and was lifted away as a spray of water shot into the air, barely missing the chopper.

An American airman grabbed her shoulders and dragged her into the Black Hawk. She could see from the faces of the crew that they were as shocked to see Mother Earth as she was to see them. Almost as shocked as they were to survey the ruins below. Their commanding officer introduced himself as Admiral Warren and shouted to the pilot over the roar of the helicopter and waters outside.

"Take us out!" Warren ordered.

"No," Serena said, her teeth chattering. "We have to find Conrad, Doctor Conrad Yeats. He's still down there."

Warren stared at her. "You mean General Griffin Yeats?"

"No, I mean his son."

Warren looked at the pilot who shook his head. "Believe me, no one's down there now."

The Black Hawk began to pull away.

"No!" Serena tried to climb in front and grab the controls. But four airmen restrained her and shoved her back against the medical supplies. She tried to get up, but all energy left her. Then the medic stabbed a needle in her arm.

"Calm down, Sister, you've been through a lot," Warren said as he wrapped a navy jacket around her shivering body. She felt dizzy and light-headed.

She brushed back wet strands of hair from her face and looked out the window. A whirlpool of water had nearly swallowed the city. Only the peak of P4 stabbed out from the murky deep. She had often imagined as a child what it must have been like when the Red Sea parted for the children of Israel to pass through and later came together again to drown all of Pharaoh's horses and chariots. Now the picture was all too clear.

She prayed to God that Conrad was safe but knew better. In her delirium, she could picture herself searching for him. Then, through the sheets of ice, Conrad would be spotted stumbling across the plain, miraculously having survived. He would emerge from the mist whiter than snow, his eyebrows and hair white, almost glowing, like he had come forth from the shiny veils of the holiest of shrines. The Americans would be forced to land the chopper. She would run to Conrad and embrace him. He would return with her to the awaiting chopper, his past buried behind him. They would hold each other tightly as snowflakes fell around them like stars.

But there was no Conrad, she realized bitterly. And God didn't always answer her prayers the way she liked. As the chopper lifted off and away, she looked down to see the flattened tip of P4 barely showing above the water. It was as if they were flying over the Southern Ocean now. Not a trace of the city below—or Conrad. It was all gone, swept clean as if it had never been there.

Warren started shouting something again. She couldn't pick up much of what he said under the whine of the blades and howl of the winds. Then she looked up to see him hanging out the open doorway. The Black Hawk swung toward whatever he was pointing at.

Serena was on her feet in an instant, clinging to Warren, peering out. There was a lone figure atop P4. The man who waved frantically was in a U.N. uniform.

"That's him!" she said with as much force as she could muster.

"Get lower!" Warren ordered the pilot, who was struggling against the wind gusts.

Serena grabbed Warren's binoculars as the Black Hawk started down. When they were no more than thirty feet away, she could see the man look up. With dismay she realized that the face she was looking at wasn't Conrad's at all. It belonged to one of the Egyptians, and his arm came up holding a machine gun.

"Admiral, pull back!" she said.

"We got him, don't worry," Warren said, and Serena looked back to see two marksmen with rifles trained on the man. "I want him alive."

Serena felt a pop of air brush past her ear and looked down to see a bullet catch the Egyptian in the leg and send him down with a splash.

Warren nodded approvingly. "Move in."

As soon as the chopper came in, however, the Egyptian rose from the water and started shooting wildly into the air.

Warren, standing in the open door, took a bullet in the throat and fell back against Serena, dead. She struggled to push his heavy body off her and called for help. But when she looked over her shoulder, she saw one of the Americans, also hit, falling backward. As he went down, his machine gun raked the cockpit with bullets. Serena heard the pilot cry out.

The Black Hawk lurched forward, and Serena grabbed at a strut for support. Then the chopper lifted violently, and she was thrown out through the open door. She felt herself falling through space. Then she splashed onto the top of P4.

She rolled onto her back and looked up. The Black Hawk bucked twenty or thirty feet up in the air, veered sharply to the left, and exploded in a great ball of fire. Burning debris scattered like shrapnel, destroying any hopes she had for escape.

Soaked to the bone and waist-deep in water, she stood up and faced the wounded Egyptian. The lone remnant of Zawas's army, blood spurting from his leg, pointed his unsteady AK-47 at her.

She didn't bother to put her hands up as he approached her with a desperate expression on his face. Or was he looking at something over her shoulder?

She turned to see another military chopper sweep in, this one with U.N. markings. Its heavy machine guns exploded and bullets kicked up water along the P4 summit, hitting the Egyptian and driving him backward over the edge and into the water.

Serena looked up as the chopper circled overhead. A ladder was lowered for her. She grabbed the first rung and started climbing. When she reached the top a strong hand helped her in. She looked up to see the face of Colonel Zawas. In his right hand was an automatic pistol and it was pointed at her.

She was numb with shock as Zawas smiled, the wind blowing his cap off.

"You do not disappoint, Doctor Serghetti." He held up her green thermos. "Now that I have the Sonchis map there is nothing to stop me from returning one day to complete that which I've begun. History, as I've mentioned, is written by the victors."

Maybe, she thought, but a quick glance told her it was just Zawas and the pilot aboard. "Tell me, Colonel, did you twist the thermos shut clockwise or counterclockwise?"

"Clockwise." Zawas eyed her dubiously. "Why do you ask?"

She smiled and said, "Oh, nothing."

Zawas's confidence began to waver. He lowered his gun to untwist the thermos. As he did, Serena tried to kick the gun out of his hand. She missed the gun but hit his arm and the gun went off. The chopper veered up, throwing Zawas off balance, but not before he put two more bullets through the window in his efforts to kill her.

Serena looked at the pilot and saw that he had been hit. She jumped in front, shoved the man aside, and grabbed the controls. She looked over her shoulder in time to see an angry Zawas rise to his feet.

"Colonel!" she screamed. "Do you know how to fly a helicopter?"

Zawas frowned. "Of course, woman."

"So do I."

She banked sharply and watched Zawas tumble out the door. He dropped like a stone, his arms windmilling until he hit the surface of the churning water and disappeared.

She took a deep breath and steadied the chopper. A quick scan of the instruments told her she might, if she was lucky, have enough fuel to make it within radio range of McMurdo and land on more solid ice. But she couldn't make herself proceed without looking back. She scanned the ice below, fighting back the tears. The city was gone and her fuel gauges were dropping.

As she hovered in the gusty skies over the hardening ice, she prayed for the soul of Conrad Yeats. Then she turned the chopper in the direction of McMurdo Station on the Ross Ice Shelf and flew away.

38

DAWN: THE DAY AFTER

At 0600 hours Zulu, Major General Lawrence Baylander, a hard-nosed New Zealander, led his UNACOM weapons inspection convoy of Hagglunds around a fissure and crossed into the target zone.

The area had been wind-whipped, and any evidence of American nuclear testing would not be visual. Dosimeter readings, thermal scans, and seismic surveys would be necessary to detect any radiation, buried facilities, and the like. Even then they would have to drill for subglacial core samples, he thought. If only they had more time.

But Baylander had already pushed the search and rescue team too far, he realized, and supplies and thus time were running low. He had already concluded they'd have to abandon the tractors and fly back once air support arrived. Worst of all, international politics and funding being what they were, he knew there would be no returning to this wasteland. About the only thing he would get out of this frozen hell was the grim satisfaction that the U.N. would stick the Americans with the tab.

He could feel his opportunity to nail the Americans slipping away. Exhausted and irritated, he was about to radio back to base to tell them that his team was ready to turn around when the convoy found the way blocked.

A red Hagglunds tractor, half protruding from the ice, had apparently sunk into a fissure, its wafer treads locked. It was still upright, slightly skewed. The forward cab was smashed.

Baylander swore and radioed the convoy to brake to a halt.

Pausing just long enough to square up his custom-made polyplastic snowshoes, he decided to keep his engine running. He yanked his cab door open, jumped down, and started across the waist-deep snow in long, slow strides.

He surveyed the wreck grimly and circled it once. Something behind the cracked, fogged-up windshield caught his attention and he leaned over for a closer look. There was a figure inside, curled up in a fetal position. A frozen corpse. If it was an American, he had his proof. Baylander straightened and ran over to the cabin door.

He knew the handle would be useless, but he tried anyway. It was frozen solid. He then took his metal staff and smashed the side window and carefully crawled in.

The man was lying across the leather seats. Baylander turned him over. The pasty white face had once belonged to a relatively young, handsome man. For a long minute Baylander stared down at the ghostly apparition, then bent down to listen for shallow breathing. There was none.

Baylander proceeded to unbutton the corpse's coat to discover a UNACOM uniform underneath. Bloody hell, he thought. He must be one of ours, from the first team. He could find no identification.

He studied the body to determine a time of death. It must not have been too long, he decided, maybe twenty-four hours, because the corpse was only now turning a dull shade of blue. Remarkable, considering how long it had been there. The cabin must have provided enough of a shield from the elements to enable the inspector to have survived far longer than he expected. Baylander suspected the man's last hours were an unforgiving mix of semiconsciousness, delirium, and the slow shutdown of vital organs. It must have been an altogether unpleasant way to go.

Baylander removed his thick gloves and put two fingers on the carotid artery. To his astonishment he could detect the faintest rhythm of a pulse.

39
DAWN: DAY TWO

Conrad Yeats awoke the next afternoon in a private room inside the main infirmary at McMurdo Station. He lay still for a long time, becoming slowly aware that his hands were swathed in bandages and one shoulder was in a sling. His head, meanwhile, pounded like a drum. He found a buzzer and pushed it with a bandaged hand, but the navy nurse who came told him to lie quietly.

So he lay and, piece by piece, recollected the events of the previous day until the middle of the morning. Along the way he drew a picture by gripping a pen between his bandaged hands. After that he dozed off again. When he woke, a woman was sitting by his bed. She smiled.

He stared at her. "Just like the hospital rooms in the old days—a bed and a sister," he said. He tried to smile, but it hurt. His voice was not much stronger than a whisper. "How long have you been here?"

"Only a few minutes," she said, her smile warming him.

But Conrad knew she was lying. He had awakened in the middle of the night and seen her sleeping in that chair. At the time he thought he was dreaming. "You're alive."

He reached for her hand, and she touched his bandage. "So are you, Conrad."

"And the rest of the world?"

"Everything's fine." A tear sparkled on her cheek. "Thanks to you."

"What about Yeats?"

She seemed to stiffen. "Past Pluto by now, I should imagine."

"You think what he said about me was crazy?" Conrad searched her eyes.

"No more than a lost city under the ice cap."

Conrad paused. "Does that mean yes it's crazy or no it's true?"

"There is no city, Conrad," she said. "The whole affair's over. Complete. Finished. Do you understand?"

"Not quite," he told her. "I've made one hell of a discovery, Serena. Look at this."

He showed her the rough sketch he had made of the Solar Bark.

Serena frowned. She looked so beautiful.

"Don't tell me I made that up, Serena," he said.

"No, you didn't, Conrad," she said. "I've seen it before. The original blueprints for the Washington Monument looked exactly like this about two hundred years ago, including the now-missing rotunda at the base."

Conrad stared at his drawing and realized that Serena was right. Suddenly he decided he would have to get back to Washington. There was his father's estate, naturally, and tying up loose ends. Maybe some of those loose ends included files from his father's office at DARPA.

A new journey was beginning to form inside Conrad's head, but apparently Serena didn't like what she was seeing.

"Listen, Conrad," she told him gently, almost seductively. "You're a great archaeologist, but a lousy amateur in every other way. You're going to publish nothing. You're going to produce nothing. For one thing, you've got nothing to produce. No Scepter of Osiris. Nothing. The only memento of our great escapade is the Sonchis map, and it's going back to Rome with me, where it belongs."

Conrad glanced over at his nightstand. "Where's my camera?"

"What camera?"

He grew still. "What about us?"

"There is no us. There can't be. Don't you see?" There was pain in her eyes. "You have no story to tell. You have no evidence. The city is gone. All that remains is your personal word. If you insist on talking, nobody will believe you except some of Zawas's friends in the Middle

East, and they'll come after you. You were the victim of your own lunatic ambitions. You're lucky to be alive."

"And you?"

"I'm director of the Australian Antarctic Preservation Society and an adviser to the United Nations Antarctica Commission investigating breaches to the environmental protocols of the international Antarctic Treaty," she said.

"You're all that?"

"It was my team that found you in the ice," she went on. "Since you're the only eyewitness to alleged events, any information you can recall would be deeply appreciated. I'll include it in my report to the General Assembly."

"They picked you to write the report?" Conrad managed a weak laugh. Of course, he realized. Who else had the international standing or passion concerning the preservation of this great white virgin continent?

Serena stood up to leave. She looked down at him, eyes tender but her body stiff with resolve. "Oh, lucky man." She leaned over and kissed him on the cheek. "God's angels were watching over you."

"Please, don't leave." He really meant it. He was afraid he'd never see her again.

She turned, hand on the doorknob. "Take a word of advice from Mother Earth, Conrad." She spoke bravely, but he could tell she was fighting back tears. "Go back to the States, bang some more coeds, and stick to university lectures and cheap tourist haunts. Forget about everything you think you saw here. Forget about me."

"Like hell I will," he said as she closed the door.

He stared into space for what felt like an eternity, thinking about Serena. Then a nurse entered and the spell was broken. "There's a phone call for you," she said. "Oh, and the doctor said it's OK for you to drink coffee if you'd like. It took me forever to find that thermos you wanted."

"Sentimental value," he said as the nurse placed the green thermos on the nightstand. "It was kind of Doctor Serghetti to keep it for me. I hope you replaced it as I requested."

"I packed her one just like it with your little gift inside," she said. "I'll come back and pour your coffee for you in a couple of minutes."

"Thanks," he said as she left.

He looked thoughtfully at the coffee thermos, then awkwardly picked up the phone with his mitts for hands.

It was Mercedes, his *Ancient Riddles of the Universe* producer in Los Angeles, laughing on the line. Everything about their last encounter in Nazca was forgiven and forgotten. "I just saw the wires on the Internet," she said. "What happened down there? Are you all right?"

Conrad cradled the phone on his good shoulder. Somehow he felt strangely content. "I'm fine, Mercedes."

"Awesome. When are you going to be mobile?"

The door was cracked open and Conrad could see a couple of U.S. Navy MPs posted outside. "Give me a couple of days. Why?"

"The sweeps are over and the networks are looking for filler. We've cooked up a special that's right up your alley. How does Luxor sound?"

Conrad sighed. "Been there, done that."

"Picture yourself standing among the ruins of a slave city," Mercedes said. "You're revealing to the world how the Exodus is true. We've even got a Nineteenth Dynasty Egyptian statuette of Ramses II to prove it. You'll get twice the usual fee. Just make sure you patch things up with the Egyptians. When can you start?"

Conrad thought. "Next month," he told her. "I have to stop over in Washington first."

"Awesome. By the way, this Antarctica thing. Is there a find?"

"No, Mercedes," said Conrad slowly. "No find."

40

DAWN: THE THIRD DAY

ROME

Serena's plane from Sydney came into Rome as dusk was setting in. She was met by Benito in a black sedan and taken to the Vatican for a debriefing with the pope. They talked in private until almost three in the morning. At the end, His Holiness placed his trembling hands on her forehead and uttered a brief prayer.

"Well done," he said simply. "The city is buried, the Americans know only half the story and will keep it to themselves, and now the U.N. can focus its energies on more productive causes. And since Colonel Zawas is gone, all evidence has been swept away."

For the most part, Serena thought, this was true. But the memories were there all the same. And she doubted she could ever sweep those away.

The pope looked her in the eye. "What about Doctor Yeats?"

"He won't talk," Serena said. "If he does, nobody will believe him. I have his digital camera and the original Sonchis map."

Serena reached into her pack and produced a green thermos. The pope leaned forward expectantly as she felt for the outer shell and frowned. There was no outer shell. It was a different thermos. When she turned it upside down, a frozen cylinder of ice slipped out. Encased inside was a rose in full bloom.

"Problems?" His Holiness asked.

Serena thought back to her visit at Conrad's bedside and the teary good-bye. "He stole it!"

The pope's craggy face broke into a wide grin, and he laughed harder than she had ever heard him laugh. So hard, in fact, that he began to cough and required a gentle pat on the back.

Serena didn't find anything funny about it. "I promise I'll find a way to get the map back."

The pope, breathing easier now, waved her off with his gnarled hand. "I believe that's his plan, Sister Serghetti."

"Sister?" she repeated. "Your Holiness, I have—"

"Been reinstated, if you so desire."

Serena paused. This was an incredible offer, a second chance that would not be repeated in her lifetime.

"But why, Your Holiness?" she asked him. "Why now?"

"I don't have long to live, Sister Serghetti," he told her. "And I do not know who will follow me. But for as many days as the Lord sees fit to keep me here on Earth, I will extend to you all the privileges of such reinstatement, including unfettered access to the Vatican Archives."

"The Archives?" she repeated in wonder. Only two or three men—and they were all men—enjoyed such access. His Holiness would be sharing with her the Church's most cherished—and cursed—secrets. "You tempt me, Your Holiness. You tempt me with knowledge, much like the serpent in the Garden of Eden."

"This is no temptation, Sister Serghetti, I assure you," the pope said. "This is a trust. This is a gift. And if I were you, I would accept it. For the one who follows me may not be as accommodating to you as I have been."

Serena understood, but hesitated. To officially declare herself a bride of Christ again would permanently keep her from Conrad and cut off any possibility of them ever consummating their relationship.

The pope seemed to sense her inner conflict. "You love Doctor Yeats," he said.

"Yes, I do," she replied, shocked to hear the words come out of her mouth.

"Then surely you must know he is in greater danger now than ever."

Serena nodded. Somehow she had sensed this ever since leaving Antarctica.

The pope said, "You will need all the resources of Heaven and Earth to protect him."

"Protect Conrad?" she said. "From what?"

"All in good time, Sister Serghetti, all in good time. Right now, we have more pressing duties."

What could be so much more pressing? she wondered when the pope showed her the front page of the *International Herald-Tribune.*

"Four nuns were raped and murdered in Sri Lanka by Hindu nationalists with ties to the government," he told her. "The crimes against Muslims have now turned against Christians once again. You must go there first thing in the morning and do what you do best, plead our case with the world watching."

"But it is the morning, Your Holiness."

"Yes, you must be tired. Rest a few hours."

Serena nodded. The concerns of the real world were too overwhelming, so overwhelming that they crowded out even thoughts of a lost civilization buried under the ice. There were larger battles to consider, she realized, battles against hate, poverty, and disease.

"I will go as you request," she told him, pausing for a moment. "First I will go to Sri Lanka to document the crimes. Then I will go to Washington, D.C., and press this issue with the American Congress before I take it up with the United Nations."

"Very well."

She let Benito drive her to her apartment overlooking the Piazza del Popolo. It was a plain room, nothing more than a bed and nightstand. But she felt better back in her own world, the one in which she first took her vows.

Next to the French doors that framed a pale moon was a crucifix on the wall. She knelt before the crucifix in the early morning light. As she looked up at the figure of Christ, she confessed to God her arrogance in thinking that she knew more about suffering and loss than he did, and she thanked him for his provision for humanity's sin in Jesus.

Then she stepped out onto the balcony and looked across the piazza at the Egyptian obelisk brought to Rome by Augustus two thousand years ago.

The monument reminded her of another obelisk, one buried in a pyramid under two miles of ice in Antarctica. And she wondered: was it really Christ's redeeming work on the cross that broke the curse of the ancient "sons of God" and saved the world? Or was it the selfless act of a godless man like Conrad, who sacrificed his life's obsession and returned the obelisk to the star chamber? In the end, she concluded that the latter could not have happened without the former.

As she listened to the cheerful sounds of traffic in a city that never slept, she reached into her pocket and removed the lock of hair she had cut from his head. In time, if she could ever let it leave her grasp, it would be analyzed.

For now she simply prayed for the immortal soul of Conrad Yeats, whoever he was, and for the forgiveness of her own, knowing in her heart of hearts that, one way or another, they would meet again.

THE ATLANTIS PROPHECY

"The only new thing in the world is the history you don't know."

—Harry S. Truman
33rd American President
33rd Degree Freemason

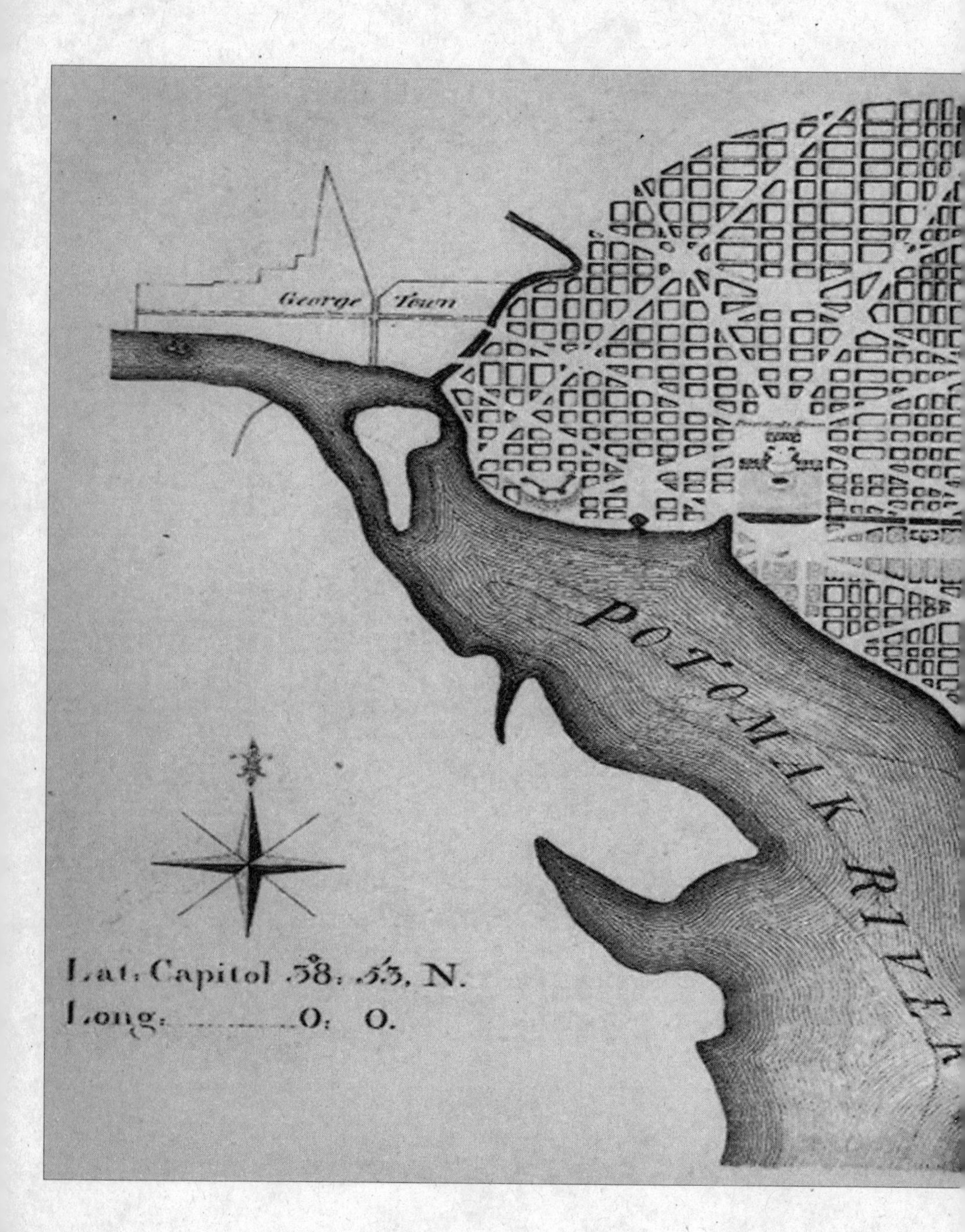
George Town
POTOMAK RIVE
Lat: Capitol 38: 53, N.
Long: ....0: 0.

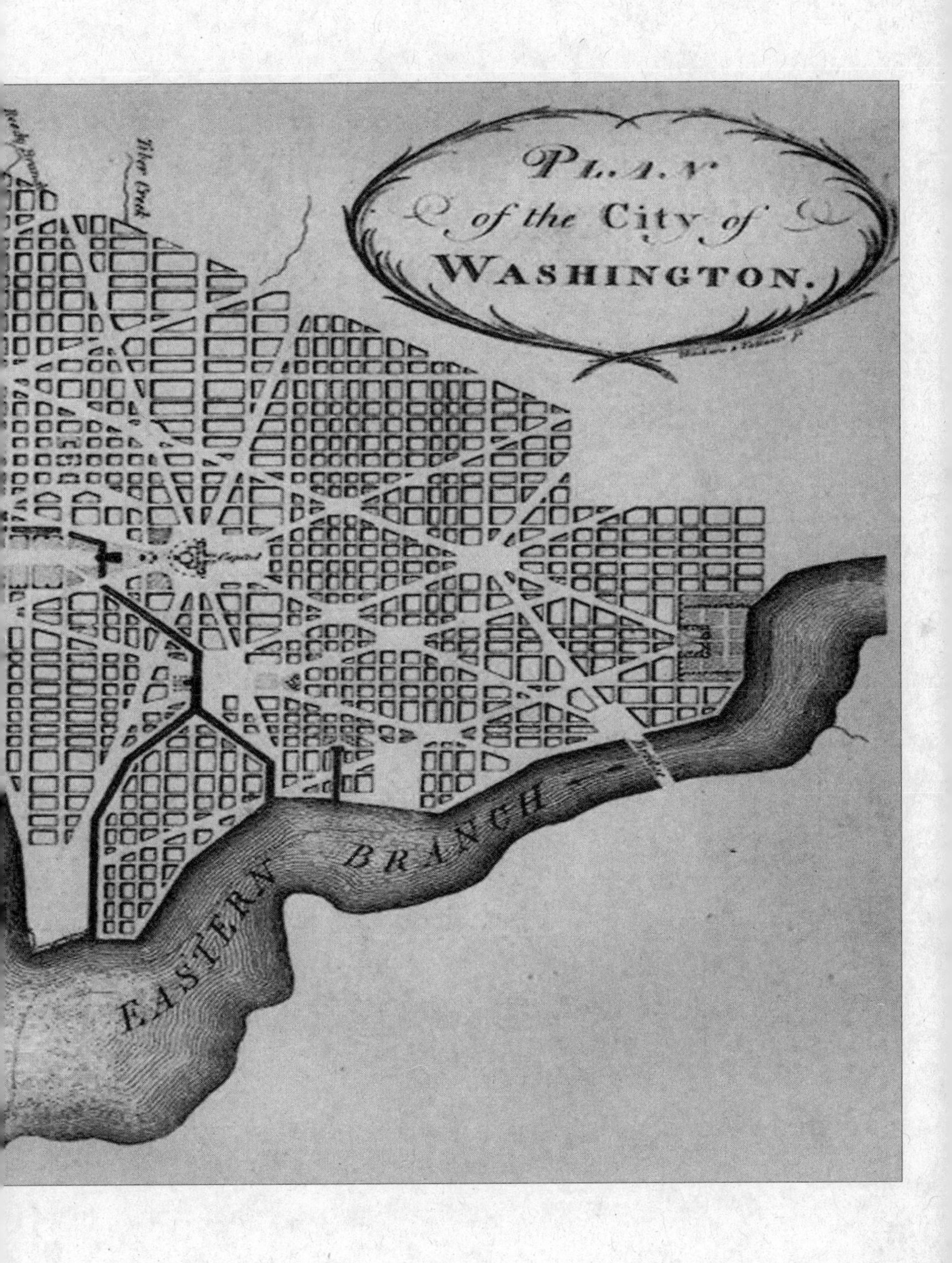

PLAN
of the City of
WASHINGTON.
Tiber Creek
EASTERN BRANCH

PROLOGUE

DECEMBER 14 1799

THE FEDERAL DISTRICT

Five soldiers of the U.S. Provisional Army came to an abrupt halt at the Georgetown wharf and dismounted their horses. The sleet had stopped, but it was bitter cold outside. The commanding officer looked out across the water at Suter's Tavern. It was the middle of the night, but he could hear music from inside. A lone lantern flickered in the middle window of the second floor.

That was the sign.

The man they were after was inside.

The officer signaled his men. They moved quickly toward the front door in single file. Their boots splashed lightly in the moonlit puddles, the bayonets at the end of their muskets glinting. Two soldiers went around the back to take positions behind the kitchen. The other two pounded the front door with the butts of their muskets.

"Open in the name of the United States of America!"

The door opened a crack to reveal the face of a small boy, who fell back in alarm as the soldiers pushed their way inside. The thirty or so revelers in the tavern sat fast in their chairs, their mugs of ale midair and their mouths open. The music stopped, the sudden silence broken only by the crackling of the fireplace flames.

The commanding officer, a head taller than most in the room, grabbed the boy by his collar and demanded, "We are looking for a runaway slave, a cook who goes by the name Hercules."

Hercules was in the kitchen, chopping onions for one last serving of his popular stew. His wiry dark hair was pulled tight to his scalp and stuck straight back like the handle of an iron skillet. Rules of the house. But he had refused to shave his beard. As his stew rose to a slow boil he suddenly realized that the noise in the tavern had died down. He cocked his ear.

The kitchen door flew open, and in stormed four Green Coats. Their commanding officer, who identified himself as Major Cornelius Temple of the U.S. Provisional Army, shouted, "Which of you is Hercules?"

Hercules froze. So did the other kitchen staff, all slaves. None of them said a word, but their anxious gazes drifted toward Hercules.

Hercules had been a slave until he ran away from his master two years ago. He had been making his way as a cook ever since, having perfected his renowned Southern dishes at the General's homes in New York, Philadelphia, and Virginia. If all he ever did was cook for his master, he would never have left. But his master made him carry out other missions, too. Secret missions. Dangerous missions. Now his past had finally caught up with him.

He just hadn't expected it to come so soon.

Hercules laid down his chopping knife on the table and stepped forward, praying that the only thing the soldiers were after tonight was a runaway slave, and not the secret his master had him bury years ago.

The major looked down his nose at Hercules. "Come with us, slave."

Hercules was only average in height, but he was as muscular as his namesake. Standing proud, he gazed directly at the commanding officer. The major's green coat reached the knee and sported yellow lapels and cuffs. His vest was white, single breasted, with white buttons. The white fringed strap epaulette on his right shoulder designated his rank. But it was the major's black three-cornered hat that had transfixed Hercules, specifically its small but spellbinding silver insignia.

The Regiment of Riflemen.

Hercules understood then that he was in the presence of killers, sanctioned by the new federal government. Until now Hercules knew of the Regiment of Riflemen by reputation only. Earlier that year Congress authorized the formation of a specialized unit of snipers that engaged in unconventional tactics. "The first in the field and last out" was the regiment's motto, and their tactics borrowed heavily from the Light Infantry and even Indians. That much was clear from the major's belt, which along with a leather cartridge and bullet cases held a tomahawk and scalping knife.

Hercules would not resist arrest, if only for the sake of the other slaves.

He turned to open a small closet door and heard the *click* of a musket hammer behind him.

"Slowly, slave."

"Jus' gettin' my coat."

Hercules calmly removed his herringbone overcoat with ivory buttons from its hook. The wool was so finely woven it gave the whole coat a glossy sheen.

The young soldier released the cocked flintlock and lowered his special model French Charleville. But before Hercules could button up, the butt of another musket smacked him in the side of his head and he went down on all fours.

"You run away with that coat, slave?" the major snarled, as he kicked Hercules in the side like an animal.

Hercules knew the drill. The major had no feelings for him one way or another. He simply needed to make him an example to any other slaves in the kitchen who might think that they, too, could one day run away.

"I bought it righteously, suh," Hercules managed to say with a grunt before four strong arms pushed him outside.

"He's a freedman by law in Pennsylvania!" cried one of the cooks.

"He's not in Pennsylvania anymore," the major barked as the door slammed shut behind him.

A flat-bottom boat, manned by four boatmen, waited at the wharf, the icy waters of the Potomac lapping at its sides. The sleet had returned, coming down even harder than before. The soldiers pushed Hercules to the stern. A moment later he was sitting between two soldiers and opposite the major and two others as they shoved off into the dark.

"The General is looking for you, slave."

Hercules shivered. The General, his master, was a just man and a great leader. But he had burdened Hercules with secrets too heavy for any American patriot to bear, let alone a slave.

Lord, please don't let this be about the globe.

Hercules gazed at the white exterior of the Presidential Palace as they floated by. Now in its seventh year of construction, it was still unoccupied; President Adams lived in Philadelphia with his family. In the distance loomed Jenkins Hill and on top of it the new U.S. Capitol Building, or at least part of it.

The General had once told him that more than a century ago the hill was called Rome and the Potomac the Tiber, because the property owner, a man named Francis Pope, had a dream that one day a great empire to rival ancient Rome would rise on these banks. But all Hercules could see was marshland, half-finished buildings, and tree stumps along what was supposed to be a grand thoroughfare—Pennsylvania Avenue—linking the great white Presidential Palace to what they were now calling Capitol Hill.

The boatmen were rowing vigorously now, as a few floating chunks of ice struck the sides of the boat. Even the major had to grab an oar. Hercules at first wondered why they didn't make him row, too. But he figured they didn't want to hand a runaway slave an oar only to have him swing it at them.

Hercules pulled at the collar of his coat as pellets of sleet slapped his face. He felt the stare of the major in the bow, whose own coat was not so heavy. But Hercules had paid for the coat himself, and his tailored wool trousers and buckled shoes, too. The General had allowed him to cook outside of the Philadelphia house in nearby taverns to earn extra money. Much of it he spent on fine clothing, which offended soldiers in the General's charge who were not paid nearly as much nor dressed as well.

Finally the sleet stopped and the boat struck the opposite shore. The soldiers pulled him out and escorted him toward steps that led up the hill to the General's estate.

Mount Vernon was ablaze with light. There were torches everywhere, and Hercules saw carriages and horsemen five deep in the court as he was marched toward the servants' entrance. An express courier galloped past on horseback, shouting for them to get out of the way, and almost trampled them.

Inside the manor, at the bottom of the back stairs, Hercules waited with several parties of private citizens and military officers and wondered what he was doing among such august company. The General's personal physician, the lanky Dr. Craik, was exchanging sharp words in hushed tones with a portly Catholic priest. Hercules couldn't hear what they were saying, and he was embarrassed by the curious glances from the others. They all seemed to know some terrible secret that he did not.

A few minutes later, a gaunt-looking man Hercules recognized as the General's chief of staff, Colonel Tobias Lear, plodded down the steps. Hercules anxiously watched the group part as Colonel Lear walked straight up to him. His military escort, seeing no chance for him to flee, stepped back and released him.

Lear looked him over. "My God, man, they were supposed to bring you, not beat you senseless."

Hercules didn't understand what Lear meant, nor Lear's glare at the major, whose expression remained emotionless.

"I been beaten worse," Hercules said.

Lear glanced about the room in search of Dr. Craik, but the General's physician was still occupied with the priest. He took out his own handkerchief and touched it to Hercules' temple. When Lear withdrew his hand, Hercules saw blood on the cloth. Instantly worried about his coat, Hercules glanced down and was relieved to find no soiling.

"His Excellency will see you now," Colonel Lear said.

Hercules glanced back at his military escort and then followed Lear up the stairs. Lear paused before the door to the General's chamber.

"Brace yourself, man," Lear said and opened the door.

Hercules at last beheld the cause of all the hue and cry: There, in his bed, writhing in pain and gasping for air, lay General George Washington, first president of the United States of America and current commander-in-chief of its armed forces. A string was tied around the great man's arm, where blood, thick and heavy, oozed from a vein.

They're bleeding him, Hercules realized. A bad sign.

Sobbing quietly at the foot of the bed was the General's wife,

Martha, who rose to her feet and smiled weakly at Hercules. Young Christopher, the General's personal servant, helped her out of the room and shut the door, all the while averting his eyes from Hercules. The guilty look on his face made Hercules wonder if he was the servant who gave him up and told Washington his whereabouts.

"The General asked for you," Lear said now that they were alone. "As you can see, he's dying."

How can this be? Hercules wondered. The last time Hercules saw his master, he seemed as robust and regal a man in his 60s as he had ever laid eyes upon. That was shortly before Hercules had run away. Terror seized his heart as he approached the bed, anxious to know what punishment his master might have in store for him.

"Massa Washington," Hercules said. "I didn't mean no disrespect. I just wanna be free, like you said the law allowed back in Philly."

"Don't be alarmed, Hercules," Colonel Lear said. "His Excellency understands the reasons for your departure and apologizes for the abruptness of your summons. He wants you to know all is forgiven. But he asks one final favor of you, not as a slave but as a freedman and patriot. Apparently, you are the only man he trusts with it."

Astonished, Hercules drew himself up to his full stature, his pride mixed with fear. For years the General had trusted him with his life—every time he put a fork in his mouth—like the Pharaohs of Egypt and their taste-testers, paranoid of conspirators who would poison them. But this was different.

Washington tried to speak but struggled with it, forcing Hercules to bend his ear. "The republic requires your services," Washington gasped hoarsely, in so low and broken a voice that Hercules could hardly understand him. He could smell vapors of vinegar, molasses, and butter on the General's breath. "I would be most grateful."

Hercules, moved deeply, bowed low. "Massa Washington, I ain't up to something like this no more."

But the General seemed not to hear him and gestured to Colonel Lear, who held out an envelope for Hercules.

Despite his protest, Hercules took the yellowed envelope and saw the bold letters written across that spelled STARGAZER. Like most of Washington's slaves, Hercules couldn't read, and he often wondered if this was another reason why the General trusted him with these sorts of communiqués. But he knew the code name all too well.

Colonel Lear asked, "Do you know the Christian name of this patriot, this agent with the code name Stargazer?"

Hercules shook his head.

"Neither do I, and I know more about the General's military papers than anybody else," Lear said. "But you know where to find him?"

Hercules nodded.

"Very well, then. Two of the General's officers will escort you to the woods outside the Federal District. From there you will take the route the General says you have taken before for him, and deliver the letter to its proper destination."

Hercules put the letter in his coat, aware of Washington's anguished eyes following the path of the letter closely. The General preferred his spies to carry secret communiqués at the bottom of their knee-high boots. But tonight Hercules was wearing his shiny buckled shoes, which the General considered far less secure, so that was not an option.

"One more thing," said Lear, and presented Hercules with a small dagger in a leather sheath. "As a token of his appreciation, the General would like you to have this. It's one of his favorites. During the Revolution you apparently proved yourself very good with a knife."

Hercules took the dagger in his hand. Engraved on the handle were strange symbols that Hercules would never understand but which, after decades in the service of his master, he recognized as Masonic. He slipped it under his coat and into his belt behind the small of his back.

The General seemed to approve and strained to say something. He gulped air to breathe and made a harsh, high-pitched respiratory noise that frightened Hercules.

"Hercules," he gasped. "There is one evil I dread, and that is their spies. You know whom I mean."

Hercules nodded.

"Deliver the letter," Washington hissed, his voice losing strength. "Rid the republic of this evil. Preserve America's destiny."

"Yessa."

Hercules rose and glanced at Lear.

"You have the final orders of His Excellency General George Washington, commander-in-chief of the United States armed forces," Lear said. "Carry them out."

"Yessa."

Hercules bowed and walked out the door just as Dr. Craik and two consulting physicians rushed in with Martha. As Hercules stumbled down the stairs in a daze and stepped out into the bitter night, the cries of the servants rang in his ears:

"Massa Washington is dead! The General is dead!"

Outside, dispatches concerning the General's demise were already being handed to express couriers for delivery to President Adams and Generals Hamilton and Pinckney.

Two military aides, meanwhile, were waiting for Hercules with the horses. Hercules faintly recalled their faces. One was a former Son of Liberty. The other was an assassin and an original member of the Culper Spy Ring who helped Washington beat the British in New York. No words were exchanged as Hercules threw a leg over his chestnut-colored horse and they galloped away from Mount Vernon.

They avoided the main roads as they rode north through the outskirts of Alexandria, cutting across farms and orchards in a wide arc until they reached the nape of the Potomac and crossed a wooden bridge a few miles west of Georgetown. Ten minutes later they reached the great woods at the edge of the federal district and Hercules brought his horse to a halt.

"What are you waiting for?" asked the former Son of Liberty.

Hercules looked into the woods. The twisted trees and strange noises had always spooked him, even before that terrible night when he and the General buried the old globe.

Oh, Lord, not here! Please don't make me come back here!

Hercules remembered the stories about the ancient Algonquin Indians that old Benjamin Banneker, the General's Negro astronomer, used to tell him when the General used the stars to draw the boundaries for the federal district. According to Banneker, long before Europeans colonized the New World, the Algonquin held tribal grand councils both at the base of Jenkins Hill, where the new Capitol Building sat, and in the ravines of these woods. What they did during those councils, Banneker wouldn't say. But he did say that the Algonquin were linked by archaeology to the ancient Mayans and by legend to the descendents of Atlantis. The chiefs of their primary tribe, the Montauk Indians, were known as *Pharaoh*, like their ancient Egyptian cousins 10,000 years ago. Banneker told him the word Pharaoh meant "Star Child" or "Children of the Stars."

Hercules craned his head up to the stars. The clouds had parted like a frame around Virgo. A chill shook his bones. Hercules knew that by making the layout of the new capital city mirror the constellation, the General benignly sought the blessings of the Blessed Virgin in heaven upon the new republic. But such mysteries spooked him, almost as much as words like *Pharaoh* and *Star Child*.

After all, slaves built the pyramids of Egypt. Would the same be true of America?

"Let's move," demanded the former assassin.

Hercules led his military escort into the woods. For several minutes he listened to the crunch of leaves beneath hooves as he weaved between the trees in the starlight, a bare branch or two scratching him along the way.

"Thro' many dangers, toils and snares, I have already come," he began to sing, repeating his favorite verse from the song "Amazing Grace." " 'Tis grace has brought me safe thus far, and grace will lead me home."

He tried not to think about old Banneker's otherworldly stories or, God forbid, the secret cave and the secret globe, which contained the greatest secret of them all. As he sang, his eyes darted back and forth, glancing at the dancing shadows all around. Then he heard the snap of a twig and stopped.

He glanced back at the two horses of his military escort in the darkness. But he could see only one rider—the former assassin. At that moment, he felt the muzzle of a pistol in his back and then heard the voice of the other escort, the former Son of Liberty.

"Get down here, slave."

Slowly Hercules dismounted and turned. Both soldiers, now standing before him, pointed their pistols at him.

"The communiqué," said the assassin. "Hand it over."

Hercules hesitated, staring down the long barrel of the French flintlock.

"The communiqué, slave!"

Hercules slowly put his hand into his coat and removed the letter. He handed it to the former Son of Liberty, who glanced at it and handed it to the assassin.

"Who is Stargazer?"

Hercules said nothing.

"Tell me or we kill your family, too, starting with your two-year-old bastard daughter. We know where to find her. She lives with her mother in Philadelphia. So, again, who is Stargazer?"

"I-I don't know," Hercules said.

The assassin's face turned red with rage and he tapped the barrel of his flintlock to Hercules' temple. "How can you not know, slave?"

"Because, be-because," Hercules stammered, "he ain't been born yet. Won't for a long, long time."

"What gibberish is this?" The assassin glanced at the other soldier and grimaced at Hercules. "Give me your coat."

Hercules stepped back, furious.

"Now, or I put a bullet hole in it."

Hercules shook his head, trying to understand what was happening. "The republic . . ."

"The republic dies tonight with the General, his slave, and this Stargazer," said the assassin. "Now give me my coat."

"*Your* coat?"

"That's right, slave. *My* coat."

Hercules suddenly felt the calm that often washed over him in moments of great danger, whenever the face behind his fear finally revealed itself. As he started to take off his coat, he used his free hand to reach into the small of his back and remove from its sheath the dagger that the General had given him. He held the coat in front of him.

"Throw it on the ground, slave."

The soldier might as well have asked him to soil the American flag. Hercules had worked too hard to buy this coat to give it up now, especially as they meant to kill him in the end. He had fed too many American soldiers with food his hands had prepared, and had sacrificed too much for his children and the General's dream of a free nation for men and women of all races and creeds.

Everything, Lord, but not my coat!

"For the last time, slave, throw it down."

"Not the ground," Hercules said. "It would get your coat dirty, sir."

Hercules tossed it through the air to the soldier. For a moment the soldier let his hand with the gun swing to the side to catch the coat, and in that moment Hercules turned to slit the throat of the soldier behind him, the blade slowed only by the catch of an artery. Before the man crumpled over, Hercules hurled the dagger at the assassin who held his coat. The blade struck him in the chest and drove him back against the trunk of a tree. The flintlock discharged aimlessly as he slid down to the ground.

A wisp of gunsmoke hung in the air as Hercules marched over to the assassin, who was gurgling up blood, his eyes rolling in surprise and fear. Hercules yanked the dagger out of his chest. The assassin opened his mouth to scream, but emitted only a low wheeze as the breath of life slowly escaped him.

"*My* coat, sir."

Hercules picked up his coat, mounted his horse, and looked up at the constellation of Virgo, the Blessed Virgin, watching over him. He slipped the letter to Stargazer into his coat and buttoned up. Then he kicked his horse to life and rode off into the night toward America's destiny.

PART ONE

PRESENT DAY

1

ARLINGTON NATIONAL CEMETERY

ARLINGTON, VIRGINIA

CONRAD YEATS KEPT A GOOD THREE STEPS behind the flag-draped coffin. Six horses pulled the caisson toward the gravesite, their hooves clomping like a cosmic metronome in the heavy air. Each resounding clap proclaimed the march of time, the brevity of life. In the distance lightning flickered across the dark sky. But still no rain.

Conrad looked over at Marshall Packard. The secretary of defense walked beside him, his Secret Service agents a few paces behind with the other mourners from all branches of America's armed forces, umbrellas at the ready.

Conrad said, "It's not often you bury a soldier four years after his death."

"No, it's not," said Packard, a fireplug of a former pilot known for his unflagging intensity. "I wish it hadn't taken this long. But you're the only one who knows the extraordinary way in which your father met his end."

Packard had delivered a stirring eulogy for his old wingman "the Griffter" back at the military chapel up the hill. What Packard had failed to mention, Conrad knew, was that he hated the Griffter's guts. The two men had had a falling out over Conrad's unusual role at the Pentagon years ago, which involved identifying secret targets for bunker-busting cruise missiles: underground military installations and nuclear facilities in the Middle East that America's enemies were building beneath archaeological sites for protection. Packard couldn't believe that Conrad, the world's foremost expert on megalithic architecture, would risk destroying civilization's most ancient treasures. The Griffter couldn't believe that Packard would risk American lives to preserve a few unturned stones that had already yielded all the information that archaeologists like Conrad needed to know about the dead culture that built them. The clash ended with an aborted air strike on the pyramid at Ur in Iraq and the revocation of Conrad's Top Secret security clearance from the Department of Defense.

"He wasn't my biological father," Conrad reminded Packard. "I was adopted."

There was a lot more Conrad could say, none of it helpful right now. Especially about how he had nothing to do with the planning of this funeral, how the Pentagon wouldn't even let him see the tombstone his father had picked out for himself before he had died, and, most of all, how Conrad was certain that the man they were burying today could not possibly be his father.

"Level with me, son." Packard glanced to his left and right. "Did you kill him?"

Conrad locked eyes with Packard, the man he called "Uncle MP" as a child and feared more than anybody else except his father. "Your people performed the autopsy, Mr. Secretary. Why don't you tell me?"

The two men said nothing more on the way down the hill to the gravesite.

Conrad suspected that the DOD had spent tens of millions of American taxpayer dollars over the past four years to locate the remains of USAF Gen. Griffin Yeats. It was all in the vain hope of finding out what happened to the billions more his father had squandered in a black ops mission to Antarctica during which dozens of soldiers from various countries had perished.

What Conrad and his father had found was none other than the lost civilization of Atlantis. And just when they were about to uncover its secrets, that ancient world was destroyed in a massive explosion that purportedly killed his father, sank an ice shelf the size of California, and sent a catastrophic tsunami to Indonesia that killed thousands.

The only other survivor of the ill-fated Antarctica expedition besides Conrad was Sister Serena Serghetti, the famed Vatican linguist and environmental activist. But the impossibly beautiful Sister Serghetti, or "Mother Earth" as she was dubbed by the media, wasn't talking to the United States or U.N. about Antarctica or lost civilizations. Nor was she talking to Conrad.

The long, bitter road ended here, at a belated funeral ceremony for a general more feared than revered, and a corpse that finally allowed the Pentagon to save face and bury the whole affair with full military honors.

For Conrad it was a homecoming of sorts to the only family he had left: the U.S. Armed Forces, even if he was its black sheep.

At the gravesite stood a gray-haired U.S. Air Force chaplain, an open Bible in hand. "I am the resurrection and the life," he said, quoting Jesus and gazing straight at Conrad. "He who believes in me, though he dies, yet shall he live."

Six Blue Angel fighter jets streaked overhead in a missing-man formation. As they peeled up into the dark skies, the thunder from their rainbow-colored vapor trails faded and an unearthly silence descended upon the gravesite.

As Conrad watched the flag being lifted off the coffin and folded, he remembered his school days as a military brat when his dad was a test pilot, like many of the other dads at the base. The sound of jets had filled the base playground. But every now and then there'd be a sputter or pop and all the kids would stop playing and listen to the long whistle, waiting to hear the poof of an ejector lid blowing. You knew who was flying that day just by looking at the faces. Ninety-nine times out of a hundred he would look up and see a chute open. But if it didn't, two days later he would be standing at a funeral just like this one, watching a friend's mom receive the flag and disappear from his life.

The miracle, he thought, was that it took this long for his turn to come.

Packard presented Conrad with his father's Legion of Merit award, his Purple Heart medal, some obscure medal from the Society of Cincinnati, and the flag from the coffin. The flag was folded neatly into a triangle of stars. The stars, so crisp and white against the dark navy blue, seemed to glow.

"On behalf of a grateful America," Packard told him, "our condolences."

The oppressive air was suddenly and violently broken by the crack of gunfire as the seven-member rifle team shot the first of three volleys.

A lone bugler played Taps, and Conrad looked on as the casket was lowered into the earth. He felt angry, empty and lost. Despite his doubts that his father was in that casket and his feeling that this whole charade was yet another attempt by the military to bring closure to a mission gone bad, the full weight of his father's death sank in, a sense of loss more profound than Conrad expected.

His father often spoke of fellow Apollo astronauts who had "been to the moon" and then came back to Earth only to find civilian life wanting. Now Conrad knew what his father had been talking about. Everything Conrad had been searching for his entire life he had discovered in Antarctica, including Serena. Now it was all lost.

Gone were the days when Conrad was a world-class archaeologist whose deconstructionist philosophy—namely, that ancient monuments weren't nearly so important as the information they yielded about their builders—led to mayhem and media coverage in many of the world's hot spots.

Gone, too, was his academic reputation after disastrous digs in Luxor and later Antarctica, where he had returned only to find that any traces of Atlantis had vanished.

Gone, last of all, was his relationship with Serena, the one ruin in his life he actually cared about.

Someone coughed and Conrad looked up in time to see the chaplain step aside from the grave, the sweep of his vestment parting like a curtain to unveil the tombstone behind him.

The sight sucked the air from Conrad's lungs.

Like some of the older stones in the cemetery, his father's tombstone was in the shape of an obelisk, just like the 555-foot-tall Washington Monument in the distance. This obelisk was a little over three feet tall. Inscribed in a circle near the top was a Christian cross. Beneath the cross were the words:

GRIFFIN W. YEATS
BRIG GEN
US AIR FORCE

BORN
MAY 4 1945
KILLED IN ACTION
EAST ANTARCTICA
SEPT 21 2004

Unlike any other obelisk at Arlington, however, this one had three constellations engraved on one side, and on the other a strange sequence of numbers he couldn't quite make out from where he was standing. The markings were bizarre by any measure, and yet familiar all the same. Four years ago in Antarctica Conrad had come across a similar obelisk.

Conrad stared at the tombstone, an uneasy feeling creeping up his spine.

It had to be a message from his father.

Conrad's heart pounded as he caught Packard watching him. Other mourners were staring, too, watching him. Belatedly, Conrad recognized the faces of five senior Pentagon code breakers and two hostage negotiators among the gathering. Then it dawned on him: This burial service wasn't meant for his father. And it wasn't meant for the DOD, to save face. It was meant for *him*. It was all some kind of setup.

They're gauging my reaction.

Conrad felt a surge of fight-or-flight in his veins, but he kept a poker face for the rest of the service. Afterward, the funeral party dispersed, and a few tourists drifted down the hillside from the Tomb of the Unknown Soldier to watch from a distance as the horses clomped away with the empty caisson. Only he and Packard were left at the grave, along with a younger man who looked vaguely familiar to Conrad.

"Conrad, I'd like you to meet Max Seavers," Packard said. "He's your father's acting replacement at DARPA."

DARPA stood for the Defense Advanced Research Projects Agency and was the Pentagon's research and development organization. Among other things, DARPA took credit for inventing stealth technology, the global positioning system, and the Internet. DARPA's mission was to maintain America's technological superiority and to prevent any other power on earth from challenging that superiority. That mission is what sent his father and, ultimately, Conrad to Antarctica four years ago.

Conrad looked at Seavers and remembered now where he had seen the sandy locks, the dimpled jaw, and the piercing blue eyes before. Seavers, barely 30, was the Bill Gates of biotech and a fixture in business magazines. A few years ago Seavers had turned over his day job running his big pharma company, SeaGen, in order to devote himself to "a higher calling" by developing and distributing vaccines to fight disease in Third World countries. Now, it appeared, he had been called to public service.

"A younger and, hopefully, wiser DARPA, I see," Conrad said, offering his hand.

Seavers's iron grip as they shook hands felt like ice. And his gaze conveyed all the warmth of a scientist in a white lab coat studying a microscopic specimen of bacteria at the bottom of a petri dish.

"We still take America's technological superiority seriously, Dr. Yeats." Seavers spoke in a baritone voice that sounded too deep for his age. "And we could always use a man with your unique skills."

"And what skills would those be?"

"Cut the bullshit, Yeats." Packard glanced both ways to see if anybody was within earshot, leaned over and rasped. "Tell us the meaning of this."

"Meaning of what?"

"This." Packard pointed to the obelisk. "What's the deal?"

"I'm supposed to know?"

"Damn right you're supposed to know. Those astrological signs. The numbers. You're the world's foremost astro-archaeologist."

It sounded funny coming out of Packard's mouth: *astro-archaeologist.* But that's what he was these days, an archaeologist who used the astronomical alignments of pyramids, temples, and other ancient landmarks to date their construction and the civilizations that erected them. His specialty hadn't made him rich yet. But over the years it had given him his own now-canceled reality TV show called *Ancient Riddles*, exotic adventures with young female fans, and the expertise to spend an obscene amount of other people's money—mostly Uncle Packard's.

"Hey, your people handled all the funeral arrangements," Conrad said. "Couldn't your brilliant cryptologists at the Pentagon crack it?"

Seavers steamed but said nothing.

Conrad sighed. "For all we know, Mr. Secretary, this obelisk is probably another sick joke to send us around the world looking for clues that ultimately lead to a statue of Dad giving us all the finger."

"You know him better than that, son."

"Obviously a lot better than you did, sir, if you and your code breakers can't figure it out. Why do you even care?"

Packard glowered at him. "Your father was a test pilot, an astronaut, and the head of DARPA. If it involves him, it's vital to national security."

"Dr. Serghetti is the real expert on this sort of thing," Conrad said. "But I'm looking around and don't see any sign of her."

"And see that you don't, son," Packard said. "This is a state secret. And Sister Serghetti is an agent of a foreign power."

Conrad blinked. "So now the Vatican is a foreign power?"

"I don't see the pope taking orders from the president, do you?" Packard said. "You are to share nothing with that girl. And I expect you to report any attempt by her to reestablish contact with you."

If only, Conrad thought, as Packard walked away with Max Seavers.

It had started to drizzle, and Conrad watched the pair march down the hill to the secret service detail, which welcomed them with two open umbrellas and escorted them to the convoy of limousines, town cars, and SUVs. Conrad counted nine vehicles parked on the narrow road. Before the funeral procession he had counted eight.

One by one the cars left, until a single black limousine remained. He was certain it wasn't the cab he called for. He'd give it another two minutes to show up before he walked down to the main gate and hailed another.

Conrad studied the obelisk in the rain.

"Now what have you gotten me into, Dad?"

Whatever answers he was looking for, however, had apparently died with his father four years ago.

He turned again toward the road and splashed toward the limousine to tell Packard's boys to take the day off.

Conrad felt a strange electricity in the air even before he recognized beefy Benito behind the wheel. Then the window came down and he saw Serena Serghetti sitting in back. His blood jumped.

"Don't just stand there, mate," she told him in her bold Australian accent. "Get in."

2

As the limousine drove out the main gate at Arlington Cemetery, Conrad Yeats set aside the folded, starry flag that had draped his father's casket and stared at Serena Serghetti with a rage that surprised him. She was the only woman he ever truly loved, and she had made it clear to him on two separate occasions, each four years apart, that he was the only man she had ever loved. Conrad always had considered it a crime against humanity that God would create such an exquisite creature as Serena Serghetti and make her a nun, forever keeping them apart.

Now here she was again, Her Holiness, the picture of effortless, earth-tone elegance in a long, belted cardigan, plaid pants, and knee-high suede boots. A gold cross hung from the columned neck of her Edwardian top. She had pulled back her hair into a ponytail, revealing her high cheekbones, upturned nose, and pointed chin. She could have just come in from a polo match as easily as from the Vatican, where she was the Roman Catholic Church's top linguist—and cryptologist.

As always, it was incumbent upon him to cast the first pebble and hope to see a ripple form across the smooth surface of her mirror-like calm.

"Ah, no medieval habit," he said. "So, you've finally come to your senses and quit that damn church."

She gave him that arch look of hers—raised eyebrow and smirk—but her brown eyes, soft as ever, told him she would if she could. She regarded his newly cut hair, dark jacket, white dress shirt, and khaki trousers approvingly.

"You clean up nice yourself, Conrad, for an archaeologist. Maybe one day you'll even discover the razor blade." She reached over and ran her soft hand across the stubble on his face. "I came because of your father."

Conrad felt her warm fingertips linger for a moment on his cheek. "Making sure he's really dead?"

"I was with you when he vanished from the face of the Earth in Antarctica, remember?" She removed her hand. "Although it's a mystery to me how anybody found his body."

"Me, too," Conrad said. "Maybe that's him following us."

Conrad looked out the rear window of the limousine, aware of Serena following his gaze. A black Ford Expedition was tailing them. Based on his reception at his father's funeral, it was obvious to Conrad that Packard thought he knew more than he was letting on—and was letting him know it.

"DOD cutouts," he said. "They're watching us."

"And we're watching them," Serena said, unruffled. "And God is watching over all of us. No worries. This passenger cabin is soundproof. They don't know who you're talking with now. When they trace the plates, they'll find a funeral home account rented out in your name for transportation to and from the service."

"I'm impressed," he said, "that you'd go to all this trouble to see me."

"Hardly." She turned from the window and looked him in the eye, all business. "I'm here to help you figure out the warning on your father's tombstone."

"Warning?" he repeated. "You're here to warn me about my father's warning?"

"That's right."

He suspected she must have had some kind of agenda all along but still he could not hide his disappointment and, again, his anger. "I don't know how I could have imagined that you came to pay respect to my father or offer me consolation for my loss."

Serena said, "I don't believe in mourning for those we may quickly follow."

Conrad settled back in the seat and folded his arms. "So our lives are in danger?"

"Ever since Antarctica."

"And you decided to tell me this, what, four years later? After you ran back to the safe confines of the Church?"

"It was the only way to gather the resources I needed to protect you."

"Protect me? You're the one I need to be protected from!" He glanced back out the rear window at the black SUV, which was doing a terrible job of trying to remain invisible three cars back. "The U.S. secretary of defense is going to string me up by my balls if he finds out I'm talking to you."

"Not until you give him what he's looking for."

Conrad sighed. "And what's that?"

She unbuttoned her jacket and slipped her hand inside her blouse.

Conrad lifted an eyebrow as she removed a key, leaned over to the soft leather attaché on the floor between her legs, and began to unlock it.

"Focus, Conrad." She removed a folder and handed it to him. "Seen this?"

He switched on the overhead reading lamp to get a better look. Upon opening the folder, Conrad saw four photos, one for each face of his father's tombstone.

"You move fast, Serena, I'll give you that."

There was the epitaph on the north face, the astronomical symbols on the east face, the set of five numerical strings on the west face, and, finally, an inscription on the back or south face of the obelisk he had missed: the number 763.

"How'd you get these? I just saw the tombstone myself."

"Max Seavers and two Homeland Security officials showed me these photos two days ago in New York," she said. "The United Nations is in session and I'm in the States for a couple of weeks. They cornered me outside the General Assembly, took me to the office of the United States Ambassador and briefed me."

Conrad considered his conversation with Seavers and Packard back at the cemetery just minutes ago. Apparently it was OK for them to talk to Serena but not him. Why was that? "You've got diplomatic immunity, and U.N. Headquarters is international territory," he said. "You didn't have to go."

"I couldn't say no to Max."

"Oh, it's 'Max,' is it?"

"Before he put his personal fortune into a blind trust and stepped into your father's shoes at DARPA, Max Seavers donated millions in vaccines for my relief efforts in Africa and Asia, on top of the $2 billion he gave to the U.N."

Conrad looked at Serena and wondered: Did Seavers and Packard really think that he was going to spill national security secrets to a nun? Or were they worried that she was going to tell him something they didn't want him to know?

"So why did Saint Max show you these photos and what did you say?"

"He said that the DOD recovered your father's body in Antarctica, which as you can imagine came as quite a surprise to me," she said. "He also said once the burial arrangements at Arlington got under way, the designs your father left for his tombstone with the cemetery raised some eyebrows, and they certainly raised mine."

"Why's that?"

"Because your father chose to make his tombstone look like the Scepter of Osiris we found in Antarctica, and to engrave it with clues he knew that only you and I working together could make heads or tails of," she said. "The only problem is he submitted his designs to Arlington before Antarctica and our discovery."

They were driving over Memorial Bridge, and Conrad could see the Lincoln Memorial, Washington Monument, and U.S. Capitol Building lined up before them on one axis, with the White House to the north and Jefferson Memorial to the south forming another axis. It looked like a model city under the stormy skies, configured like a giant white marble cross on the wet green lawns and reflecting pools of the National Mall.

He handed the sketch back to her. "Big deal. So my father obviously knew what we were looking for in Antarctica. For all I know, you probably did, too. What else is new?"

"Your father's tombstone, Conrad. He wanted us to figure it out together."

"Us?"

"Why else would he leave his clue in the form of an obelisk that only you and I could decipher? You saw those astrological signs. They're celestial markers. They have terrestrial counterparts on the ground, as you bloody well know. It's a star map to lead us to a specific landmark."

"You told Seavers this?"

"Of course not, Conrad. I told him I didn't have a clue. That you're the only one on the planet who can figure it out."

Conrad grinned. "That's what I told him just now back at Arlington, but about you."

Serena didn't grin back. "He wanted me to tell him if you tried to contact me," she said. "To let him know what you tell me and what we find out."

"Thanks for the heads-up, Serena," Conrad said, the anger he had been suppressing now rising again. "But what are 'we' supposed to find at the end of this treasure trail? The lost treasure of the Knights Templar? A sinister secret that could destroy the republic? Or maybe you've forgotten that besides the occasional Discovery Channel documentary, I now make my living as a technical advisor for Hollywood movies about these sorts of fantasies? That's because nobody wants to fund any real-world digs for me anymore. You saw to that when you kept your mouth shut after Antarctica and destroyed whatever reputation I had left as an archaeologist. So, Serena, what do you think my father wants 'us' to find?"

Serena listened to his outburst calmly. She had absorbed his fury like a palm tree planted firmly in the sands of some South Pacific island, bending gracefully in a monsoon only to rise taller in the sun afterward.

"I don't know," she said. "But it's obviously something important enough for the Pentagon to investigate. Something even my superiors in Rome won't reveal to me."

"Ooh, I have chills," Conrad deadpanned, although secretly he had been hooked from the second he saw the obelisk. "Guess the new pope isn't as fond of you as the old one, huh? But if you could just tell His Holiness the meaning of some cryptic ciphers on some dead American general's tombstone, then the Church would know what we'll find at the end of that celestial treasure trail and you'd be 'Mother Earth' again."

She frowned and said nothing, obviously not appreciating the dig.

"I have a deal to make with you, Conrad. You figure out the meaning of those astrological signs and numerical strings, and I'll help you figure out the meaning of 763."

"Or else?"

"Or else Max Seavers and the Pentagon will beat us to whatever secret your father left behind," she said, "at which point there's no reason to keep you around anymore—or the republic."

"The republic?" Conrad was incredulous. "What makes you think this has anything to do with the republic?"

"Fine," she said. "Then at least let me help you save your life. That's all you seem to care about these days." She gave him her card, which was blank except for a ten-digit number. "That's my private number, Conrad."

Conrad stared at it for a moment and didn't know which excited him more: seeing secret ciphers on his father's tombstone or securing Sister Serghetti's private number after all these years.

Serena said, "Call me if you figure something out."

Conrad realized the limo had stopped. He took her card and looked out to see that they were parked in front of Brooke's house at 3040 N Street. She knew where he lived.

"Too bad Ms. Scarborough couldn't make it to the funeral to offer her own condolences," Serena said.

And she also knew about Brooke. She probably knew a whole hell of a lot more than that, too.

"Just because you chose to be a nun doesn't mean I have to live like a monk," he told her, and stepped out of the car into the rain, angry that he felt it necessary to justify himself to her, and even angrier that her opinion meant so much to him.

"I'm sorry, Conrad," she said through her lowered window, a

single drop of rain falling on her face like a tear. "God called me. And now he's called you."

She raised her window and signaled her driver.

Conrad watched the limo drive away, aware of a black SUV slowly rounding the corner and parking across the street, its tinted windows too dark to see anybody inside.

3

CONRAD BOUNDED UP THE FRONT STEPS to Brooke's brownstone in two strides and unlocked the front door. She had given him the key to her place months before he agreed to move in with her, a decision made only after he had finally accepted that he would never get another chance with Serena Serghetti.

Inside the foyer, he threw his coat on the bench and began to disarm the alarm. His mind was already on the book that awaited him in the study, and he absently punched the wrong numeric code on the keypad.

As he cleared the alarm and put in the correct code, he wondered what kind of other surveillance besides the SUV outside the SecDef had on him. Probably audio but no video, he concluded, and even that from directional microphones in the SUV and not from any bugs in the house. Packard wouldn't risk the ire of Brooke's father, Senator Joseph Scarborough, who oversaw half of Packard's black ops appropriations from his seat on the Senate Armed Services Committee. Then again, Senator Scarborough had an even lower opinion of the man his daughter was living with than the Secretary of Defense. "Never did any woman see so much in a man with so little," the Senator once mused. He wouldn't overlook any opportunity to terminate their relationship.

Conrad walked into Brooke's study and placed the flag from the funeral on the fireplace mantle. He pulled out an old, brown cloth hardcover book from the third shelf.

The title was gilt stamped on the book's spine—*The Adventures of Tom Sawyer* by Mark Twain. His father had given it to him when he was ten. It was the only thing his father had ever given him except pain and grief.

Conrad grabbed a pen and a pad of stationery that read *Brooke Scarborough / The Fox on Fox Sports* and dropped them with *Tom Sawyer* on the coffee table in the living room. He then went to the kitchen to heat up some leftover pasta from Café Milano before he sat down on the living room sofa with his bowl of carbs, bottle of Sam Adams, and *Tom Sawyer.*

He tore off three sheets from Brooke's notepad.

On the first sheet he wrote the number from the back of his father's tombstone: 763. He was clueless as to its meaning for now.

On the second sheet he wrote out the names of the constellations he had seen on the east face of the obelisk:

Boötes
Leo
Virgo

Next to each constellation, he wrote down the name of its anchor or "alpha star," which was usually the brightest to the naked eye as seen from Earth:

Boötes (Arcturus)
Leo (Regulus)
Virgo (Spica)

In theory, each alpha star had a terrestrial counterpart or landmark. In places like Giza or Teotihuacán, the ancients placed their pyramids or ziggurats to point to key stars in the heavens. The effect was an astronomically aligned city that mirrored the heavens on the ground. Symbolically, it was intended to achieve some kind of cosmic harmony between man and the gods. Practically, it created a secret "treasure map" to the city known only to its founders.

He quickly drew the alpha stars in relation to each other from memory and came up with a triangle:

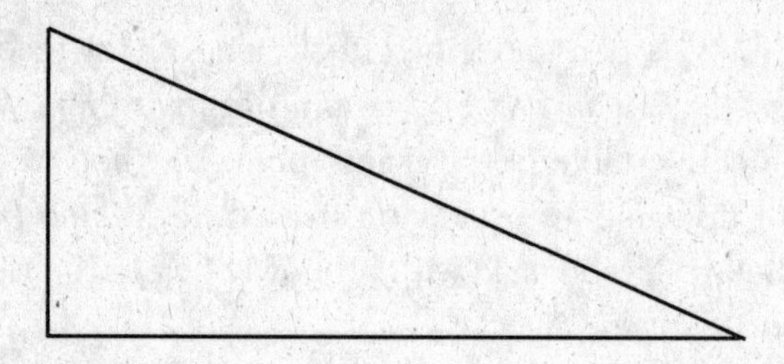

That makes no sense at all.

The way it worked in places like the pyramids in Egypt and the Way of the Dead in South America, each landmark linked to a star would lead to another landmark and then another. In theory, you could follow the star map written across the heavens on the ground until you reached a fixed destination. Usually it was a monument or shrine of some kind whose true meaning and purpose would finally be revealed —along with whatever treasure or secret knowledge it contained.

Unfortunately, this triangle of stars was no map at all. It had no direction. In effect, it was an endless loop, going in circles. This, too, would take time to crack.

Finally, on the third sheet, he quickly scribbled out the numeric code—a sequence of five numerical strings—he had memorized:

155.1.6
142.8.1
48.7.5
111.2.8
54.3.4

Ah, finally something familiar.

From the looks of them, Conrad guessed the numbers were in "book code." Each string of three numbers represented a word. The first number was the page of the book. The second was the line on that page. The third was the actual word on that line. So the five sets of numbers meant there were five words, which together formed a phrase or message. That message would be key to unlocking the meaning of the star coordinates.

The problem with book codes was that they were impossible to break—unless you had the book on which they were based, usually a specific book and edition possessed by both the sender and the recipient.

This has to be the book, Conrad thought as he picked up *The Adventures of Tom Sawyer*. It was the only book his father ever gave him, and his father had taught him the cipher when Conrad was into codes as a Boy Scout at age ten, the same age as Tom Sawyer in the book.

Conrad sat back in the sofa and cracked open the front cover of the novel. It was an unauthorized, non-illustrated edition published in Toronto by Belford Brothers Publishers in July 1876, months before the authorized American edition came out. Conrad remembered how, like Tom Sawyer, he wanted to be a pirate as a child. And this edition was the "pirate" version that a furious Mark Twain claimed was stolen from the typesetters.

He glanced at the string of numbers he had copied down and flipped through the pages of the book. The first of the five strings—155.1.6—directed Conrad to page 155, line 1, word 6.

Conrad flipped to page 155 and deciphered the first number:

SUN

He quickly deciphered the next two numbers and stared at the note:

SUN SHINES OVER

The sun was probably a final, invisible celestial marker, and what it was shining over was the final terrestrial landmark—the location of something his father thought was so important.

He flipped to page 111. The next word was SAVAGE.

SUN SHINES OVER SAVAGE

He was about to flip to page 54 and the last word when he heard the bathroom door creak upstairs and he froze.

"Conrad?" a voice called out. "Is that you?"

Brooke! She had been home the whole time. He didn't expect her so early, but a glance at his watch told him she finished her show two hours ago.

Conrad slapped *Tom Sawyer* shut, slipped it under the sofa, picked up a remote and turned on the plasma television. Brooke TiVo'd her weekend sports show on Fox. He found it on the program guide and tuned in.

On the screen the logo for her show came up with the Wagnerian music score before the commercials. It mixed sports and politics. All of the sponsors, it seemed, were powerful, industrial global giants involved in "communications" and "energy" and "financial services." The average viewer was a white, middle-aged man with a bulging stock portfolio and golf pants to match as he ogled Ms. Scarborough and sipped his Arnold Palmer in the clubhouse.

"Why don't we declare war on Muslim terrorists?" she chirped to baseball's A-Rod, shown on the field. The New York Yankee looked at her like he had woken up in an alternative universe. "They've declared war on us for years," she went on. "The Crusaders had it right: We need to sack them or put them in our jerseys."

Conrad had fought his own battles with Islamofascists and was all for winning the war on terror. But he couldn't believe they let her say this stuff on the air. Yet hers was one of their highest-rated political talk shows. It was better watching her with the TV muted, but instead he turned up the volume for the benefit of anybody listening.

The real show involved gratuitous, low-angle full shots of her legs and her flipping her long blonde hair while she blathered conservative social commentary—lower taxes, no more affirmative action, and guns for everybody. He knew she kept a loaded .357 Magnum in a Manolo Blahnik shoe box at the top of her bedroom closet upstairs. Of course, since she had about 200 shoe boxes, he could never be sure which one it was.

He craned his neck and looked up the stairs as a pair of long legs stepped into view. It was Brooke in a pair of strappy Jimmy Choos and a green Elie Saab evening gown that showed off her faultless figure to full effect.

"There you are," she said, eyeing the pasta bowl and Sam Adams on the coffee table. "Where were you?"

"The graveyard," Conrad said.

"I know, sweetie, I'm sorry I wasn't there." Brooke walked over and kissed him on the lips. "But that's why we planned to go out tonight, remember? To put the past behind you and to celebrate us and the future. The Olympics reception at the Chinese Embassy is tonight. Everybody from the network is going to be there."

Conrad stared. He had completely forgotten.

"I just buried my father, Brooke," Conrad said, his thoughts on the book under the sofa. "I'm not in a party mood."

She frowned and her crystal blue eyes, which at times could look vacant, seemed to come into sharp focus like the automatic lens of a camera.

He expected her to say, "You hated your father," but what came out was sugary sweet. She was great that way.

"I know it must be hard, Conrad," she cooed. "But at least yours went out with a bang. My grandfather was a veteran who died in a retirement condo in Florida while he nodded off watching Errol Flynn in *Night of the Dawn Patrol*."

"So you think I'm going to kick off watching *Top Gun* while you're out?"

"No, you're going to kick off being my Top Gun tonight," she said with shining eyes. "If you're lucky."

Conrad smiled as he looked at her. Although she had quite a killer body now, with a kick-ass personality, Conrad had met her and dated her when they were but gawky teenagers at Sidwell Friends School after his father had dragged him to live in D.C. for two years. Now she was poised, confident, sexy, having filled out her curves and buffed her body to perfection. She seemed to have all the answers.

"Wake me up when you get back," he told her.

Brooke sighed, picked up his raincoat from the bench and put it in the closet. She turned to the foyer mirror and started to apply more lipstick. "I might bring somebody home with me."

"More the merrier." Conrad turned the sound back on the TV. "Make sure she's a brunette."

"I hate you," she said.

"Everybody does in time."

She marched over and took the remote from him.

"Hey, I was looking for *Top Gun*."

"The only thing you're watching tonight is me."

"But I was watching you."

"In the flesh, Con. We're staying home together."

She leaned over, her cleavage practically enveloping his head, and kissed him full on the lips with passion. That she would stay home for him spoke volumes about her devotion, and her soft lips lifted his mood in spite of himself.

"What about the Chinese?" he asked.

She smiled. "We'll order take-out."

She took him by the hand and led him upstairs. Only once did he glance back at the book under the corner of the sofa.

4

Conrad lay on his back in bed, staring at the ceiling, thinking of Serena. Sex with Brooke had certainly released his pent-up energy, but he felt guilty as hell.

He looked over at Brooke. They had gone out together in high school, and she was the first girl he'd ever made love to. Now that his father was gone, she was the only connection to his past. After school, he had left her behind to go off on his digs and to other women, catching clips of her colorful commentaries now and then on NBC and later Fox.

Then Serena had made him forget his previous life entirely, made him forget everything the moment he first met her in South America.

It was only after Serena had deserted him after the disaster in Antarctica and he had come back to D.C. that he and Brooke reconnected. He had been jogging through Montrose Park just a few blocks away, as he did almost every morning. She was walking her dog. They practically collided in front of the park's sphere-like sun dial. It was fate. Almost instantly, it seemed, she had brought him home with her. The dog must have known it had lost its place in Brooke's heart to Conrad, because it ran away the day before he moved in. Ever since, it was like they had never been apart.

Until now. Until Serena had shown up at Arlington.

Conrad's thoughts turned to *Tom Sawyer* downstairs and the incomplete message he had deciphered. Just one more word to finish it.

He looked at Brooke, watched her full breasts rise and fall rhythmically and was convinced she was asleep. He slipped out of bed and glanced out the bedroom window. The black SUV was gone, but that didn't mean someone or something out there wasn't watching or listening.

He quietly walked downstairs, where he headed for the living room and retrieved the book from under the sofa. He didn't like hiding things from Brooke, mostly because he knew how much she hated it when he did. But he doubted he could bring up the book code without bringing up Serena—or looking like a liar if he failed to mention their encounter and she found out. And Brooke would. She always did.

He walked into the hallway bathroom, put the toilet lid down and sat with the book in the soft glow of the nightlight over the sink.

He looked up the last word from the book on Page 54: It was the word "land." When he finished writing it down, Conrad stared down at the note in his hand and the complete message his father left him:

SUN SHINES OVER SAVAGE LAND

What the hell did that mean? Was it simply the misguided musing of an old, disillusioned former Apollo astronaut and much despised Air Force general? Or did it mean something more? It had to mean something more, because it was intended only for Conrad—just like the astrological symbols on the obelisk. But why? And what was with the stand-alone numeric code 763 from the back of the obelisk? It had no correlation to the book code.

Conrad stared at the binding of *Tom Sawyer*, which lay open on the last page he had looked up. Something about it bothered him.

Conrad noted a slit where the binding separated. He opened it wider and realized there was a hidden pocket of some sort inside the cover of the book. He flipped through the rest of the book. All the other pages were fine and there was no other break in the binding. This secret slot was meant to hide something.

He carried the book into Brooke's study and found a letter opener in the drawer of her colonial rolltop desk. He folded the book back at page 54 and reached in with the letter opener to drag out an envelope.

It was yellowed with age. The word STARGAZER was written in faded bold script across it.

Conrad opened the envelope carefully and removed a folded document from inside. Unfolding it, he realized there was text on one side and some kind of map on the other.

Conrad instantly recognized the topography of the Potomac. He also recognized the layout. It was a terrestrial blueprint for Washington, D.C. In the upper left corner was the moniker WASHINGTONOPLE. In another corner was a watermark: TB.

Serena had to see this.

More fascinating still was the text on the other side of the map. It was a coded letter of some kind, and someone—his father, he assumed, based on the handwriting—had deciphered the salutation and signature. It was dated September 25, 1793.

The body of the letter was written in an alphanumeric code he didn't recognize. Probably a Revolutionary War–era military code. But the translated salutation was plain to see, and his hand trembled when he saw the signature. It was from General George Washington, and it began:

To Robert Yates and his chosen descendent in the Year of Our Lord 2008. . . .

5

THAT MORNING CONRAD FOUND Brooke downstairs at the breakfast table scanning five newspapers while the morning news shows blared on the TV, which she had split into six screens to follow the major broadcast and cable networks simultaneously. She was having her usual half grapefruit and Wasa cracker along with her coffee—some diet that she religiously followed from a Beverly Hills doctor to the stars. It required her to take a tiny scale with her wherever she went to weigh her food—no more than three ounces of anything at a time, no less than four hours apart.

"You're up early," she said as she poured him some coffee. "The *Post* ran a nice obit on your dad."

She showed him the picture and headline: *Body of Former Air Force General Found in Antarctica Laid to Rest.*

Conrad glanced at the photo of his dad, circa 1968, back in his "Right Stuff" days with NASA, a genuine American icon.

"I figured I might as well get a jump on the documentary for the Discovery Channel," he told Brooke. "You know, put the past behind and look ahead. So I'm going in early this morning to the offices in Maryland. See if Mercedes goes for it."

"Just see that she doesn't go for you, Con," Brooke said without looking up from her newspapers. "That one, unfortunately, isn't a nun."

Conrad paused, wondering if he had talked about Serena in his sleep. But then he noticed Serena on four channels of the TV screen. She was talking about the state of human rights in China on the eve of the Olympics, as well as China's status as the world's biggest polluter because of its high carbon emissions. The two other channels had segments about the bird flu, which had landed in North America and caused some poultry deaths but had not yet jumped to human-to-human contagion. That, of course, the expert with the mask on TV droned, was only a matter of time.

"I'll be careful," he laughed and kissed her goodbye.

Outside on the front steps, he looked out and noticed no suspicious vehicles. No spy types lurking in the shadows. He hurried down the sidewalk toward 31st Street and hailed a cab. He climbed inside and said, "Union Station."

Brooke watched Conrad disappear around the corner, then went into her study and stopped. Something was off. She scanned the shelves and noted a gap on the third shelf that caused some books to slant. Conrad had removed and replaced a book. *The* book, she suddenly realized, the one everybody had been looking for.

So he cracked the book code.

She walked over to the bookcase, removed *Tom Sawyer,* and flipped through the pages. She was about to put the book back and call it in when she noticed a break in the binding. There was a slit, revealing some sort of hidden pocket. She swore.

Hands shaking, she went to the kitchen and returned with a razor blade. Carefully she traced the inside cover until she formed a kind of flap. Ever so gently she peeled it back to reveal the empty pocket and, inside the flap, a smudge trace of writing. An imprint of some kind.

In a fog of dread she marched into the foyer and held up the book to the mirror, barely able to force herself to look. There in the mirror the word shone clear: STARGAZER.

"Holy shit," she gasped.

The map had been in her house all along, inside the book, right under her nose, and she had missed it.

She speed-dialed a local number in Georgetown on her coded cell phone. She identified herself to the agent who answered.

"This is SCARLETT," she said. "I've got a Priority One message for OSIRIS."

6

Conrad didn't recognize the tail until the young male attendant in the first-class compartment of the Acela Express came by to present a choice of hot or cold breakfasts. Conrad chose the bran flakes. The only other passenger in the compartment, a man who looked like an NFL linebacker crammed into a suit, ordered the Big Bob Egg Scramble.

That's how Conrad knew he was a federal agent. Only a fed on the taxpayer's dime would go first-class and order the Big Bob Egg Scramble, which sounded like Amtrak's version of a shrimp cocktail.

So much for the privacy he had sought by upgrading from business class after the attendant told him the first-class car was empty: Apparently none of the other passengers thought the Egg Scramble was worth the extra $80.

Except Big Bob a few seats back.

Conrad swore to himself and looked out the giant picture window at the barren pastures of Pennsylvania flashing by. The Acela Express was the fastest train on the continent, racing at speeds up to 150 miles an hour between Washington, D.C., and New York City. Conrad had hoped to reach Serena before lunch and make it back to Brooke by dinner without anybody knowing. Obviously, he wasn't moving fast enough.

Because there sat Big Bob, smiling at the attendant as he took a couple of tubs of cream and three blue packets of artificial sweetener with his coffee and pretended to peruse the *Wall Street Journal* until his Egg Scramble arrived.

Conrad got up from his seat and, without looking back, walked down the aisle to one of two bathrooms at the end of the car closest to the locomotive.

Conrad closed the door and braced himself. "Acela" was one of those names made up by some New York branding company that combined the words "acceleration" and "excellence." The secret to the Acela's speed was its ability to tilt in curves without slowing down or spooking passengers. Conrad could feel a slight tilt coming on now as he looked at himself in the mirror and thought about what he was doing.

He couldn't involve Brooke in any of this, for her own sake. At least that's what he told himself. Maybe he just didn't want her to know he was involved at all with Serena. But Brooke was a big girl. She knew he had never made her any promises. She probably also knew, better than he perhaps, just how slim the odds were of his ever getting together with Serena.

Facing the mirror, he slowly unbuttoned his shirt to reveal the envelope he had taped to himself. He removed the map from inside and flipped it over to look at the text:

763.618.1793

634.625. ghquip hiugiphipv 431. Lqfilv Seviu 282.625. siel 43. qwl 351. FUUO.

179 ucpgiliuv erqmqaciu jgl 26. recq 280.249. gewuih 707.5.708. jemcms. 282.682.123.414.144. qwl qyp nip 682.683.416.144.625.178. Jecmwli ncabv rlqxi 625.549.431. qwl gewui. 630. gep 48. ugelgims 26. piih 431. ligqnniph-cpa 625.217.101.5. uigligs 2821.69. uq glcvcgem 5. hep-ailqwu eu 625. iuvefmcubnipv 431. qwl lirwfmcg.

280. qyi 707.625. yqlmh 5.708.568.283.282. biexip. 625. uexeqi 683. ubqy 707.625. yes.

711

All his father had translated was the alphanumeric salutation —*To the chosen descendent of Robert Yates in the Year of Our Lord 2008*—and the numeric signature—*General George Washington.* Perhaps his father thought that was enough information for him to crack the rest of the cipher. Or perhaps his father could never figure it out.

All Conrad really knew about Robert Yates was that his father's side of the family had adopted the "Yeats" spelling to distance themselves from Robert Yates, who was one of America's more controversial Founding Fathers. Besides helping to draft the first Constitution for the State of New York, he represented New York as a key delegate at the convention in Philadelphia to draft the U.S. Constitution.

That's where things got ugly.

For it soon became clear to all that the Constitutional Convention, under the leadership of George Washington, wasn't tweaking the Articles of Confederation among the thirteen states as advertised. It was creating a new, centralized power: the federal government. A new sovereignty with the power to levy taxes and maintain an army.

That's when Robert Yates berated Washington, stormed out of the proceedings, and did everything in his power to defeat ratification of the U.S. Constitution, going so far as to run for New York governor in 1789. He failed. But in 1790 he became Chief Justice of the New York Supreme Court, and for the rest of his life was one of America's fiercest and most outspoken defenders of state rights and critics of federal authority.

Even the grave couldn't silence Yates. In 1821, twenty years after his death, his notes from the Constitutional Convention were published under the title *Secret Proceedings and Debates of the Convention Assembled . . . for the Purpose of Forming the Constitution of the United States*. By then, of course, the Louisiana Purchase had doubled the number of states in America, and the notion of still questioning the constitutionality of the federal government became, well, embarrassing for the family.

That's about the time, Conrad recalled, that his father's branch of the family stopped calling itself "Yates" and joined their cousins by spelling their surname "Yeats."

At least that's what Conrad could recall. He never paid much attention to the Yeats family tree growing up because he was adopted.

Conrad felt another tilt and acceleration as the Acela took a curve. He taped the map with the text to his chest and buttoned up his shirt. Somehow he had to elude Big Bob and reach Serena.

He pulled out his Vertu cell phone and was tempted to dial Serena's private number to arrange a pickup at Penn Station. But he slipped it back into his pocket, figuring that somehow Big Bob's friends would be listening. Ditto for any text messages.

Instead he would have to use one of the train's onboard phone booths in the dining car. And for that, he'd need a credit or debit card, and it would have to belong to somebody else.

When Conrad emerged from the lavatory, breakfast had been served on the extra large tray tables. He walked past his seat, which still said OCCUPIED on the LED readout in the overhead bin console, picked up his coffee, and went straight up to Big Bob, who had already scarfed down half his Egg Scramble.

Conrad said, "Looks like you overdid it with the Tabasco sauce."

Big Bob glanced down at the orange smudge on his tie and swore. He dabbed it with his napkin as the train took another curve.

Conrad went with it, swaying enough to spill his coffee on Big Bob. The guy bolted in his seat, knocking the tray table up and hitting his head on the overhead bin.

"Gosh, I'm sorry," said Conrad, steadying Big Bob as he slipped his hand inside the guy's suit and lifted his wallet.

Big Bob said, "What's the matter with you?"

"Let me get something from the snack car for you," Conrad said, slipping the wallet into his own pocket and walking away. "My apologies."

Conrad approached two pneumatically operated sliding glass doors. They whooshed aside like the deck of the *Starship Enterprise*, and he passed through the spacious and quiet intercar passageway into business class.

Both business cars were half full, maybe forty passengers each, most busying themselves with their newspapers, laptops, and iPods when they weren't cursing at their BlackBerries and mobile phones for cutting out in the middle of conversations.

He passed through two more sliding doors to reach the snack car. About a dozen patrons were in the lounge area, perched uncomfortably on the high and low stool seating. A plasma TV on the wall flashed highlights of the weekend in sports.

At the far end of the snack car was a business center with a fax machine, copier, and two onboard Railfones, one of them in an enclosed booth. Conrad stepped inside. The Railfone didn't accept coins or bills and required payment by a major credit card. Fortunately, Conrad had a Visa card with the name Derrick Kopinski, Sergeant Major of the Marine Corps, aka "Big Bob."

Conrad dialed Serena's number and looked at Kopinski's ID card while the other end rang. The driver's license had him in Oceanside, CA. That meant Kopinski had until recently been stationed out of Camp Pendleton. Kopinski was a Marine. Probably green at the Pentagon. Definitely DOD, one of SecDef Packard's men. An E-9 Special pay grade.

Besides forty dollars in cash, Kopinski's wallet included a picture of his wife and kids in a Sears portrait, for sure. She looked like Goose's wife from *Top Gun*, a young Meg Ryan. Very nice. Same with the kids, who fortunately looked more like their mother. Even a little baby baptism card. Eastern Orthodox. And coupons for Starbucks coffee, McDonald's Extra Value meals, and Dunkin' Donuts. Lots of Dunkin' Donuts coupons. Jeez, they didn't pay this guy enough.

The call finally connected and Conrad got a voicemail from Serena speaking French that asked him to leave a voice or text message. Before he could punch in anything the signal cut out and the call was dropped.

Conrad hung up and paused for a moment. He removed the envelope from his body and taped it to the underside of the shelf beneath the phone. Then he buttoned up and stepped out of the booth.

Back in first class, Sergeant Major Kopinski was waiting for him. As soon as the glass doors opened, Conrad saw him standing there, jacket open to reveal a shoulder-holstered gun. The stain on his tie looked even bigger.

"I want my wallet, Dr. Yeats."

"Yes, sir." Conrad handed it over and looked back to make sure they were out of view of the business car and alone in first class. They were.

"This mission can't be what you intended for your life when you enlisted in the Marines, Sergeant Major," Conrad said. "You tell Packard to give you a real assignment."

Kopinski nodded, then to Conrad's dismay started convulsing. Kopinski's eyes rolled back in their sockets and something green began to leak out his nostrils.

Then he saw a tiny dart in the Marine's neck as the head tilted to the side unnaturally and the heavy body crumpled to the floor with a thud. He was dead. Conrad spun around to see the glass doors into first class wide open and the attendant pointing some sort of dart gun at him.

"You just killed a federal agent," Conrad said.

"Hand it over," the assassin said. "Slowly."

Conrad reached into his pocket and pulled out Kopinski's wallet.

"Forget the wallet." The assassin stepped forward, still pointing the gun.

"Who are you?" Conrad asked.

"The Grim Reaper, as far as you're concerned." The assassin waved the dart gun at him. "Turn around."

Conrad turned to face the picture window. More bland pastures passing by. He felt the assassin pat him down.

"Take off your boots."

Conrad removed his boots.

The assassin looked at them and then back at him. "Unbutton your shirt."

"I'm not that kind of guy."

The assassin tapped the point of his dart gun on Conrad's chest. "Open your damn shirt."

Conrad could see the guy's eyes were on fire, meaning business. He unbuttoned his shirt and pulled it open to show nothing but his chest. "I work out, as you can see."

"Where is it?"

"Where is what?"

"Whatever you took from that little book of yours."

Conrad said, "If you people did anything to hurt Brooke, I'll kill you."

"You should be worried about what we're going to do to you."

The assassin whipped the butt of the gun against the side of

Conrad's head, and lightning flashed across Conrad's field of vision. The searing pain made it a struggle for him to stay standing.

"Give it to me," the assassin ordered, "or I'll open your ass to look for it."

"You know, that's just where I've got it." Conrad, his head throbbing, began to unbuckle his belt. "You look like the kind of guy who'd like to search for it there."

Conrad bent over, his butt up to the assassin's face, his own face inches over poor Kopinski on the floor, the guy's Egg Scramble and Tabasco sauce all over his shirt. He thought of the guy's wife and kids. A *Marine*, for Christ's sake. And this little shit behind him killed him.

"Now take a good, hard look," Conrad said. "You don't want to miss anything."

Conrad dropped his pants with one hand and reached into Kopinski's jacket with the other. He suddenly straightened up and turned around, his pants around his ankles. The assassin's eyes were looking down where they shouldn't, missing Conrad's arm swinging up with Kopinski's gun.

"Surprise," said Conrad, and shot him in the stomach.

The bullet blew the assassin against the wall, and he crumpled to the floor in a fetal position.

After pulling up his pants, Conrad looked back through both sets of glass doors into the other car to make sure nobody heard the shot, then leaned over and dug the pistol into the guy's neck. "Who are you people?"

The assassin's mouth broke into a wide, wicked grin. Conrad saw the cyanide capsule between his teeth. But before he could bite down on the suicide pill, Conrad smashed his front teeth with the butt of the pistol. The assassin started choking on his teeth and swallowed the capsule.

"Gonna take you a little longer to die now," Conrad told him. "And you don't have to. You can still get some medical help. But only if you tell me who you people are."

The assassin only glared at him.

"I see you still have a few teeth left." Conrad held up the pistol for another blow. "I think I can fix that."

The assassin didn't flinch, even as he coughed up some blood. "You'll be dead by sunset."

Conrad bent closer. "Says who?"

"The Alignment," the assassin gasped through his bloody teeth, and then slumped over, dead.

Conrad ripped open the man's uniform and found a BlackBerry device. There was nothing else on him except the strange dart gun on the floor. Conrad took the BlackBerry and tucked Kopinski's gun behind his back.

He dragged both corpses to the port galley in the first-class car, where he found the body of the real attendant. He stood and looked at all three bodies and shook his head. He'd have all of twenty minutes tops before they were found after they pulled into New York. He looked at his watch. It was 10:30. They were due in Penn Station in a half hour.

Back in the snack car, he had to wait five minutes to use the Railfone booth. He slid inside, felt beneath the metal shelf counter and pulled out the envelope with the map inside that he had taped to the underside. Then he called Serena.

7

UNITED NATIONS HEADQUARTERS

NEW YORK CITY

In the pantheon of modern megalithic architecture, China's new 25-kilometer-long venue for the 2008 Olympic Games—humbly dubbed the "Axis of Human Civilization"—was a sure bet to join America's interstate highway system, Central America's Panama Canal, and Europe's Chunnel as one of the great wonders of the modern world.

But to Serena Serghetti, now standing before the General Assembly, it was an environmental disaster, a state-run catastrophe that was endangering animals, destroying ancient temples, and driving more than a million people from their homes. All because China wanted to show the world that it had come of age.

"Now we have reports of avian influenza—or 'bird flu'—spreading in the squalor of the countryside where the homeless have been exiled," she said. "But the government has refused to even acknowledge the threat of a global health pandemic, let alone help the poorest of its own people."

Naturally, the Chinese ambassador to the United Nations didn't see it that way and seemed visibly annoyed. This morning alone he had been forced to deny accusations that his country actively suppressed free speech and systematically imprisoned and executed people to harvest their organs. Now he had to contend with reports of avian flu just weeks before the Olympic Games in Beijing.

"We beg to differ," was all he said through a translator. "The industrialization and development of Beijing has created a rising standard of living for our people and better health care."

"At least allow us to help your needy, Mr. Ambassador."

Serena cited a report on relief efforts following the 2004 tsunami in Indonesia and the 2005 hurricane that wiped out New Orleans, events that also displaced more than a million people.

"As the head of FEMA has stated, some of the world's problems are just too big for governments," she said. "But the global church —Catholics, Protestants, and Orthodox together—is present in more than a million distribution plants worldwide. For food, shelter, vaccines, relief supplies, and helping hands, there's a local church on the ground wherever disaster strikes. And we're ready to help you."

"I am sure you are, Sister Serghetti, but we can take care of our own people," said the Chinese ambassador, and further discussion was tabled.

As Serena returned to her seat, she could think of at least one other person who would beg to differ: Conrad Yeats. She had left him for the work of the Church, the very hope of the world she was proclaiming in this chamber. But in Conrad's mind it was the Church that had denied him her love.

She picked up her bulky but lightweight white earpiece and sat down. Most delegates needed translators from the interpreter booths overhead to follow along. But not Serena, who was fluent in many of the world's languages. She used the earpiece to pick up messages unobtrusively and write them down. Now a voice in Italian told her that the media room said that "Carlton Yardley" from *The New Atlantis* magazine was there for his scheduled interview with her.

Her heart skipped a beat.

He must have found something, she thought, although she was embarrassed to realize she didn't care if he had nothing to show her but his face. His unshaven, stubbled face.

As soon as she could step outside the chamber and into the crowded visitors' lobby, Serena pulled out her iPhone and called Benito to bring the car out from the private garage. She scanned the cavernous glass atrium. The media line was at the entrance, behind the blue velvet rope. She started walking in that direction when Max Seavers stepped into view, blocking her path to Conrad.

"Serena!" Max said, smiling.

Serena stopped in her tracks.

Before he was tapped by the American president to help with the Department of Defense, Max Seavers had helped her humanitarian efforts in Africa and Asia on a number of occasions by donating vaccines. She couldn't just blow him off now.

"*Déjà vu,* Max. Weren't we standing here just a few days ago with you showing me some rather unusual photographs? What brings you back?"

"Sounding the alarm here and on Capitol Hill about the coming flu pandemic. What about you? I hear you were telling the Chinese where to stick their new dam."

Serena couldn't help glancing over his shoulder toward the media line, where various cameras were set up to catch the comings and goings of dignitaries. She spotted Conrad, and he saw her and motioned.

"I suppose you have an opinion on the new Beijing?" she said as she started walking away from the entrance and toward the delegates lounge.

"A technological marvel," Max said, keeping pace with her. "You've got to give the Chinese credit for that. They've left nothing to chance. Even the date of the opening ceremonies on August eighth was chosen because the number 8 represents good fortune to the Chinese."

"I see: That's the eighth day of the eighth month of the eighth year of the new millennium," Serena said, pretending to marvel. "And I used to think three sixes in a row was the devil's number. Tell me, Max, what about the million souls the Olympics are displacing?"

"You mean driving from their homes which had no running water or electricity in the first place?" he said. "Sounds like progress to me."

Serena glanced sideways at him as she walked. "And the destruction of the ancient temples, their history?"

"Obviously the Chinese don't care about their ancient temples as much as you do, Serena. That's because the Chinese are looking to the future. They know that in time some other civilization is going to do the same thing to their Olympic Park that they're doing to those ancient temples."

She came to a halt. "I wonder if you'd feel the same way if these temples were the ones about to be destroyed?" She pointed out toward the Manhattan skyline—away from Conrad in the media area.

Max Seavers followed her finger and smiled. "If it was some act of God—like the tsunami, I'd be devastated. But if it was our government doing the submerging, for the betterment of the country, like the Chinese, then yes. Have you seen this?"

Serena realized he was referring to the nearby display of a model city in the lobby. It was the official Olympic Venue Construction Plan for Beijing. A nameplate read "Axis of Human Civilization." More PR.

"Impressive, Serena, isn't it?"

Serena looked at the model of the city's new Central Axis. The Chinese had successfully constructed a 25-kilometer-long boulevard connecting the new Olympic Park in the north with the Imperial Forbidden City and Tiananmen Square in the city center. She noted a stretch of avenue labeled "thousand-year path."

"It's certainly audacious, Max," she said. "This Beijing axis looks like the New Berlin that Hitler never got to build."

Max chuckled. "Funny you should say that. Because it was designed by Albert Speer Jr., the son of the architect who designed the New Berlin for Hitler's grandiose empire, the 'world capital Germania,' the capital of the so-called Thousand Year Reich."

Serena said, "You're joking."

"No." Max shook his head. "Charming old man, incredibly gifted. Tried to hire him myself for SeaGen's corporate headquarters in La Jolla, but the Chinese outbid me."

Serena stared at the model city. "Is Speer trying to copy his father or outdo him?"

"That's what the German news magazine *Die Welt* asked when the plan was unveiled," he said. "But it's all nonsense, of course. The Chinese insist Speer's design simply fulfills their own intentions of creating a central axis, and that the idea was laid out in the planning of the imperial capital centuries ago. I think the real point of interest is where the elder Speer found his inspiration for the New Berlin in the first place."

Serena shrugged. "You've got me, Max."

"Pierre L'Enfant's design for the National Mall in Washington, D.C.," he said. "What's more, Speer maintained that L'Enfant's plan was itself based on earlier source maps going back to ancient Egypt and Atlantis. That's Doctor Yeats's specialty, isn't it?"

Serena wasn't going to bite. Nothing good could come out of lingering here even a moment longer.

"Atlantis?" she asked, giving him a dubious look. "Now don't get all mystic on me, Max. We need you to keep those vaccines coming."

With that, she turned and briskly walked away, exhaling slowly. As she approached the media line by the entrance, she was aware of Conrad in the pack. She walked right past him without a glance to the waiting limousine and got in. Benito closed the door, slid behind the wheel and drove away.

8

Furious to see Serena pressing the flesh with none other than that pseudo-philanthropist-billionaire Max Seavers, and feeling helpless because he couldn't risk being seen, Conrad walked out of the U.N., weaving between the flagpoles in front until he was far enough away to hail a cab and climb inside.

"Christie's," he said as the driver pulled away from the curb and into the lunch-hour traffic. The driver glanced at him in the mirror and asked where Christie lived. "Rockefeller Center. She's an auction house."

Conrad didn't know where else to go until he could reach Serena, and he didn't want to tell the driver to just "drive." Worst case, there was a cute assistant curator at Christie's that he had seen off and on whenever he was in New York. Ironically enough, her name was Kristy. Maybe she could make some sense of the map, or at least its monetary value, and refer him to somebody outside the federal government who could help him decode the text.

Conrad took out the cell phone he had lifted off the body of the assassin aboard the Acela. He had tossed his own phone under the tracks before leaving the platform at Penn Station. The question was whether anybody had found the bodies yet and been sharp enough to start tracking this phone. Probably not. Hopefully not.

He keyed in Serena's number from memory and listened to it ring on the other end.

The driver's phone beeped at the same time. "Yeah?" he said.

Conrad heard the cabbie loud and clear—on his phone.

"Yeah?" the cabbie repeated.

A cold shudder passed through Conrad's body. He stared at the phone's display and realized he had redialed the last number the assassin called. Conrad looked up at the rearview mirror in time to see the slits of the driver's eyes widen.

"You're one of them," Conrad said and pointed the gun he lifted from the dead Marine at the driver's head.

Too late Conrad noticed the driver had only one hand on the wheel and ducked as a bullet burst from the front seat and shattered the rear window.

Conrad pumped a bullet into the back of the driver's seat. The bullet shattered the driver's spine and he slumped forward onto the steering wheel, his arms loose at his side.

Conrad felt sick to his stomach. He tapped the driver on the back of the head. The man's head rolled to the side, revealing a trickle of blood running down his neck.

The cab suddenly accelerated wildly.

Conrad lunged over the seat and put his arms over the corpse to reach the steering wheel, but the car was careening out of control.

A flash in the rearview mirror caught his eye and he looked back through the blown-out rear windshield to see an unmarked Ford Explorer with federal plates and red lights coming up from behind. Suddenly Conrad's shock turned to rage. He wrenched the steering wheel toward the road and the cab shot off.

The federal car gave chase, but Conrad quickly turned the wheel while pulling the brake lever, sliding the cab sideways with a long skid. Then he turned it against the street direction, driving straight toward the Explorer.

The driver of the Explorer didn't have a chance to remove his seat belt and pull out a gun. And he couldn't swerve in time before Conrad drove the cab head-on into the black SUV. Conrad's face slammed into the corpse on impact and bounced back in time for him to see the airbags inflate in the federal car.

He heard sirens closing in a minute later. He staggered out of the cab, his ears still ringing from the crash. Or was that the sound of police sirens growing louder? There was a squeal of brakes. A voice called, "Hey!"

It was Serena calling from the open window of a Mercedes limousine. She kicked open the rear door with the Vatican emblem on it and motioned him inside.

Conrad paused for a second, thunderstruck. She was a vision from heaven. Her lips were moving but he couldn't hear anything. He dove into the back, the door slamming shut behind him as the limousine peeled away.

"Anything else you want to destroy, Conrad, or are we finished for now?" said Serena as Benito swung them into traffic on First Avenue.

He stared at her, incredulous. In her black Armani suit and white silk blouse, she looked completely unruffled.

"I'm fine, thanks."

"Too bad I can't say the same for that poor Amtrak attendant and Marine the police band says you killed," she said softly. "Please tell me the Alignment was responsible."

He stared at her. "You know about the Alignment?"

"If you're referring to the secret, centuries-old organization of military imperialists, then yes," she said. "What an amateur you are, Conrad. The Church has been at war with the New World Order for eons. From the way you talk, you'd think you discovered it. Now hand it over so I can at least make sure you found the proper document."

He produced the map and Serena took it from his hands.

Conrad watched as Serena slowly scanned the map and then flipped it over to study the text. Her hands began to tremble, and Conrad swore he saw what looked like the tiniest pearl of perspiration on her smooth forehead long before she had reached the last paragraph. Conrad had never seen Sister Serena Serghetti, the Vatican's top linguist, ever break a sweat.

She looked up at Conrad in wonder. "You're Stargazer."

"What?"

She pushed a button on the partition to reveal Benito in front. "Benito," she said. "The jet."

"Si, signorina."

Conrad recalled that Benito was a former Swiss Special Forces soldier, a crack marksman, and the only Vatican bodyguard who could keep up with Serena on the slopes at Davos during World Economic

Forums. He hoped the same was true for the streets of New York City.

"What's going on, Serena?" Conrad asked. "Less than twenty-four hours after you show up on the scene, people die, and my life goes into the crapper."

"That's why we have to get you out of here. You're in grave danger, and so is America and the whole world."

Suddenly a phone started ringing up front and Conrad jumped. The ringtone sounded familiar. It was an old Elton John song, "Benny and the Jets." Benito the driver didn't bother to pick up.

"The jet is fueling up at the airstrip, *signorina,*" Benito said. "If we can reach it."

They turned a corner and Conrad saw the flashing lights of several blue-and-white police cars blocking the road. A young cop approached the limo, hand on his weapon.

"Alignment?" Conrad asked.

"God knows, these days. Say your prayers."

Conrad looked at Serena, who crossed one leg over the other and then pulled out a flap revealing a space beneath the rear seat of the limo.

"You're kidding me, right?" he asked.

"Get under and shut up," she told him.

"Whatever happened to the missionary position?"

"May God have mercy on your soul, you wanker." She gave him a final kick inside and pushed the flap back into position behind him.

"Easy does it, Benito." Her voice sounded muffled to Conrad in the dark. He could feel the car slow to a halt. The squeak of a window lowering came next, then Serena's voice. "Yes, officer?"

There was a long pause, and Conrad crouched very still in the darkness. Then he heard the young cop clearing his throat. "Sister Serghetti," he said. "It's an honor."

"Is there a problem, Officer O'Donnell?" she said, reading his badge.

Thank God, thought Conrad. An Irish Catholic cop.

"Nothing concerning you, Sister. Looks like terrorists failed at both Penn Station and the United Nations."

"Is everything OK?"

"Nothing was stolen or destroyed," the officer told her. "But two federal agents, an Amtrak employee, and a cabbie were killed."

"I'm so sorry. Is there anything I can do to help? Do you need to search my car?"

Beneath the seat Conrad punched her in the rear.

"No, ma'am. That won't be necessary. To begin with, you've got diplomatic plates and a search would be illegal."

Conrad heard a shout and then a screech as one of the squad cars reversed and the Mercedes lurched forward as they were waved on through.

"God's angels watch over you, *signorina,*" said Benito.

No, Benito, Conrad thought. *She's the angel.*

9

ROME

JUNE 24

The next morning Serena stared out through the tinted glass of another limo at the towering ancient obelisk in St. Peter's Square as Benito drove through the gates of Vatican City. She thought of Conrad and wondered if it was wise to have left him back at the secret safe house outside New York City before flying here to press their case.

There were a few police outside on the plaza, but no tourists or *paparazzi* this early in the day. More pigeons than people, really.

"Not like the old days, *signorina,*" said Benito, referring to the protestors and media circus that once surrounded her arrivals at the Vatican.

Back then she was only in her 20s but had already made a lifetime's worth of enemies as "Mother Earth" in the petroleum, timber, and biomedical industries—anyone who put profit ahead of people, animals, or the environment. Today she was an older and wiser 31, but the damage was done: Those inside the Vatican who had ties to these outside governments, corporate CEOs, and other "deep pockets" still didn't trust her and never would.

Which was why she had decided Conrad was better off back at the safe house.

"That was another era, Benito."

"Another pope, *signorina.*"

They curved along a winding drive and arrived at the entrance of the *Governorate*. The Swiss Guards in their crimson uniforms snapped to attention as Serena walked in.

The old pope, by favoring her with his friendship, had protected her within these walls. In one significant way he still did. Before he died, he shared with her a vision he believed God had revealed to him about the end of the world. And he let others know as much. The halo effect ensured that at least some door would always be open to her here.

The new pope she hardly knew. He was a good man, although she had heard that he had voiced his displeasure at the special favor his predecessor had shown her. Which was reasonable, she concluded, given that the new pope knew her only by her nickname among his former peers in the College of Cardinals: "Sister Pain-in-the-Ass."

That included Cardinal Tucci, gatekeeper of the secret maps collections. She had called Tucci from somewhere over the Atlantic to demand access to the Vatican archives, an extraordinary privilege she had enjoyed under the old pope but which Tucci had revoked with the new pope.

"Sister Serghetti," Tucci said flatly when she entered his office, which was tucked away at the end of an obscure hallway, reached only by an old service elevator. "Welcome back."

Tucci rose from his high-back leather chair, a pair of seventeenth-century Bleau globes on either side, and extended his hand. Only in his late 40s, Tucci was a "secret cardinal." That is, he was appointed by the pope to the position and nobody else was informed of it, although Serena was aware of two others besides herself who also knew.

A secret cardinal to hide the secrets of the Church.

Every Christian, Serena knew all too well, must wrestle with the tension of living in this world without becoming a product of it. But she suspected that Cardinal Tucci had lost that battle a long time ago.

"Your Eminence," she said, and kissed his ring with the Dominus Dei insignia. *Dominus Dei* meant "Rule of God" and was an order within the Church that predated the Jesuits and traced itself back to the first Christians who served in the palace of Caesar in the first century. Secrecy was their highest value, as it meant survival in the early days of Christianity. Serena didn't like secrecy. It had become an excuse over the centuries for a host of crimes, crimes that made the fictionalized evils of Dominus Dei's upstart cousins in Opus Dei look like acts of charity.

"To what do I owe this pleasure?" he asked suspiciously as they sat down.

"I want to see the L'Enfant Confession," she said, just like that.

Tucci looked at her with undisguised disdain. He seemed tired of her already, and perturbed. Perturbed because she had pressed his aides to wake him up in the wee hours of the morning to take her call. Perturbed by her very existence.

If Tucci wondered how she got as far as she had within the Church, the feeling was mutual. He was boyish by Vatican standards and yet mature enough to sport the smile of a man who experienced enough of life to find it a bad joke. Even his name was ironic, implying he was some indigenous Italian bureaucrat when, in fact, his mother's side of the family came to America on the Mayflower and was Yankee through and through. He came to the Vatican by way of Boston, where he was known as a raucous but brilliant student at Harvard and an even more brilliant priest and professor of American history at Boston College. He had risen very far in Rome, very fast.

Even now, as she awaited a response, Serena couldn't help noticing, with some envy, the medallion that Tucci wore around his neck. In its center was an ancient Roman coin, a silver denarius with the image of the emperor Tiberius. Legend had it that this coin was the very "Tribute Penny" Jesus held up when he told his followers that they should "render unto Caesar what is Caesar's and unto God what is God's." It had been passed down through the ages, from one leader of the Dei to the next. Some argued it represented power greater than the papacy.

"The L'Enfant Confession?" Tucci repeated, as if he had never heard of it.

Serena said, "The deathbed confession of Pierre L'Enfant, the original architect of Washington, D.C., to John Carroll, the first Catholic bishop of North America."

Tucci looked mystified. "What exactly did Pierre L'Enfant confess?"

"Something to the effect that the major terrestrial monuments of

America's capital city are aligned like a map to the stars, as are Egypt's pyramids and South America's Way of the Dead," she said.

"What do you mean, the monuments are aligned like a map?"

She showed him a digital photo of General Yeats's tombstone at Arlington, of the side with the four astrological symbols. "These are the zodiac signs for the sun and the constellations Boötes, Virgo, and Leo. Each celestial coordinate has a terrestrial counterpart in the city of Washington, D.C."

"And you're telling me that George Washington had L'Enfant use these constellations to anchor America's capital city?" He inflected his voice in a tone to hint at just how ridiculous and a waste of time the idea was. He glanced at the antique clock on the wall to underscore his displeasure.

"Yes," she said without flinching. "And we can follow those monuments that correspond to the stars like a treasure map."

"And where does this heavenly treasure trail lead?"

"To a specific place beneath the National Mall, or perhaps even a specific date in America's future," she said. "I was hoping you could tell me."

"My forte is American history and cartography, Sister Serghetti, not eschatology," Tucci said, amused. "But, as a historian, I know that Pierre L'Enfant was a Freemason. And I don't have to refer to my *Freemasons for Dummies* book to tell you that his secret society—like all those who seek the light of God outside of the Holy Church—has had a long and tortured history with us. So you'll have to forgive my skepticism when I ask you why on earth would L'Enfant confess anything to a Catholic priest, let alone Archbishop John Carroll, about this alleged secret geography of the American capital?"

"You mean why under the earth," Serena said, confident that Tucci knew full well what she was about to say. That's why she had come to him in the first place. "It was Daniel Carroll, the Archbishop's brother, who owned Capitol Hill and sold it to Washington. All that land, by the way, once belonged to a Catholic named Francis Pope who called it Rome."

Tucci tapped two fingers to his lips as he looked at her thoughtfully. Finally, he cleared his throat and sat back in his chair.

"There is no L'Enfant Confession, Sister Serghetti," he said. "Never was."

"Like the Alignment?" she asked.

Tucci frowned, aware that she had him there. After all, the sole reason his own group, Dominus Dei, still existed was allegedly to fight the Alignment threat to the Church. Without the Alignment—fact or fiction—there could be no funding, no foot soldiers for Tucci's order coming from the pope.

"The Alignment is simply an umbrella term for all secret societies aligned against the Church and operating in the shadows of power around the world," Tucci said. "Don't tell me you sincerely believe it's an actual group of warriors who trace their ancient knowledge to the survivors of Atlantis and use the stars to control world events to their own ultimate agenda? Please."

"I didn't until now," she said. "But George Washington was a Mason. As was his chief architect, Pierre L'Enfant. As were fifty of the fifty-six signers of the American Declaration of Independence. Perhaps you could humor me and tell me what link the Masons have to the Alignment—if the Alignment were, in fact, an actual group."

"Why, the Knights Templar, of course," Tucci said, obliging her with a conspiratorial smile.

Tucci was referring to a tiny band of nine French Crusaders at the end of the first millennium who for nine years protected pilgrims visiting Jerusalem. Legend, Serena knew, suggested they were really searching for some priceless relic like the Holy Grail or a piece of the cross on which Jesus was crucified. Whatever it was, they apparently found it, because the Knights Templar over the next two centuries exploded in membership and money among Europe's nobility. The Church, threatened by the power and influence of its holy defenders, suddenly and expediently decided that the Knights Templar were conspiring to destroy it, and in 1307 launched a seven-year war that ended with the Grand Master of the Knights Templar being burned at the stake.

It was only last year, seven hundred years too late, that the Vatican issued a formal apology for its persecution, and Serena knew that Tucci was that apology's key architect.

Serena said, "I thought the Church, through Dominus Dei, took care of the Knights Templar centuries ago."

"Not quite," said Tucci. "A few Knights escaped to Britain and formed a new network called Freemasonry, once again hijacking another society, this one formed of the builders and bricklayers of the great cathedrals and palaces of Europe. It was only a matter of time before the Masons came to America, penetrated its elites like George Washington, and used their influence to establish a new country and, they hoped, a new world order."

"So do you still consider the Masons to be a threat to the Church?"

"Hardly," Tucci said. "The Alignment long ago left the Masons, having moved on to controlling U.S. policy through the Council on Foreign Relations, the Trilateral Commission, and your friends at the United Nations."

There was a twinkle in Tucci's eyes, a glimmer of triumph that he had succeeded in utterly humiliating her for her gullibility and in drawing their little meeting to a resounding close.

"We could go on all day about this, Sister Serghetti," Tucci said. "But like I told you, there is no such thing as the L'Enfant Confession. It's a myth."

"So is this," she said, and produced the map Conrad gave her.

Tucci bolted upright as she unfolded it on his desk. "Where did you get this?"

"From Stargazer," she said, and watched a flicker of recognition at the code name register in Tucci's horrified eyes.

"Conrad Yeats," he muttered, putting his knowledge of her long-standing and controversial relationship with Conrad together with his knowledge of the Yeats family's history in American politics and the Masons. "Yeats is Stargazer. But, of course. I should have known."

"What matters is that it's the genuine article," Serena said, sensing she was on the verge of getting more out of this meeting with Tucci than she ever imagined.

Tucci grabbed a magnifier and leaned over the map. The upper left corner had the word WASHINGTONOPLE, the original name for George Washington's namesake city.

"Mother of God!" Tucci exclaimed, truly awed.

He then passed the magnifier over the city radiants. The ornate, crown-like seal with the initials TB must have jumped into view, because he snapped his head back in wonder.

"That's the seal used by the English papermaker Thomas Budgen for paper he manufactured from 1770 until 1785," Serena told him, letting him know she had done her own analysis on the map.

"I know what it is," he said sharply.

Serena said, "I always thought L'Enfant's original blueprint for Washington, D.C., was either on display or in preservation at the Library of Congress."

"That one is a later draft that Washington submitted to Congress in 1791," Tucci said automatically. "What you have brought me is the original terrestrial blueprint for America's capital city, which L'Enfant's own handwriting here says is based on an earlier star map drawn by Washington's chief astronomer, Benjamin Banneker."

Tucci sank back in his chair and stared at her, his eyes sizing her up for the first time. It was obvious that he had underestimated her, and she could actually see the wheels turning in his head as he contemplated just how much she knew that she wasn't telling him, and just how much she knew that *he* knew.

"What else did the pontiff tell you before he died, Sister Serghetti?" Tucci asked. "I've heard the rumors. A fifth Fatima? A revelation of the Apocalypse?"

"Many things, Your Eminence," she said. "But today I come to discuss only one."

She could see the white flag of surrender waving in his eyes. "And so he still protects you."

"God alone is my refuge and strength," she demurred.

Tucci removed a leather binder from the center drawer of his desk, and out of the binder withdrew a single sheet of parchment that looked very much of the same stock as the map she had shown him. He passed it across the desk to her.

"This is what you wanted to see, Sister Serghetti."

Serena Serghetti slowly read the handwritten testimony of Pierre L'Enfant that had been signed by John Carroll. Her heart began to race long before she reached the last paragraph.

"L'Enfant claims that the relic that the Alignment found in

Jerusalem through its proxies, the Knights Templar, was a celestial globe," she said, translating from the French as she studied the confession.

"Yes," said Tucci. "The globe once stood upon one of two pillars in King Solomon's temple. Masonic lore says that this globe was hollow and contained ancient scrolls detailing the history of human civilization and its sciences before the Great Flood, and thus before the Book of Genesis."

Serena read on.

L'Enfant claimed that the Alignment brought the globe to America through the Masons in order to use the ancient knowledge it contained to establish a new world order. By no coincidence, the globe came into the direct possession of General George Washington, perhaps America's most visibly prominent Mason and a Grand Master in the order.

But then Washington discovered that his Masons, and perhaps even his armies, were in fact controlled by the Alignment, whose vision of a new world order had little in common with the cause of freedom. Rather, they saw the United States as a blunt weapon they could use to smash the world's dynasties and pave the way for resurrecting Atlantis and its ancient faith in the stars and fate.

Washington knew he couldn't expose and destroy the Alignment without criminalizing the Masons and jeopardizing the fledgling United States itself. So immediately upon becoming America's first president in 1789, Washington secretly instructed L'Enfant to use astronomical charts drawn by his chief astronomer, Benjamin Banneker, to align the proposed capital city of Washington, D.C., to the constellation Virgo—as a warning sign for future Americans. His hope was that in time the American people would be free enough and strong enough to reject the Alignment's agenda.

L'Enfant concluded his confession by saying that he did not know the significance of the specific date in the distant future that Washington chose for the conjunction of monuments and stars, only that Washington buried the celestial globe containing the horrible secret he had discovered somewhere under the Federal Triangle.

Serena looked up from the text at Cardinal Tucci, seated in

his massive throne-like chair with a Bleau globe on either side, one terrestrial and the other celestial. She stared at the celestial globe.

"Impossible," Serena said in disbelief. "Washington's celestial globe has been on display in his study at Mount Vernon for more than 200 years."

But Tucci looked sure as ever. "That globe is an inferior replacement made in England during the 1790s. Its surface, which is only papier-mâché, has been flaking so badly in recent years that it's been moved to the new museum at the estate for preservation. The original globe, according to L'Enfant, was made of bronze or copper and etched with the constellations. Washington buried it someplace under the American capital sometime before he died."

Serena shifted uncomfortably in her seat as she glanced again at L'Enfant's confession.

"The handwriting holds up to analysis," Tucci said. "Whether it's true or the blatherings of a madman is another thing entirely."

Tucci was known for playing things very close to his vestments. He was *not* known for wild speculation or outright disinformation. If he was sharing this information with her, it was because he believed it to be accurate.

"So L'Enfant says he followed Washington's instructions to lay out the city of Washington, D.C., so that key monuments would lock with key stars at a specific date in the future," Serena said. "A doomsday warning, if you will. And what's going to happen on that date is revealed by the celestial globe Washington buried."

"Or by what's inside the globe," Tucci said. "Not since the War of 1812 has anyone in Rome believed L'Enfant's confession. But if this map you've shown me is real and Stargazer is real, there can be little doubt that L'Enfant's confession is true. Which means America is in grave peril. Look at the end date."

She stared down at the date: July 4, 2008.

"So you see, Sister Serghetti, Stargazer has six days to stop the alignment of the monuments with the stars or the United States of America will cease to exist."

Serena said, "You mean stop the organization we call the Alignment."

"They are one and the same, Sister Serghetti," Tucci said. "If anything is going to happen in heaven and on earth in six days, you can be sure the Alignment will make it happen. They have been gathering strength for centuries. This conjunction of landmarks and stars—this metamorphosis of America into something its founders never intended—is their *raison d'état*. Their twisted sense of destiny is searching for any moral or legal justification to use the United States to unleash their will on this world and wipe out their enemies *en masse*."

Serena couldn't hide her shock or skepticism. "By what power, Your Eminence?"

"Perhaps by some new technology or weapon of mass destruction or some natural wonder that can be exploited," Tucci said. "I don't know. Like I told you, I'm a historian and not an eschatologist. But there is one thing that I do know about America in Bible prophecy."

"What's that?" Serena asked.

"It isn't there," he said. "It's as if America never existed."

Serena grew very still, the utter insanity of everything sinking in still deeper.

"So Washington set up the alignment of monuments as a warning to Americans in the future," she said slowly. "And Stargazer—Dr. Yeats—is a kind of ultimate 'sleeper' agent that Washington essentially sent into the future to stop the Alignment."

"Crazy, I know," Tucci said. "And all from the lips of Pierre L'Enfant, the pompous architect of the American capital who spent his last penniless days wandering the boulevards he laid out and bemoaning the changes from his grand designs."

"So you think L'Enfant was a delusional *l'enfant*."

"I did until you gave me the original L'Enfant map along with Washington's orders for Stargazer."

Serena looked Tucci in the eye, to avoid any doubt. "You want me and Dr. Yeats to go under the capitol of the New World Order to dig up this globe and save America from the Alignment."

"No," he said firmly. "I want you to bring the globe back to Rome."

Serena stared at him, feeling a tingle of fear creep up the back of her neck.

"The world is a better place because of the United States of America," Tucci said. "But world civilizations come and go. The Church is forever. If America should collapse as an imperial power or morph into something else, we must be prepared to confront a new New World Order."

"But Conrad . . . Dr. Yeats."

"Is never to see the inside of that globe should you come upon it," Tucci said. "Not if you want to save America, or him."

10

ABBEY OF OUR LADY OF LETTERS

WESTCHESTER COUNTY, NEW YORK

While Serena had run off to Rome with his map, Conrad was in hiding at her safe house way out in the hills of Westchester County, two hours north of New York City. Here at the Cistercian Abbey of Our Lady of Letters, the brethren wore robes, sang Gregorian chants, and ran an Internet retailer called TonedMonks.com, which sold discounted printer cartridges and other office supplies to churches and charities.

According to the literature picked up by the school groups and tourists that visited the abbey by day, TonedMonks.com was the brainchild of the honorary abbot, "Father McConnell," a member of the Catholic lay leadership organization known as the Knights of Columbus. In his former life McConnell had been a billionaire Wall Street hedge fund manager who decided it was far better to have something to live for than enough to live on.

The real story, however, was in a dimly lit, dank crypt beneath the abbey, where Conrad was working around the clock with a team of researchers to crack the codes from his father's tombstone and Washington's letter to Robert Yates.

The abbey and its front, TonedMonks.com, apparently did for Serena and the Vatican what venture capital fund In-Q-Tel did for the CIA: fund new technology to advance the kingdom, in this case the Kingdom of God. The abbey's specialty was document analysis. Serena ran the nuns and a secret archive of historical documents out of nearby Mount Saint Mary's, a local Dominican college on the

Hudson where she taught on occasion, while McConnell ran the brothers and analysis in these crypts beneath this abbey.

The monks also made a mean espresso, and by his third day codecracking Conrad was sleepless, fatigued, and jittery as he reviewed his progress on the screen before him.

He clicked on his digital chart table and reviewed the three constellations of Boötes, Leo, and Virgo. Using a digital pen he connected the alpha stars from each constellation—Arcturus, Regulus, and Spica—to draw a triangle.

He then called up a second window on his desktop, a scan of the terrestrial L'Enfant map, and placed it next to the celestial map. He used his digital pen to connect the three key markers on the terrestrial map labeled "Presidential Palace," "Congressional House," and "equestrian statue to honor Washington." Those were the early monikers for the White House, U.S. Capitol, and Washington Monument.

These, too, formed a triangle.

As he suspected all along, the star map mirrored key landmarks on the ground. The White House was aligned to the star Arcturus in the constellation Boötes, the U.S. Capitol to the star Regulus in the constellation Leo, and the Washington Monument to the star Spica in the constellation Virgo.

But a triangle pointed nowhere.

That's what had stumped Conrad at the beginning. In the past he had used star maps to help find a specific location on earth—a secret chamber under the left paw of the Sphinx in Egypt, for example, or the Shrine of the First Sun in Atlantis. But this star map might as well be a circle, an endless loop. A star map was supposed to point to a specific location on earth.

Or a date in history.

That's when it all clicked for Conrad: These three key monuments along the Mall were not only each aligned to certain stars, but collectively to a celestial clock, to a single moment in time and space that any astronomer—or astro-archaeologist—conversant with the precession of equinoxes would know comes along only once every twenty-six thousand years.

It took him a few hours to work the astronomical calculations and correlate them with the astrology of L'Enfant's day, always a tedious task. That was because astrology was a bogus science, based on discredited beliefs. But it was upon those beliefs that ancient pyramids and monuments were once built. So not only did Conrad need to know some hard science, he had to reconcile it with the flawed worldview of a structure's builders during a particular era in history.

Finally, he was done.

Conrad typed in the password to launch his program and watched the screen. The triangles of the celestial and terrestrial maps slowly began to merge, the former on top of the latter. As they did, a digital calendar at the top of the desktop screen flashed like a cosmic odometer.

"Behold, the secret design of Washington, D.C.," he announced to himself.

He stared intently as the terrestrial and celestial triangles became one and the calendar clock froze at 07.04.2008.

July 4, 2008.

Conrad let out a breath. That was only five days away.

What's going to happen in five days?

"I'm wondering the same thing," said a voice from behind.

Conrad turned to see the abbot, Father McConnell, looking over his shoulder. Conrad must have spoken aloud. That or he was going crazy, which by the looks of his surroundings was becoming more plausible by the day.

"So you broke the astrological code, Dr. Yeats."

"The first level," Conrad said. "There's more to everything than meets the eye."

"There always is, son."

Conrad asked, "When is Serena coming back to return my terrestrial L'Enfant map with the Stargazer text on the back?"

"Tomorrow. Meanwhile, I found something for you from the archives at Mount Saint Mary's."

McConnell showed him a text written by Pierre L'Enfant in March of 1791, just after arriving to begin his preliminary survey. His work, L'Enfant wrote, would be like "turning a savage wilderness into a garden of Eden."

Conrad said, "So you think Washington's use of the term *savage* is referring to the original L'Enfant map Serena took, and that the map will show us the way to whatever we're supposed to find?"

"That's my bet," McConnell said. "But you don't look so sure."

"I think that's partly right. I get the impression that this savage is a person, but we'll need more to go on."

"Then we'll keep looking and leave you alone." McConnell walked away.

Conrad felt like he was getting his second wind after his breakthrough with the star map code. He was afraid he'd lose momentum if he stopped.

He turned his attention to the coded letter to Stargazer. The digital scan he had taken of the text remained a jumble of numbers.

763.918.1793

634.625. ghquip hiugiphipv 431. Lqfilv Seviu 282.625. siel 43. qwl 351. FUUO.

179 ucpgiliuv erqmqaciu jgl 26. recq 280.249. gewuih 707.5.708. jemcms. 282.682.123.414.144. qwl qyp nip 682.683.416.144.625.178. Jecmwli ncabv rlqxi 625.549.431. qwl gewui. 630. gep 48. ugelgims 26. piih 431. ligqnniphcpa 625.217.101.5. uigligs 2821.69. uq glcvcgem 5. hepailqwu eu 625 iuvefmcubnipv 431. qwl lirwfmcg.

280. qyi 707.625. yqlmh 5.708.568.283.282. biexip. 625. uexeqi 683. ubqy 707.625. yes.

711

He tried to use what little translation his father had given him to figure out the rest, but he didn't have enough to go on. He ran the message through every old military code Washington used as president and then commander-in-chief, all to no avail.

Finally, he tried something else: an obscure Revolutionary-era military code. It was a secret numerical substitution code invented in 1783 by Colonel Benjamin Tallmadge, America's first spy chief. Tallmadge substituted strings of numbers for words that Washington would insert into secret communiqués. "New York," for example, became the number 727 in Tallmadge code.

I wonder if there's a word for the number 763.

According to his database, there was: "Headquarters."

Suddenly the dateline at the top of the Stargazer letter made more sense:

Headquarters September 18 1793

But many words in the rest of the text didn't have a number code. For those words, he would have to use Tallmadge's letter-substitution cipher:

a b c d e f g h i j k l m n o p q r s t u v w x y z
e f g h i j a b c d o m n p q r k l u v w x y z s t

Conrad thought it a long shot since Washington was not the kind of spymaster to resort to sixteen-year-old codes on his deathbed. But he applied the letter-substitution cipher, and when he looked at the display of his digital chart table, the translation, clear as day, read:

Headquarters September 18 1793

To Robert Yates and his chosen descendent in the Year of Our Lord 2008:

My sincerest apologies for any pain I have caused you and your family. If we do not deceive our own men we will never deceive the enemy. Failure might prove the ruin of our cause. There can be scarcely any need of recommending the greatest caution and secrecy in a business so critical and dangerous as the establishment of our republic.

The fate of the world is in your hands, and your reward is in Heaven. The savage will show you the way.

General Washington

Conrad was so excited he accidentally knocked his coffee mug off the table and it shattered on the floor. He didn't bother to pick up the pieces. He was too busy staring at the translation, pondering its implications.

He quickly got back to work. The word *Headquarters* appeared to be the Tallmadge translation for the mysterious number 763 engraved on his father's tombstone. That solved that mystery, only to raise another: What did *Headquarters* actually mean?

Then there was the date: September 18, 1793. That was a good six years before December 14, 1799, the night Washington died. Had Washington written the letter years earlier and only released it on his deathbed? Or had he written the letter the night he died and the date carried some significance for Robert Yates?

The phrase "the fate of the world," meanwhile, looked like a double entendre to Conrad. He didn't know what "the world" meant but sensed it was important, and that the key to unlocking both it and the "reward in Heaven" was the "savage" Washington mentioned.

Sun sets over savage land.

He remembered the message his father left him from the tombstone along with the number 763 and the astrological symbols. It was almost as if his father wanted to draw special attention to the word "savage" in case Conrad never found the L'Enfant map.

So who is the savage? he was wondering when McConnell breathlessly walked up to him with a document.

"We pulled this from the archives," he said. "It's dated the night of Washington's death on December 14, 1799."

Conrad took the letter and looked at it closely. It was a letter addressed to Bishop John Carroll and purported to be an eyewitness account of George Washington's last hours at Mount Vernon as seen by Father Leonard Neale, a Jesuit from St. Mary's Mission across the Piscatawney River.

From what Conrad could tell from the report, Father Neale was distraught that he wasn't allowed to perform last rites or baptize Washington before he died. Neither were the Episcopalians, Presbyterians, or Baptists. Only the Masons would be allowed to bury the body, Neale noted, even though Washington hadn't set foot in a Masonic Lodge more than a couple of times in the last thirty years of his life, nor practiced Masonry outside of a few public cornerstone-laying ceremonies.

The reason, according to Tobias Lear, Washington's chief of staff, was that while Washington believed the republic owed its freedom to men and women of faith, he had seen the sectarian strife in Europe and wanted no part of it for America. As a result, he would not allow himself to be allied to any particular sect or denomination.

But it was what followed in Neale's account that riveted Conrad:

> *Lear told me that it was Washington's duty to the unity of the republic that he be complimentary to all groups and to favor none, in death as in life. When I protested and asked if such duty meant a death of civility without Christian hope, he said, "Aye, even so." As I took my leave and wept, I saw Lear escort to Washington's bed chamber a runaway slave, Hercules, whose food I had occasion to taste. I had little chance to ponder this strange sight as the cries of the servants rang out in the courtyard, "Massa Washington is dead!" I was nearly run over by three horsemen—the slave Hercules with two military escorts.*

Conrad reread the text to be sure he got everything right. Then he looked at McConnell. "So you believe that Hercules delivered the Stargazer text with the L'Enfant map on the back to my ancestor Robert Yates. You think Hercules is the savage?"

"Maybe." McConnell called up a portrait of Hercules.

Conrad looked at the picture of the slave with a proud look and fine clothing. There probably weren't too many slaves in those days who merited a portrait.

"Hercules may have delivered the Stargazer letter to my ancestor Robert Yates," Conrad said, excitedly. "But he's not the savage we're looking for."

Conrad called up another portrait, and McConnell did a double take.

The Washington Family was a gigantic life-size portrait of President Washington and his wife seated around a table at Mount Vernon with Mrs. Washington's adopted grandchildren. Spread across the table was a map of the proposed federal city. To the left of the family stood a celestial globe and to the right a black servant. In the background, open drapes between two columns framed a magnificent view of the mighty Potomac flowing to a distant, fiery sunset.

"This is hanging in the National Gallery of Art?" McConnell asked.

Conrad nodded. The map on the table was practically a live-scale model of the L'Enfant map to Stargazer. And the celestial globe and servant completed the picture.

"That slave isn't Hercules," McConnell said. "That's Washington's valet, William Lee. He's not the savage."

"No, he's not," Conrad said. "The painting is the savage."

McConnell looked confused. "Say what?"

Conrad clicked on the link with information about the painting and up popped the window:

> *Edward Savage*
> *American, 1761–1817*
> ***The Washington Family**, 1789–1796*
> *oil on canvas, 213.6 x 284.2 cm (84 3/4 x 111 7/8 in.)*
> *Andrew W. Mellon Collection*
> *1940.1.2*

"The savage is the artist Edward Savage," Conrad said triumphantly. "And this painting is Washington's way of pointing us to whatever it is he wants us to find."

11

The Washington Family.

As the Gulfstream 550 began its descent over the Atlantic toward the northeastern tip of Long Island, Serena rubbed her tired eyes, opened her window shade, and took another look at the high-resolution printout of the Edward Savage portrait from the image that McConnell had e-mailed her. The original oil, which she had seen herself in the National Gallery of Art in Washington, D.C., was larger than life, like America itself. Seven feet tall and nine feet wide, the picture was the only group portrait of the Washington family developed from live sittings.

"The savage will show you the way," she muttered to herself. "How could I have missed it?"

There was the celestial globe, plain as day, along with a map and clues to its final resting place. The answer was right in front of her, if she could just crack the portrait's secret. If the L'Enfant confession was to be believed, she and Conrad had four days to unravel this prophecy before America would go the way of Atlantis.

She looked closely at the Washington family sitting around a map of the federal city. According to Savage's catalogue, Washington's uniform and the papers beneath his hand were allusions to his "Military Character" and "Presidentship." With the L'Enfant map in front of her, Martha was "pointing with her fan to the grand avenue" —Pennsylvania Avenue. Their two adopted grandchildren, George Washington Parke Custis and Eleanor Parke Custis, along with a black servant, filled out the scene.

Well, it's no Mona Lisa.

However iconic today, *The Washington Family* was hardly accurate in its details, let alone any sort of masterpiece. In the seven long years it took to complete the portrait, Savage had never even seen Mount Vernon. That explained the two columns in the background. They didn't exist. As for members of the Washington family, Savage apparently took individual portraits of each family member in his studios in New York City in late 1789 and early 1790 after Washington's first inaugural. He then threw them all together in his imagined scene at Mount Vernon.

That would explain the awkward grouping of the family and their stiff poses. Each one stared off into every direction but the map on the table.

Conrad, however, had another explanation.

According to the report McConnell had e-mailed her, Conrad insisted that this bland portrait contained a great secret, one that Washington needed to get just right to preserve for centuries. And Conrad had demonstrated a simple test at the abbey to prove to the monks that the firm hand of George Washington was behind Savage's seemingly slapdash composition.

Repeating Conrad's experiment, she laid the picture flat on her tray table and with a marker drew two diagonal lines across opposite corners—one giant "X." Smack-dab in the center of the portrait where the lines intersected was Washington's left hand resting on the L'Enfant map.

The controlling hand of George Washington.

This "secret geometry," Conrad argued, was a sure sign that Washington wanted to show that nothing about this portrait was left to chance. Rather, he was communicating an important message.

And she had to agree.

Conrad Yeats, you clever wanker.

The question, of course, was what that message could be. And clever as Conrad was, she knew he would never guess that "the fate of the world" Washington referred to in his letter to Stargazer was the location of the mysterious globe that America's first president had buried somewhere under his eponymous capital city.

Or would he? She had underestimated Conrad before, only to regret it later.

Impossible, she concluded. Not without knowledge of the L'Enfant confession. Which she possessed and Conrad did not.

Using Conrad's experiment with Washington's left hand as a clue, she decided to take a fresh look at the portrait and what he was doing with his right hand. It was resting on the shoulder of his adopted grandson, a symbol of the next generation, who in turn rested his hand on the globe.

Just as interesting was what the boy was holding in his hand: a pair of compasses, Masonic symbols of the sacred triangle. It was as if he was about to measure something on the L'Enfant map.

An unbroken chain from the globe to the map, she marveled, *with nobody to witness it save for the black servant.*

Truly, Washington intended this portrait to work with the original L'Enfant map to lead Stargazer to the final resting place of the celestial globe.

All of which made Serena wonder about the more important question that Cardinal Tucci had warned her neither she nor Conrad should ever try to answer:

What was *inside* the globe?

Serena stepped off the plane at the Montauk airstrip to find a sober McConnell waiting for her with a black Mercedes. Dressed in a dark business suit, he stood coolly in the late June heat and opened a door for her.

Serena rode in the back of the town car with McConnell while Benito drove them through the pristine woods and moorlands. The land had once belonged to the Montauk Indians until the federal government of the United States took it a century ago and built a now-abandoned military installation. All that was left of the base now were the ruins of an old, enormous SAGE radar dish and the airstrip. Private jets owned by wealthy men like McConnell could land without much attention.

"So how is our friend Dr. Yeats?" she asked.

"Popular."

He handed her a printout of an FBI alert to various law enforcement agencies about Conrad's exploits last week. "They're not accusing him of anything. He's only 'a person of interest' at this point. Meaning they don't want any cop shooting him, or even letting his name leak to the press. They just want their eyeballs peeled in case he pops back up on the grid."

She looked at the picture of Conrad the FBI used. Somehow his face always came out looking far more menacing in photos than in person.

"Well, I can't wait to see him as a monk."

"I'm afraid he won't give you that satisfaction. In the process of deciphering the letter to Stargazer, Dr. Yeats cracked the meaning of 763."

Serena felt a pit in her stomach. "Please tell me he's still at the abbey, Father."

"I'm sorry." McConnell shook his head.

Serena stared at him. "You let him disappear on us?"

It was bad enough that Conrad probably suspected she had known about the Savage painting all along, which wasn't true, and that he couldn't trust her, which unfortunately, thanks to Cardinal Tucci, was true: her counter-mission was to let Conrad figure out the location of Washington's globe but take it herself back to Rome. It was the only way to protect him from the Alignment, she rationalized, even at the risk of him hating her forever.

"You know our mission statement requires that we can't keep anyone against his will, Sister Serghetti. But Dr. Yeats has little incentive to flee far from the only sanctuary he has right now. And a plainclothes security detail is following him."

She held up the FBI alert. "Others might be, too."

"Don't worry. Dr. Yeats is in disguise."

"Disguise?"

"You'll need one, too," he said. "It's in the bag on the floor."

Serena looked down at the black bag and pulled out a white bonnet, blue blouse, and white puffy skirt. She couldn't hide her reaction at this reversal and knew she would have to confess it later.

"And just where in bloody hell did Conrad go?"

12

HEADQUARTERS

NEWBURGH

Dressed in boots, britches, and a blue Continental Army coat, Yeats circled the large 25-foot-tall obelisk. It was made of fieldstone, like the Washington Monument, and built more than a hundred years ago by the Masons of Newburgh, New York, to commemorate Washington's greatest yet least-known military victory.

For it was here at Newburgh and not at Yorktown that the last battle of the American Revolution took place. On this very spot Washington was offered the chance to be America's first king by his officers. But Washington refused the crown, which he considered anathema to the cause of liberty to which he and his soldiers had dedicated themselves. His officers then attempted America's first and only military coup.

Washington quelled the coup at the eleventh hour by appealing to their better instincts with a speech that came to be known as the Newburgh Address. Moved to tears, his officers reaffirmed their support for their commander-in-chief.

It was the Revolution's darkest hour and Washington's greatest victory.

At least that's what the history books say.

Today, this last encampment of the Continental Army is known as the New Windsor Cantonment State Historic Site, a state park just off the New York Thruway. Here interpreters in period dress reenact military exercises and show what everyday life was like for the camp's 7,000 troops and 500 women and children. Nobody on the staff at the visitors center gave much thought to the lone "cast member" wandering about the 1,600-acre enclave and winding up in front of the obelisk memorial.

Except maybe one. A ruddy, middle-aged man dressed as a Redcoat had given Conrad a funny look inside the gracious Edmonston House when he asked for records of names of those who may have visited Washington at the encampment. There were none officially, but Conrad was allowed to peruse a few journals of the day kept by members of the military. It took hours, but he finally found an entry dated March 15, 1783, which mentioned Washington had a visitor, Robert Yates, in his base home shortly before addressing his mutinous troops.

But there was nothing about the nature of the visit that Conrad could find.

Now he stood outside, bending over to examine the inscription on the obelisk monument, trying to discern what business his nominal ancestor and George Washington had conducted under these extraordinary circumstances.

He found what he was looking for in an inscription on the granite tablet on the south face of the obelisk:

> *On this ground was erected the "Temple" or new public building by the army of the Revolution 1782-83. The birthplace of the Republic.*

The birthplace of the republic, he thought when a voice from behind said, "My, don't you look fetching in breeches."

He turned to see Serena dressed in a white bonnet, puffy white skirt, and busty blue blouse that simply could not safely contain her natural endowments.

"Don't you dare say a word," she warned him. "Or I'll introduce you to the pleasures of spending the rest of your life as a eunuch. Now, why are we here?"

Conrad walked her over to a long, rectangular log cabin with a line of small square windows, like a church without a steeple. Serena recognized it from her visitor's guide as a full-scale replica of the camp's original "Temple of Virtue," erected at Washington's command to serve as a chapel for the army and a lodge-room for the fraternity of Freemasons which existed among the officer corps. On the parade grounds beyond, a musket and artillery demonstration was under way. Every now and then she heard the boom of a canon.

"Picture the scene," he said. "The British are defeated at Yorktown. End of war, happy ending. All the same, things aren't looking so good in early 1783. The peace negotiations in Paris are dragging on and on. Congress is balking about the army's back pay, pensions, and land bounties. High-ranking officers led by Major General Horatio Gates, Washington's second-in-command and commandant of this Cantonment, threaten to ruin the cause of independence by mutiny."

"Right, so he confronts them in the Temple of Virtue with his famous Newburgh Address," she said, wishing right now she had Conrad's and Cardinal Tucci's encyclopedic knowledge of American history.

"Except the speech doesn't work and his words fall on deaf ears," Conrad said. "So with a sigh he removes from his pocket a letter from a member of Congress that he wants to read to them. But he has trouble reading it and reaches into another pocket and brings out a pair of new reading glasses, which he has never worn publicly. Then he says, 'Gentlemen, you will permit me to put on my spectacles, for I have not only grown gray but almost blind in the service of my country.' "

This much Serena knew from the visitors guide. "Yes, and moved to tears by the unaffected drama of their venerated commander's spectacles, the officers vote to affirm their loyalty to Washington and Congress. The Newburgh conspiracy collapses. A month later the Treaty of Paris is signed and the eight-year War of Independence comes to an end. Washington resigns his commission and retires to Mount Vernon. The army disbands. Everybody goes home. End of story. You have a point, mate? Because this blouse is itchy."

"What if old George's bit with the spectacles didn't work?" Conrad asked. "It's really hard to believe it did if you think about it. What if this wasn't the birthplace of the republic? What if this was the birth of the empire and this group called the Alignment?"

"You're reaching, Conrad," she said. "You haven't even told me how you came up with Newburgh in the first place."

"The number 763 on my father's tombstone. You know, the code you were going to give me if I helped you."

Serena felt the intended sting of Conrad's remark. "I thought the Tallmadge code you used on the Stargazer text translated 763 as 'Headquarters.' Washington had many headquarters throughout the Revolution."

"But Tallmadge invented the code for Washington in 1783, when Washington was encamped here at Newburgh," he said, looking about. Serena could tell he was oh, so close to putting his finger on it. "This is where the paths of my family and Washington intersected. That's why Robert Yates stormed out of the Constitutional Convention in Philadelphia six years later and then wrote a book called *Secret Proceedings and Debates* about the formation of the U.S. Constitution. Something happened here."

Obviously something happened, Serena thought. *Otherwise this historical state park wouldn't exist and we wouldn't be standing here dressed like fools*.

"Just think about it, Serena," he said. "Washington delivered everything the Newburgh conspirators demanded. The soldiers got their pay. The oldest military hereditary society in the United States was formed with the Society of Cincinnati. Then the U.S. Constitution was ratified, establishing a strong national government and military."

Which was all true, Serena realized.

According to her literature, Washington served as the first president general of the Society of Cincinnati from 1783 until his death in 1799. The Society was named after the Roman farmer-general Cincinnatus, who like Washington centuries later left his fields to lead his republic into battle. Its noble motto: "He gave up everything to serve the republic." These days Serena knew the Society of Cincinnati to be a decentralized and outstanding charitable organization, one that she had worked with on occasion. But she wondered if originally it had been something more. Perhaps the Alignment had forced Washington's hand into creating for them a new host so they would leave the Masons, much like the biblical account of the demon that Jesus cast out of a man and into a herd of pigs. By the time Washington died in 1799, the Alignment may well have abandoned the Society if they had succeeded, as Washington feared, in penetrating every level of the new federal government. Thus his warnings to future Americans.

Serena said, "You think Washington cut some kind of deal with the military, something that's coming home to roost now."

"In four days," he said, staring at her with his warm, intense hazel eyes. "But we won't know for sure until we find whatever Washington buried under the Mall in D.C."

Serena gasped. *He knows.* "What are you talking about?"

"We're looking for a celestial globe," he told her. "Just like the one in the Savage portrait. Washington buried it for his ultimate sleeper agent, Stargazer, to recover at the end of time. By some cosmic joke, it appears that I am Stargazer. And only when I find this celestial globe will I fulfill my mission."

Suddenly it hit her. Not only did Conrad figure out what they were looking for, he knew where it was! How did he know?

"You know where the globe is buried?" she asked, thunderstruck.

"You had the answer in your hands all along. Do you have my letter from Washington? I thought I saw something in there," he said playfully.

He was referring to the cleavage her blouse exposed. Embarrassed, she turned her back on him, retrieved the letter and handed it over.

"Father Neale told Bishop Carroll that he saw the slave Hercules leaving Washington's chamber just before Washington died on December 14, 1799." He unfolded the letter with the map on back, looking around to make sure nobody was watching. "But the letter itself is dated September 18, 1793. See? That's the date he buried the globe."

Serena nodded anxiously, berating herself for having missed the discrepancy in dates. "It's got some astrological significance, doesn't it?"

"Enough significance that Washington chose that date to lay the cornerstone for the U.S. Capitol—on the hill that Bishop John Carroll's brother Daniel sold him."

With that, everything came together, wholly and horribly.

"The globe is in the cornerstone of the U.S. Capitol," she said.
Conrad nodded. "And I'm going to steal it."

An hour later they drove south out of the New York tri-state area in separate cars, Conrad in McConnell's black Mercedes making a list of everything he'd need for his operation, Serena in her limo with Benito calling ahead to make sure the new safe house would be ready.

As Conrad and Serena headed toward their designated rendezvous in Washington, D.C., the man in the Redcoat costume was sitting in Horatio Gates's old headquarters at Edmonston House, calling a number in Virginia as he looked at a picture of Conrad Yeats he had torn from his fax machine the day before.

"This is Vailsgate," he said. "I need to get a message to Osiris."

13

PENN QUARTER

WASHINGTON, D.C.

Dressed in a fresh Armani suit that Serena had provided with his new cover, Conrad stood at the rail of the penthouse balcony and listened to the sounds of a summer jazz concert drifting up from the glowing fountains of the Navy Memorial plaza. He looked out at the lit-up dome of the U.S. Capitol, rising above the National Archives like a glowing moon.

It would have been a perfect evening, Conrad thought as he swirled his wine. If only Serena wasn't a nun and true romance between them hopeless. If only big Benito wasn't standing guard by the door.

"We should have more dates like this," he told Serena as he walked back inside. "Definitely a step up from the abbey."

The penthouse atop the Market Square West Tower overlooked Pennsylvania Avenue, halfway between the White House and the U.S. Capitol. It once belonged to the late Senator Daniel Patrick Moynihan of New York. Now it belonged to yet another one of Serena's mysterious patrons. This one was an architect whose firm had a hand in the construction of the new underground Capitol Visitors Center and who had provided them with blueprints of the Capitol Building dating back to William Thornton's original 1792 design for the building.

"This is crazy, Conrad." Serena looked up from the pile of schematics spread across the large dining table. "The U.S. Capitol has to be one of the most heavily guarded structures on the planet. You're never going to pull this off. You may not even come out alive."

"I'll get the globe and whatever's inside it," he told her calmly. "All you have to do is get me inside the Capitol, and I think your friends at Abraxos have already done that."

He tapped the special identification pin on his lapel, made for him courtesy of an executive at a company of ex-CIA types who handled covers for the agency and were now handling Conrad's cover pro bono for Serena.

"As one of 435 relatively anonymous members of Congress, I get to bypass security. So for tonight, let's pretend I'm a powerful lawmaker and you're my sweet little intern who is going to get me into a lot of trouble."

She gave him her "not-a-chance" death stare. "I can get you in, Conrad. But how the bloody hell are you going to get out?"

He could tell where her intensity was coming from. She really didn't think he was coming back.

"I'm going to trigger a false positive result for chemical agents. Doesn't take much more than household Lysol to set off the alarms in the Capitol if you know where the sensors are. I'll clear out the whole building and escape in the process."

Serena raised an eyebrow. "With the globe under your arm?"

"I told you, I've taken care of my exit strategy."

"No, Conrad, you haven't told me bloody much of anything. You forgot to mention, for example, that the U.S. Capitol doesn't even have a cornerstone. Not one that anybody has been able to find after two hundred years of excavations."

"True." Conrad leaned over her shoulder and saw that she was studying the 1793 map of the U.S. Capitol foundations by Stephen Hallet. "You'd think that the most technically advanced nation in history would know where it laid its first cornerstone."

"So what makes you think you're going to find this cornerstone where everybody else has failed?"

"Because I'm not everyone else," he said. "But then you knew that since you measured this suit perfectly. Let's say I get rid of this and we go up to the roof. There's a pool if you want to take a dip."

He smiled and offered her some wine. But she wasn't biting, and his mock bravado did little to erase the furrow in her brow.

Serena returned to the Hallet map, all business. "History records that Washington laid the cornerstone at the southeast corner of the building in a Masonic ceremony. But nobody knows if that was the southeast corner of the original north wing that went up in the 1790s or the southeast corner of what would eventually become the entire Capitol Building."

"Neither," he told her. "The Masons typically lay the cornerstone in the northeast corner of their buildings."

"I've crossed all the records, Conrad. Washington definitely laid the cornerstone in the southeast corner."

"Look." Conrad guided her hand across the Hallet map. "Here's the original north wing of the Capitol, which was built first. And here right next to it is the proposed central section, which would ultimately support the dome and connect the north and south wings."

"I can see that, mate."

"Really?" He guided her finger to the southeast corner of the north wing, where Conrad was betting Washington laid the cornerstone. "What do you see now?"

"Holy Mother of God," she said, staring at her finger. "The southeast corner of the north wing is also the northeast corner of the central dome section."

"And the dome represents not only the heart of the U.S. Capitol, but of the entire city of Washington, D.C., as well," he said. "So my location for the cornerstone is both historically accurate and Masonically correct."

Still she refused to let go of her doubts. "Very clever," she said. "But a lot's changed since the cornerstone was laid. For starters, everything built on top of your cornerstone was razed to the ground by the British in the War of 1812. And the original turned out to be so heavy the entire East Front of the building had to be rebuilt—directly over your bloody cornerstone—just to hold the thing up. So how are you going to find it under all that modified rubble?"

"Come with me."

He took her hand and they walked out onto the balcony thirteen stories above Pennsylvania Avenue. The concert was still going on down in the plaza, and Serena looked positively radiant, the view marred only by the FBI building looming behind her.

"This is supposed to be the city's grand avenue, linking the White

House to the U.S. Capitol," he said. "By design the buildings were supposed to be within each other's line of sight. And for years they were, until the Treasury Building went up and obstructed the view."

"Money usually does," Serena said, still letting him hold her hand. "But the symbolism was that the executive and legislative branches of the American government could keep a watchful eye on each other. I get it. So what?"

"So this terrestrial arrangement is mirrored in the heavens," he said. "Look up at the stars. There's the star Boötes over the White House. And over there is Regulus over the U.S. Capitol. See?"

"Actually, Conrad, I can't."

"The city lights make them harder to see. But they're there, and there's an invisible radiant connecting them right over our heads."

She raised an eyebrow. "Stars I can't see? Connected by an invisible radiant? Does this work on other women?"

She was joking, but he could hear the tension in her voice. For all her spirituality, Serena Serghetti was the most practical, down-to-earth woman he had ever known. She was scared for him, and all his mumbo-jumbo wasn't going to change that.

"All I'm saying is that Pennsylvania Avenue by design extends to the center of the U.S. Capitol, somewhere under the basement crypt, which is directly below the rotunda, which is directly below the Capitol dome, which itself is a representation of the celestial dome."

Serena looked frustrated and upset. "I told you, Conrad, the shape of the hill beneath the Capitol has been altered over the centuries with all the terracing, let alone the structure above."

"But the stars haven't, Serena. Which is why you and the feds can't find the cornerstone. You're looking at blueprints. I'm looking for the *intended* center of the dome. And my cosmic radiant in the sky, with the assistance of the Pentagon's Global Positioning System, is going to lead me to the cornerstone and the celestial globe."

Serena took a deep breath and looked him in the eye. "Now how can I argue with a man who has the logic of Don Quixote. Or is it Don Juan? It's so hard to tell with you."

She wiped an eye, and Conrad couldn't tell if it was a tear or the wind.

"Maybe a nightcap would clear things up for you," he said. "After all, this could be my last night alive."

"I hate you," she said and punched him hard in the chest.

Laughing, he rubbed an aching rib. "So why save America?"

She looked conflicted. "Because the cliché is true: America is the world's last best hope."

"I thought you believed Jesus was."

"I meant right now, politically, America is the best we've got for the unencumbered work of the Church and freedom of religion, which isn't going over too well in other parts of the world like the Middle East and China."

"Is that you or Rome talking?" he asked, hoping to raise her ire and get her worries off him. "Because there are some people, mostly in Europe, the Middle East, and Asia, who feel that the Church *is* the problem and that the world would be better off without it."

His ploy seemed to be working.

"The Church, however corrupt an institution, is a symbol of the kingdom of heaven in a world that is passing away," she said. "As such it stewards the eternal, life-changing message of redemption."

"Oh, so the Church is the last best hope?"

She looked him in the eye, lost in some dark thought, and then glanced away.

"No, Conrad. Unfortunately, as things now stand, you are."

Scary thing was, Conrad felt she really believed it, because she started to cry softly. He held her tight in the dark and looked out at the dome of the Capitol glowing in the night, wondering if she was in his arms for the last time.

PART TWO

JULY 1

14

U.S. CAPITOL BUILDING

WASHINGTON, D.C.

Inside a secret room in the Capitol, Max Seavers sat before congressional leaders with officials from the intelligence community and Health and Human Services. Three years ago, as the Chairman and CEO of SeaGen Labs, he had told this same group that a bird flu pandemic could one day kill millions of Americans. This morning, as the head of DARPA, he was there to announce that that day had come.

"This was taken yesterday from a village in the northeastern province of Liaoning in China," he said, wrapping up his confidential briefing with a slide stamped "top secret" across the bottom.

The slide showed Chinese health officials in protective gear burning the bodies of men, women, and children outside a poultry farm.

"As you can see, our intel raises serious questions about Chinese disclosure of the spread of bird flu among their population. They want nothing to cloud the upcoming Olympic Games next month. And they have already warned us that any attempt to publicize our concerns will be taken as a political act to undermine the Games and international relations. Unfortunately, by then it will be too late. Worse, the Games themselves, with people attending from all over the world, may prove to be the ultimate launching platform for a global pandemic when they go back home."

Seavers moved on to his next slide. It was a grainy black and white.

"The Spanish flu pandemic of 1918, which was a form of bird flu, killed fifty million people. The new H5N1 mutation is far more dangerous today, targeting adults in the prime of life, and killing more than half of those it infects. No one in the world is immune, putting all six billion of the planet's human population at risk."

Senator Joseph Scarborough, the chairman of the committee, turned red with anger. He peered over his glasses at the man seated next to Seavers, an official from the Centers for Disease Control, and demanded, "And what the hell is the CDC going to do about this?"

"The messy medical reality is that people can spread flu a full day before they show symptoms," the official said, meekly tap-dancing around the fact that "nothing" was his real answer. "So even shutting U.S. borders against an outbreak at the Beijing Games offers no reassurance that a super-strain isn't already incubating here. Should an outbreak hit American shores, the best we can do is limit international flights, quarantine exposed travelers, and restrict movement around the country. That could slow the virus's spread and give us time to dispense our stockpiles of the SeaGen super-vaccine to limit the inevitable economic and social chaos."

The senator now fixed his gaze on Seavers. "I thought the SeaGen vaccine wasn't designed to fight this new strain."

"On the contrary, we've always known that human-to-human contact of the virus would one day be widespread. But advance preparation is always iffy because a vaccine developed to combat today's bird flu may be ineffective against tomorrow's mutation. SeaGen's smart vaccine solves that problem with its ability to 'dial up' or 'dial down' certain genes, modulating the immune system to combat whatever mutation the virus assumes."

"And how exactly does your vaccine 'dial down' a person's immune system?"

"Through a microbiobot inside the vaccine that can receive instructions via wi-fi signals."

"You mean from outside the body?"

"Yes, sir."

"What if somebody doesn't have the flu, Dr. Seavers? Could signals from the outside instruct this 'biobot' to dial down targeted genes?"

"Theoretically, I suppose, yes, but the chance—"

"Goddamn it, Seavers. You people did it again. You took federal dollars to develop a vaccine to save lives and instead you weaponized it. Now you want to give it to every American."

"Not yet," Seavers said. "The first step is to inoculate first responders. To keep a country's basic infrastructure working in the event of a pandemic, an estimated 10 percent of the population must be inoculated—including all doctors, nurses, police, and other emergency personnel—as soon as the virus strain is identified and the first batch of vaccine becomes available."

"Is that all?"

"And I'd want mandatory vaccinations of armed personnel and elected officials as well, since a pandemic could disrupt government and render the Twenty-fifth Amendment useless. If need be, we can scale up to the general population once the bird flu lands in the U.S."

Max Seavers and Joseph Scarborough stared at each other, the silence in the chamber thick. Behind the tension was the complexity of a symbiotic relationship in which Scarborough held the purse strings for the Pentagon while the Pentagon's contractors underwrote Scarborough's reelection campaign and lifestyle. Seavers often found it hard to tell when Scarborough was posturing for effect or genuinely incensed.

"As a former Boy Scout, 'be prepared' was my motto growing up," the senator said, and Seavers felt he was on the verge of getting what he had come for today. "As a senator, that sentiment rings true even . . ."

Seavers's BlackBerry, on silence mode, vibrated.

He glanced down at the text message. It was an official alert from the Capitol Police. The subject line read:

> *10:45 a.m.: "Subject: An Emergency Exists for the Capitol Building—Evacuate Building. Importance: High."*

Seavers could see vibrating phones throughout the chamber jumping on tables. Almost simultaneously, the doors to the chamber opened and Capitol Police officers rushed in from the corridor to direct people toward the exits.

He looked at Scarborough. The Senator, who hated being cut off by anyone or anything, stood up with a scowl and left the chamber.

As Seavers and the rest were hustled down the corridor after the senators, he saw the incoming Haz-Mat teams in protective gear and clicked the message header on his BlackBerry for details:

> *This is a message from the U.S. Capitol Police. If you are in the Capitol Building, then evacuate. Chemical sensors detect a biotoxin threat. Haz-Mat teams are responding.*
>
> *If nearby, grab Go-Kits and personal belongings. Close doors behind you, but do not lock. Remain calm. Await further instructions outside. Do not remain in the building.*

Seavers heard a loud whine and a thud and looked up. They were shutting down the ventilation system to prevent the spread of any biotoxins.

He tugged at the multisensor badge on his lapel. Developed by the counter-bioterrorism group at DARPA, the badge could detect the presence of biotoxins in the atmosphere in real time. That's because DARPA was able to package dozens of photothermal microspectroscopy procedures onto a single microchip, including the electrokinetic focusing of bioparticles. Durable, lightweight, and with no external power requirement, this "lab in a badge" provided an immediate visual indication of the presence of any contaminants.

Except there were no contaminants, according to his sensor.

Outside on the east lawn of the Capitol, Senator Scarborough was waiting for him, his face red and puffy.

Scarborough said, "This sure as hell better not be some stunt you're pulling to convince us to go ahead with your program, Seavers."

"Absolutely not, Mr. Senator," Seavers replied hotly. As a billionaire he hated begging for federal funding or agency approval, especially from politicians. They were worse than his private equity investors. "And I don't think there's anything to worry about."

"Why the hell not?"

"My sensor says so." He handed the senator his biodetector.

Scarborough turned it over in his hands and glanced at Seavers with the faintest hint of respect. "Maybe I should have one."

"I think you should. I think all senators should, along with a shot of the SeaGen vaccine."

Scarborough grumbled something about waving the white flag and walked off toward a cluster of his staffers who were waiting for him by a police barricade.

Seavers looked at his badge detector again. There was nothing, absolutely nothing in the air that was deadly, not even in trace amounts.

He looked back at the building. False alarms happened all the time in Washington, D.C. But something felt wrong as he paced outside the Capitol's east entrance. Beyond the police barricades, rows of news vans crammed the street, and he could hear the reporters breathlessly blathering on about nothing. There was little to report so far. Everybody was standing around talking or watching the Haz-Mat teams enter the building and people coming out: senators, staffers, and Serena Serghetti.

An alarm went off in his head, the one that never gave false readings. What was *she* doing here?

Then it hit him: *Conrad Yeats.*

15

A few minutes before the alarms went off, the public tour of the U.S. Capitol was running behind schedule. So Conrad was still inside the original north wing, impatiently standing outside the Old Supreme Court chamber, staring at a plaque that read: *Beneath this tablet is the original cornerstone for this building.*

Like most things coming out of Washington, D.C., the plaque wasn't entirely true, as the pleasant docent explained to the group, which included a dozen Boy Scouts from Wyoming.

"The plaque on the wall refers to the tablet on the floor before you, and the tablet on the floor only marks the spot where a former Architect of the Capitol once believed the cornerstone resided."

Conrad looked down at the stone, which was about four feet wide and two feet tall and embedded into the floor, and read the engraving:

LAID MASONICALLY SEPT. 17, 1932
IN COMMEMORATION OF THE LAYING
OF THE ORIGINAL CORNERSTONE BY
GEORGE WASHINGTON

"So we've got plaques commemorating stones in commemoration of other stones," muttered the scoutmaster next to Conrad in the back as the group finally headed to the crypt. "Am I missing something?"

"Just your federal tax dollars," Conrad replied and looked at his watch. The Capitol Police were probably already sending text alerts to higher-ups and it was all going to trickle down in a very loud display of alarms any second now.

The tour ended at the crypt under the rotunda, where George Washington was supposed to be buried. It was a vast chamber with 40 massive Doric columns of Virginia sandstone, upon which rested the rotunda and dome above, much like America itself rested on Washington. In the center of the black marble floor was a white starburst.

"This crypt is the heart of Washington, D.C., and the end of our tour," the docent said. "Following Pierre L'Enfant's design, the city's four quadrants all originate at the U.S. Capitol. The starburst on the floor of this crypt is the center."

The starburst marked what was to be a window into the tomb of George Washington beneath the crypt. The idea was that Washington could look up from his tomb and ultimately see his glorified self in heaven as painted on the ceiling of the Capitol dome. Only Washington wasn't in the tomb below—his widow Martha had insisted he be buried at the couple's Mount Vernon estate.

As the tourists took turns standing on the starburst, Conrad drifted off to the wide marble staircase nearby and walked down to the subbasement level of the Capitol, passing several glass-enclosed offices packed like mouse cages.

He took an immediate right back under the stairs and passed a sign that read "No visitors allowed," just as the public alarms went off.

Now he had to move fast. He had only minutes to find the cornerstone before the Haz-Mat teams reached the subbasement levels.

He glanced back at the small warren of offices behind him. Staffers, mostly scruffy middle-aged types with PDAs, were shaking their heads, gathering belongings and heading for the exits. Conrad proceeded up a few crumbling stone steps, passing a nuclear fallout shelter sign as he entered a long, yellow brick tunnel.

He pulled out his modified smartphone and looked at the screen with the schematics and GPS tracker. Conrad was the white flashing dot in the maze.

At the end of the tunnel was a black iron gate like something out of a medieval church, and beyond the gate the tomb intended for George and Martha Washington. The only thing inside the tomb was the catafalque, the structure on which the corpse of Abraham Lincoln, the first president to die in office, rested when he lay in state for public viewing in the rotunda after his assassination.

Conrad turned to his right and saw the rust-colored access door he was looking for. It was marked:

SBC4M
DANGER
Mechanical Equipment
Authorized Personnel Only

It had no handle or knob, but he thought he could pry it open. As he did, he heard the scrape of metal against stone behind him, and turned to see the metal door marked SB-21 on the opposite side of the tunnel open.

A technician emerged in a work outfit and a look of surprise when he saw Conrad. "There's an evacuation alert, sir."

"Yes, they're passing these out." Conrad pulled a surgical mask from his suit pocket. "Take it," he said and smothered it over the man's mouth.

Conrad pushed him back through the door, and the man crumpled to the floor next to some electrical machinery. Conrad closed the door behind him, picked up the chloroform-soaked mask and dragged the technician past a bank of equipment and exposed piping to a utility room.

Inside he found a single marble bathtub, a relic of the old Senate spa that offered members of Congress and their guests hot tubs, haircuts, and massages. He put the man inside the tub, closed the utility door and moved down to the old furnace area.

According to the GPS marker on his phone, he was near enough to the northeast corner of the central portion of the Capitol to use his pocket sonar. He popped what looked like a memory card into the slot atop the handheld device. A thermal-like image of red and yellow splotches against a glowing green backdrop filled the small screen.

DARPA had developed the pocket sonar for Special Ops forces searching for small underground structures like caves that could serve as hiding places for weapons of mass destruction or tunnels for smuggling weapons and terrorist infiltrators across borders. Conrad had adapted the sonar for exploring megalithic pyramids and temples in order to find and map his own secret chambers and passageways. Today he was looking for a hollow space in a foundation stone—the cornerstone.

He had done it once before, under remarkably similar circumstances, when he helped historians in Hawaii find a long-lost time capsule buried by King Kamehameha V in the cornerstone of the landmark Aliiolani Hale building. They knew the cornerstone contained photos of royal families dating back to Kamehameha the Great and the constitution of the Hawaiian kingdom. What they didn't know was its exact location. Conrad helped them find it within ten minutes, using his pocket sonar to locate the hollow spot in the northeast corner of the building.

He had to beat that record now.

Conrad watched the screen of the sonar as he made his way toward the southeast corner beneath the original north wing. For a second he thought he had something, but it turned out to be an old grating in the stone that led to the massive steam pipes.

There are miles of underground utility pipes that provide heat and steam from the Capitol Power Plant to the Capitol campus and surrounding areas. And these miles and miles of pipes were maintained by a team of ten employees from the office of the Architect of the Capitol.

Ten men to maintain miles of underground pipes.

His GPS tracker beeped and then he saw it, the dirt trench he was looking for. It was about three feet wide and four feet deep, dug by a previous Architect of the Capitol along with members of the U.S. Geological Survey. They had used metal detectors to look for the silver cornerstone plate beneath the stone, but had never found it.

If only they had used sonar, he thought. *If only they had dug a few feet in the opposite direction.*

Conrad aimed the sonar at the wall of large foundation stones to his right. The metamorphic sandstone had been ferried here on boats from quarries in Aquia, Virginia. And on the other side should be the northeast corner of the central section.

He watched the screen . . .

Ping!

He found a hollow space within the rock and made a crooked X on the stone with a marker. His hand was shaking.

The cornerstone of the U.S. Capitol. This is it! The very stone that Washington laid on September 18, 1793.

Based on the way it was set in the bedrock, it was slightly bigger than he expected—about two feet high and four feet wide.

This was the good part, he thought, the part the Hawaiians wouldn't let him do with the cornerstone back at the Aliiolani Hale. They said digging it up would destroy the building above, which was also a historic treasure. But you didn't have to dig it up to dig out what was inside.

He pulled out his pocket microwave drill, an incredibly useful tool originally developed at Tel Aviv University. The drill bit was a needle-like antenna that emitted intense microwave radiation. The microwaves created a hot spot around the bit, melting or softening the material so that the bit could be pushed in.

Conrad had used it beneath the Great Pyramid in Giza to slip a fiber optic camera into a previously closed shaft, much to the dismay of the Director General of the Egyptian Supreme Council of Antiquities, who liked to stage live "opening the tomb" spectacles for the American television networks.

If only this were televised, he thought, *I'd be an American hero, maybe get "Ancient Riddles" back on the air. The feds could keep the damn globe so long as I got credit for the find. Then Serena and I . . .*

The dream always got fuzzy in the end, because it was never going to happen with him and Serena. Not in this life, which was about to come to an abrupt end if he didn't finish this job.

With steady hands now, he began to bore a hole a centimeter wide through the sandstone, watching the tip of the drill bit glow an intense purple. The beauty of the microwave was that it was silent and didn't create dust. The only downside was the intense microwave radiation the drill produced. The shielding plate in front of the drill bit seemed awfully small to Conrad, who began to drip with sweat.

It was done in less than sixty seconds. Conrad cut the heat and pulled out the drill wire. He then snaked the fiber optic line through the hole and looked at the screen on his handheld device. The hair-thin cable emitted its own light and would give him a view inside the cavity of the cornerstone.

A few seconds later he saw it: nothing. The cavity was there, but it was empty.

Damn.

He leaned back in the dark, dumbfounded. Why would the Masons drop a recessed cornerstone and not put anything inside? It made no sense.

There was a movement behind him. Conrad turned. A man in a Haz-Mat mask stepped forward into the dim light. He removed his mask and reached for a radio.

"This is Pierce," he called in. "Alert sublevel 2, old furnace area. Suspect cornered."

"You people got here sooner than I thought," Conrad said, clenching his right fist around his handheld. "That's some nifty gear you've got."

"Who are you?"

"I'm you," Conrad told him and delivered a right hook to the man's temple that took him down.

The radio of the unconscious Haz-Mat technician squawked. The signal was breaking up in the subbasement, but Conrad heard enough to know he needed to get out, and he had known from the beginning he'd never get out the way he got in. Now, he could use the technician's gear for where he was headed.

As Conrad zipped up his Haz-Mat suit, a Capitol Police officer entered the old furnace area and saw the body on the ground. The CP drew his weapon and ran over. Conrad stood very still, pointing to the man on the ground.

"He was down here doing God knows what," Conrad said in a muffled voice through his mask.

The CP was bent over the body when he noticed Conrad's dusty wingtip shoes protruding from his newly donned suit, and quickly drew his pistol.

Conrad blocked the officer's arm and the gun fired. The sound of the shot inside the old walls was deafening. Conrad stiff-armed him in the neck, knocking him back against an electrical box, then raced for the grating to the network of old gas pipes.

He heard shouts and looked back to see a team of CP officers, rifles at the ready, running toward him, attracted by the sound of gunfire.

Conrad gave the grating a good hard yank and it came free.

The police were firing now and his mask was fogging up in the dark. A bullet ricocheted by Conrad's ear, sending him to the floor. He popped up again and, on all fours, lunged forward. A moment later he plunged into the steam tunnels.

16

By the time Max Seavers arrived on the scene at the old boiler room in the subbasement, a dozen Capitol Police were crowded around the piping entrance.

"What are you waiting for?" Seavers screamed.

But the Capitol Police officer halted his men and pulled out his radio to speak: "Suspect is in a Haz-Mat uniform and has entered the steam tunnels. Repeat, suspect is in the tunnels."

Seavers stared at him. "You're not going after him?"

"We won't even let our dogs go after him," the officer said. "Not down there. Too dangerous. All that crumbling concrete and carcinogenic asbestos. And our phones and radios don't work in the tunnels."

"This is a national security issue! That terrorist could be planting a suitcase nuke to blow up Capitol Hill!"

"That doesn't seem to be the case, sir, based on what we're seeing down here."

"And what the hell do you know?" Seavers said. "It was a CP officer who staged one of the last false alarms here a couple of years back. You know how they knew it was a CP officer? He was so stupid he couldn't even correctly spell out his 'anonymous' warning note."

"Easy, sir," said the CP officer. "The R.A.T.S. are coming."

"Rats?"

"Recon and Tactics Squad," the officer said. "A select group of us have undergone special training to access the miles of utility tunnels underneath the Capitol complex. They're arriving now."

Seavers turned to see the elite unit march up with their navy blue baseball hats, flak jackets that said R.A.T.S., and special night-vision Haz-Mat masks. The laser-sighted automatic machine guns in particular impressed Seavers, as he instantly recognized them to be German-made G36s by their distinctive translucent magazines. Their short-stroke gas system enabled them to fire tens of thousands of rounds without cleaning, perfect for use in the tunnels. And he especially admired the commanding officer's AG36 40mm grenade launcher.

"Well, it's about time," he said.

The knife-thin commanding officer lowered her mask to reveal a young, dark-skinned face. "I'm Sergeant Randolph, sir."

"Have you ever done this before?" he demanded.

She ignored him as she unfolded her classified schematics of the steam tunnels and reviewed choke points with her team.

"We won't have any radio signals down there," Sergeant Randolph said. "We'll stick to light signals. Converge at point C."

Seavers said, "Where is point C?"

"I'm sorry, sir," she said, folding up her blueprints and slipping them inside a hidden vest pocket. "But the Capitol Police can't provide any further details about how we protect the tunnels. You know, national security."

Seavers watched her put on her mask. She motioned a man to widen the open grating and a blast of scalding steam came out. Seavers covered his face and watched Sergeant Randolph and her R.A.T.S. vanish into the pipes.

17

Conrad ran through the dilapidated network of steam tunnels beneath Capitol Hill, hands up to brush aside falling debris from the crumbling ceilings. He could hear his heavy breathing inside his mask and feel the sweat drench his body. He had found the cornerstone but no globe, and right now his only mission was survival.

He knew that all the buildings in the U.S. Capitol complex could be entered through the steam tunnels. But he never imagined their state of repair to be this poor. Not after the feds just spent a billion dollars on the underground Capitol Visitors Center. They must have just sealed off the new construction and said to hell with the steam tunnels.

He came to a cross tunnel. Something inside prompted him to stop and listen. Besides a continuous low rumble in the background, he couldn't hear a thing. But when he looked over his shoulder, he saw the green glow of night vision gear.

He started to run.

A shot rang out, and he ducked as a bullet ricocheted off the tunnel wall. He froze as several chunks of the ceiling came down around him. Slowly he turned around and squinted in the dark.

A thin shadow was wafting toward him. He looked down and saw the glowing red dot on his chest.

Suddenly a beam of white light blinded him and a voice in a ringing alto shouted: "Hands up where I can see them!"

It was a woman's voice, and she was mad as hell.

Conrad put up his hands and heard a deafening crack. But he wasn't shot. It was the floor—it was beginning to crumble.

The policewoman yelled: "Stop!"

But Conrad stomped on the floor as hard as he could. His knees began to buckle. The tunnel floor gave way under him and he plunged into darkness.

Sergeant Wanda Randolph kept her G36 steady in spite of the tunnel collapse, both eyes peering through her electronic red dot sight. But when the smoke cleared, her man was gone.

Quickly but cautiously, she moved through the dust to the crater in the tunnel floor, coughing through her mask. Finger on her trigger, ready to unload a round, she pointed her G36 down and hit her high beams, bathing the rubble below in light. There was no suspect underneath the chunks of concrete.

There was, however, another tunnel, one not on her schematics.

"Sweet Jesus," she said, although she wasn't surprised.

Before she joined the Capitol Police, Sergeant Wanda Randolph spent two years in Tora Bora and Baghdad crawling through caves and bunkers and sewers ahead of American troops in search of Bin Laden and later Saddam Hussein. She was tall and lean, with narrow shoulders and hips that enabled her to slip through holes and places people just weren't created to go. And while dogs could sniff explosives with their noses, they couldn't see tripwires, so they sent her ahead of even the dogs.

It was a year later that ten employees who worked in the Capitol Power Plant tunnels sent a letter to four members of Congress to express their concern that there was no police presence in the underground tunnels. The tunnels provided steam to heat and cool the Capitol campus and ran from the Capitol Power Plant to the House and Senate office buildings, the Capitol and surrounding buildings.

Now she was "Queen Rat," chief of the Hill's special Recon and Tactics Squad. The mission of the R.A.T.S. was to police the crumbling, asbestos-lined tunnels that had become a giant health trap to federal employees and a gaping hole in national security. As dirty and humble as her life's work had turned out to be, she was the best at it and proud to serve the United States of America.

"All R.A.T.S., report," she called into her radio, but knew it was no use even before static filled her earpiece. She flashed her call sign twice into the dark. No response.

As usual, she was on her own.

She climbed down into the new tunnel, using the rubble like a staircase until she reached the bottom and straightened up with her G36 pointed ahead. She hit her high beam again and gasped.

The tunnel wasn't a steam tunnel at all, but something else, like something out of ancient Rome. With one arm still holding up her weapon, she ran her other hand along the stone wall, awed by the solid construction of the stonecutters. She had seen enough tunnels beneath centuries-old cities to know this tunnel was older than the steam tunnels above, which themselves were more than a hundred years old. For all she knew, this tunnel was older than the republic.

Either the government had forgotten this tunnel was here, or knowledge of its existence was way beyond her pay grade. In any case, she had an intruder to capture or kill, and she marched down the corridor.

About three minutes later she saw the perp in his yellow Haz-Mat gear standing before a fork in the tunnel, his back to her.

"Turn around, hands up, or I shoot in three," she shouted, her G36 up and locked on the perp. "One . . ."

His arms seemed to waver but he wasn't turning around.

She aimed the glowing red dot between his shoulder blades.

"Two . . ."

Now his right leg seemed to waver, but still he didn't turn around.

She took a breath and tightened her grip on the trigger.

"Three."

One of his arms came down and his body twisted toward her. She wasn't about to wait for him to get off a shot and pulled the trigger, letting loose a burst of fire.

The bullets hit her target in the chest, blowing him back into the tunnel.

She ran down the stone floor to the crumpled body, her G36

pointed at the mask. She lowered the barrel and lifted the mask to see that it was empty. The perp had shed the suit and strung it up.

She looked down one tunnel with her high beams and saw nothing, then down the other and saw a glint of metal. She gave a war cry and ran down the tunnel only to find a shiny vaultlike door at the end.

It was an emergency hatch. All the old sublevel hatches were replaced several years back with new ones. And like all the safety precautions in place in the tunnels, it was designed to keep people on the outside from getting in, not people on the inside from getting out.

She opened it and climbed out of the ancient tunnel and into a machinery room. A minute later she popped through a metal door into an underground passageway and startled a group of young Capitol pages. They were exiting the Capitol complex with their supervisors and heading back to their school on the top floor of the Jefferson Building at the Library of Congress.

At this point, Sergeant Randolph knew that even if she saw the perp she wouldn't know him now. She wanted to scream, but it would only scare the Hill staffers.

Her radio, now in range of the command post, squawked.

She picked it up and said, "Suspect's gone native. Time: 1304 hours."

The Jefferson Building at the Library of Congress was the most ornate building in Washington, D.C., the greatest library in history since the Library of Alexandria burned to the ground two thousand years ago. Besides a fifteenth-century Gutenberg Bible, there were ancient maps of Antarctica that showed the subglacial topography of the continent before it was covered with ice, complete with curious addenda by the U.S. Air Force. Then there was a nineteenth-century manuscript copy of U.S. Senator Ignatius Donnelly's worldwide bestseller *Atlantis: The Antediluvian World.* Most prophetic, perhaps, was a sixteenth-century essay of Francis Bacon's on "The New Atlantis," all about the New World and the land that would become America.

Not that any of that interested Conrad right now as he split from the procession of Capitol pages and passed through a deep arch into the library's central atrium a few minutes later.

The ornate Great Hall was flanked by two grand staircases and constructed almost entirely of white Italian marble. Floating 75 feet overhead was a spectacular ceiling with stained glass skylights, paneled beams, and 23-karat gold leaf accents.

The street exit was just a stone's throw away. He started for it when he saw several Capitol Police officers coming in, talking on their radios.

He turned around and ducked into a public restroom, where he removed his dirty suit jacket and jammed it into a trash can. Then he ripped off his fake goatee and threw cold water on his face. He rolled up the sleeves of his blue dress shirt and looked at himself in the mirror, a relatively new man. After he wiped the dust off his shoes, he walked back out into the Great Hall.

Seeing police at the security station by the main floor exit, he crossed the wine-dark marble floor and climbed one of the marble stairways to the second floor level. There a crowd was pressed against the glass overlooking the East Lawn of the Capitol across the street.

With the polite authority of a Library docent he pushed his way through the bodies toward the window. Then he looked down and realized he had a skybox seat to the mess he had made across the street—police vans, news crews, the works.

All for naught, he thought as he stared out the glass. He had followed his precious "cosmic radiant" in the sky above Pennsylvania Avenue to the dome of the U.S. Capitol only to find an empty cornerstone.

All that remained for him now was to wait for an opportunity to escape the Library, meet Serena at their designated rendezvous, and tell her that he had failed.

Even now, the Statue of Freedom atop the Capitol dome across the street seemed to be mocking him. Made of bronze, it was six meters tall and, standing on the dome, the tallest statue in D.C. since 1863. By law no statue was permitted to be taller. Maybe that's why the statue's back was turned to the Washington Monument rising high into the sky beyond.

Or maybe not.

He caught his breath.

The U.S. Capitol was built to face west. But the Statue of Freedom faced the Library of Congress in the east. In theory this reversal was decided on so that the sun would never set on the face of Freedom, but Conrad suddenly wondered if there was another reason.

He looked again at the gleaming dome of the U.S. Capitol under cloudy skies—the cosmic center of Washington, D.C. What if the cosmic radiant in the sky that paralleled Pennsylvania Avenue didn't end over the dome? What if it kept going? In his mind's eye, he extended the radiant to the east . . . to right about where he was standing in the Library of Congress.

He turned and walked back through the crowd toward the balcony overlooking the Great Hall and looked down twenty feet below. In the center of the marble floor was a giant sunburst, around which were 12 brass inlays of the signs of the zodiac arranged in a giant square.

This must be what the Masons wanted Stargazer to find: A marker of their own design, laid directly along the path of the city's central radiant.

Conrad could feel his heart beating out of his chest.

A zodiac in the shape of a square rather than a circle symbolically linked the constellations to the flat plane of the earth, not the vast space of the heavens. And a sunburst in the center, if he recalled correctly, represented the cardinal points of the compass.

Meaning the zodiac on the floor of the Great Hall was pointing to a hidden direction on Earth—or under the earth.

The Masons moved the globe. And it was right here, under the Library of Congress.

18

OFFICE OF THE SECRETARY OF DEFENSE

THE PENTAGON

THAT AFTERNOON MAX SEAVERS marched down corridor nine toward Secretary of Defense Packard's suite of offices on the third floor of the Pentagon. It had taken a half hour for his black Escalade to get there from the media circus at the U.S. Capitol on this overcast Monday afternoon, and he dreaded the inevitable confrontation in store.

This meeting had already been on the books. Seavers was supposed to debrief Packard after his testimony on the smart vaccine before Scarborough's committee. Only now, thanks to Conrad Yeats, Packard would be asking about what, if any, connection there was between the empty cornerstone beneath the Capitol and the bizarre codes on General Griffin Yeats's tombstone at Arlington, and how a dead American general and his elusive son could make them all look like jackasses.

Two MPs saluted as he approached the vault-like doors, and Seavers surrendered his BlackBerry to the receptionist before passing through. Packard's office was classified a SCIF, or sensitive compartmented information facility. No mobile phones, BlackBerries, or other wireless devices were permitted inside. The idea was to ensure that the most classified conversations could be held in this office in confidence, without fear of being overheard.

This afternoon the only other person in the room besides Packard and Seavers was Packard's intelligence chief, Norman Carson, Assistant Secretary of Defense C3I, who sat in one of two chairs in front of Packard's desk. A wiry egghead with thinning hair and a thinner sense of humor, Carson was in charge of all command, control, communications, and intelligence for the DOD, which these days pretty much covered all of America. He was also the executive agent responsible for ensuring the continuity of government should some unthinkable attack or natural cataclysm hit the United States.

Carson didn't bother to get up and shake hands when Seavers walked in, and Packard was already behind his stand-up desk. Seavers took his seat. The vaultlike doors closed heavily behind him in the lobby, then another set in Packard's office closed likewise, sealing them and whatever they said inside.

Packard glared down at Seavers from his desk, which looked like a giant lectern, the ultimate bully pulpit. "What the hell is going on, Seavers?"

"Security cameras in the Capitol confirm it was Conrad Yeats, Mr. Secretary. We ran the tapes through the facial recognition software. He circumvented security and bypassed the detection gates by posing as a congressman from Missouri."

"And the biotoxin scare?"

"Haz-Mat teams found an open bottle of industrial cleaning solvent in a janitor's closet. The vapors set off the false alarm. It was a diversion."

"Dammit, Seavers!" Packard said. "How the hell did you let Yeats get away?"

Seavers didn't flinch. "The Capitol Police, who are in charge of security, failed to apprehend Dr. Yeats when he escaped through the steam pipes under the complex. He popped up in the Jefferson Building at the Library of Congress. By the time the Capitol Police reviewed the security feeds, he had left the building."

Packard nodded gravely for effect, and Seavers resented this flogging for something outside his operational control, especially in front of Packard's lapdog Carson, no less. "All this after he found the cornerstone beneath the Capitol, something we haven't been able to do in two hundred years."

Seavers calmly replied, "And this is important to my initiative with the vaccine because?"

Packard ignored him and turned to Carson. "Norm, what do the symbols on the obelisk mean?"

Carson passed two copies of a leather-bound brief to Packard and Seavers that included four photos, each showing one of the obelisk's four sides.

"We worked up another interpretation of the astrological symbols," Carson said. "Based on Yeats's actions today, we now feel the symbols represent celestial counterparts to the U.S. Capitol, White House, and Washington Monument. Teams have already been dispatched to the White House and Washington Monument to search for their cornerstones."

Packard nodded. "And the number 763?"

"We confirmed it's the Major's code."

"The Major's code?"

"Major Tallmadge," Carson said. "He was George Washington's spy chief during the Revolution, although by the time he created this alphanumeric cipher system he was a colonel."

Packard said, "So Yeats is using a code more than 200 years old?"

"He's using, in effect, the DOD's very first code, Mr. Secretary."

"And what exactly does 763 stand for?" Packard demanded. "Should I be quaking in my boots like the president?"

The Pentagon's top intelligence chief said nothing, although the look in his eyes implied that, yes, they should all be quaking in their boots. "In general terms, sir, 763 is the numeric code for headquarters. Specifically, in this context, it clearly means this."

Carson wrote a name on a sheet of paper and slipped it to the SecDef. The SecDef picked it up and stared. "Oh, gawd," he groaned, and was about to crumple it up and toss it into his wastebasket until he thought better of it. "You mean the president's paranoia might have some basis in fact?"

"General Yeats seemed to think so, sir."

Seavers, unable to read the text on the paper Packard was holding, cleared his throat. "The president is paranoid about what, Mr. Secretary? I'm afraid I'm lost here."

"We all are if this prophecy is true." Packard pulled out a lighter and touched it to the corner of the paper.

Seavers sat forward on the edge of his seat and watched the paper burn. This stage of the briefing was news to him. "What prophecy?"

Packard said, "Let's just say we think George Washington buried something under the Mall, and every U.S. president since Jefferson has been trying to dig it up, all under the guise of building or restoring monuments over the past three centuries."

"Buried what?" Seavers pressed.

"Something very embarrassing," Packard told him. "Not just for this Administration, but for every president since Washington. Something that casts doubt on the American experiment itself, its origins and destiny. We have to stop it from coming to light."

Seavers could feel Packard studying him, clearly conflicted. Packard had brought him to DARPA to develop new vaccines and create the perfect soldier, impervious to chemical and biological weapons. That was his reputation as one of the world's greatest minds in genetic research. Coded tombstones and buried artifacts were not his forte.

Unless he knows about my great-grandfather, Seavers thought, and suddenly wondered if there had been more to his appointment at DARPA than he had given Packard credit for.

"Mr. Secretary," he said, breaking the silence, "it would help me a great deal to know what exactly you think Washington buried."

"A globe, Seavers."

"A globe?"

"A celestial globe," Packard said. "Probably about two feet in diameter. The kind of floor globe you find on a stand in the library of lavish estates."

"Like those Old World bar globes you open and inside you find liquor?"

Packard glared at him. "This has nothing to do with the Old World, Seavers."

Seavers could only shrug. "But how important can this globe truly be?"

Packard was adamant. "Nothing could be more important to the national security of the United States of America."

Seavers nodded to show he understood the gravity of the situation. "And you think Dr. Yeats has a shot at finding it?"

"He found the cornerstone of the U.S. Capitol, didn't he?" Packard began to pace back and forth behind his desk, obviously wrestling with some decision. "Seavers, I want you to find this thing before

Yeats does. Or let him lead you to it, I don't care. But if he does, he'll uncover a secret he's not authorized to know. Nobody is."

Seavers glanced at Carson, who looked shocked that Packard had assigned him the task, and said, "You'll give me what I need to do this job, Mr. Secretary?"

"The president has authorized me to have the entire resources of the federal government at your disposal," Packard said. "You've got the gizmos, I'll give you some muscle, your own black ops domestic response team." Packard looked at Carson. "Norm, your ass is covered. Just give Seavers whatever intel he needs to find Yeats. It's embarrassing that he's walking around D.C., which has more security cameras than galaxies in the heavens, and we still can't find him."

"I'll track down Yeats and whatever it is he's looking for." Seavers looked at Packard and Carson. "And Dr. Yeats can take whatever he knows to the grave and join his father."

"General Yeats may have been a four-star bastard, but I always tried to treat his son like my own. So I hope it doesn't come to that, gentlemen," Packard said. "But if it does, Conrad Yeats sure as hell isn't going to be buried at Arlington with full military honors."

19

MONTROSE PARK

ROCK CREEK NATIONAL PARK

It was set for 6 p.m. However things went down at the Capitol, Serena was to rendezvous with Conrad in Montrose Park at the edge of the vast Rock Creek National Park north of Georgetown. But it was half past six already, and there was no sign of Conrad. She was worried sick.

Carrying a backpack and dressed like a college coed in a white tank top, sunglasses, shorts, and flip-flops, Serena strolled past the tennis courts, picnic tables, and playground in search of what Conrad told her would be "an unmistakable celestial marker."

And suddenly there it was: the Sarah Rittenhouse armillary, a sundial of sorts. Actually, on closer inspection, it was a classic Greek celestial sphere comprised of three interlocking rings that represented the motion of the stars encircling the earth. The outermost band of the ecliptic featured the raised constellations of the zodiac. Piercing through the rings was an arrow that pointed to true north.

But still no Conrad.

She set her sunglasses atop her brushed back hair for a moment and adjusted the volume of her iPod as she waited, pretending to admire the armillary. It stood on a marble pedestal and according to the plaque was dedicated in 1956 in memory of some society woman named Sarah Rittenhouse.

"Sarah Rittenhouse was some matronly preservationist who saved this park from nasty developers back in the early 1900s," said a voice from behind her. "Reminds me of somebody I know."

She turned to see Conrad in a dress shirt and suit pants, a hard-cover book clutched in his hand. He looked like a university professor. "So where's the globe?"

"I'm fine, thanks." He stared at the celestial armillary. "This is where I first saw Brooke after you disappeared on me. She was walking her dog."

"We have all of three days to stop the Alignment," Serena said, frustrated. "Did you find the globe?"

"No, but I know where it is."

She started walking briskly away from the armillary, where they might be seen if they stood together too long. "You told me the globe was in the cornerstone of the Capitol."

"It was," he said, guiding them down a cobblestone walkway called "Lovers Lane" to the ravines of Rock Creek Park. "The Masons moved it for safekeeping."

"But it was already safe in the cornerstone, right?"

"Not after the British burned the Capitol down to its foundations during the War of 1812. I think the Masons felt they had to move it before the Alignment got to it. At least that's my guess."

"Your guess?" she repeated, unable to disguise her dismay. "And where do you guess the Masons moved it?"

"Under the Jefferson Building at the Library of Congress."

Serena shook her head. "That site was never in L'Enfant's original plans for the city."

"No, but the cosmic radiant cuts right through the Capitol dome to the Library's Great Hall."

Serena had heard enough. Time was running out and they had nothing. "You and your blasted radiant, Conrad! We could follow it around the world a dozen times and still never find the globe."

"But the Masons knew that," he said, and stopped them in their tracks near a stream that she assumed was the eponymous Rock Creek. "They knew they were 'going off the grid,' so to speak. So they left clues for Stargazer in the form of zodiacs."

"Zodiacs?"

"The Jefferson Building is a hive of them," he said. "Scholars have counted seven zodiacs, but the docents have counted eleven. I counted fifteen."

Serena stared at him. "Wait a minute. When did you count the zodiacs?"

"This afternoon."

She nearly screamed. "I'm out of my bloody mind wondering if you're alive, and you're loitering around the Jefferson Building after breaking into the U.S. Capitol across the street?"

"Calm down," he said, looking around and taking her by the arm. "I was already there, so I took advantage of the opportunity."

Serena angrily twisted her arm out of his grip. "Well, if you found the accommodations so comfortable, why didn't you just spend the night?"

"I thought of it. But I couldn't crack the zodiacs. Then I saw the central arch to the east of the main zodiac in the Great Hall. The top of the arch is inscribed with the names of those responsible for the construction of the Library, starting with Brigadier General Thomas Lincoln Casey."

Serena huffed. "And Casey is important because?"

"He was a Mason like Washington and L'Enfant," Conrad said. "He not only supervised the completion of the Washington Monument, but he also built the Library of Congress from the ground up."

They were deep in the ravines of the park now, and Serena was wondering where Conrad was leading them.

"So you believe that Casey and the Masons built the entire Library of Congress as some kind of cosmological citadel to protect the celestial globe?"

"I do."

"It's a nice theory, Conrad, but we need hard evidence to link Casey to the last known resting place of the globe. You said it was the cornerstone of the U.S. Capitol."

"It was," he said. "And after the British destroyed the original north wing of the Capitol in 1814, it was Casey who wrote up the damage report for the Architect of the Capitol at the time, then Benjamin Henry Latrobe."

Serena knew the name of Benjamin Henry Latrobe. He had designed America's first cathedral in Baltimore for Archbishop John Carroll with input from Thomas Jefferson. Suddenly Conrad didn't seem so crazy.

"So that's when you think Casey and the Masons removed the globe from the ruins of the Capitol."

"Exactly."

"You were busy at the Library." She jabbed at the old hardcover book he held—*Elements of Astronomy* by Simon Newcomb. "Did you check out that book?"

"I'll bring it back when I break into the Library."

There wasn't much Serena could say at that point. There was no going back, and Conrad was determined to go forward. "So who is Simon Newcomb?"

"He was an admiral in the U.S. Navy and probably America's most brilliant astronomer of the 19th century," Conrad explained. "And years before Casey became Chief of the Army Corps of Engineers and built the Library of Congress, he was Newcomb's assistant. Amazing how everything connects, isn't it?"

"So you think by reading Newcomb's popular astronomy guide you'll tap the minds of the people who built the Library of Congress."

"That's the idea" he said. "Once D.C. started deviating from the original L'Enfant plan, the Masons had to find a way of communicating outside the hard landscape of astronomical alignments. So they resorted to symbols in the form of zodiacs. If I can reconcile the zodiacs with the Library's extensive renovation plans on file, I bet I can find a sealed-off access tunnel somewhere that will lead us to the globe."

Conrad paused to scope out the surrounding woodlands. Convinced they were not being watched, he stepped into some nearby brush. "Follow me."

Serena followed him through the dense foliage, her hands up to keep the branches from her face, wondering what he wanted to show her. They were off any beaten trail now. Conrad stopped a couple of minutes later in front of a small cliff in the ravines, and parted a curtain of vines to reveal the mouth of a cave.

"I used to hide out here as a kid," he told her. "There's an old Indian well in the back. The cave collapsed at least a hundred years ago, so my dad and I used to come out here and dig it out, bit by bit. Every spring we'd plant shrubs to cover any trace of the path."

Serena nodded. She wasn't even sure if she could ever find it again herself if she had to. But this cave was certainly a better safe house for Tom Sawyer here than the penthouse, which was surely under surveillance now.

She said, "Tomorrow night I'm at the Hilton for the annual media dinner and then the Presidential Prayer Breakfast the following morning. The day after that is the Fourth of July."

"I get it, game over," Conrad said. "I'm going to have to hit the Library of Congress tomorrow night at the latest if we're going to have any chance of nabbing the globe and making any kind of sense of it to stop the Alignment."

"Stop them from what, Conrad?" she pressed. "If we know what they're going to do, then maybe we don't need the globe."

"Oh, we need the globe," Conrad assured her. "And I'm guessing the Alignment is going to do what it failed to do in 1783."

"Stage a coup?" Serena asked. "American citizens would never sit still for it."

Conrad shrugged. "What if it's a coup and nobody knows it?"

Serena grew very quiet.

"Astrological symbols are quite different than astronomical alignments," she said softly. "They're open to all sorts of interpretations, not the clean lines and calculations you're used to. Admiral Newcomb may not shed enough light for you to find the globe."

"That's OK," Conrad said. "I know an old Mason who can help us."

"A Mason?" Although Serena knew that most Masons were constructive "builders" of structures and people, their secret society had been corrupted by the Knights Templar, warriors, to say the least. Worse, it now seemed clear that the Alignment itself had infiltrated and controlled the Masons at one strategic point during the American Revolution. Who knew how many of their lieutenants and informants they had left behind in the brotherhood? "Can you trust this Mason?"

"My father did."

"Like I said, can you trust him?"

"Serena, I can't even completely trust you. But our options are limited at this point. I don't even know if he's still alive."

Serena looked at Conrad, still stung by his comment about her being untrustworthy, though of course she was, wasn't she? "How are you going to find out?"

"I know someone who might know. I'll contact him at his office at 5 a.m."

"Your friend's in the office at 5 a.m.?"

"Yep."

"What are you going to do until then?"

"Camp out here," he said, looking into the cave. "You want to spend the night with me in the catacombs?"

Little did Conrad know, she thought, but she would like nothing more in this life than to hide out with him in a cave and never come out. And if God and people and the world around them didn't mean so much to her, she would.

"Tempting," she said. "But at this point it's best for both of us if I'm seen out and about and far away from you. If I can break away to join you and this Mason tomorrow, I will. But I'd rather be safe than sorry."

He gave her a funny look. "You said the same thing at Lake Titicaca."

Conrad was referring to when they first met years earlier in the Andes, and as she looked around these wild ravines she felt the same sense of mystery and foreboding.

"Well, you better have these." She removed her backpack and gave him a toothbrush, lightweight trench coat, and a change of clothing.

Conrad studied the underwear. "You know I prefer briefs."

"Please watch yourself, Conrad," she begged him. "This isn't some boy's adventure. Those are real bullets they're firing at you."

It was getting dark in the ravines now, and Serena turned to leave while she could still find her way out. As she began to weave between the twisted branches, she thought she heard Conrad whisper something. By the time she looked over her shoulder, he had disappeared into the darkness.

20

Later that night Max Seavers stood naked in the bedroom of his Georgetown house and looked at himself in the mirror. There was much to admire—his golden hair, sapphire eyes, aquiline nose, and strong chin, not to mention his rock-hard six-pack abs. This was not the face of a monster. Moreover, it was what one couldn't see in a mirror—his towering intellect, his genius—that was intrinsically noble.

Soon, he thought, *everybody will see it.*

He heard the shower in the bathroom turn off. He walked across the plush carpet to his bed, slipped under the sheets and waited for her. As he did, he mulled over the SecDef's directive about finding this thing that Washington had buried and marveled at the absurdity of it all.

For it was in another country, in another time, that his own great-grandfather was asked to help run an organization quite similar to DARPA and to pursue similarly bizarre research for his boss, Adolf Hitler.

Before and during the Second World War, Hitler had German scientists and archaeologists roaming the earth for evidence of the biological superiority of the Aryan race. Few were hard-core Nazis, but fewer still were about to spurn the overtures of the Führer and his ax man Heinrich Himmler, who in exchange for keeping them out of concentration camps offered these academics the kind of funding and resources no university could match.

The Ahnenerbe, as the think-tank was called, was an SS agency established to prove once and for all that Aryans were not just the "master race" or pinnacle of human evolution but also the "mother race" of human civilization. At its peak it counted more than 200 scholars, scientists, and staff among its ranks. And its teams fanned out across the globe in search of evidence in places like Lake Titicaca in Bolivia, the Canary Islands, the Greek Islands, even Tibet. All these places were alleged to have been built by Aryan colonists, and research efforts soon crystallized into one final quest to find the place from which those colonists came.

That place, they concluded, was Atlantis, and its location was determined to be Antarctica. If only they could find its ruins beneath the ice, they could prove once and for all the superiority of the Aryan race and the inevitable triumph of Hitler's Thousand-Year Reich.

Toward that end, Hitler sent U-boats to Antarctica, where teams of Nazis disembarked on the ice cap in search of ruins. They also planted Nazi flags still buried to this day in order to claim the last continent for Nazi Germany.

They came back empty-handed, of course, those who managed to come back at all. Many perished in the otherworldly cold. Those who survived had no relics to show for their pains. Some had no fingers or toes either, as they were lost to frostbite.

None of this surprised Seavers's great-grandfather, Wolfram Sievers, who considered much of archaeology the domain of crackpots. Whereas half of the Ahnenerbe was focused on the past, Wolfram was focused on the future, on genetics and human evolution. Much of his work was inspired by the American eugenics movement of the early part of the twentieth century.

Unfortunately, research required Wolfram to experiment on living subjects, which could be found in great supply among the Jews in the concentration camps. The results yielded a treasure trove of data and the creation of new biotoxins.

Hitler hoped to place the biotoxins in the tips of his V-2 rockets and launch them against the Allies. But the tide of war turned against Hitler and his Nazis, and the work of Wolfram was cut short.

In the end, Germany was split in two by invading Allied forces. "Good Germans" who had served the Ahnenerbe were free to resume their respectable chairs at elite universities. Some, like rocket scientist Wernher von Braun, were even invited to the United States to help the Americans land a man on the moon. "Bad Germans" linked to the Holocaust like Seavers's great-grandfather, however, were executed in Nuremberg for their "crimes against humanity."

Growing up in Southern California with relatives, Seavers hid his true paternity with shame. At Torrey Pines High School he announced his resolve to dedicate his life to creating vaccines that would eradicate pandemic diseases and extend human life. By the time he was a junior at Stanford, he got the backing of venture capitalists to launch his own biotech company back in San Diego.

He made billions but ran into trouble when America's religious fanatics got in the way of his stem-cell research, which required the destruction of aborted fetuses. They called him a baby killer, these Catholic and evangelical Christian hypocrites, who themselves benefited from his drugs and who carried out "God's work" in Third World countries by administering his vaccines to the poor and sick.

It was then that he began to consider that his great-grandfather, who didn't even work on live embryos but on prisoners as good as dead, may have been misunderstood.

Politics from Nazis or the White House had no place in science, he realized, and neither did religion. But the burdens of government regulations on his company's research became too much to bear. He had nowhere to turn in the private sector—except the Homeland Security–Industrial Complex.

And it was here, outside the gaze of Wall Street and the world, that Seavers found not only billions of dollars at his disposal but the cloak of "national security" to perform the kinds of research and experiments—mostly on enlisted soldiers—that he would never have been able to pull off in the private sector. Literally decades of research had been compressed into less than 36 months. The result was the SeaGen smart vaccine, his crowning achievement.

Now, however, like his great-grandfather, he was reduced to dealing with imbecile masters at the Pentagon, hunting for buried globes, and crossing swords with "astro-archaeologists" like Conrad Yeats.

What an insane world, he thought. *Time for a new one.*

Seavers heard the bathroom door open and saw a whiff of steam from the shower billow out. Then a long, tan leg emerged from the mist and the naked form of Brooke Scarborough stepped toward him.

Seavers admired Brooke's body as she walked over and slipped under the sheets next to him. It had been weeks since they had sex, and it infuriated him that he had to share Brooke with Conrad Yeats.

Worse, she had put him in a bind with the Alignment, which wanted her dead after she had allowed Yeats to find the code book right under her nose and slip away. He had intervened on her behalf, arguing that the death of Senator Scarborough's daughter would only bring even more unwanted scrutiny at the eleventh hour. Moreover, if there was anyone Yeats would turn to once he popped back up on the grid, it would be her. The Alignment bought his argument, and she had won a reprieve.

So far, however, Yeats seemed to be able to live without her. Brooke was certain that Yeats felt so guilty about reconnecting with Serena Serghetti that he was hiding from her as much as he was the Alignment. If so, Yeats was a weaker man than he thought.

"The president and Packard told me about the globe," he said. "Did you know this was what that tombstone and book code nonsense was all about?"

Her silence said yes. He didn't know which annoyed him more: that the Alignment had kept him out of the loop or that she had. As a biological legacy of the Alignment, he always resented it when those adopted into the organization knew more than he did. Especially the true identity of one or more of the 30 who ruled the Alignment and knew all the names and faces. In two days so would he.

"They want me to find it."

"You?" She looked at him with frightened eyes. "Have you told Osiris?"

"Of course. Nothing's changed. I simply have to keep this globe from falling into the hands of either the Church or the State. And now the federal government has given me the men and muscle to do that. Meanwhile, you're going to have to be on the lookout for Yeats. He has few places to turn now. One of them is bound to be you."

She said nothing.

It was an awkward pause, but Seavers didn't mind her discomfort. In fact, he took perverse pleasure in it and the knowledge of pleasure soon to come.

"Max, you're as cool and confident of yourself as ever," she told him. "But you only know Conrad Yeats the specimen. Not the man."

"Unlike, say, you?" he replied with ice in his voice.

She was terrified. He could see it in her eyes. "I'm just saying that there's always a body count when people go after him."

Seavers let out a loud laugh and couldn't stop laughing. It was too funny, really.

"After tonight, Brooke, the only body you'll need to worry about is yours."

21

The next morning Conrad stood in his change of clothes outside the Starbucks on Wisconsin looking at his watch. It was barely 5:30 a.m., and already the line to see his old friend Danny Z was out the door.

Daniel Motamed Zadeh—"Danny Z" to friends—worked as a barista behind the counter. Danny had let his hair grow long since his days at the Pentagon and had it in a ponytail, looking like Antonio Banderas in *Zorro*. But Conrad could tell it was him even from the back of the line. Ten minutes later Conrad stepped up to the counter and looked Danny Z in the eyeballs for the first time in a decade.

"Tall nonfat latte," he told Danny as he slipped him three George Washingtons. "The name's Bubba."

Danny marked up the order specs on the outside of an empty white Starbucks cup and looked over Conrad's shoulder and said, "Next customer, please."

Just like that, they were done.

Conrad ambled over to the far counter where several patrons waited to pick up their orders—K Street types, a couple of diplomats and a college intern fetching orders for her congressman's entire staff. He couldn't help but notice the headline below the fold of the front page of the *Post* that one of the K Street guys was reading:

False Bioterror Scare
Clears U.S. Capitol

Then the guy lowered his paper and looked straight at him. Conrad shifted his gaze quickly to scan the mugs on the shelves to the side. They were always coming up with new ones. He was tempted to buy a pair—one for him and one for Serena.

When a barista called the name "Bob" nobody answered. Conrad figured "Bob" was "Bubba," lost in translation.

One sip told him that was the case, and as he walked out to the street he looked at the side of his cup and noticed the peculiar markings for his latte: there were the three symbols for the constellations from his father's tombstone, along with a new, fourth symbol which Danny had inserted.

Strung together the translation on the side of his Starbucks cup read:

Boötes + Leo + Virgo = Bad Alignment.

Tell me something I don't know, Conrad wondered, but when he looked back inside the store Danny Z was no longer behind the counter. Another barista, a blonde, was taking orders.

Conrad went round back to the alley and stood by the trash bins behind the store. It was starting to drizzle. He sipped his coffee and waited. Danny Z made slamming good coffee, although this probably wasn't what his parents in Beverly Hills had planned for their little genius when he went off to MIT.

Danny came from an Iranian family that fled Tehran when the mullahs toppled the government of the Shah of Iran decades ago. They settled in the Trousdale Estates part of Beverly Hills with other Persian Jews and pretty much kept to themselves while sending their kids to Beverly Hills High School, which eventually had so many Persians that by the time Danny was going there the school was printing its programs in English and Farsi. It was only a matter of time before the CIA recruiters called, always looking for a few good Iranians with connections to the old country. Daniel Motamed Zadeh, tired of his cars and Persian princesses and prospects for more of the same, was ripe for a higher calling and became a spy for his beloved America, the Great Satan, so far as the current regime in Tehran was concerned.

Danny Z had left National Intelligence at the Pentagon a few years back under a cloud of bitter recriminations on both sides. This after he was brought on board to become, in effect, the chief astrologer for the Joint Chiefs of Staff.

Apparently Danny was under the impression that Conrad still worked for the Pentagon. The first thing he did coming out the door with a bag of trash was take a swing at Conrad with it.

Conrad ducked, spilling some coffee and scalding his hand. "Hey, Danny, I'm one of the good guys."

Danny stuffed the bag into the stinking trash bin. "Bullshit. Your name is Yeats, isn't it? Just like your old man."

"He's dead, remember?"

"Promise?"

"There was a funeral, Danny. You were the only one from the old days not there."

"Meaning what?"

"Meaning, you're the only one I can trust."

Danny gave him a napkin from his pocket. "Better drink it now, it loses its oxidation and flavor in a few minutes. Don't make me waste a cup of good coffee."

Conrad wiped the cup and then his hand. He took a sip and nodded his approval.

Danny calmed down, pulled out a cigarette, and started blowing smoke, eyeing him nervously.

Conrad said, "I thought you preferred hookah pipes to sticks."

"I got religion and gave up all that shit."

"Since when are cigarettes a sacrament?"

"Since Genesis says that when Rachel saw Isaac from afar 'she lit off her Camel.' " Danny blew smoke out of both nostrils. "So you're trying to figure out your old man's tombstone like the rest of them?"

"The rest?"

"Packard's people came to me asking about the stars on the tombstone weeks ago. How else do you think I knew about the constellations? You think I'm a psychic now, too?"

Conrad looked at the once-happy Danny and wondered what must have happened to him after the DOD's intelligence branch stole him from the CIA. It was all bullshit, of course. But the Russians, al-Qaeda, the Chinese and others often timed their rocket launches, terrorist attacks, and nuclear tests to significant dates. The head of the Russian rocket program had gone so far as to state on record that he believed astrology was a "hard science." And as long as America's enemies, both real and imagined, believed in hocus-pocus, the Pentagon figured they had better, too. They plotted every day and date, both historically and astrologically, visible and invisible, in order to predict threats and prepare accordingly.

Danny was a natural, coming from a long line of mystics who allegedly traced themselves back to the Persian Empire, to the Jews exiled to Babylon and taught by King Nebuchadnezzar and his staff of astrologers six centuries before Christ. It made all the Bible-thumper evangelicals in the Pentagon wet their pants to have "the real deal" on their side. The kicker was his name was Daniel, just like the prophet who spelled out the rise and fall of the world's future empires until the end of time itself.

Conrad said, "Danny, what happened to you?"

"You don't know?"

"No."

"You don't fucking know?"

Conrad shook his head. "I heard they had you working out dates and stuff, right? I figured you got tired of the grind and living in the heads of psychos living in caves halfway around the world."

Danny took the cigarette stump out of his mouth and dropped it to the wet pavement, stamping it out. He looked up at Conrad. "They were using my charts against special ops."

"I thought that was the idea, Danny. You think like the enemy and tell the brass, like that splinter Red Cell group of astrologers and psychics they use."

"No." Danny laughed bitterly and lit another cigarette. "They started using my charts to mount *our* special ops."

Conrad's jaw dropped. "American troops?"

"Like I'm giving 'em a regular meteorological report, only they launch an air strike when Mars is at the Dragon's Head, screw the full moon." Danny took another drag. "Admiral Temple told me they've been doing it since the Revolution. It's how we won the War of Independence. It's how we've won every stinking world war since. It's why the armed forces of the United States are invincible, Yeats."

"Invincible?"

Danny shrugged. "Stars say so."

Conrad said nothing, just watched Danny, a man clearly conflicted and depressed. In other words, after enough time at DARPA himself, Conrad was ready to believe him.

"At first, I thought they were bullshitting me, putting pressure on me. Then I decided to give them a bogus chart, just to see what happened. Next day I find out twenty Delta Force troops die, just like that. I get called in. Stars never wrong. I must have been. I promised I'd do better."

"But obviously you didn't."

Danny gave him the evil eye, offended.

Conrad glanced away at the trash bins all around them. They weren't exactly conversing in the situation room these days.

"So what was it, Danny? Another special op gone bad?"

Danny shook his head. "June 30, 2004," he said and then paused. "That's almost four years ago exactly. Holy shit! Now you turn up."

Conrad scratched his head. Four years ago Conrad was long gone from the Pentagon himself, off in the Andes doing his *Ancient Riddles* show. Then his father mysteriously resurfaced in his life, as was his pattern, and dragged him down to Antarctica.

"So what happened on June 30, 2004?"

Danny told him: "U.S. handover of Iraq."

Conrad blinked. "The Joint Chiefs had you chart the day the U.S. would return sovereignty to the Iraqis?"

"To the second: 10:26 a.m. in Baghdad, which was 2:26 a.m. here in D.C.," Danny said. "But then they fucked up. They got word of some assassination attempt in the works on the interim prime minister, Ayad Allawi. So Paul Bremer, the coalition's civil administrator, bumps up the transfer and gives Allawi the leather-bound transfer document and a handshake two days ahead of schedule."

Conrad stared at him. "And you believe that's why we screwed up the occupation in Iraq?"

"Fuck, no. But some brass in the Pentagon did. Beats looking in the mirror, I guess. It's all fucked, man. Axis of Evil. Bullshit! We found shit in Iraq. Meanwhile, the nut jobs in Iran and North Korea are building nukes and passing them around to every lowlife terrorist group. They're gonna blow up the whole fucking world. Because we got our heads up our asses."

Conrad had heard enough to know where Danny stood on the issue. Now he needed to get from Danny what he came for, without sending the poor son of a bitch over the edge.

"Danny, listen to me." Conrad took a deep breath. "I need to find SENTINEL."

Danny looked at him like he was the boogie man. "Now you wanna do business with the Masons?"

"Maybe."

"You're fucking nuts! All of you!" Danny started turning circles, waving his arms like an inmate in some asylum. "The whole world is fucking nuts!"

"Look, I told you, Danny. You're the only one from the old days I can trust. You and Sentinel."

Danny stopped turning, his eyes looking the crazier for it.

"Yeah, well, he's from your old man's days, the old-old days. I heard he's dead. Him and all his Masonic bullshit."

"Is he?"

Danny finally looked like he was calming down. "Maybe. I don't know."

"If he were still alive, where would I find him?"

"Some nursing home in Richmond, I think. Near the VA hospital."

"Really?"

"We can't all go out in a blaze of glory like your old man, Chief."

They said nothing for a moment. Conrad listened to the morning rush hour picking up on Wisconsin. The sky was getting lighter, though it was still drizzling. Then Danny seemed to regain his sanity and sight. He looked at Yeats in his rumpled suit and suddenly figured it out.

"Holy shit, Yeats. That was *you* yesterday at the Capitol?"

"Maybe."

Danny shook his head. "I could have told you it wouldn't work."

"The moon in the wrong house or something?"

"Something."

"How's tonight look?"

"Seriously?" Danny worked up a quick chart on another Starbucks napkin. "Problem with you is you don't even know your own birth date. That screws things up some. But based on all your personality quirks, we always figured you for a Pisces. Definitely a water sign."

A minute later Danny showed him the chart.

It was completely unintelligible to Conrad's eyes. "And what's that supposed to mean?"

"You're fucked."

"Seriously?"

Danny nodded and stamped out his second cigarette. "So am I, if I'm spotted with you."

Conrad pocketed the napkin and turned to go. "You never saw me."

"I wish," Danny said, and disappeared back into the Starbucks.

22

DARPA HEADQUARTERS

ARLINGTON, VIRGINIA

THE SIX-STORY OFFICE BUILDING in Arlington that houses the headquarters of DARPA attracts scant attention from the commuters emerging from the nearby Metro station or the patrons of the neighboring fast-food joints, gas stations, and multiplexes. Only the lone security guard at the entrance to the anonymous steel-and-glass office tower hints of something inside to passersby, but something no more exciting than a nondescript local bank branch.

Max Seavers was in his glass office on the sixth floor when the call came in: Conrad Yeats had turned up on the grid, and Norm Carson's team at the Pentagon wanted to move in.

Seavers called them off. "I'll handle it." He hung up and placed another call. "This is Nebulizer. I need a Medevac at the helipad. See you in ten."

Meanwhile, I'm going to need some more juice.

Seavers took the elevator down from his office to the other sixth floor—the one six stories below the building's underground parking garage. The Meat Locker on sublevel 6, as it was called, was built by his predecessor General Yeats to house an astounding discovery. The Griffter had kept it a secret even from the Pentagon. Seavers learned of its existence only upon taking over the old man's job, and its revelations affirmed in a thousand ways his choice to heed the Alignment's call and leave SeaGen for DARPA.

Seavers walked down a long tunnel to a thick metal vault. He swiped his right index finger on the scanner next to the door. He heard a lock thud and then a series of clicks as bolts moved inside. The two-foot-thick door opened to reveal a contamination room and another vault beyond.

Seavers put on a protective germ "bunny suit" and opened the second vault. Inside was a secret prison that housed one of the most unique enemy combatants America had ever captured.

His code name was HANS, and he was discovered by American troops in Antarctica in the 1940s during Operation Highjump, which was the massive U.S. invasion of Antarctica based on information gleaned from the Nazis in the waning days of World War II. Almost every major American base on the ice continent could trace its origins back to Highjump.

Hans was a corpse, the frozen corpse of a German officer who was part of a secret Nazi base in Antarctica established by the "Baron of the Black Order" himself, SS General Ludwig von Berg. It was at this base that Hitler's "Last Battalion" apparently stored biotoxins. These biotoxins had been smuggled out of the collapsing Third Reich on U-boats, along with senior Nazis, who then went on to establish new identities in Argentina.

Hans didn't talk much, but his diseased lung tissue had provided Seavers with the second most important discovery of his life: the Nazis had weaponized the 1918 Spanish flu that had killed more than fifty million humans. In the end, it also killed the Nazis safeguarding their ultimate doomsday weapon. But it breathed new life into Seavers' research and set him on his present course.

Specifically, Hans's frozen lung tissue had given Seavers the perfectly preserved live bird flu virus itself. The trouble had been converting it into an easily dispersible aerosol version. In the process Seavers also discovered a prion mutation in the corpse's brain cells. One drop of fluid drained from the tissue could create a dozen lethal injections. A simple prick by syringe or dart gun caused instant death from apparently natural disease. But it had to be used within 24 hours of extraction or it would lose its effectiveness. Hence his periodic visits to the Meat Locker.

Seavers smiled at his frozen friend. "We're going to have to make this one fast today, Hans," he said, looking forward to extracting some cells from Conrad Yeats.

23

MISSION SPRINGS NURSING HOME

RICHMOND, VIRGINIA

IT WAS A THREE-HOUR CAR TRIP for Conrad and Serena, and Conrad could tell she had grave doubts about meeting this Master Mason known as Sentinel. But dressed in her traditional nun's attire, she said nothing as they walked through the front entrance of the Mission Springs Nursing Home. The home specialized in scooping up the half-dead human leftovers from the nearby VA hospital, keeping their juices and benefits going for a few weeks, and then dumping them in the grave.

The administrator at the nursing station, seeing clergy had come to visit, directed them down the hall to 208. They came to a room with the door partially open. Conrad gave it a rap with a knuckle. It opened wide and a big nurse with the name tag Brenda came out with a bottle of urine.

"We're all done, Father," Nurse Brenda said, noticing the white collar Conrad sported under his trench coat, courtesy of Serghetti Couture.

They entered the room and there was Reggie "Hercules" Jefferson, who had gone by the name Sentinel for as long as Conrad could remember. Herc, short for Hercules, was one of his father's few true friends from the Air Force, maybe his only one. Born in New Orleans, Herc's father was a bricklayer who became a Tuskegee Airman, one of the first African-Americans to fly for Uncle Sam.

Herc wanted to do even better and aspired to be an astronaut. But

NASA wasn't ready for an African-American Apollo pilot, so he ended up flying Hercules C-130 transports on black ops missions for General Yeats. In time he, like most anybody associated with Conrad's old man, literally crashed and burned in an impossible landing that snapped his spinal cord and left him crippled for life at the age of 40.

That was thirty years ago.

Before Conrad could say a word, Herc said with a low, gravelly voice, "Took you long enough, son."

"I finally figured out that it was you who carved my father's tombstone."

"Just like your daddy wanted."

Herc was an unlikely Mason, not of the dead white male variety. His family claimed to have descended from a line of slave Masons since the Revolution. General Yeats believed it, having witnessed both Herc's encyclopedic knowledge of Masonic esoterica and his advanced skills as a stonecutter and site planner for forward-based military ops. As for Herc's claim that his family had blood ties to Founders like Washington and Jefferson, who allegedly had had affairs with female slaves, that seemed like wishful thinking to Conrad when he heard it from Uncle Herc as a boy. Looking at him in bed it seemed even more fanciful now.

Conrad said, "The globe's not in the cornerstone of the Capitol building."

"Of course not. Casey moved it after the War of 1812. I could have told you that, boy."

Conrad sighed. "You could have come to the funeral."

"On these legs? Besides, your old man and I never thought I'd make it this far. We thought you'd be on your own. Had to build a message into the tombstone and hope you'd be smart enough to figure it out. Guess you ain't."

"So how long have you been waiting for me?"

"How long since the Griffter died?"

Four years, thought Conrad, ashamed for having not even thought of Uncle Herc until now. Conrad could see that Herc had expected him to pay a visit as soon as his dad died. But Conrad had been wrapped up in his own worries following the death and destruction in Antarctica. Little did he know that poor Herc had been waiting here all this time, scratching sores in the bed his father had put him in.

There wasn't much Conrad could say, so naturally Serena said it for him, getting directly to the business at hand. "Hello, Uncle Herc. I'm—"

"I know who you are, Sister Serghetti," old Herc said. "Pleased to meet you."

"We figure the globe is buried beneath the Library of Congress," she said. "Casey and his son Edward, who was responsible for the interiors, appear to have left clues in the form of zodiacs as a map. But Doctor Yeats can't crack the secret, and we hoped you could."

Her bold Australian accent immediately perked up old Herc, and he smiled at Conrad approvingly. "She's a handful, ain't she?"

Conrad glanced at Serena. "That she is. Now, about the globe—"

But Herc asked Serena, "So you think we Masons are all devil worshippers?"

"I think you worship knowledge," she said without batting an eyelash. "The danger comes in ever learning but never coming to the knowledge of truth."

"We ain't a religion, Sister Serghetti. We promote enlightenment, not salvation."

"Thereby making an idol of enlightenment," she countered. "The very temptation that Lucifer offered Eve in the Garden of Eden."

"So you *do* think we worship the devil."

She smiled. "In a roundabout way, yes."

Conrad said nothing as a heavy silence filled the room.

"You know, Yeats, your girl reminds me of another lady named Anne Royall," Hercules finally said. "She was America's first prominent female journalist, a real rabble-rouser screaming about government corruption and all in the 1800s."

"Anne Royall?" Conrad repeated.

"Yeah, she used to live on B Street near 2nd Street and the Capitol back in her day," Herc said. "Her husband, Captain William Royall, was a Freemason. For years their basement was used as a secret meeting place for Masons dedicated to preserving the federal city's alignment with the heavens. But in time they couldn't even preserve the house. Got torn down by the Army Corps of Engineers."

Conrad could feel a tingle racing up his spine. Something was coming. He could see it in old Herc's eyes. "Why did the Army Corps of Engineers tear down Anne Royall's old house?"

Herc smiled. "Casey had to raze it to make room for the Library of Congress and the laying of its northeast foundation stone in 1890."

There it was. He looked at Serena, who got it, too: *The Masons moved the globe to the basement of Anne Royall's house. Then they built the Library on top of it. The house was gone, but not the basement. It was buried under the Library of Congress.*

Then Conrad thought of something and frowned. "The radiant I've been tracking cuts across the Library's Great Hall in a southeasterly direction. Shouldn't the basement be somewhere under the northeastern corner of the building?"

Hercules nodded. "It is, but the access tunnel is in the southeast corner."

"What access tunnel?" Serena pressed.

"Go get me my file, and I'll show you."

Conrad and Serena looked around the small room and saw only a wooden dresser with an old picture of Herc and Conrad's father from their glory days.

"It's inside the back."

Conrad walked over, removed the backing from the picture and peeled out a very old and thin schematic that had been folded several times over. He brought it over to Herc, who motioned for him to unfold it.

"Ain't hardly readable, but I can interpret."

It took a minute, but when Conrad was done he and Serena found themselves looking at plans, elevations, and details from the Jefferson Building. They were stamped "Edward Pearce Casey, Architect, 171 Broadway, New York" and signed by Bernard Green "Superintendent & Engineer" for the Library of Congress.

"See, the radiant crosses the sign Virgo across the zodiac on the floor of the Great Hall," Hercules pointed out with a gnarled finger. "At the end of the day, when it comes to the federal district, it's all about Virgo. The whole city is aligned to the Blessed Virgin in the sky."

"I beg to differ," Serena said. "The astral virgin is Isis, not Mary, despite attempts by Vatican astronomers to Christianize her in the Middle Ages. As such, the zodiacs are part of a deterministic philosophy of astrology that worships fate, not free will. And there can be no human rights without the recognition of free will."

"Maybe it means all that to some people," Herc said. "But to Masons the Virgin represents the hearth and home, the milk of the breast and the promise of the harvest. Like the New World to the Founders."

"Well, then your stars are sexist."

Herc seemed delighted with Serena. "You got a point, Sister. Anytime you deal with God or the stars, it seems you gotta have a Virgin. Very important." He looked at Conrad. "You ain't gonna pull this thing off without a virgin, son, and now you've got two of them—one in the heavens and one real live wire here on Earth."

24

Herc awoke with a start in his bed later that afternoon at the nursing home. He had dozed off after the Griffter's son and the nun had left. He lay still, pondering everything they had discovered, wondering if he should have said more.

Because there was certainly a lot more he *could* have said.

Slowly he reached his shaking hand under his bed and pulled out an old dagger with Masonic letters. It had been passed down through the generations, and he was told it once belonged to George Washington. He wondered if that was true. The only reason he kept it under his bed these days was to make sure some orderly didn't steal it.

He had intended to give the dagger to the Griffter's kid but forgot. His memory was slipping, along with just about everything else.

He heard footsteps and slipped the dagger under his gown as two young orderlies appeared at his door with a wheelchair and Nurse Brenda chirped that it was time for his physical therapy.

As they wheeled him down the hall, he noticed that he was feeling a bit queasy. Damn nursing-home food.

"I know you want to keep the feeding tube in, sweetie, but your mother is trying to tell you she wants to leave this earth," Nurse Brenda was telling the daughter of the woman down the hall as they passed by.

Forget the feeding tube, Herc thought, they just needed to give that woman some water. She was going to die of dehydration, not dementia.

Suddenly Hercules realized they had passed the physical therapy room, and when he looked ahead they pushed him through two double doors to the parking lot outside where an ambulance was waiting.

"Hey, where you taking me?" Herc said as the orderlies lifted him up and dropped him on a gurney inside the ambulance.

A blond doctor with a syringe inside welcomed Hercules as the doors closed and the ambulance moved off. "I'm disappointed we missed Dr. Yeats," the man said. "But maybe you could tell us where he's going?"

Herc said nothing, although his gown was wet. He must have pissed in his pants. That's because he saw the other guy strapped down in the ambulance—young Danny Z, his mouth gagged and eyes wide.

"Don't know who you talking about, Doctor. Now please tell me where we're going."

"For a ride, Mr. Hercules," the man said with some amusement. "If you help me, you might get off. If you don't, then I'm afraid you'll suffer the same fate as your friend here."

Danny Z started to scream as the doctor slipped a long needle into Danny's neck.

"A body is a terrible thing to waste," the doctor told Danny as he slowly pushed the syringe. "So I'm only going to melt your brain."

25

GEORGETOWN BALLROOM

WASHINGTON HILTON

"A FUNNY THING HAPPENED to me yesterday on my way to Capitol Hill."

There was laughter in the Georgetown Ballroom at the Hilton Hotel as Serena Serghetti addressed the Washington Press Corps at the annual Media Dinner on the eve of the annual Presidential Prayer Breakfast.

"I was testifying about human rights in China, or lack thereof when it comes to your personal body parts and organ transplants, when I realized that the Chinese are right."

The room grew quiet, just a few forks clinking on plates as the journalists enjoyed their choice of beef or salmon. Meanwhile, here she stood as an ambassador for Christ covering up a federal crime in progress. The guilt was almost too much to bear.

"If a human lives for four score years and the state is forever, then the state should be able to do whatever is necessary for the so-called greater good," she explained. "But if it's the soul that is immortal, as that old Oxford don C. S. Lewis used to say, then it's the state that is passing away. Which means individual rights are paramount."

She was getting nervous as she saw the clock in the back of the room. Secret Service teams with dogs would be sweeping the hotel in a matter of hours and then the security would clamp down like a fortress, and nobody would be able to come in or go out until the president left the breakfast in the grand ballroom at 10 a.m. If Conrad didn't get back soon . . .

"The whole point of 'one nation under God' in the American pledge of allegiance is recognition that the government isn't God. Individual rights are the basis for the foundation of the United States, and much of this philosophy came from American preachers like Thomas Hooker, who argued for the 'priesthood of believers,' insisting that since the Holy Spirit resided in the heart of every person, each person should be able to vote and live their conscience. In short, we're the government. You and me and all the people."

She looked at the sea of faces in the room, many of them familiar talking heads on TV who would have plenty to talk about if they only knew the truth.

"Sometimes I wonder if my evangelical friends in America have forgotten this. Are we people *of* faith in the halls of power? Or are we people who have faith *in* the halls of power? It's an important distinction. One leads to an open, diverse society. The other leads to something like we have in Russia today, where the former KGB spy agency has effectively taken over the government. One begins to wonder if something like that could even happen here."

She was thinking of the Alignment and the average American citizen. The Romans had bread and circuses. The Americans had TV and the Super Bowl. The members of the "chattering class" represented in this room were part of this Great American Conspiracy. But they also reported on it and thus shaped it. Which is why she had accepted this invitation in the first place.

"All of this underscores the primary role the Fourth Estate or free press performs in a democratic society, for it is you who inform the electorate and help us make sense of our world so that we, the people, can decide the fate of nations, not the other way around."

It was over soon enough and she was standing before a line of appreciative journalists. And then Brooke Scarborough walked up.

Serena hadn't seen her until now in the room, and never in person. She was much . . . taller than she expected, with very big hands that now clasped her own.

"Sister Serghetti," Brooke said. "I think we have a mutual friend who is in trouble."

Serena feigned ignorance, but knew from Brooke's eyes that each woman completely understood the other.

"You'd tell me if you've seen Conrad, wouldn't you?" Brooke pressed.

"Ms. Scarborough, I had assumed that you would be the first person Dr. Yeats would go to if he were in trouble. Are you no longer together?"

It was Brooke who feigned ignorance now, as she was forced to move off and let the person behind her say hello to "Mother Earth," but even out of sight Serena could feel Brooke's eyes watching her every move.

26

JEFFERSON BUILDING

LIBRARY OF CONGRESS

Conrad listened to the soft strains of Mozart on his iPhone's earbuds as he walked along Constitution Avenue in the rain. The dome of the Jefferson Building at the Library of Congress gleamed proudly under dark skies tonight, its grandeur almost eclipsing that of the U.S. Capitol across the street. It was already a few minutes past midnight, which meant it was already July 3, and meant he was running out of time. He turned up the collar of his trench coat and walked into the researchers entrance.

The guard on duty looked up from his station and immediately recognized Conrad from all his previous, legitimate visits to the Library over the years. Conrad's heart sank. Good ol' Larry was shaking his shaved head, whistling the spooky theme song to Conrad's old reality series *Ancient Riddles of the Universe*, which could be seen only in syndicated reruns on late-night TV and which said everything Conrad needed to know about Larry's social life.

"The Library closed to the public at 5:30 p.m. and to researchers at 9:30 p.m., Dr. Yeats. Only congressmen or their staff allowed now. You know the rules."

"Still a little wet behind the ears, Larry, as you can see." He wiped his wet hair back and put on a smile, his gut churning at the thought that Larry might get hurt.

"If you'd just stick to the tunnels connecting all the buildings here, Dr. Yeats, you'd stay nice and dry on a night like this." Larry, unable to resist, had to repeat the show's tag line. "After all, 'the truth is DOWN there.' "

"You know I'm claustrophobic, Larry. Besides, I needed some fresh air."

"What you need is to get yourself a date," Larry said. "Say, whatever happened to that blonde Nazi babe from Fox News Channel? She didn't like your salute?"

"My salute's just fine, Larry. It seems I have trouble following orders."

Larry chuckled, but Conrad could tell he was disappointed. The guard's head was filled with images of Conrad in Egyptian pyramids and Mayan temples, with beautiful graduate "researchers" assisting him on his digs—when they weren't working auto shows. What on earth was an astro-archaeologist like Dr. Conrad Yeats, "the world's foremost authority on megalithic architecture and the astronomical alignments of Earth's oldest monuments," doing roaming the musty hallways of Washington, D.C.?

Conrad emptied his pockets of his wallet and keychain and made a face.

"Let me guess," Larry said. "You forget your user card again?"

Conrad nodded. In truth he had a bogus ID card with another name, which he obviously couldn't use now. And even if he had his own ID, Larry wouldn't be able to swipe it without all sorts of "apprehend and detain" directives popping up on his screen.

"I won't be long in the stacks," Conrad promised, looking at his watch. "Just give me twelve minutes."

Larry looked doubtful as he handed him a clipboard. "Just give me your John Hancock and ID number."

Conrad scribbled a signature, put down a bogus six-digit number and hoped that Larry would manually key it in later.

Larry took the clipboard without a glance. "Come on through."

Conrad turned up the volume of his iPhone and approached the multisensor detection gate. Serena had told him this particular piece of music would throw off the new brainwave scanners the feds had installed around the Mall. As he passed through the gate, he watched Larry study the thermal-like images on the bank of monitors. It was the curious monitor at the end Conrad kept an eye on, which could detect what the feds called "hostile brainwave patterns." The colors changed, and Conrad could see that Larry saw it, too. But Larry's voice betrayed nothing, and his hand hadn't reached for the silent alarm yet.

"Your iPhone, Dr. Yeats."

"Oh, I'm sorry." Conrad removed his earbuds and handed the iPhone to Larry. "You want the fedora and bullwhip, too?"

"Hee, hee."

Larry passed the phone through the detector, but Conrad only motioned to pick it up along with his wallet and keychain.

"You have yourself a good evening, Dr. Yeats. Don't go reading so many old books you scare yourself shitless."

"Too late," Conrad said as he walked away.

"Hey, Dr. Yeats," Larry called after him. "You forgot your—"

Conrad turned, pressed the remote on his keychain and heard the crack of the iPhone explode behind him. Larry started coughing, and Conrad waited for the invisible knockout gas to work. But it didn't. Larry staggered a bit, down but not out. He was reaching for his radio to call for help.

Damn sufentanyl, Conrad thought. So much of its effect depended on the biology of the individual.

Holding his breath, Conrad marched over to Larry and gave him a good, sharp chop to the back of the neck, knocking him out the old-fashioned way.

"Sorry, Larry."

Conrad removed Larry's radio transceiver along with his iPhone and earbuds and walked away. He looked at his watch as he entered a low hallway with yellow walls and white trim. Larry would be up in a few minutes if he wasn't discovered sooner.

Conrad's twelve minutes had just been cut in half.

27

JONES POINT PARK

VIRGINIA

Across the Potomac at Jones Point near Alexandria, Max Seavers looked over schematics at his makeshift command post inside the old lighthouse while the special warfare dive team searched the seawall below for the original foundation stone.

According to the crippled vet they broke under torture, the Masons had moved Washington's globe from the cornerstone of the U.S. Capitol to an even more auspicious location "back in time": the very first boundary stone that Washington laid for the Federal District itself.

Seavers's own research confirmed that it was Daniel Carroll, the man who sold Washington Capitol Hill, who laid the stone here with Washington and an old black astronomer named Benjamin Banneker.

Today Jones Point is a big municipal park under the shadow of a giant bridge. For several years the bridge had proved to be a security headache for the feds, but it also proved to be a perfect cover for Seavers and his special ops team of Marines.

They were part of an elite 86-man unit known as Detachment One, oriented toward amphibious raids, at night, under limited visibility. "Extreme circumstances" were their theater of war, and they were trained and equipped to carry out special missions including embassy evacuations, airfield seizures, underwater demolitions, and down-pilot rescues within six hours of notice.

Normally, they fell under Naval Special Warfare Squadron One, which operated out of the U.S. Special Operations Command.

Now they were under his command.

The lighthouse door opened and a Marine stepped inside from the rain, which was picking up now.

"The dive team found the foundation stone, sir. It's embedded in the seawall."

"Bring it up," Seavers ordered.

28

Conrad passed under a thick arch and entered the Great Hall. He felt a tight knot in his stomach as he stepped onto the huge zodiac embedded in the marble floor and faced east toward the Commemorative Arch leading back to the former entrance to the Main Reading Room. He was acutely aware of the six security cameras, two visible and four hidden, all watching him. But what he was looking for was invisible and in a moment he would be, too.

Conrad looked back over his shoulder, due west, toward the library's main entrance. Were it open, he would see the gleaming dome of the U.S. Capitol. And were it visible to the naked eye, he would see a radiant from the center of that dome pass through the zodiac on which he was standing, cutting through the signs of Pisces and Virgo and projecting to a point beyond the arcade at the east side of the Great Hall.

Conrad followed the radiant under the archway to the other side. The air smelled like bubble gum—the peculiar odor of the antiseptics they used to scrub the floor. To his right and left were two working antique elevators used by the Library staff. Above each elevator was a mural by the American Symbolist painter Elihu Vedder, one depicting the effects of good government and the other the effects of bad government.

The message was clear: America faced two possible and diametrically opposite fates.

The fresco above the staff elevator to the right showed America in all her glory, with full leaves in bloom and fruit in season—a land flowing with milk and honey. The fresco over the service elevator to his left depicted a barren America, bare trees, and a bomb with a lit fuse under the rubble of overturned marble and monuments.

Conrad considered the two opposing fates.

He walked to the staff elevator beneath America the beautiful and pressed a black button. The doors opened to reveal an ornate cage with a marble tile floor, brass bars, and glass. Conrad stepped inside and looked at the column of five buttons: 2nd Floor, 1st Floor, Ground, Basement, Cellar. He glimpsed the horror of America the damned before the doors closed and the elevator began its descent.

When the elevator doors opened again in the musty cellar of the Library, Conrad could see the staff elevator on the opposite side of the gray linoleum floor, just a few yards away. He was about to step out when he heard something down the corridor, out of his field of vision. He stayed in the car and pulled out a telescoping rod with a mirror, carefully sticking it out of the elevator at floor level. The mirror showed another security guard coming his way, probably to use the elevator.

Conrad retreated to the back of the elevator and took out the radio he lifted from Larry at the researcher's entrance. He pressed the Channel 6 button and waited.

There was a crackle down the hall. The sound of approaching footsteps stopped. A voice said, "Kramer here."

Conrad kept the talk button pressed, to avoid the guard hearing his own voice coming out of the speaker. Conrad said in a soft voice, "Central Security. A sensor in the Asian Reading Room is acting up again. Need a visual check."

"Copy," Kramer said, backtracking in the opposite direction.

Conrad waited for the steps to die away before he crossed the cellar floor to the staff elevator on the opposite side and pried its doors open. He stuck his head into the shaft and looked up to see the bottom of the staff elevator stopped at the basement level overhead. Then he looked down and could see the bottom of the shaft six feet below. Feeling the doors pressing him on both sides, he jumped.

He landed on an iron grate embedded in the floor, heard a painful pop and immediately dropped to his knees. For a second he could have sworn he blew his Achilles tendon. But it was only an ankle sprain. It would hurt like hell, but it wouldn't slow him down.

He heaved on the grate with his fingers. The heavy iron bulkhead lifted an inch or two, revealing a narrow crawl space and steep well that dropped into nothingness. He slid the grate with a heavy scrape across the floor. He wanted to avoid severing a finger as he lowered it. But in doing so, he dropped it the last quarter inch and it fell with a deafening thud. He froze. Had any of the audio sensors in the floor above picked up the sound? He closed his eyes and waited for a few seconds. His pulse thundered in his ears. Nothing.

He opened his eyes and looked down into the well. He then heard a hum and looked up to see the elevator coming down on top of him. He quickly jumped into the crawl space.

He waited in the darkness until the elevator started back up. Then he reached up and with a strong tug pulled the grating shut. At one time the staff elevator could descend to this subcellar level. But years later the Architect of the Capitol decided it was an error, that the shaft was in fact unfinished and abandoned by Casey, so the Army Corps of Engineers ordered modifications that raised the floor. When the Library was closed for a 12-year renovation in the 1980s and 1990s for its centennial, the hollow was used only to house a modernized electrical power plant.

Conrad looked around, the light from the shaft overhead dimly illuminating his makeshift command center. His pocket sonar had confirmed a tunnel on the opposite side of the north wall of the well.

He could barely contain his excitement as he unrolled the Primasheet explosive from the lining of his jacket and stuck it on the wall. He then attached the wafer-thin cardboard backing and popped in the remote fuse.

He had honed his skills in demolition over the years through numerous illegal explorations of Egyptian and Mayan pyramids. But this was no Third World dust bin. This was the Library of Congress of the United States of America. And he was about to detonate an explosive device on American soil, in a sacred national institution, no less.

If he properly attached the Primasheet, the explosion would blow in one direction—into the tunnel on the other side of the wall. That was the beauty of it—you could shape, direct, even stand next to it with only a piece of cardboard in between. If you did it right.

If he was wrong, Conrad could burn the place down and himself with it. Actually, even if he was right, he could still die in a matter of minutes. But at least he would know why.

He stepped behind another wall, which his radar had proved rock solid, and looked at the remote detonator in his hand—his cell phone. He then made the sign of the cross, did a Hail Mary, and pressed speed dial button No. 2.

29

The rain was driving down hard at Jones Point as Seavers watched the crane plop the dripping foundation stone onto the ground. He marched over while the Detachment One divers shone lights on the sides and he examined the markings.

"This is it. Drill it."

The demolitions diver came over with a drill and started boring a core sample. But a minute later he shook his head.

"It's solid, sir. There's nothing inside."

Seavers felt the frustration rising inside him. "Then split it open."

The divers looked at each other, as if some higher permission was necessary to open the original foundation stone for the Capitol of the United States of America.

"Split the goddamn rock!" Seavers shouted.

The diver hit the drill and made four holes before he took a special pick and gave one big whack. Seavers heard the clink of the metal to stone, heard the crack spiderweb across the surface and watched as the stone crumpled open into solid chunks.

He could only stare as the wind and rain whipped off the Potomac.

The Mason lied! That goddamn cripple!

Just then his cell phone rang. It was his office. This was an official alert. The voice on the other end said, "Something's going down at the Library of Congress, sir."

Conrad Yeats!

Seavers shouted into the phone: "Seal the whole frickin' Library, I don't care if you have to kill all the Capitol Police to do it. Nobody gets out. Nobody. I'm on my way."

30

The blast had blown Conrad back against the wall and the grating up the elevator shaft. The grating struck the bottom of the elevator car on the floor above, creating a series of sparks that set off a dozen different fire alarms and the sprinkler system. Then it came back down toward the well. Conrad crouched for cover as the grating landed with a deafening crash. He put his hands to his ringing ears and choked on particle-filled air.

When the dust settled, he could hear alarms blare overhead and his radio squawking like a duck. Every sector was rushing to the shaft. He stood up and, stepping through the debris, peered anxiously into the swirling dust through his goggles to see stone steps declining steeply into the earth.

He left behind another gas explosive with a sensor to slow his pursuers and started down the steps. The air coming up from the bottom of the passageway was cool and dank. Conrad felt a chill. The end of the stairs loomed abruptly from out of the shadows.

A wrought iron gate blocked the bottom of the stairs. Conrad kicked the gate open. It was the only damn thing that had opened as planned so far.

There before him was a long sloping tunnel with a dirt floor. He broke out his flashlight and started sprinting, catching his sprained foot on a tree root and falling face down into the dirt. He picked himself up and started running. Suddenly it dawned on him that the topography beneath his feet was that of George Washington's time.

Despite the nonsense of this hill's alleged supernatural origin, Conrad sensed the logic of everything as he neared the end of the tunnel. As the city grew bigger, monument by monument, the entire American republic had been built upon Washington's dream.

As he reached the bottom of the hill and the end of the tunnel, he was drenched in sweat, barely able to breathe. The path he had followed, illuminated a dozen feet at a time with the beam of his flashlight, came to an abrupt halt at a wall. There was a small marker with a symbol—the constellation of Virgo—and an iron gate, beyond which lay the vault.

Conrad stared at the star pattern for Virgo on the wall. He had seen one like this only once before in his life, at the bottom of the earth in Antarctica.

"The Beautiful Virgin," he said aloud, and then heard himself laugh as he remembered old Herc. For all their genius, America's founding fathers had peculiar fantasies. He slapped another Primasheet patch with a five-second timer on the gate and blew the vault open.

Dust filled the tunnel, forcing Conrad back. Suddenly he heard another explosion from behind and realized that security forces had set off his flash explosive. They were entering the tunnel. Conrad took a deep breath, choking on the dust, and ran headlong through the cloud and into the vault.

The vault was a large bunker similar to those beneath the Pentagon, dominated by a big stone table with an old model of the city on it. He recognized the White House and U.S. Capitol and the Washington Monument. But to the south was an enormous, never-built pyramid.

It's a monument to America itself, Conrad realized. Roman numeral markings at the foundation of the pyramid struck him as odd at first glance.

But he had little time for closer inspection. At any moment security forces would be entering the tunnel outside.

A few feet beyond the table was what he was looking for: a golden celestial globe, like something out of Dutch master cartographer Wilhem Bleau's studio in the sixteenth century.

This was the original globe that Washington kept in his study at Mount Vernon for years before it disappeared, Conrad knew instantly. Not the inferior papier-maché replacement from London that Washington later commissioned as America's first president and which now stood on display in the estate's museum.

Or at least Conrad prayed to God it was the real deal.

Conrad dropped to his knees and felt the smooth contours and constellations of the globe, marveling at its three-dimensional, holographic look. The artifact itself would fetch a small fortune at auction.

The corner of his eye caught a glint of metal on the table beside the globe. He looked over and saw a silver plate—*the* silver plate made and engraved by Caleb Bently, a Quaker silversmith, upon which the U.S. Capitol's cornerstone was set.

That's why the U.S. Geological Survey could never find the cornerstone with metal detectors. The Masons had taken the plate when they moved the globe.

He read the engraving on the silver plate:

> *This South East corner Stone of the Capitol of the United States of America in the City of Washington, was laid on the 18th day of September 1793, in the thirteenth year of American Independence, in the first year of the second term of the Presidency of George Washington, whose virtues in the civil administration of his country have been as conspicuous and beneficial, as his Military valor and prudence have been useful in establishing her liberties, and in the year of Masonry 5793, by the Grand Lodge of Maryland, several lodges under its jurisdiction, and Lodge No. 22, from Alexandria, Virginia.*
>
> *THOMAS JOHNSON,*
> *DAVID STUART,* *Commissioners*
> *DANIEL CARROLL,*
> *JOSEPH CLARK, R.W.G.M.—P.T.*
> *JAMES HOBAN,*
> *STEPHEN HALLET* *Architects*
> *COLLEN WILLIAMSON,* *M. Mason*

Conrad's hands began to shake as he slipped the silver plate into his coat pocket and looked at the globe.

The fate of the world is in your hands, he marveled, recalling Washington's words. *Let's see what the world has to offer me.*

He ran his finger along the 40th longitude of the globe, feeling for a seam. When he found it, he traced it to a spring-loaded latch. He pulled the latch and stared in amazement as the globe split open.

PART THREE

JULY 3

31

Conrad ran out of the vault at the same time two red laser beams shot through the dust at the end of the tunnel and federal agents in night goggles poured in. The agents started firing as soon as they spotted Conrad. The sound of the shots in the ancient tunnel was muffled, but Conrad felt the force of bullets whiz past his ear and plow into the wall behind him. He hurled a flash puck down the tunnel. It exploded with a bright light, blinding the agents temporarily and buying him a moment to escape.

Conrad ducked back inside the vault and searched for a second, secret exit. The Masons usually had one somewhere. He found it behind a wall-sized tracing board depicting the entrance to King Solomon's Temple with two giant pillars on either side. The rich gold hue gave it the look of a Byzantine icon, and it was very heavy. Conrad needed to give it a good hard shove with his whole body to slide it even two feet across the floor. But when he did, an opening in the wall behind the board revealed a small spiral staircase.

This picture of the Temple portal was itself a portal.

The smell was rank as Conrad ran up the spiral staircase and into a sewer tunnel. He was a hundred yards down, sloshing through God knows what, when he found a stairwell to street level. A moment later he burst out a metal door and found himself not in some alley between a couple of federal buildings like he had hoped, but inside a small book bay in the Main Reading Room of the Jefferson Building.

Damn.

He could feel his heart pounding in the silence of the cathedral-like room. Father Time and his clock said it was a quarter past midnight. The life-size statues of history's greatest thinkers looked down on him from near the top of the dome. The room was empty. Not even a lone Library or Congressional staffer was around here this time of night. Security cameras would catch him the second he stepped out from the alcove and into the open.

His only choice was to turn left and run along the stacks of books through the exit to the yellow corridor which led back to the researchers' entrance. Overhead he noticed what looked like a large metal duct running along the ceiling of the corridor. It was the conveyor belt that distributed books throughout the Library and U.S. Capitol complex.

He followed the beltway to two metal doors, which automatically slid open to reveal a large processing room. Large bins of books surrounded a conveyor belt on which blue bins carried books to an elevator-like chute. They were too small to carry a person. There was no escape.

He pulled out the parchment he had taken from inside the celestial globe and gazed at it. On one side was a strange sort of celestial chart or star map. The other side was blank save for a signature at the bottom—President George Washington.

He stared at it intently to burn it into his memory. Then he folded it several times over and removed a book from a bin—*Obelisks,* of all things. He carefully inserted the star map into the spine of the book and placed it back in a blue bin. Glancing at the code key sticker on the wall, he tapped a four-digit code into the chute's keypad and sent the book on its way to join the millions of others in the Library of Congress, the world's largest.

As he watched it disappear he heard the doors slide open from behind and turned to see Larry the security guard stagger in, gun waving at him.

"Hands up where I can see them, Professor Yeats." His voice broke above the low hum of the processing equipment.

"Larry," Conrad said, slowly raising his arms. "This isn't how it looks."

"I'm sorry, sir. But it looks pretty bad. You can't just go around stealing books."

"Larry, it's not a book. It's something very different."

The doors opened again and Max Seavers stormed in with a gun pointed at him.

"Excellent job, officer."

Larry nodded, his eyes on Conrad. Then Conrad watched in horror as Seavers turned his gun to the security guard and shot him in the head.

"Larry!" Conrad shouted, but the bullet had already blown splinters of skull fragments and brain against the machinery. Stunned, Conrad watched the security guard crumple to the floor.

Seavers bent down and picked up Larry's gun. "So you found the globe, Yeats."

Conrad put this reference to the globe together with the brazen slaying he just witnessed and instantly knew that Max Seavers was not acting on behalf of the United States but the Alignment. And Seavers knew he knew.

"Yeah, it's in front of the Cartography Room," he said, referring to a public display globe in the basement of the Library's Madison Building. "I can show you if you want."

"Your file said you were a cool one in a tight spot," Seavers said with a hint of admiration. "There might even be a place for you in our organization if you hand over whatever you found inside."

"Oh, so they didn't tell you? I bet the Alignment's having second thoughts about you already. What happens to you when you can't deliver what I stole?"

That seemed to touch a nerve. Seavers pointed Larry's gun at him. "I'm thinking this poor son of a bitch you killed got a lucky shot off as he went down and hit you in the heart."

"Really? Because I'm thinking I have a better chance of walking out of here alive with what I know than you do with what you don't. And all your billions won't save you."

"No, but maybe this will," said Seavers as he extended his gun to Conrad's chest and fired.

The bullet pushed Conrad back against the conveyor belt,

knocking two blue bins to the floor. He slid down, breathing hard as Seavers marched over.

Conrad lay there, the world spinning around. Then he felt Seavers's hands patting him down. He opened his eyes a crack to see Seavers remove the silver cornerstone plate from Conrad's inside coat pocket.

As Seavers stared at it in wonder, a small piece of metal fell from it into his hand. Seavers studied it before realizing it was the slug from his gun, and that the silver plate had stopped it cold.

Conrad grabbed Seavers's balls and squeezed hard. Seavers winced and fell back, then swung Larry's gun at him.

Conrad slammed Seavers's hand against the conveyor belt and the gun went off. They wrestled as Conrad tried to pry it loose from Seavers's grip. Again he slammed the back of Seavers's hand against the belt. This time the fingers loosened and the gun dropped onto the belt.

Seavers tried to grab it, but Conrad tackled him from behind, driving him into the machinery. Seavers tried to strike back, but seemed to have caught his finger in some gears. With a shout Seavers pulled out his bloody hand, sending a severed finger flying through the air.

The finger landed on the conveyor belt, Seavers helplessly watching it make its way to the inner recesses of the Library.

Conrad grabbed his hair and slammed his head against the conveyor belt. Seavers crashed to the floor, out cold.

Conrad quickly fetched the severed finger from the belt before it disappeared and put it in his pocket. At some point, if he ever survived the night, it might prove useful when the police ran the ballistics on who shot Larry.

He then pried loose the silver cornerstone plate from Seavers's other hand and stood up and stared at the two bodies on the floor, aware of shouts outside growing louder.

32

When the U.S. Capitol Police burst into the processing room on the main level of the Jefferson Building, Sergeant Wanda Randolph found three bodies on the floor: Max Seavers, a security guard with bloody hair matted across his face, and a third man with a bullet hole in his shaved head—obviously the perpetrator who detonated the explosives.

A few minutes later, outside the researchers entrance on 2nd Street, she watched the coroner zip up the corpse of the stranger when Officer Carter, one of her R.A.T.'S., walked up.

"So who is he?" she asked.

"They're telling me his name is Dr. Conrad Yeats," Carter reported. "But I couldn't run the security feeds through the facial recognition software to confirm, because somebody up there pulled them."

Wanda could feel her blood begin to boil. "Did they make that secret tunnel in the subbasement disappear, too?"

"No, but there's a detachment of Marines down there now."

"Marines?"

"Sealed the tunnel off and won't let us in."

She looked on as two emergency technicians used backboards to immobilize an unconscious Max Seavers before placing him on a stretcher and securing him in the ambulance for transport to George Washington University Hospital.

"This is our turf, Carter, not theirs."

"Sure, and you can bring that up with the president next time you lunch with him," Carter said. "Meanwhile, what do we do?"

The EMTs moved the big stretcher with Seavers to the side and put the folding one with the security guard on the bench seat next to him in the back of the ambulance. An attending paramedic was on hand to check his wound.

"That guard is our only chance of finding out what really happened in the processing room," she said. "I'll see what I can get out of him before he goes into surgery. You keep working the DOD detail. They can sweep the tunnel clean but they can't seal it off forever."

The ambulance was getting ready to go. The first EMT had gone behind the wheel and the second one was about to close the doors in the back.

Wanda sprinted up before the doors shut and flashed her card from the ERMET. "I'm a certified EMT-2 and need to talk to the security guard if he comes to," she said to the attending EMT. "What's his status?"

"Looks like he's lost a lot of blood, but I couldn't find the entry wound. I was going to clean him up some more on the way over and start a transfusion."

"And Dr. Seavers?"

"Lost a finger and consciousness. Possible concussion from a nasty blow to the back of the head."

"I'll handle it. You stay in touch with the ER up front with the driver," she said as the EMT closed the doors on her.

The ambulance shot out down 2nd to Pennsylvania with its lights full on and siren blaring. Wanda, seated on an uncomfortable, foam-padded vinyl seat with one hand on a stainless steel grab handle, looked down at the guard.

He lay on a fold-out stretcher, held with three straps and a white blanket. She adjusted the light blue pillow behind his head.

The guard stirred and she held his hand. His hair was matted with blood.

"He shot me," he groaned, eyes still closed.

"I know," she told him. "His name was Conrad Yeats. But you killed him. They just zipped up his body and sent him to the morgue."

"No, him."

He lifted his finger and pointed to Max Seavers in the other gurney, who was just beginning to stir with consciousness.

"Max Seavers?"

The guard nodded and seemed to pass out again by the time the ambulance pulled up to the emergency entrance on 23rd Street. The ER at George Washington University Hospital, just blocks from downtown D.C.'s monuments and government complexes, was a Level 1 Trauma Center. It was where President Ronald Reagan was rushed after being shot in 1981, the year Wanda was born, and it was where she herself had been sent on more than one occasion for smoke inhalation and suspected carbon monoxide poisoning from the subterranean tunnels she frequently explored beneath the city.

A reception team was waiting to transfer the guard and Seavers to the ER. The security guard was carried in first while Wanda helped the hospital paramedics roll a moaning Max Seavers into the ER.

Seavers seemed to be regaining strength quickly, and Wanda bent her ear to listen to what he was trying to say. Then she noticed his bloody finger stump pointing to the empty gurney inside the ER.

"Don't worry," she told him. "The guard made it out alive, too. Probably in surgery already."

Seavers's eyes widened and he bolted upright, startling her and the attending ER technician. He angrily pulled the IV drip out of his forearm and looked around.

"You stupid bitch," he said to her, his eyes on fire. "That was Yeats in the ambulance. He pulled a switch!"

She ran out of the ER and saw a discarded, bloody uniform stuffed into a trash bin. The security guard from the Library of Congress was gone.

33

HILTON HOTEL

WASHINGTON, D.C.

Conrad, now wearing a white dress shirt and raincoat stolen from a doctor's locker back at GWU Hospital, got out of the cab at Dupont Circle. He walked several blocks in the drizzling rain up Connecticut toward the Hilton, which even at 1 a.m. was swarming with cabs, limos, and security as visitors from around the world were checking in for the next morning's Presidential Prayer Breakfast.

The way it was supposed to work, Conrad would walk into the lobby, ride the elevator to the tenth floor and go to room 1013, where Serena had already seen to it that he was checked in under an alias, Mr. Carlton Anderson. Then he was to call room service using the room phone and order a pastrami sandwich. Some mole on the staff under her control would then let her know that he had arrived safely and she would come to his room and see what he found in the globe and plot the best way to get it to the president at the prayer breakfast.

The problem, he immediately discovered upon entering the Hilton, was that his picture was on every TV screen in the hotel bar. News reports called him a "person of interest" in connection with a terrorist attack on the Library of Congress, in which a Capitol Policeman was slain. The FBI was pinning the blame on former Pentagon analyst–turned–Starbucks barista Danny Z, now an "Islamic extremist" and the "mastermind" behind the attack.

Those bastards, Conrad thought.

He slipped into the mainstream of boisterous late-night patrons and followed them past the gift shop to the elevator banks, which were packed with still more people. It was a mob, many of them smiling and making conversation.

Who are these people? he wondered. *And why were they alarmingly cheerful at this hour?*

Conrad stood in the middle of the mob, aware of a few glances from a couple of bodyguards around the president of some African country. He just had to grin and bear it.

It took three elevators before one opened with enough room for him. He stepped in, saw that every single button was lit up, and sighed. It would be a long ride up. At every floor it stopped, a couple of people would step off, and four more would be outside waiting to catch the elevator on the way down.

"Suck it up!" ordered a loud one from Texas, whose wife, a petite blonde, kept eyeing Conrad. "Always room for one more for Jesus!"

Finally, it was just him and the couple from Texas.

"Thought you could escape, huh?" the husband said, smiling. His nametag read Harold from Highland Park, Texas. "My wife says she knows you."

Conrad stood there, flat-footed.

"She says you're Pastor Jim. You wrote that book *A Church of One*."

Conrad paused for a moment and smiled. "So you liked it?"

"No, but Meredith did," Harold said, and turned toward his wife, whose lipoed waist and silicon breasts defied the laws of natural aging. She could have been anywhere from 30 to 50 years old, depending on where she was between her Botox injections. "See, honey, I told you we'd meet all the big shots here."

"You look much younger than your picture," she said and squeezed his arm enthusiastically. But her husband Harold didn't seem to notice.

Conrad remembered something Serena always used to tell him and said, "Now don't go looking at the outside, Meredith. The good Lord looks at the heart."

She sighed. "So true, Pastor Jim."

The elevator door opened on the tenth floor, and Conrad exhaled as he stepped off along with Harold and Meredith. He turned down a hallway and walked briskly to Room 1013, hearing Meredith's heels clack behind him. He looked over his shoulder to see the couple wave good night and enter their room across the hall. He looked both ways and then inserted the coded plastic key card Serena had given him to unlock the door.

Once inside he immediately picked up the phone on the nightstand and called room service. "I'd like a pastrami from your all-night menu. Thanks. Oh, and a Sam Adams." Then he went to the bathroom and turned on the shower.

As the water heated up, Conrad removed the silver cornerstone plate from inside his raincoat. He rubbed his thumb over the dent from the bullet Seavers intended for his heart.

He placed the silver plate on the dresser next to a golden ticket that Serena had left for him. The embossed letters read:

57th Annual
Presidential Prayer Breakfast
Thursday, July 3, 2008

Next to the ticket was a 10 x 14 souvenir reproduction of *The Washington Family* portrait by Edward Savage. Apparently Mr. Anderson had taken a day trip to Mount Vernon and the new museum. There was even a sales slip from the gift shop.

Nice, Serena.

Then he took a shower and found a complete wardrobe hanging for him in the closet. Instead he put on a bathrobe and waited for Serena, hoping she'd really bring him that pastrami, because he was famished.

As the minutes passed with no Serena and no pastrami, he found his eyes drifting back to the souvenir copy of Edward Savage's portrait *The Washington Family*. He had used it to find the globe. Perhaps it held some secret to the meaning of the contents of the globe, namely, the star map.

But the only thing new he noticed in the portrait was the column —or rather, two columns on either side of the panoramic view of the Potomac. Mount Vernon, of course, had no columns like that.

He remembered the giant Masonic board depicting King

Solomon's Temple in the secret chamber beneath the Jefferson Building. It, too, had similar columns. But something about those pillars was different from Savage's. He couldn't put his finger on it, but he was sure of it.

Then it hit him: The columns at the entrance of King Solomon's Temple had two orbs on top of them.

Two globes.

The Savage portrait hinted at it all along. That's why there were two suns on the celestial map.

There's a second globe!

But, of course, he realized. They always came in pairs.

Old Herc must have known there were two. Why didn't he tell me?

He looked again at the Savage portrait, realizing that if there were two suns representing two globes, there were probably two landmarks designating their location. If Martha Washington's fan pinpointed the cornerstone of the U.S. Capitol in the east, then perhaps . . . yes, young Eustice—a virgin, no less, at least in symbol—was holding the L'Enfant map at the western horizon. Her fingers pinched the horizon just behind the starburst in the guard of Washington's sword—surely a symbol of the sun.

That would place the location of the landmark somewhere in . . . Georgetown.

Only there was no celestial landmark in Georgetown, at least none that Conrad knew of, and he knew them all, or so he thought.

Conrad sat quietly, running through any correlation he could think of when he heard a knock at the door.

He rose to his feet and walked over to the door. He looked out the peephole to see Brooke standing in the hallway.

His heart stopped.

"I know you're in there, Conrad," she said. "I saw you in the lobby. Please let me in. Everybody's been looking for you, and I've been worried sick."

Conrad, his mind racing ahead to Serena's impending arrival and the resulting fireworks, realized it was better to have Brooke inside the room than outside, so he opened the door.

Brooke came in wearing an expensive but modest dress that still managed to show off her amazing figure. Her eyes swept the room, resting on the silver cornerstone plate on the dresser. She wrapped her arms around him and kissed him.

"Thank God you're OK, Conrad. Where the hell have you been? What's going on? The police have been asking questions, the FBI, and now your face is plastered all over the news. My news director called me and asked me if I had seen you and said you were about to join America's Most Wanted."

"You'd never believe me."

"Try me."

"The feds think I attacked the U.S. Capitol and Library of Congress and killed some people."

Her eyes widened. "And did you?"

"Well, yes. But I didn't kill the people they say I did."

"You just killed different people?"

"Yes."

"Oh, my God, Conrad. You better tell me everything."

34

Goddamn you, Yeats.

Minutes after refusing treatment at the hospital, Max Seavers was back at the Library of Congress. He ordered it sealed in the name of national security. Kicking over what was left in the secret chamber Yeats had discovered, he nursed his bandaged stump of a finger and examined the split-open celestial globe in the corner.

The globe was an incredible work in its own right, Seavers thought, and looked like it had been fashioned from a single block of fiery bronze or copper.

But the globe was empty.

Yeats had gotten away with whatever was inside.

Until now Seavers had convinced himself that the Alignment's quest for the celestial globe was a distraction from its mission. But now that Conrad Yeats had cut off his finger and gashed his head, he was furious. The smooth, unruffled veneer he had cultivated since his days at Stanford had been punctured forever. Never again could he do a handshake deal with somebody without the knowledge that he was missing something, even if it was only the tip of a finger. For that he would always hate Yeats.

Worse, Seavers knew he would have to report his failure to Osiris, something he had never had to do before.

Seavers stared at the globe in morbid fascination for a full minute before he heard footsteps and turned. It was the wide-eyed black cop, Sergeant Wanda Randolph, nipping at him like some federal terrier with two of her R.A.T.S. The Marines shouldn't have let her in.

"Sir, we've got a problem."

Once again, he'd have to set her back on her heels. "You lost the suspect again, Sergeant?"

"The security tapes from the processing room where you were shot, sir. They're gone. Without them we can't verify your story."

"Why don't you stop trying to cover your ass and start looking for Yeats, Sergeant. While you're at it, maybe you could find my finger, too."

He saw the fury in her eyes, which he actually thought made her more attractive.

"Yes, sir," she said.

The sergeant turned and vanished into the tunnel.

Seavers waited until she was gone before he turned his gaze to the Masonic mural depicting King Solomon's Temple on the opposite side of the chamber. The two pillars in front with the orbs atop caught his eye. Like a gateway.

He walked over and ordered two of his Marines from Detachment One over. They lifted the mural away to reveal a small alcove with a Mason's compass symbol to the side. He pushed it and the wall slid open.

So this was how that son of a bitch Yeats got away.

Whatever cool he still possessed disappeared as he ran through the damp tunnel like a madman, even though he knew the chance of catching up to Yeats was nil. A minute later Seavers emerged through a metal door into an alcove in the corner of the ghostly, empty Main Reading Room.

He stopped and looked around. And it suddenly hit him that the silver plate and whatever else Yeats may have taken could still be in the Library, buried somewhere among the thousands of stacks with millions of books. Even if he found Yeats, it could take days or weeks to find whatever the Alignment wanted, if ever.

He looked up at the statues of the world's great teachers ringing the dome looking down at him. He could almost hear their jeers at his failure.

Suddenly all the anger, the frustration and fury building inside him burst forth. In that moment he knew he would do whatever it took to get back whatever Yeats stole from him—starting with his own dignity.

You goddamn bastard, Yeats. I'm going to slice you alive and make you eat your own brain.

He listened to the deafening silence around him, feeling only his raging pulse. And vibrating cell phone.

He had a text message from Brooke:

YEATS AT THE HILTON.
ROOM 1013.

Seavers smiled. He wouldn't be making that call to Osiris after all.

35

"**My father always said** your father was one sick bastard," said Brooke, who sat on the bed after Conrad finished the pastrami sandwich that room service finally delivered and recounted the events since his father's funeral. Everything except Serena, which admittedly was leaving out a lot. "You can't actually believe you're a sleeper agent sent by George Washington into the future to save America? This isn't about the future of the republic, Conrad. This is about your father continuing to mess with your mind from the grave."

Conrad paced back and forth, aware of Brooke looking at him like a crazy person and all the while expecting a knock on the door from Serena.

"Brooke, this is what I know: Washington entrusted a secret to Robert Yates, a secret passed down through the generations to my foster father, who then spent the better part of my childhood training me to unlock it. And I also know that the L'Enfant map, the celestial globe, and the people trying to kill me are for real."

"Who is trying to kill you, Conrad?"

"I told you, the Alignment."

She sighed. "A mystical group of warriors who use the stars to chart the rise of their master civilization?"

"Yeah, and Max Seavers is one of them."

She blinked. "The head of DARPA?"

"Yep. This belongs to him." Conrad showed her the finger of Max Seavers.

"Oh, my God!" She stared at it in horror and looked like she was about to vomit. "What have you done?"

"Relax, he's alive." Conrad pocketed the finger in his bathrobe. "Which is more than I can say about the guard he shot in the head."

Brooke sat still on the bed, her eyes darting back and forth as if she was processing everything he was telling her. He realized just how crazy it sounded. But at some point he was going to have to deal with the feds, and Brooke through her father, Senator Scarborough, was his best shot for exoneration. Unless, of course, he wanted to spend the rest of his days hiding out in a monastery and refurbishing toner cartridges.

"Show me this document you found inside this globe."

"I hid it somewhere."

She narrowed her eyes. "You don't have it with you?"

"No, but it had a kind of star map on one side and George Washington's signature at the bottom of the other side."

"And this is the reason you walked out on me and got mixed up in this crazy conspiracy? Some map and a signature?"

"Maybe," he said. "I think the star map was originally drawn in invisible ink. But it's what's on the other side that got me into trouble."

"But you said there's nothing on the other side, just a signature."

"I think the rest of that side was written in dissolvable ink. Washington sometimes signed iffy contracts in an ink that would dissolve after a while, effectively making them disappear."

"And you found this invisible-visible parchment in a golden celestial globe?"

"It looked more like copper, really, but yes. And I think the star map leads to the other globe."

Her eyes widened. "There's another globe?"

"Yeah, but I don't know where just yet. I can't believe I was so stupid. There are always two—a celestial globe and a terrestrial globe. Even the old Mason knew it, I could see it in his eyes, but he said nothing."

He was aware of her looking at him in shock and awe. Shock at his lunacy and awe that he apparently thought it was true.

"Do you hear yourself, Conrad? How am I or my father or

anybody else supposed to believe you? Show me something other than chopped-off fingers to back up your story, Conrad!"

"How about this?"

He showed her the silver cornerstone plate. The markings captured her attention immediately. He recalled her family had some Masonic background.

"This is the cornerstone plate, Conrad. You actually found the cornerstone of the U.S. Capitol."

"I told you I did."

She looked up at him, hope in her eyes. "No, you don't understand. *This* is a legitimate story. This is something you unveil on July 4, a piece of Americana. I'll get you to tell your story on Fox. Whatever crazy-ass stuff you add, well, nobody can deny you found this."

"Or that I was the one responsible for the incidents at the Capitol and Library of Congress."

"Let me work on this, work with my dad, bring you in somehow."

"Bring me in? You make me sound like a dog you're afraid is going to come in out of the rain and crap on your carpet."

"If the paw fits, Conrad. Now get dressed."

Conrad walked into the closet and removed his bathrobe. He slipped the finger from Max Seavers into his expensive suit pants and put one leg in after the other.

"Say, Brooke," he called out. "What was his name?"

"Whose name?" she answered from the bedroom, sounding preoccupied, like she was on the phone.

"Your dog's name."

"His name was Rusty," she called back absently as she spoke quietly in the bedroom.

That's right, he thought, remembering that day in the park. Her dog was named after some early American scientist her father admired—David Rusthouse or something like that.

Conrad slid his belt through the last loop of his pants, eager to bolt. Any minute Serena would walk in and find him with Brooke, and then he would have still more explaining to do. But the reality was that after what happened at the Library of Congress tonight, nobody was going to believe anything he had to say. Not Serena nor the feds.

His only hope was to find that second globe. To do that he had to find some kind of landmark in Washington, D.C., that aligned with the setting sun, just like in the starburst on George Washington's sword at the western edge of the L'Enfant map in the Savage portrait.

The problem was that the land at the western edge of the district was developed as residential housing or preserved like Rock Creek Park. In other words, there were no obvious monuments or landmarks he could think of.

And then it hit him.

Ritty. The name of Brooke's dog wasn't Rusty. *It was Ritty.*

As in David Rittenhouse, a famous astronomer during the founding of America who worked closely with Ben Franklin and Benjamin Banneker.

As in Sarah Rittenhouse, the grand dame who two centuries later "saved" Montrose Park in Georgetown from development.

But what was Sarah Rittenhouse *really* trying to preserve the parkland for?

Conrad felt his pulse explode:

The terrestrial globe!

The armillary dedicated to Sarah Rittenhouse was in fact the landmark he was looking for—a monument to the terrestrial globe that Washington buried somewhere below!

How could I have missed it?

Then he knew the answer: In his mind he had always associated the armillary sphere with Brooke's dog, who was urinating on the memorial's base that day he followed the canine back to Brooke's shapely legs and they reconnected.

He quickly tucked in his shirt, and then froze.

How could Brooke forget her own dog's name?

Suddenly their meeting in the park—their entire "reconnection" —smelled like a setup from the start. She must have known that he liked to jog in the park and simply put herself in his path. The irony was that he must have jogged past that armillary a thousand times and never imagined its secret. And neither, he guessed, did Brooke.

Brooke had stopped talking in the bedroom.

From behind Conrad could hear the *click* of a slider. Slowly he turned and saw her pointing an automatic pistol at him.

"I'm sorry, Conrad." She shook her head. "That fucking dog."

36

Conrad stared in shock at the 9mm Glock in Brooke's manicured hands, his mind trying to make sense of how he could have so thoroughly misinterpreted the nature of their relationship, and how long he had before whomever she called arrived.

"You've got to understand, Conrad, I had no choice," she said. "But you, you still have a choice: Give up the globe or die."

She's either with the feds or the Alignment, he thought. If it's the feds, he could live with it. *But, God, not the Alignment.*

"Some choice," he said, and coolly walked into the bedroom. Brooke followed him, and he could sense her gun pointed at his back until he sat down in a chair and looked up at her. "So everything we had was a lie?"

"No, Conrad," she said, her voice shaking with emotion. "Everything *but* us is a lie."

"Like you and Max Seavers?" he said, putting it out there.

"Tell me where you put the star map from the first globe, Conrad, and I'll let you go before he gets here."

Damn. She's Alignment.

He said, "What about the second globe?"

"Max doesn't have to know. But I need something to give him."

Conrad nodded, trying to figure his way out of this. "Does your father know about any of this?"

"No. He's a Mason. That's why it was a coup for the Alignment to nab me as a teenager and then use me to get to you, the son of General Yeats."

"But I'm not his son. Not his real son."

"No, you're much more special," she said. "I know about Antarctica, Conrad. I know about your blood."

Conrad looked at her. "What about my blood?"

"It's the basis for Max's flu vaccine."

Conrad started. "And how's that?"

"Max came to DARPA to genetically engineer the perfect American soldier," she said. "Along the way he discovered certain immunities to disease in the bloodlines of native Americans, specifically the Algonquin Indians. Immunities that had been diluted over the generations. So Max launched a global DNA testing program to connect the lost cousins of the Algonquins in the Americas, Europe, Africa, the Middle East, and Asia. It was called Operation Adam and Eve. By studying the mutations in Y chromosomes and mitochondrial DNA, Max was able to reconstruct their tribal migrations throughout the globe and trace their roots to Antarctica and one common ancestor: You."

"Me?"

"You're more American than any of us, Conrad. The last of the Atlanteans."

"Atlantis?" Conrad had thought he was ready for anything, but not this. This was over the top even for Brooke. "What on earth are you talking about?"

"You may be of this earth, Conrad, but whatever is in some of your dormant DNA strands isn't. You're one in six billion. Why else do you think your father was so hell-bent on going to Antarctica in the first place? Or didn't Her Holiness, Sister Serghetti, and her friends in Rome tell you?"

No, she hadn't, Conrad thought, and he hoped to God she was going to beat Seavers to the room so he could personally hash this out with her.

"So I take it you're not going to help me with the feds?"

"The Alignment IS the federal government, Conrad. That's what I'm trying to tell you."

"You cannot seriously expect me to believe that every low-level grunt in the federal government is Alignment."

"No, but they all work for the Alignment, whether they know it or not."

"Not me," he said, and with a quick move of his right arm grabbed her arm holding the gun, slammed her body against the wall with his own, and then with a hard twist snapped her wrist.

"Ahh!" she cried, but wouldn't drop the gun. She was almost as tough, physically, as Seavers.

He gave her a sharp elbow in the stomach, spun out as she doubled over and then hit her on the neck, sending her to the floor.

He picked up her gun and pointed it at her head as she slowly rose on all fours.

"You broke my fucking wrist, Conrad," she said.

He dug the barrel of the gun into her temple. "Why do the monuments line up with the stars tomorrow, Brooke? Why now? Why 2008?"

"Something about the transit of Venus or something."

Conrad knew the transit of Venus—when Venus crossed the path of the sun to the naked eye on Earth—came once every couple of hundred years. But when the transit came, it came in pairs—eight years apart. As it happened, the world was in the middle of such a transit. The first crossed the sun in 2004, the year he and Serena had their adventure in Antarctica. The next transit was due in 2012. There wasn't anything scientifically significant about such a conjunction, but it held great meaning to the ancients.

"We're between the two transits, Brooke. Why 2008?"

"Something about solar years and the number 225. It's all Alignment esoterica. I'm not at that level."

But Conrad was. The planet Venus took about 225 Earth days, or about 7½ months, to go around the sun. At the same time, Venus took more than 243 Earth days to turn on its own axis, making its days longer than its years. Conrad subtracted 225 from the current year, 2008, and came up with 1783.

"Newburgh," he said, recalling the coup attempt Washington allegedly quelled in 1783 at his final winter encampment. "It has something to do with Newburgh."

"I don't know!" Brooke screamed.

He kept pressing her. "What's the connection to my family,

Brooke? What did Robert Yates have to do with it? Was he responsible for this?"

Brooke bared her teeth. "He was nobody, Conrad, a side note to history like you want to be. He was the goddamn lawyer."

Conrad paused. "For what?"

Brooke rammed her head into his, and with a scream lunged for the gun in his hand. Caught off-balance, Conrad fell back and brought the butt of the gun down on the back of Brooke's head, knocking her out.

With a heave he pushed her body off him and dragged it to the bed. He then tied her hands to the posts, spread-eagled, as she came to.

"What's going to happen tomorrow, Brooke?"

"I don't know," she moaned. "Only that the Alignment is going to make it happen."

"Not good enough." He tightened the knot around her broken wrist until she winced in agony.

"I'm just trying to save your life!" she cried.

"Funny way of showing it," he said, waving her gun in her face. "Now, for the last time, what's going down tomorrow?"

Her voice, when she finally spoke, had a dead tone. "Max is going to release a weaponized bird flu contagion."

Conrad stared at her. "Where?"

"Somewhere on the Mall, I don't know. But it's got a 28-day incubation inhibitor so that it won't jump human-to-human until August 1. Everyone will assume it originated at the Olympic Games in Beijing."

"So Seavers kills a billion Chinese," Conrad said. "What happens to all the Americans who get saved with his vaccine?"

"You know that, thanks to Congressional gerrymandering, there are only seventeen competitive districts left in America that can swing a national election. Undesirables, including representatives, get their vaccines turned off and die. By the time the voters elect replacement officials—Alignment types—it's too late. A democratically elected coup."

"And this thing from Newburgh is their moral, if not legal justification."

"Oh, God, I loved you, Conrad."

He gagged Brooke and left her writhing on the bed as he placed the gun on the dresser and walked to the door. He slowly opened it and looked down the hallway just as the ding of the elevator sounded.

He quickly walked across the hall and knocked on the second door to the right. It was Meredith from Texas who answered. "Harold, it's Pastor Jim!"

Harold was in the bathroom, vomiting up his dinner.

"May I come in?" Conrad said, stepping inside and closing the door behind him. As he did, he looked out the peephole and saw Max Seavers walking toward his room.

37

The elite club room on the tenth floor of the Hilton was on the same level as Conrad's room, but Serena felt a world away. What she had hoped to be a brief meet-and-greet after the media dinner had stretched into the early hours of the next morning. It was against her nature to not sympathize with and pray for those in need, whatever their station in life. And it was also the perfect alibi for her whereabouts during those hours between the media dinner and the prayer breakfast.

A Hollywood producer was confessing to her that his reason for attending the Presidential Prayer Breakfast was to meet well-heeled "Christian coin" to fund "family movies" to cover his alimony payments and cocaine habits. As he spoke in hushed tones, she couldn't help but steal glances at the large flat-panel TV screen on the wall flashing pictures of Conrad and the swarm of police outside the Library of Congress. The dateline flashed July 3, 2008, across the screen, and it was clear the story was going to dominate the morning news shows in an hour or so. This was what America was going to wake up to.

Dear Lord, she prayed, *I hope he's OK.*

Her iPhone vibrated and she looked down to see a text message from Benito that Conrad had made it to his room and had called the hotel's room service. Serena let out a low sigh of relief. She wanted to bolt right then, and struggled to maintain a calm expression before this reprobate of a producer who saw American Christians not as a flock to be fed but a market demographic to be fleeced. His "career," it seemed, consisted almost entirely of living off other people while he indulged his talent for making box office flops.

That moment a concierge walked over to tell her that there was a gentleman outside the club lounge who would like to see her. *Could Conrad really be that stupid and have left his room?* She casually stood up and politely excused herself, pausing only to shake a few hands on her way out.

Max Seavers was waiting for her in the foyer, along with two Secret Service agents.

"What did you do to your finger, Max?" she said, trying to hide her alarm. "And is that a gash on your forehead?"

"Follow me," he said sternly.

He led her down the hallway to the third door on the left—the room she had reserved for Conrad. She tensed up.

The game's up, girl.

The door was open and two more Secret Service agents were inside. But she couldn't see Conrad.

Only Brooke Scarborough, tied to the bed, spread-eagled, a bullet hole in her head.

Oh, my God, she thought with a shudder. *Conrad, what have you done?*

"I'm sorry you had to see this, Sister Serghetti, but I need to ask you if you've seen Conrad Yeats at the hotel."

"No," she said, still staring at Brooke. "What does he have to do with this?"

"He's a wanted man," Seavers said. "This was his room. He checked in under the alias Carl Anderson. I thought you might know something."

"I don't."

Seavers turned to the Secret Service agents. "Not a word to Senator Scarborough or anybody until after the prayer breakfast," he ordered. "We have a killer on the loose. We don't want to give him a heads-up that we're onto him by creating any unusual disruptions. Seal off the room and post two security guards outside the door. I want room-to-room sweeps during the breakfast while everybody is downstairs in the ballroom. This killer isn't getting out of this building."

The lead special agent nodded. "Yes, sir."

Seavers took her by the arm and escorted her out the door.

"Where are you taking me, Max?"

"Somewhere safe," he told her. "There's no telling what this maniac might do."

He led her down the hallway to a service closet that turned out to be an express service elevator. It linked the small kitchen of the 10th-floor club room to the hotel's main kitchen on the ballroom level. They took it all the way down and emerged in the service corridor between the back of the ballroom stage and the main kitchen.

Waiting for them were six Secret Service agents, who instantly formed a protective ring around them.

They turned down another hallway behind the back of the ballroom, a curving corridor with wood-paneled walls and portraits of every president and first lady since George Washington. Step by step they passed through succeeding epochs of administrations until they came to the portraits of the sitting American president and his wife and then a small, unmarked door.

Inside was a special VIP room with red carpets and gold walls that reminded Serena of a funeral parlor. The president's advance Secret Service detail was there. So, too, were Secretary Packard, Senator Scarborough, and several Chinese officials, all awaiting the president.

"Sister Serghetti," said Packard. "You know Senator Scarborough."

She was caught off guard but smiled and shook the hand of the father of the dead woman she had just seen. "How are you, Senator?"

"On behalf of the Presidential Prayer Breakfast, I'd like to personally thank you for offering up the opening prayer."

"The honor is mine, Mr. Senator."

"And this is Mr. Ling, China's top Olympics ambassador. Max Seavers is going to show him and all the Olympics delegates some real fireworks tomorrow on the Fourth."

Mr. Ling was all smiles. "I told my wife I was going to see the Fourth of July from the ultimate skybox—the observation deck of the Washington Monument. She didn't believe me."

Senator Scarborough looked at his watch. "Well, Mr. Ling and

I have to get backstage. Sister Serghetti, you simply walk out when Bono is finished performing and open the breakfast in prayer. The rest of the program will take care of itself."

Serena nodded. "Yes, Mr. Senator, thank you."

She watched Scarborough leave with Ling and two Secret Service agents. It was just her, Seavers, and a glaring Packard in the room now, along with the president's personal advance team.

"What the hell is going on, Seavers?" Packard burst out.

"We found the body of Senator Scarborough's daughter in a room checked out to Yeats. Yeats murdered her."

"God Almighty!" Packard said. "This is a nightmare!"

"I don't believe Dr. Yeats murdered Ms. Scarborough," Serena said quickly. "Not for one second. Dr. Yeats is an American patriot of the first order and comes from a family of patriots. I also know he had feelings for her and would never kill without just cause."

Packard looked at Max Seavers. "What's Yeats doing here at the Washington Hilton of all places, anyway?"

Seavers said, "We believe his primary target is the president, sir."

"What!" Serena cried. "You can't be serious."

She was astounded, considering his relationship with Conrad, that Packard seemed to think it plausible.

"I suggest you mass e-mail a photo of Yeats to all agents on the premises immediately, Mr. Secretary," Seavers pressed. "He's wanted not only for the death of a security guard and an attack on the Library of Congress, but now the slaying of a U.S. senator's daughter. And the senator will have all our heads if we fail to apprehend Yeats."

That was enough for Packard, whose purse strings were controlled by Scarborough as chairman of the Senate Armed Services Committee.

"OK, do it."

Max Seavers nodded, clearly proud of himself.

Serena realized that Seavers had cleverly managed to turn the one person she and Conrad needed to reach—the president of the United States—into the one person he would never be able to get close to.

"What about Sister Serghetti, sir?" Seavers asked. "She has a history with Yeats and might pass along intel to him. Or some key or means to escape."

"That's absurd, Mr. Secretary." She then looked at Seavers. "You want to frisk me, Max?"

Seavers motioned to a couple of the stone-faced Secret Service agents but was cut off by Packard.

"This is the Presidential Prayer Breakfast, goddammit," Packard said. "Sister Serghetti is in the program for the opening prayer. We can't hold her, Seavers. We'll just watch her."

A Secret Service agent walked up and said, "Mr. Secretary, the presidential motorcade is two minutes away."

"I'll be back in a minute to walk with the president to the ballroom." Then Packard offered her his arm. "Ladies first."

"Thank you, Mr. Secretary."

Packard looked back at Max Seavers and the security detail. "After the breakfast we'll meet here with the president and break the news of his daughter's slaying to Senator Scarborough," Packard barked. "By then you better pray that you've got Yeats in custody. Now go find that goddamn bastard."

38

If Conrad had his way, right now he'd be digging for the second globe beneath the Sarah Rittenhouse armillary in Montrose Park. He had already figured out that the secret access tunnel had to be the cave that his father had shown him as a child, and that the globe was probably at the bottom of that old Algonquin well in the back. It all made sense now, every wacky thing his crazy ass father had put him through.

But by 5 a.m. all entrances and exits to the Hilton had been sealed off in anticipation of the president's arrival. He was trapped in a hotel room with Harold and Meredith from Highland Park, Texas.

The most he could hope for now was to warn Serena and the president about the second globe and Seavers's plan to release a bird flu contagion. His best shot at reaching them was the prayer breakfast. And thanks to some bad blowfish the night before, Harold was going to be saying his prayers in the toilet while Conrad—or rather "Pastor Jim"—escorted Meredith to the breakfast.

Together they stood in the long line of thousands of prayer breakfast attendees who had emerged from packed elevators and stairwells to follow the directions of young ushers in blue blazers down two escalators to the ballroom level for the 57th Annual Presidential Prayer Breakfast. And dead ahead, just before the ballroom's open doors, the Secret Service had set up an elaborate and impenetrable security checkpoint.

"This is just like the end of time when God's angels will separate the sheep from the goats," Meredith joked.

Conrad chuckled nervously. He had pulled a switch with the tickets back in Harold and Meredith's room, taking Harold's ticket and leaving him his own. But he also had the silver cornerstone plate. Whatever hope he had of slipping through the checkpoint would vanish as soon as he tripped the metal detectors and drew unwanted attention.

Meredith slipped her arm under Conrad's and looked up at him starry-eyed. "Ooh, I feel so dangerous, Pastor Jim!"

As the metal detection gates at the checkpoint began to loom larger, Conrad felt his chest tighten. There was no way the trained agents were going to miss the fact he looked nothing like Harold's picture unless Meredith distracted them first.

"Hey, Meredith," he said, and removed the silver cornerstone plate from his inside breast pocket. "This souvenir I bought from Mount Vernon. I want you to have it."

"Why, thank you, Pastor Jim!" she said, and took it from his hand and ran a perfectly manicured fingernail across the surface. "How pretty! I'll treasure it," she cooed, and slipped it into her little pink purse.

When they reached the security gates a few moments later, Conrad could see there were checkpoints about ten feet apart. Armed agents in windbreakers stood at one table next to the first gate.

"Please empty your pockets and place any metal objects on the table," said a young female officer. "Thank you."

Beyond the gate an impossibly large black agent stood with a wand in his hand for full body scans.

"Oooh, this is so exciting," she said to the officer as she emptied her purse. "Oh, wait, hon, you go through first, I better turn this over," she said, and pulled out the cornerstone plate from her purse. "Don't want to set off any alarms with my souvenir."

Conrad presented his ticket, walked through the metal detector, and looked back to see the officer return the cornerstone plate to Meredith.

"Please move on, ma'am."

Conrad let out a low breath as Meredith bounced over to him with a smile. He calmly led them away from the security checkpoint and toward the open doors of the giant ballroom. Soon as they crossed the threshold, he tried to ditch her.

"I'm at table 232," he told her. "Where are you?"

She had trouble letting go of his arm. "I'm over in the 700s."

"I just realized something," he said. "That souvenir I gave you—I had promised it to someone else. I feel horrible."

"Oh, now don't you worry about a thing, Pastor Jim." She looked disappointed, but gave it back without a second thought. "You gotta be a man of your word."

Conrad smiled at her as they parted ways. "You're a saint."

Seavers left the gold room with a couple of Secret Service agents and marched toward the security checkpoint outside the ballroom. He showed the agents on duty Yeats's picture. None of them had seen him.

"Are you sure?" Seavers pressed one young man, who had hesitated.

"I'm almost positive," he swore, though Seavers could see the doubt in his eyes.

"Almost?" Seavers seethed.

Just before he killed her, Brooke had told him that Yeats had discovered the existence of a second globe. Seavers knew he had to find out what Yeats knew and stop him before he told the good sister or the feds.

Seavers then heard some kind of row and turned to a man being frisked at the metal detection gate by two agents.

Seavers hurried over. "What's going on?"

"We flagged his ticket—Carl Anderson."

Seavers looked at the man. He obviously wasn't Conrad Yeats, but the man must have had contact with him. "I take it your name's not Carl?"

"My name's Harold," the red-faced man said. "I don't know how I got that ticket. Look, my wife is already inside with Pastor Jim Lee. You know, the bestselling author?"

"Does Pastor Jim look like this?" Seavers held up the photo of Yeats, which looked familiar enough to startle Harold.

"That's him!"

"Not quite," Seavers said. "You just handed off your wife to a terrorist wanted for the slaying of law enforcement agents and attacks on America's most sacred landmarks."

"Dear God!" Harold cried. "I didn't know! You have to believe me!"

"Can you recognize your wife, at least?"

Harold shot him an angry look. "I'm pretty sure I can."

"Then take me to her in the ballroom," Seavers said.

The gigantic ballroom was as big as a football field. The domed ceiling a couple of stories high only added to the aura of an indoor sports stadium.

Conrad, now free of Meredith, slipped between hundreds of round tables with white cloths and gold chairs toward a table to the right of the stage. It was near the staff door to the hotel's main kitchen, where hundreds of waiters shuffled in and out.

He picked an empty seat at the table, the least desirable chair because its back was to the stage, but perfect for him. He sat down and faced the wall by the kitchen entrance and six smiling table companions: a young couple from California, an older self-proclaimed "Lake Wobegon" couple from Minnesota, a middle-aged rabbi from New York, and a tall black woman from D.C. It was a United Nations of faith.

"You're never going to see anything good looking this way," joked the rabbi. "Would you mind passing the cantaloupe? They pray later."

Conrad looked down at the table full of fruit, pastries, juices, and coffee. Because of security issues and the crowd, everything had been prepped beforehand, and he had to remove a clear plastic wrap from the chilled plate of cantaloupe.

"Here you go," he said, and passed it over. As he did, his eyes swept the ballroom for Serena. She was already on stage with various generals and senators, including the presumptive Democratic and Republican party nominees for the presidency in November. They were waiting for the president.

Most everybody else in the ballroom was seated, except hundreds of waiters attending to the tables. Conrad helped himself to some coffee and looked over the navy blue program with gold leaf trim in front of him. The opening prayer was to be offered by Sister Serena Serghetti following a contemporary rendition of "Amazing Grace" by the rock group U2's lead singer, Bono.

Conrad was about to pour himself a second cup of coffee when the young California man, who was Asian-American, said, "You might want to think twice about that. Security won't let you go to the bathroom while the president and first lady are in the ballroom."

"Thanks, I'll hold off . . ."

"It's Jim," the man said, offering his hand, and Conrad shook it. "Jim Lee."

Conrad cocked his head. "Like Pastor Jim, the bestselling author?"

The black woman and the rabbi snorted a giggle. Conrad didn't get the joke.

"Pretty much," said Pastor Jim. "That's me."

"Oh!"

Conrad suddenly realized that Meredith from Texas had known from the start he wasn't Pastor Jim.

The old-timer from Minnesota said, "Is it true that there are more Christians in China than America, Pastor Jim?"

"Yes," said Pastor Jim. "But my family is Korean."

"From Seoul?"

"Burbank."

The old-timer, realizing he perhaps made some sort of faux pas, nodded enthusiastically. "You people make good citizens."

"Thank you." Pastor Jim smiled.

The black woman next to Conrad said, "He sells almost as many books as Bishop Jakes, you know."

Conrad nodded absently and, scoping the room for any sign of Seavers, said, "You sure don't see this kind of event in any other country on Earth."

"You mean elected officials acknowledging they're not God?"

"You got it," Conrad said, surprised by her dig. "You must work for one of them?"

"All of them. I'm a sergeant with the Capitol Police."

"I'd have never guessed," Conrad said slowly. There was something very familiar about her. But if she was feeling likewise she wasn't showing it. "Tell me, is it true what they say about politicians here in Washington?"

"What's that?"

"That the only ones with convictions are in jail?"

"You're funny! I'm Wanda, by the way. Wanda Randolph."

"J-Jack," he said, glancing over at Pastor Jim, who was now talking to the rabbi.

She put out her hand. "Pleased to meet you, Jack."

"The pleasure's mine."

The instant Conrad grasped her hand he knew it belonged to the woman who held his in the ambulance the night before, the same one who pumped several bullets his way in the tunnels beneath the U.S. Capitol a couple of days ago.

She knew it, too. Her smile froze and she looked down at his hand, not letting go. Her eyes widened like she had just been shocked with an electric buzzer.

"This your first time here, Jack?" she asked him, even as she glanced over her shoulder at the small army of plainclothes security surrounding the ballroom.

"First and probably last," he told her, not taking his eyes off her.

"Why is that, Jack?"

"I just feel like I don't belong, you know? Like I'm a criminal here with all the saints."

There were glances around the table. Then a few vigorous nods.

"We all are, brother," said the man from Minnesota. "But too few of us are honest enough to admit it and seek forgiveness at the foot of the cross. Isn't that right, Pastor Jim?"

Pastor Jim, his mouth full with an almond croissant, could only nod.

Conrad looked at Wanda as her hand reached into her purse. He slipped both of his own under the table and for a wild second was ready to upend it if necessary.

But her hands emerged with a card and a pen. "I know from the ballistics report that you didn't kill my man Larry last night," she whispered to him as she wrote a phone number on the back of her card. "But I can't yet prove that Max Seavers did." She slid the card across the tablecloth to him.

"What's this?" he asked.

"That's the number to Prison Fellowship. It's a charity that ministers to men and women behind bars. You're going to need it if you don't scram this second."

Conrad looked at her. "And why is that?"

"Because I see Max Seavers and two Secret Service agents walking straight toward our table."

From the stage Serena saw Max Seavers, too, and decided to jump the gun on the prayer breakfast by standing up, walking to the microphone stand, and offering up her opening prayer a good seven minutes ahead of schedule.

"Let us rise for the opening prayer," she said, and bowed her head, aware that the president hadn't arrived yet and that she had caught the senators on stage off guard. But there was nothing they could say at this point as everybody in the ballroom rose to their feet and effectively blocked Seavers from reaching Conrad.

"Almighty God," she prayed. "We make our earnest prayer that Thou wilt keep the United States in Thy Holy protection, and Thou wilt incline the hearts of the citizens to cultivate a spirit of subordination and obedience to government, and entertain a brotherly affection and love for one another and for their fellow citizens of the United States at large. . . ."

She kept her eyes open, along with every member of the security detail stationed throughout the ballroom, and she could see Seavers seething in the back, craning his neck as he searched for Conrad.

". . . And finally that Thou wilt most graciously be pleased to dispose us all to do justice, to love mercy, and to demean ourselves with that charity, humility, and pacific temper of mind which were the characteristics of the Divine Author of our blessed religion, and without a humble imitation whose example in these things we can never hope to be a happy nation. Grant our supplication, we beseech Thee, through Jesus Christ our Lord, Amen."

As soon as everybody sat down again, Seavers, a furious frown on his face, marched toward the corner of the room where Yeats sat. Bono, who was supposed to open the breakfast with a song before the opening prayer, now began to sing "Amazing Grace."

This prayer breakfast was like an absurd nightmare, Seavers thought, walking among the well-dressed deluded whose minuscule brainwaves were directed to a deity that did not exist, and who actually believed that the Founding Fathers sought to establish a Christian nation. That Conrad Yeats believed he could find refuge here was even more absurd.

Yeats had his back to him as Seavers approached and recognized the policewoman from the Capitol. Was there any place he could avoid that woman?

Seavers glared at Sergeant R.A.T.S. as the two Secret Service agents took positions behind her opposite Yeats. Seavers then placed his left hand with the stump of a finger on Yeats's left shoulder.

"Time's up, Yeats."

But instead of Yeats, Seavers found himself staring at the face of a Latino server, who was holding a pot of coffee.

"This is Pablo, our server," Sergeant Randolph explained. "We had an extra seat and in the spirit of this event invited him to join us in prayer."

"Goddamn you, where is he?" he said, drawing sharp glances from nearby tables.

"Relax, Dr. Seavers," she said, eyes like daggers. "Where's he going to go? He's not armed and you've got an army of security people down here."

Seavers snapped his head and scanned the ballroom for Yeats as the Irish lilt of Bono's voice swelled to an unearthly decibel level. No sign of him, only servers with coffee and breakfast items heading into and out of the kitchen entrance.

"The kitchen," he barked.

39

By the time Serena followed the president out of the ballroom after his remarks to the attendees, it appeared from the anxious faces of the Secret Service agents in the hallway that her prayer had been answered and that Conrad had escaped.

"I heard you did a good job with the opening prayer, Sister Serghetti," the president said as she followed him and his Secret Service detail past the portraits of previous leaders. "Wish I had heard it myself."

"I simply recited the official prayer that George Washington offered for the United States of America in the year 1783," she said. "It was printed in the program."

The president frowned and said nothing more until they entered the gold room, where Packard was waiting beside an American flag and a small spiral stairwell that led to a secret outside door and the president's waiting limousine.

"You've got sixty seconds before I step outside," the president said.

Packard broke the news. "That item we've been searching for is waiting for you in the Oval Office, but it's empty," he said, providing no particulars with Serena present. "Brooke Scarborough is dead. Conrad Yeats killed her and is at large on the premises. Seavers is sweeping everything room-by-room."

The president looked at her. "And I'm to understand that the Vatican has been helping Dr. Yeats?"

"No, Mr. President, but I have," she said boldly, seeing the shock in Packard's face. "You should, too. And he did not kill Brooke Scarborough."

She slipped her hand inside her blouse and removed Washington's letter to Stargazer. Packard looked like he was going to pass out at the very sight of it.

"I had hoped to press my case with you once I had everything, Mr. President, but I'm afraid I don't." She handed him the letter. "But you have everything I do, sir."

The president looked it over and handed it to Packard. "DARPA will analyze this?"

"Right away, Mr. President."

Serena watched Packard slip it inside his dress uniform pocket. She doubted it would ever see the fluorescent light of a lab at DARPA or anywhere else if Packard were foolish enough to pass it along to Max Seavers.

She said, "What you'll find out, Mr. President, is that Dr. Yeats is simply following the orders of George Washington, commander-in-chief."

"I'm the commander-in-chief, Sister Serghetti," the president said emphatically.

"What I'm trying to say is that he believes he is serving the highest interests of the republic. If you could offer him immunity from prosecution, he might come in and give you whatever he took from the globe."

"I appreciate that, Sister Serghetti, and maybe yesterday we could have cut him some kind of deal," the president said. "But now that he's been caught detonating explosives on U.S. landmarks, slaying federal agents, and has murdered the daughter of one of America's most prominent senators, well, I don't think even I can help him. I swore an oath to protect America."

"No, Mr. President, you swore an oath to protect the Constitution."

The president was not pleased with her impudence. "I'll say a prayer for Conrad Yeats, Sister Serghetti. God bless you."

"And you, Mr. President."

With that, the president marched up the spiral staircase behind two Secret Service agents. He was followed by Packard, who looked back at her with undisguised animosity. She saw a square of light thrown on the curving wall and heard the roar of running engines outside before the thud from an unseen door left her alone in the room.

She pulled out her cell phone and pressed a button. Benito answered. "Bring the car around. We're leaving."

40

Inside the Hilton's underground parking garage, two policemen stood on either side of the service door as dozens of waiters carried crates of fruit, muffins, and croissants from the prayer breakfast to awaiting vans, which in turn would deliver the food to local homeless shelters.

One of those waiters was Conrad Yeats. He carried not one but two boxes of ice-packed fruit on his shoulders to the nearest van, but he never went back inside. Using the vehicle line to shield himself from the policemen, he walked out into the garage in search of Benito so he could hitch a ride in Serena's limo with the Vatican emblem and secret cargo compartment.

The garage was alive with activity now that the president had left and the senators, congress members, and foreign dignitaries were free to leave as well. The limousines and SUVs were already lining up to pick up their VIPs in front of the hotel entrance.

"Conrad Yeats?" a voice called from the shadows.

Conrad cursed himself for having ended up in a well-lit place in the garage. He turned to see a young brunette whose face he recognized but whose name he had forgotten. She was in her mid-20s, an aide to a female senator from California.

"Hi, there!" he said, faking excitement as he walked over to her.

She frowned at his generic response. "It's Lisa from San Francisco," she said. "And what are *you* of all people doing at a prayer breakfast?"

"Mending my ways, Lisa."

He pulled out a knife he had taken from the kitchen and put it to her side as she gasped. He hated himself for doing this to her, but he had no choice.

"OK, I confess," he whispered in her ear. "I haven't really changed. If you scream or make a sound, I'll kill you. You've seen the TV reports. You know I will."

"Please," she begged him. "I'll be better for you next time. You can wear the fedora and I'll learn to like the whip."

"Quiet," he said, jabbing the knife in the fold of her skin. "You're going to help me get out of here, Lisa. Nod if you understand."

Lisa nodded.

Seavers stationed himself outside the main entrance of the Hilton and watched the VIPs get into their taxis, limousines, and SUVs. The prayer breakfast was over, incident-free as far as its guests were concerned. The announcement about Brooke Scarborough's death would not reach them until they were on their way back to Kansas or Iowa or wherever the hell they came from. By then, of course, the Alignment's agenda would be unstoppable.

The only X factor, he thought with rage, was the elusive Yeats.

Seavers watched the junior senator from California and her aide get into her limousine and drive off as a sleeker limousine with a Vatican flag pulled up. He turned his head to see Serena Serghetti emerge from the front entrance and make her way to the open rear door and climb in.

Seavers motioned two Secret Service agents to the limousine. They halted the driver and swept the underside of the car with long, extended mirrors.

The rear door opened and Serena stepped back out and watched the scene. And because she did, a small crowd behind her did also.

"Lose something, Max?" she asked, putting on a great show of being held up. "I confess I brought out a couple of chocolate croissants for Benito. He loves them so."

"Tell your driver to open the trunk," Seavers demanded, and walked to the back as two agents drew their guns.

He was aware of the scene he was causing with the curious dignitaries, but he didn't care, even when a press photographer started taking pictures. He knew he couldn't force her to open up—the car had diplomatic plates, after all—but if she didn't the world would know she was hiding something, and so would he.

Her swarthy driver came out and, getting the nod from Serena, opened the trunk. Besides a garment bag and small suitcase, it was empty.

Serena put her hands on her hips and an amused expression on her face for the cameras. "You want to search those, too, Max?"

Seavers turned red with rage when one of his agents came up. "Sir, we found something," he said and led Seavers to the rear seat of the cabin.

Seavers then waved the good Sister over from her photo op and pointed into the limousine. "Open that seat compartment or I'll tear it open with a knife. Your choice."

"Max." She turned serious. "You do understand that in some countries I've been forced to smuggle out missionaries and political prisoners. If you let the press and public know about this, then some of those prisoners will lose their last option."

"Your choice, Serena."

She leaned into the back of the limousine and felt for a hidden latch that released the flap beneath the rear seat. As it opened, she was pushed back by one of the Secret Service agents.

"Step back, please, ma'am," he said and pointed his gun into the secret compartment.

But it was empty.

Seavers burned inside as Serena turned to face him with her beatific smile. "Told you, Max."

Aware of the television cameras, he leaned over and whispered. "Your friend the fugitive is a murderer and an American traitor. You don't want anything to do with him."

"No, Max. I don't want anything to do with *you* anymore. You can keep your vaccines." She got inside and nodded to Benito to go.

Seavers watched the limousine drive off and turned to the Secret Service agent who had examined the secret compartment. "Did you place the GPS nano tracker on her person?"

"Yes, sir. Stuck it under her shoulder when we hustled her down to the holding room. She'll never know."

"Have a team follow her signal," Seavers ordered. "At some point she's bound to lead us to Yeats."

Serena leaned back in her seat and breathed a sigh of relief as Benito turned the limousine onto Connecticut.

"You OK, *signorina*?"

"Now that I'm breathing, yes. But I don't know where Conrad is."

Benito looked up in the mirror. "He was in that limo ahead of us back at the Hilton."

"No, there was a senator in that limo. I saw her get in."

"But Dr. Yeats was driving," Benito said. "He found me in the underground garage and told me to give you a message."

Serena sat on the edge of her seat. "Give it to me."

"He said he will meet you at Sarah's house."

As Conrad drove the senator's limousine, he listened carefully to the senator gossip with Lisa about some of the individual speakers at the breakfast even as she expressed being moved by the event itself. Lisa said very little. He had warned her that he was strapped with explosives and that any attempt to alert the senator or send a text message from her cell phone would blow them all up.

It worked until they crossed Washington Circle.

"What's that knocking?" the senator asked Lisa.

Conrad could see Lisa squirm in his rearview mirror.

"Could be the 87 octane level of the gas, ma'am," he told the senator, pulling into a Union gas station across the street from the Ritz-Carlton. "Let me check, maybe top off the tank with some premium."

"You should have done this earlier," the senator barked as he stepped out in his chauffeur's uniform and walked to the pump.

A minute later, the knocking got even louder inside the limousine.

The senator looked out the window and couldn't see the driver. "Find out where he is, Lisa."

But her aide started breaking down in tears for no reason.

"I don't have time for this today, Lisa."

The senator opened her own door and saw the gasoline hose in the limousine's gas tank, but no driver. The knocking, she realized, seemed to be coming from the trunk. She stepped out and walked to the trunk and opened it.

There was her driver, tied up and gagged.

By the time Seavers and his men arrived at the gas station, two D.C. cops were questioning the senator's aide, who apparently knew Yeats from their previous, albeit brief, relationship and provided a detailed description. An ATM camera across the street at the SportsClub fitness center, meanwhile, had captured Yeats on video.

Where are you going, Yeats? Seavers wondered as he climbed into his SUV and they drove off. *To the second globe perhaps? To meet your lovely Serena?*

"You set it up so I can track the nun on my own phone?" he asked the driver, a Marine named Landford from Detachment One.

"Yes, sir," Landford replied. "Check your Google Maps."

Seavers looked at his cell phone and followed the red blip that represented Sister Serghetti. It was moving up R Street past Montrose Park. Then it stopped.

He looked closely at the screen and clicked the zoom button. Slowly the fuzzy pixels sharpened and he realized he was staring down at a statue of some kind. He clicked on the image and a Web page automatically popped up with a picture of the Sarah Rittenhouse Armillary.

The armillary, he realized, staring at the image of the sun dial-like sphere on its marble pedestal. *The second globe that Brooke had told him about, the one Yeats was after now, could be buried beneath the armillary!*

"We're here, sir," said the driver in the mirror.

Seavers looked out his window to see the armillary a mere 20 or so feet away from the street, potentially holding a treasure but in plain daylight for all to see.

But there was no sign of Serena or Yeats.

He looked back down at his phone. The red dot—the GPS tracker—was still stationary, still blinking next to the armillary.

"She must be under the armillary," he said. "There must be another entrance, a sewer line or something beneath the monument. Get the drill team from Jones Point over here and send a plainclothes unit to sweep the park."

"Excuse me, sir," Landford said, hanging up his phone. "We picked up a call from the National Park Service station inside the park. An officer nabbed a man in a chauffeur's uniform fitting our APB."

A few minutes later Seavers entered a small, damp NPS station, which stunk from the dung of the horses in the stables. The watch officer escorted Seavers to a small holding cell, where the man in the chauffeur's uniform sat in the corner.

"Yeats!" Seavers shouted.

The head looked up and Seavers found himself looking into the wrinkled, warted face of a homeless man who had traded his rags for a suit.

"You imbeciles!" Seavers shouted to the watch officer.

But the watch officer was talking on his radio. "Copy that," he said, and switched it off before addressing Seavers. "Looks like your man stole one of our horses, too."

41

Conrad left his police horse at the old Peirce Mill. He then walked along the creek at the bottom of the ravine in the direction of the cave. That cave, he was now convinced, would lead him directly to the final resting place of the terrestrial globe beneath the Sarah Rittenhouse Armillary.

As he crossed the creek, exhausted but determined, he thought of Washington's crossing at Valley Forge and the courage that saw America through the Revolution. It was that same courage and resolve which must have driven Washington on the fateful night in these woods when he stood up to the Alignment to save the republic.

George Washington galloped through the woods on his horse in the rain. It was almost three o'clock in the morning when he cleared the trees and came to an abrupt halt by the wharf in Georgetown.

Slowly Washington led Nelson to the old stone house, listening to the old war horse's hoofs clapping lightly in the night. He tied him to a hitching post and walked to the front door, anonymous in his civilian raincoat and hat. Even so, he could not hide his regal bearing as an officer and gentleman.

He knocked on the door three times. He paused a moment and again knocked. He tried the latch and the door opened on its own. Washington stooped to enter, his towering 6-foot-3-inch frame filling the doorway, and stepped inside.

The man he was to meet, his top forger, sat limply in a chair by the flickering fireplace, blood on his face and a bullet hole in his forehead. On the rough-hewn table before him were charts, maps, and documents.

"A treacherous affair, this new republic." A voice spoke from the shadows. "Who knows where it will end?"

Washington grew very still, then slowly turned his head.

Several feet away, beneath a doorway, stood a mountainous silhouette. He was a bull of a man, with a ruddy face and white, curly hair. His eyes were black and soulless. The man drew a pistol from his coat and aimed the barrel directly at Washington. "You should not have tried to fool the Alignment." His voice, though familiar, was not easy to place. "Now tell me where your copy of the treaty is."

"There on the table," Washington said warily. "I came to pick it up."

"Liar." The man emerged from the shadows.

"You!" Washington said, staring at one of his most loyal officers through the years. The man was a former Son of Liberty. A Patriot. One of the original members of the Culper Spy Ring who helped Washington beat the British in New York. His top assassin.

"This is a forgery," the assassin said as he picked up a document from the table and waved it in Washington's face.

Washington felt a surge of dread. He knows. How does he know?

"The ranks of the Alignment are everywhere. Its destiny and America's are one." The assassin leveled his gun at Washington's chest. "Now sit down next to your friend."

Washington did as he was told. Dawn was still hours away, and the room was very dark. He removed his hat and coat and set them on the table, and sat down opposite the assassin.

"A lot of good your brotherhood of builders did you," the assassin sneered. "What match are they against the warriors of the Alignment?"

Washington watched as the assassin unfolded the forged document on the table and examined it by the light of the fire.

"Brilliant," said the assassin approvingly. "This looks exactly like the amended and updated treaty you are to sign and exchange with the Alignment for the original treaty. Except that you used that special ink that becomes invisible after a few days, rendering your

signature meaningless because the articles of this treaty will, in effect, disappear. By the time the Alignment would have discovered your treachery, you would have no doubt destroyed the original treaty. Was old Livingston here your man in the Alignment?"

Washington said nothing.

"You always did like to play the double spy game." The assassin turned, holding the official treaty that Washington was supposed to sign. "And what did you intend to do with this?"

The assassin held up the amended treaty that Livingston had copied, the one that would have bound Washington and America to an unthinkable fate.

Washington stared at the fire wordlessly. That infernal treaty! he thought. I never should have signed the first one ten years ago.

"No matter," said the assassin. "Your game is nearly up. Our friends will be here soon. They will decide if you attend your ceremony tomorrow."

He was pointing to a flyer posted on the wall inviting all to join the president and members of Congress on a procession from Alexandria to the top of Jenkins Heights for the laying of the cornerstone of the new United States Capitol building.

Washington could feel a cold chill coming on, the life of the republic passing away.

"How about some ale?" Washington asked.

"So what drink shall it be? Fate or free will? Destiny or liberty?" He reached for some glasses on a shelf and for a moment turned his back.

"I choose freedom," Washington said, leaning back in his chair until his feet came up toward the table. "I can't help it."

Washington rammed the table with his feet into the assassin's back, driving him into the wall. Several glasses crashed to the floor. The assassin turned, his face a bloody mess as his arm swung up with his pistol. Washington rose from his chair, his left hand deflecting the pistol as his right knee came up into the assassin's groin. The assassin's head jerked forward, his leg hooking behind Washington's, sending them both crashing to the ground. As Washington went down with him, he reached for the wrist of the hand that held the pistol, smashing his fist into the side of the assassin's neck, aware of the pistol exploding between them.

There was the distinct smell of burning flesh and the assassin lay still, dead.

Washington got to his feet, picked up the official treaty and tossed it into the fire. He signed the forgery and slipped it into his overcoat. Then he paused.

The rain had stopped outside.

"Blast it," he cursed, realizing that he had to hurry for his rendezvous with the Alignment to exchange his forgery for their copy of the countersigned and amended treaty he first signed ten years ago. It was the only binding document left and, God willing, would shortly be in his possession.

In the center of the Federal District was a hill known as Jenkins Heights. Washington had always known it as Rome, because a century earlier a Maryland landowner named Francis Pope had a dream that a mighty empire to eclipse ancient Rome would one day rise on the banks of the Potomac, which he called the Tiber.

Washington, steeped in the history of the land he surveyed as a youth, knew the hill's history stretched well before that, and he felt as if he were riding back in time as old Nelson climbed the hill for the exchange of treaties.

Long before Europeans colonized the New World, the Algonquin Indians held tribal grand councils at the foot of this hill. The Algonquin were linked by archaeology to the ancient Mayans and by legend to the descendents of Atlantis. The chiefs of their primary tribe, the Montauk Indians, were known as Pharaoh, like their ancient Egyptians cousins. And the word was spelled like it was in the old Arabic languages 10,000 years ago, meaning "Star Child" or "Children of the Stars."

Which was why Washington had chosen this hill as the heart of the new federal city, and why his hand-picked surveyors Ellicott and L'Enfant had oriented the proposed Congressional House to the star Regulus in the constellation of Leo—key to both Atlantis and

Egypt—and the entire federal city to the constellation Virgo, like Rome.

Washington himself was ambivalent about astrology.

As a Mason, he felt it made sense that new cities and churches and public buildings be aligned to the stars, if only to acknowledge the necessity of heaven's blessings on so vast and corruptible an earthly enterprise as the founding of a new republic. And it made sense to him to cast astrological charts for the laying of cornerstones at the most opportunistic, astronomically favorable moments, such as the time set for the laying of the cornerstone of the U.S. Capitol on this very hill at 1 p.m. later that day. The stars, after all, were more permanent fixtures in the heavens than the passing politics of men.

The officers of the Alignment, however, were no builders like the Masons, but rather warriors who traced their origins to Atlantis and who had infiltrated and manipulated the armies of various empires throughout the ages. They used the stars to wage war and destroy those they considered their enemies. Moreover, their astrology was not elective, like his, employed only to make the most of a favorable astrological climate. No. Their astrology was fixed, fatalistic, and filled with doom—a self-fulfilling prophecy. They never considered the irony that they were merely using the stars to justify their actions.

At strategic points in history, the Illuminati, the Masons, and even the Church had served as ignorant hosts to the infernal ranks of the Alignment, who had now set their sights on the federal government of the new United States. During the Revolution, even Washington himself had gone so far as to rely on certain officers trained in their arts to turn the tide of battle.

It was a mistake he had lived to regret.

They were waiting at the top—12 representatives of the Alignment on horseback with torches. They included officers, senators, and bankers Washington knew well, but clearly not as well as he had thought.

Washington rode up to the group, stationed around a trench dug for the laying of the cornerstone.

A few feet beyond the trench was the golden celestial globe.

The official Alignment negotiator, known by the pseudonym Osiris, ran his hands around the smooth contours and constellations of the globe until it cracked open to reveal the wooden axis that kept the two halves together. He pulled the globe apart and removed the axis. It was hollow.

"The treaty, General," he said.

Washington handed over the forgery he had brought with him from the old stone house, complete with his signature as president of the United States.

Osiris rolled it up into a scroll, placed it inside the axis and closed the globe. Then Osiris handed over the original treaty signed in Newburgh in 1783, back when Washington was commander-in-chief of the Continental Army and the United States of America and its Constitution did not yet exist.

Washington slipped the Newburgh Treaty into his pocket, then watched as the sealed globe with the forgery penned with dissolvable ink was lowered to the bottom of the trench into a hollow stone block. On the reverse side of the forgery was something the assassin back at the stone house missed: a star map in invisible ink that would reveal itself later should the globe ever see the light of day.

But that would be centuries from now, Washington thought.

Mortar was poured on top of the trench to seal it. Then a few spades of dirt to cover it. Come morning a silver plate marker would be placed at the bottom of the trench and on top of it the cornerstone to the U.S. Capitol.

"You have what you want," Washington told them. "Why not be rid of me?"

"You have been indispensable, sir. And we salute you. If only you were of more sturdy character, you would have let us crown you, and then you could have led us and America into her destiny this generation instead of forcing her to wait for another."

"America will prove you wrong," Washington said.

Four soldiers were posted to guard the celestial globe until the cornerstone-laying ceremony, and the 13 officers dispersed in every direction. Four each to the north, south, and east, and one lonely horseman, Washington, to the west.

It took Washington a half hour to reach the wild outskirts of the Federal District and make it to Peirce Mill along Rock Creek. He followed the winding waters through rocky ravines and dense, primeval woods. At the end of his journey was a cave, hidden among the dense ferns, shrubs, and other foliage. A shroud of gray moss and tangled vines over the entrance made it all but invisible.

Washington tied Nelson to a hickory tree, parted the curtain of tangled vines and stepped inside, where a flicker of light was visible in the distance. He followed the cave to the end, where a larger cavern or hollow appeared and a shaking Hercules, his most trusted slave, held a torch over an ancient Algonquin well surrounded by several barrels of gunpowder.

Washington gazed at Hercules and the round sackcloth by Hercules' buckled shoes. He bent down and removed the sackcloth to reveal another copper globe.

The globe was almost identical to the one he had just seen buried atop Jenkins Heights. But this one was terrestrial, originally paired with its sister but now separated for a special purpose. He stared at the unique topography the cartographer who crafted the globe had carved so long ago, marveling at it.

Washington moved his finger along the 40th parallel on the globe, feeling for the seam. He found the spring, and the globe cracked open. He removed the signed document from his overcoat, placed it inside the globe and closed it up. Then he nodded to Hercules, who knotted some rope around it and lowered it down the well.

Washington watched as the coil of rope by Hercules' feet unwound. Deeper and deeper the globe descended until it rested at the bottom of the well. Putting on his Masonic apron, Washington took out a trowel and threw a simple spade of dirt into the well. Then he sat down on a barrel of gunpowder and held the torch as Hercules rolled up his sleeves, picked up a shovel and began filling the bottom of the well with dirt.

Every now and then Hercules would pause to dust himself off, and Washington could only marvel at his slave's fine clothing, gold pocket watch, and ornate buckles. Hercules was probably the best-dressed slave in the United States. It was a shame to involve him in all this nasty business.

"Do you realize you are a finer specimen of fashion than I am, Hercules?"

"You allow me to sell leftover foodstuffs, sir."

"And your profit?"

"About $200 last year, sir."

Washington shook his head. This was a new world.

Finally, they lowered two kegs of gunpowder down the well, and left a long trail of powder behind them as they exited the cave.

Outside in the dark, Washington took in the fresh air and looked at his nervous slave.

"You'll be going back to Philadelphia by way of New York," Washington told Hercules, and handed him an envelope intended for Robert Yates, chief justice of the New York Supreme Court. "You know where the designated drop box is buried?"

Hercules nodded. "Just outside that farm."

"That's right," said Washington. "You best be going now. We'll talk again when I'm back in Philadelphia."

"Yessa," Hercules said, and ran off through some branches to his horse and untied him.

Washington watched Hercules gallop off and then turned to the cave and removed his pistol.

Washington raised his arm and leveled his pistol at the cave. "God save America," he said, and fired a single shot.

There was a flash from somewhere deep inside the cave, and then a deep, thunderous explosion, setting off several more as the entire back of the cave collapsed. A blast of dust and the smell of sulfur billowed out from the mouth of the cave, burying the globe until Kingdom Come or until Stargazer could come for it, however fate would have it.

When the smoke cleared, Washington was gone.

Conrad found the cave on the other side of the creek behind its cloak of vegetation. He parted the curtain of roots and entered the damp passage. It felt like he was going back in time, searching for his lost childhood, his origins, his father. In a way, he was. Because here in this cave everything came together: *Tom Sawyer*, those many days with his dad digging out the cave, even the Sarah Rittenhouse Armillary in the park a hundred feet up where he used to jog.

It was always here, he marveled. *All this time.*

There was a movement in the dark, then the blinding glare of a headtorch. Conrad blinked for a moment until he saw Serena's angelic but dirty face, a halo of light behind her, and a shovel on her shoulder, ready to bring it down on his head.

"Thank God, Conrad," she said. "You made it. I wasn't sure if I got your directions right."

He wanted to wrap his arms around her, tell her how much he loved her and drag her away from all the nonsense that kept them apart. Instead, he grabbed her by the throat.

"You dirty, pretty liar," he told her. "You knew there were two globes all along, and you didn't tell me."

"They always come in pairs, Conrad," she said, choking. "Terrestrial and celestial. I assumed you knew that."

He tightened his grasp. "Or maybe you and your friends at the Vatican wanted to keep them for yourselves."

"Please, Conrad, I know you didn't kill Brooke."

He looked into her dark, smoky eyes and let go.

She gasped for air.

"Brooke," he muttered, remembering his last glimpse of her tied to the bed in the hotel room, feeling the hurt of what must have happened to her after he left pressing down on him. "Seavers did it, I swear."

"I know," Serena said, swallowing hard, trying to catch her breath. "Here, take this. We don't have much time."

She handed him a shovel.

42

SARAH RITTENHOUSE ARMILLARY

MONTROSE PARK

IT WAS JUST AFTER 7 P.M., the sun setting over the horizon, when the corporal from the Army Corps of Engineers crawled out of the sewer on R Street near the armillary to break the news to Max Seavers, who had the area roped off by his disguised Detachment One Marines.

Seavers, who was hunched over a geological survey of Rock Creek Park in the relative quiet of the playground by the armillary, had noticed the drilling had stopped. "What's wrong, Corporal?"

"We tagged something, but we're not sure what," the corporal said. "So we're tripping right now."

"English, Corporal."

"The casing—er, the tube we dropped down to set off the charges developed a spur of some kind. So we're bringing the drill bit back up. Once we've tripped the bit back up, we'll send down a mill to bore out the casing. After we retract the mill, the bit will have to be tripped down again."

The only thing Seavers understood was that this was going to cost him even more time. And he had already allowed Yeats too much. "How long is this going to take, Corporal?"

"It's going to cost DARPA about a hundred grand for the new drill bit and about a million for the day, as far as the GSA is concerned," the corporal said. "We've got seventy-five men and a lot of equipment down there, sir. This is a massive operation to throw together so fast."

"I didn't ask about the cost, you penny-pinching bureaucrat," Seavers seethed. "I asked how long."

"The trip is going to take about twelve hours each way."

That was 24 hours from now, Seavers realized, just when he was going to be accompanying the Chinese Olympic officials to the Washington Monument.

"That's unacceptable, Corporal. How much further do you have to go?"

"About two hundred feet before we hit what looks to be a cavern, although it's partially collapsed," the corporal said. "But we've hit the harder, more resilient metamorphic rock that's in the way, sir. It's got schists, phyllites, slates, gneisses, and gabbros."

At this point, Seavers knew more about the geology of America's fourth-oldest national park than he ever wanted to. Designed for the preservation "of all timber, animals, or curiosities . . . and their retention, as nearly as possible," the park was 15 kilometers long and almost two kilometers wide, a sanctuary for "many and rare and unique species," according to the act of Congress that created it.

Those species right now included Conrad Yeats and Serena Serghetti.

"Hold on, Corporal," Seavers said, and radioed Landford at the mobile command post. "Where is the NPS in the hunt for our terrorists?"

"Nothing yet, sir," Landford reported. "But they've got all available rangers and police on horseback and foot sweeping the creek area."

Unfortunately, as Seavers now knew, Rock Creek itself ran almost 53 kilometers, and the entire Rock Creek "watershed" covered almost 50,000 acres. Worse, it cut through deformed metamorphic crystalline rocks that were dotted with innumerable sinkholes, caves, and caverns. A quarter of the area was within the boundaries of the federal district, making it a virtual urban Tora Bora in which Yeats could hide for some time.

Seavers looked down at his geological map showing the vast cave systems throughout the area. He was positive Yeats and the nun had followed one of them to wind their way back beneath the armillary. At some point, if he didn't beat them to the globe, they would have to come out, and when they did, he wanted them captured immediately.

But he was taking no chances.

"Corporal, you're done drilling," Seavers said. "We're going to drop a suitcase bunker buster bomb down the casing. It should easily penetrate the remaining two hundred feet of rock to hit the cavern."

The corporal looked shocked. "You drop a mini bunker buster, sir, and you'll probably collapse the cavern, burying whatever it is you're looking for."

"We can always dig it up," Seavers said. "I just don't want it going anywhere."

43

The walls of the ancient well were lined with stone, which made Serena wonder if it had been used for something sacred or ritualistic. It appeared to have been originally constructed with pure Algonquin muscle, probably two or more Indians working side by side. As such it was wide enough to accommodate both her and Conrad. He did the digging while she hauled up the dirt.

"Mother Superior always told me that if you ask God to move your mountain, don't be surprised if he gives you a shovel."

"Did she teach you to lie and cheat, too?" Conrad asked with a grunt, digging his shovel deep into the dirt. "You knew Brooke was Alignment from the start, Serena, didn't you? But you didn't warn me. You didn't lift a goddamn finger until after I found my orders as Stargazer from Washington."

"What did Brooke tell you, Conrad?"

"That Seavers is going to release a bird flu virus at the Olympic Games in Beijing next month." He tossed a shovelful of dirt into a bucket. "Actually, he's going to release it tomorrow at the National Mall. But the contagion won't start until the Olympics so that everybody will assume it started in China. America gets to give the smart vaccine to its friends and deny it to its enemies at home and abroad. Seavers is just the Alignment's trigger man for the Apocalypse. The globe we're after is what they're going to use to somehow justify the 'cleansing' and their New World Order."

Like a dark shadow the revelation came upon her and she shivered.

"The bird flu," she repeated. "Oh, my God, Conrad. I should have known. As a linguist I should have known."

"Known what?"

"The word *influenza* comes from the Old Italian," she said. "It means a 'bad alignment of stars.' The ancients associated the outbreak of plagues with astronomical conjunctions."

"Yeah, well, this time the Alignment is going to make it happen."

"We have to stop him, Conrad. But how in the world are we going to get to him?"

"We're never going to find that needle in that haystack," he said, breathing hard. "There are going to be a half million people picnicking on the Mall for the concert and fireworks. And security has never been tighter."

As she watched him redouble his digging, Serena tried to make sense of this new revelation. Suddenly, she said, "I know where he's going to do it."

Conrad stopped digging for a moment, to catch his breath and listen.

"I heard Seavers talking to a Chinese official at the prayer breakfast. He's going to the top of the Washington Monument when all the visiting Olympic officials go up to see the fireworks. We have to call it in to the president and Secretary Packard."

Serena tried her cell phone, but of course there was no signal, not this deep under the earth.

"Like they're going to believe us, anyway," he said, and she heard a definitive clank of the shovel.

She got down on her knees and helped him clear the remaining dirt away to reveal the bottom of the well. She felt her stomach turn over.

"It's not here," she said, desperation in her voice. "The globe is gone. We have to leave and warn the White House about Seavers. We have no choice now."

"No, it's here." Conrad wiped his brow and looked up the walls of the well. "I know it. We haven't gotten below the water table yet. Step back."

Serena moved aside as he lifted his heavy shovel into the air like a man with a sledgehammer at a county fair about to ring the bell and impress his girlfriend. "What are you doing?"

"This is a false bottom." He brought the shovel down on the stone bottom of the well. Sparks flew from the thunder of the blow. Conrad lifted the shovel up again and brought it down even harder, and she heard a loud crack. "Help me lift these out."

It took a half hour to haul up the stones, and another hour of digging before Conrad's shovel produced a distinctive clink. He had struck something metal.

It was the globe.

Conrad set the shovel against the wall of the well, pulled out a cigarette from the pocket of the shirt he had lifted from a homeless man and lit it.

Serena stared at him. "What the bloody hell are you waiting for!" she said, worried that Max Seavers and his armed dupes could be on top of them any moment.

Conrad took a slow drag from his cigarette and blew out a perfect ring of smoke. She watched the "O" hang in the air, expand and break up as it floated away into nothingness. Finally, he spoke:

"Brooke said something else back at the Hilton."

She could feel her stomach tighten. He always did this—chose the worst moments to bring up something he had been turning over for hours, days, weeks, or even years. "Not now, Conrad. Please."

"She said you knew something about my blood. Something you've always known. Something I had to see to believe."

Serena took a deep breath, walked over, and removed the cigarette from Conrad's mouth. She took a slow, deep drag, returned the cigarette and blew smoke back in his face. "You really want to play this game now, of all times?"

"Yep."

She got down on her knees in the bottom of the well and started digging desperately with her hands while Conrad watched her. "It's not your blood so much as your DNA."

"You had my DNA analyzed?"

"After Antarctica," she said, her voice tightening.

"What did you take from me?"

"A lock of hair," she said. "We can do this later, Conrad. Please help me. Help yourself."

"Why did you have my DNA analyzed, Serena? You didn't really believe what my father said there, did you? There's nothing special about my DNA. You don't think I had myself tested? I've seen the numbers, read all the tables. No unusual strands or combinations, Serena."

"Conrad, you're impossible!" She could see the top of something metallic just beneath the dirt.

"You know something I don't, Serena? You usually do."

"It isn't explained in analysis, Conrad. You have to see it."

"What the hell are you talking about, Serena?"

She rose to her feet and looked at him. "You want to know, Conrad? Fine. Your DNA strand spirals to the left."

"Of course it spirals. That's what the double-helix is all about."

"Except that the DNA of every indigenous organism on planet Earth spirals to the right."

She watched his hard face, watched his penetrating eyes study her, until his mouth softened and he dropped his cigarette and stamped it out. "So what do you believe, Serena?"

"I don't know what to believe now, Conrad. Only that I love you and want to be with you if we get out of this mess. I realized that the moment I thought it was you who was dead in the room and not Brooke. But we have to pull out whatever is under our feet and get it before Seavers does, or we're history."

She wrapped her arms around Conrad's neck and leaned up and kissed him full on the mouth. She could feel her heart pounding out of her chest and his arms wrapped around her waist, pulling her tight. Then he slowly let go and she looked up at his face, grim with determination.

"Let's dig this thing up."

44

CONRAD DUG A CHANNEL around the globe with his hands while Serena brushed the surface protruding from the dirt with a rag. Soon the outline of North America, etched across the northern hemisphere, came into view.

"Look!" Serena said excitedly. "This is clearly the terrestrial globe —it shows the land, not the stars. How do you open it?"

"Like this." Conrad pushed the blade of his knife under the edge by the equator and pressed hard. There was a crack and the hemisphere began to move beneath his hand, opening like a lid to reveal a sealed wooden cylinder. "Here it is."

They climbed out of the well and knelt on the dirt floor of the cave. Conrad removed a scroll from the wooden cylinder and began to unfold it.

"You're smudging it with your dirty hands," Serena scolded. "Let's get out of here and look at it someplace safe."

"Your hands are just as dirty as mine, Serena." He refused to budge. "And no place is safe until we know what this thing says. Right here, Serena, right now. Information, not preservation."

She flashed a light on the document. "I hate you."

"Get in line, it's a long one." He angled the document to the light.

The paper was like the star map, almost a parchment. But this was no map. Rather, it was a formal document, written in English, with a bold sort of preamble. Certain dates and titles from 1783 had been amended and initialed in 1793.

"A Treaty of Peace," he began to read, "concluded this Present Day ye eighteenth day of September One Thousand Seven Hundred & Ninety Three between the Regency of New Atlantis and its Subjects and George Washington President of the United States of North America and the Citizens of ye Said United States." He looked at Serena. "The Regency of New Atlantis?"

"The Alignment," Serena said. "A regency is simply a person or group selected to govern in place of a monarch or other ruler who is absent, disabled, or still in minority."

"So they're saying there's some new Caesar waiting in the wings to take over the world?"

"We in the Church prefer to call him the Antichrist."

The preamble was followed by a series of articles Conrad had a hard time following. He handed her the treaty and took the flashlight.

"You're the linguist and expert on international treaties, Serena. What's this New Atlantis?"

"The federal government," Serena said, scanning the articles. "This treaty says that the federal government has the right to secede from the United States on July 4, 2008, and form its own entity, New Atlantis, the very superpower that Sir Francis Bacon predicted would arise in the New World through its technology and power. The United States of America would be dissolved and power would be returned to the states."

"Holy shit. If it's legal, this thing's nuclear."

"You mean neutron: the regimes would change, but D.C. and all public lands acquired by the federal government since its inception—about one-third of the country, mostly in the West—would remain as territories of New Atlantis, including all U.S. military bases both here and around the world. Meaning the New Atlantis would have the means to enforce its will on the former United States and the rest of the world."

He shook his head. "The U.S. Supreme Court would never back it."

"How could it?" she said. "If anything, this Charter is not only unconstitutional, it's *anti*-constitutional. It clearly holds itself as both the precursor and successor to the U.S. Constitution. But it definitely looks genuine. As such, it's an embarrassment to America and casts doubts on its very founding at a time when its critics are wondering whether the world is better off without it. No wonder every president since Jefferson has been after this. What I can't understand is why Washington would ever sign such a thing."

She handed it back to Conrad, who looked at the bottom. There was an endorsement of the articles dated April 23, 1783, by George Washington, commander-in-chief of the Continental Army. Lastly, there was a second endorsement dated almost a decade later, September 13, 1793. This was followed by the signature of President George Washington and the official seal of the United States of America—or rather the front of the seal. Opposite thereto were twelve signatures and the reverse or "New World Order" side of the seal.

One seal, Conrad thought, *and two Americas.*

"I can see why he'd sign it," Conrad said, the years of American history drilled into him by his father kicking in. "Put yourself in Washington's boots in 1783."

"But to endorse it as president after the U.S. Constitution was ratified? What was he thinking?"

"He was thinking like most Americans that the federal government and its lands were all of a few square miles of marshland on the Potomac, dwarfed by the giant states like Virginia, Pennsylvania, and New York. He had no idea it would consume the continent as an empire with warships controlling the seven seas and military garrisons around the world and in space."

Conrad looked at the two seals, the eagle and talons for the United States and the pyramid and Lucerific eye for the New Atlantis, and recalled what Brooke had said: The Alignment wasn't merely a shadow government, it *was* the government. Or, rather, *the other side* of the federal government. It always had been; it just hadn't come to light—yet.

"What's wrong, Conrad?"

"I know why the Alignment signed this and why Washington had to go along at the time. And it's obvious why every president aware of its existence has tried to keep it from coming to light, if only to preserve the Union. But to a large extent the Alignment has already succeeded beyond its wildest dreams and the federal government is so strong—taxes to boot—that in a *de facto* way America IS the New Atlantis. So, aside from some historical or perverse moral justification, what possible reason could the Alignment have for risking its agenda to grab the treaty?"

"I can think of twelve, Conrad."

She showed him the signatures of those representing the Regency of the New Atlantis.

Conrad looked through the signatures. Members of Congress, American patriots, Founding Fathers who supported a strong federal government. "Holy shit. These names."

"Some of the most famous in America, along with some I've never heard of," she said. "These are the ancestors of those who are going to make the Atlantis prophecy happen one way or another. This is what Washington was trying to warn us about, and to do it he used L'Enfant's layout of the city and Savage's portrait in the National Gallery and the letter to Robert Yates for you to open more than two centuries later. To lead us to this Newburgh Treaty and its signatories. So we could know the families, trace them to the present day and have a fair idea of who its leaders are."

Conrad said, "Which means if we can find their descendants today . . ."

"We can find out who is behind what's going to happen—who Seavers is really working for—and stop them." Serena paused as she scanned the treaty, her face pale.

Something had struck her, and Conrad realized it wasn't in the body of the charter. Rather, it was one of the signatures.

Conrad brushed off bits of loose dirt that had fallen onto the treaty from the ceiling. He looked at the names again, starting with Alexander Hamilton, and one in particular, the designated Consul General of the Regency, jumped out at him: John Marshall.

Conrad's mind whirred. Marshall, a lawyer at the time of the Revolution, became chief justice of the Supreme Court within a year of Washington's death and over the next 30 years did more than anybody else to expand the powers of the federal government. Then he made the connection:

Marshall was also a cousin of Thomas Jefferson and, as such, the sitting president's great-great-grandfather on his mother's side.

"Holy shit!" he said as the walls began to shake violently. "We've got to get out of here."

Serena grabbed her backpack as the roof of the cave started to collapse. Suddenly smoke filled the cave. Then everything went black.

PART FOUR

JULY 4

45

AN UNDISCLOSED LOCATION

CONRAD WOKE UP IN COMPLETE DARKNESS, a black hood over his head, chilled to the bone. He sensed he was deep underground and could feel the low rumble of large, powerful machinery nearby. Something very sharp was pressing on his chest.

"Serena?" he called out.

He heard a laugh. It belonged to Max Seavers. "You're an inspiration, Yeats, I'll give you that."

Then the black hood came off and Conrad looked up to see Seavers standing over him, pointing an ornate dagger at his chest. Conrad tried to move, but his arms and legs were strapped to a restraint chair, bolted to the floor of a windowless room with stone walls and a metal door.

"Do you like my dagger, Yeats?" Seavers said, pushing the point into Conrad's sternum. "Your old friend Herc gave it to me before he died and joined Danny Z in the Great Beyond. He said it once belonged to a legendary 33rd Degree Mason of the Scottish Rite or some such, and that the Masons used the dagger in rituals to initiate candidates into a perverse system of levels or degrees by which they replicate themselves. Apparently the candidate for the First Degree is hooded and brought into the Lodge. There, at the point of a dagger, he undergoes ritual questioning. Welcome to my Lodge, Yeats. Maybe you can work all the way up the ranks like Herc."

As he struggled to get his bearings, Conrad remembered what Brooke had told him about the weaponized bird flu virus Seavers was going to release, and what Serena said about Seavers hosting the Chinese at the Washington Monument for the fireworks.

"The Fourth of July concert on the Mall," Conrad said. "You're going to release your contagion on Chinese officials during the fireworks. At the only moment in history that the monuments will be directly below their designated stars."

"Impressive, isn't it?" Seavers said as he walked out of sight behind him. "I was surprised to discover there's actually some science behind what you allegedly do for a living as an astro-archaeologist. The stars in the sky rotate like some giant odometer every 26,000 years or so. Washington one-upped the Egyptians by ordering his chief architect L'Enfant to align the sites of as-yet-constructed monuments not to the position of the key stars of their day, but to their positions on this day, July 4, 2008, when the Regency of New Atlantis could make its claim and dissolve the United States."

"Tell me something I don't know, Seavers."

Seavers obliged. "When my masters in the Alignment thrust this great responsibility upon me, I knew that I had to make it special for them, seeing as they actually believe in mystical astrological signs and all. So I took a page from your book and decided to coordinate our strike with the heavens."

"Is that what you call killing, what, a billion Chinese and a third of the world's population?"

"It's written in the stars, sport. Today the sun begins a 28-day path across the skies from Washington, D.C., to Beijing, where it will experience a total eclipse at dusk on August 1, exactly seven days before the opening ceremonies of the Olympic Games. My time-delayed virus on Earth mirrors the sun's path in the heavens like some cosmic fireball. As above, so below. By the time they light the Olympic torch, the first symptoms of the global human-to-human bird flu pandemic will appear, igniting international chaos and cries to build a new Great Wall to quarantine China. Poetic, isn't it?"

"You're deranged."

Conrad craned his neck to see a dozen syringes, needles, and tubes laid out on a table along with rolls of adhesive tape, bags of saline solution, handcuffs, and leg irons. He shivered. "Are you really going to use all that on me, or is it just for effect?"

Seavers put on a pair of surgical gloves, selected a vial and held it up to the fluorescent light. "This is for somebody else."

As he spoke, the door opened and two lab technicians rolled Serena in on a gurney. She was strapped down flat and showed little movement.

"You bastard!" Conrad snarled.

Seavers slid the vial into a syringe gun and put it to Serena's neck.

"This is a special formula of the bird flu virus minus the incubation inhibitor," Seavers said. "Tell me where you put that star map you stole from the celestial globe or I pull the trigger and Sister Serghetti is the first to die."

"Don't you dare, Conrad," Serena warned from the gurney. "You know all those stories through the ages about Christian martyrs? This is one of them. But if you cave to this bastard, he'll just off us and it's plain murder. We'll be as much his victims as the ones who get the bird flu."

Not if we survive, Conrad thought, and he wondered why Seavers wanted the star map. It only led to the terrestrial globe and the Newburgh Treaty, which Seavers already possessed. "It's inside a book at the Library of Congress."

"Shut up!" Serena screamed.

Seavers dug the syringe gun into Serena's carotid. "Tell me the title of the book, sport."

Conrad shifted in his restraining chair. In pressing the point of the dagger to his chest, Seavers had nicked one of the straps. Conrad felt it would tear and snap with enough force, but that he still wouldn't be able to free his hands or feet.

"It's in a book called *Obelisks*," Conrad said, hearing the desperation in his voice and seeing the disappointment in Serena's eyes.

"You bloody fool," Serena said in defeat. "I hope you've made your peace with God."

"You know I did," Conrad said. "In Antarctica. But not with you."

"And you won't in this lifetime, you wanker," she said. "But when I wake up in the next and see the face of Jesus, I want to see yours, too." She began to utter something in Latin.

Seavers began to laugh. "Are you performing last rites for your beloved Yeats?"

"For you, Seavers," she said. "Because there's no air conditioning where you're going."

"Now, now, Sister Serghetti," Seavers said, in a soothing tone Conrad found very creepy. "Even Jesus forgave his enemies when he was dying on the cross."

"Well, you can go to hell, Seavers!" she screamed. "You have no excuses. You know exactly what you're doing."

Max Seavers's face screwed up into a twisted mask of pure hatred, and Conrad anxiously watched him walk to the instrument table and return with a roll of duct tape.

"That mouth." He tore off some tape and slapped it across Serena's lips. "Somebody in Rome should have shut you up a long time ago."

Then he plunged the syringe gun into her neck again, this time deep enough that Conrad could see a trickle of blood.

"Give me the call number for the book, sport, or I shoot."

"I don't know the call number," Conrad said, panicking as he saw Serena struggle, her eyes wide and her cries muffled. "But it's an old book and there can't be more than a couple of copies in special collections. I'm telling you the truth."

"We'll see when I come back from my previously scheduled engagement," Seavers said, and pulled the trigger.

Serena's neck twitched like she'd taken a bullet.

"No!" Conrad shouted.

Seavers laid the syringe gun down, studying Serena as he spoke to Conrad. "She'll be fully infected within a few hours unless I administer the vaccine. But once she starts showing symptoms nothing can save her, not even my own vaccine, and she'll be dead by dusk. So you better pray to her God that I find that map. Or you'll watch her die before your eyes, and then I'll kill you."

With that, Seavers walked out past two Marines posted outside the door, which rumbled shut and locked with a thud.

46
THE NATIONAL MALL

MORE THAN 20 SECURITY CHECKPOINTS had been set up around the National Mall in preparation for the day's Fourth of July parade and festivities, which slowed an impatient Seavers on his way to retrieve the star map from the Library of Congress. That map, together with the Newburgh Treaty, was his insurance policy just in case he pulled the trigger on the bird flu contagion and Osiris suddenly decided he was of no further use to the Alignment.

Sitting in the rear of the black SUV with a Marine driving, Seavers pulled out a laptop computer from his briefcase and called up the Library of Congress website. He typed in the name of the book on obelisks that Yeats had given him. It was in special collections on the second floor of the Jefferson Building. He jotted down the call number.

He then removed the folded Newburgh Treaty from the left breast pocket of his suit jacket and reviewed the signatures, some famous and others obscure. He typed the names into his laptop to cross them against current U.S. political leaders. He wanted to see where the genealogies matched ancestor with descendant. A far more detailed analysis would be required later on, he knew, but almost immediately several names popped up and surprised even him.

"Well, would you look at that?" he said to himself with a soft whistle.

First, there was the sitting U.S. president himself, a "man of faith" that Seavers would not have guessed in a million years. Could he be

Osiris? The president's lineage didn't necessarily mean he was Alignment, only that it was likely.

Then there were the leading Democratic and Republican presidential candidates. Both had blue-blood family ties to the Alignment, ensuring that whoever was elected in November would stick to the Alignment plan. These names he more readily accepted as leaders of the Alignment.

Finally, there was Senator Scarborough—a real shocker since Brooke had been led to believe otherwise. So had Seavers.

He could only imagine what Scarborough was feeling now that the senator most surely had been given news of his daughter's death. And Seavers could definitely thank his lucky stars that Conrad Yeats was taking the rap. As soon as he grabbed the star map he would call in the orders to kill Yeats, before anybody in the Alignment could interrogate him.

Seavers shut the laptop and looked out his window. It was going to be a hot and sticky day.

By the time he walked into the special collections room at the Jefferson Building, his shirt was soaked with sweat. The Library was closed to the public today but not to members of Congress and the executive branch. He flashed his ID to the lone female staffer at the desk, wrote out a request for the *Obelisks* book and waited. She returned with a copy.

He took the book to a cubicle and opened it. Nothing!

He returned to the desk and asked the woman for the second copy. She checked her computer and said, "It's still in the carts, we haven't shelved it yet."

As calmly as he could, Seavers said, "Well, do you think you could check the carts? Please."

She flinched at his intensity. "It may take me a few minutes. We only have a skeleton staff today."

Seavers said nothing, and quietly fumed for almost fifteen minutes before she returned with the book.

"Here you go," she chirped. "It was between—"

"Thank you," he said, cutting her off and taking the book to the opposite corner of the room, out of her line of sight.

He cracked the book open and found the paper folded lengthwise and tucked inside the spine, in the space between the cover and the binding. He unfolded it and saw Washington's signature on one side and the star map on the other.

Seavers reluctantly had to give Yeats credit for not only finding both globes but thinking clearly enough to hide the star map among the millions of books at the Library of Congress as a bargaining chip.

But now that chip was cashed.

Seavers pulled out his BlackBerry and made the call. "This is Seavers. Terminate prisoner 33."

47

Serena heard the door to the cell open and looked up from her gurney as two Marines, their faces all business, walked in. One of them went to the table with the syringes. The other marched straight for Conrad in the restraining chair and started thumping Conrad's left forearm with his finger, looking for a vein.

She tried to shout, but her cries were muffled by the duct tape across her mouth.

"You strapped him so tight, you cut off his circulation," the Marine complained to his comrade. "I can't find a vein."

The other Marine, who was preparing an IV apparatus, said, "Keep poking him with a needle until you find a gusher."

Serena watched as the Marine attending to Conrad loosened the strap on his left hand to allow for more blood flow. Still without luck, he then tried the right arm and struck blood with a needle. He slipped a catheter into Conrad's vein. The catheter tube was connected to two bags of a clear solution.

Conrad glanced at her and then spoke to the Marines. "Max Seavers was responsible for the deaths of Brooke Scarborough and a Capitol Police officer," Conrad said. "And he's going to be responsible for a billion more if you don't help me."

Either the mention of Brooke or the CP seemed to get their attention. But it didn't slow their work. The Marine with the syringes placed them in order. "He gets sodium pentothal sedative first, then the potassium chloride to paralyze him, and then the lethal injection."

Serena suspected the Marines wouldn't even need the lethal injection, because the only thing potassium chloride paralyzed was the heart: it stopped it cold. She started squirming in her straps, moaning as loud as she could. But the Marines ignored her.

Conrad said, "Seavers is working with terrorists against the U.S., and now you're working for them, too."

The Marine securing his catheter said, "Then why are you the one on death row in a black ops prison?"

"Because I know what Seavers is going to do," Conrad said. "He's going to release a weaponized flu virus on the Mall today during the fireworks."

The Marine looked at him in disbelief. "On Americans?"

"On a Chinese delegation watching the fireworks from the Washington Monument. They won't become infectious until the Olympics when it spreads worldwide."

Something in the Marine's eyes told Serena that he knew at least enough about Seavers to consider Conrad's story in the realm of the possible. "And what are we supposed to do? Let you go?"

"No, call the Pentagon. Tell them you have a message from me for Secretary of Defense Packard. My name is Conrad Yeats. And that's Serena Serghetti."

Serena nodded up and down as the Marine walked over to her. He turned her gurney around so that her feet touched the wall and he looked down on her face with amazement. "Holy hell, I think it's Mother Earth!"

The other Marine scowled. "You can't possibly believe him, Hicks."

"No, I really think it's her," Hicks said, and suddenly turned red-faced as he stared at her. "Remember those . . . pictures . . . I downloaded from the Internet."

"That was her face on some stick model's body," the other Marine said. "This one's got curves."

Serena felt the bewildered gaze of Hicks. "Look," Hicks said. "It can't hurt to at least call in a potential security threat."

With great relief Serena watched Hicks turn for the door when suddenly the other Marine shot him in the back of the head. Hicks's arms went up in shock, and then he went down with a crash.

Serena stared at the dead Marine sprawled on the floor face down. The other Marine, obviously Alignment, holstered his sidearm and picked up a syringe with a nasty yellow-greenish color to it. Serena started to panic as the Marine took the syringe over to Conrad, who looked at her with determined eyes.

"Good thing the Pentagon ordered up that stockpile of bird flu vaccines," the Marine said and pushed the syringe into the catheter.

Serena watched the yellow-green line of fluid wind its way down the long tube toward Conrad's arm. The Marine watched it, too.

"Say night-night, Yeats," the Marine said when Serena used her feet to push off the wall and launch the gurney into the Marine's back.

The Marine shouted in surprise and turned to strike her.

As he did, Conrad snapped his left hand free from the loosened strap, yanked the catheter out of his right arm and plunged it into the Marine's groin.

"You son of a bitch!" the Marine grunted, eyes wide in shock as he pulled the catheter out. But it was too late. Whatever he had intended for Conrad was in his system now. His eyes glazed over and he collapsed next to his fallen fellow Marine.

"And then some," Conrad said, and began to unfasten the rest of his straps.

Serena's heart leapt as Conrad stood up and wobbled, weak at the knees from the hours in the restraining chair. He staggered to the Marines and lifted their swipe cards and guns. Then he walked over to her and with a quick yank pulled off the duct tape.

"Let's go," he said.

Her lips stung, but finally she could move them as Conrad freed her.

"I can't go, Conrad. If I've got the bird flu, I'm going to infect everybody. I may have already infected you."

"Impossible," he said, and she watched him take a Masonic dagger from the table and put the blade to his forearm. "I'm immune."

"What are you doing?" she cried as he slit his arm. A scarlet line of blood oozed out.

"Brooke said Seavers used my blood for his vaccine."

She stared at him. "And you believe her?"

"You said my double-helix spirals to the left instead of the right." He took an empty syringe and unwrapped a sterile needle and drew his blood out. "Should I believe you?"

He offered her the syringe filled with his blood.

"But it's just your blood, Conrad. It's not the vaccine. We don't know if it will work."

"It can't work if we don't try."

She took the syringe from him and ran the needle along her arm until she found the right spot. She hated getting shots, but her travels throughout the Third World long ago made them a regular part of her life. She had rolling veins but not deep, which meant she wouldn't have to penetrate far beneath the skin.

"Do you want me to do it?" Conrad asked impatiently.

"No, I've got it," she said and stuck herself with the needle.

Slowly she pushed Conrad's blood out of the syringe and into her vein. It felt warm and strange. Then she pulled the needle out, put her thumb on the puncture and held her arm up.

"So how in bloody hell do we get out of here?" she said, standing up. "Those swipe cards can't open every door in this facility."

"No, but I bet this will," Conrad said, and held up a finger—Max Seavers's missing finger.

48

Conrad led Serena through the dark corridor to another metal door, the sixth they had encountered. They hadn't seen any more Marines, and security cameras were nowhere to be found. But Conrad was beginning to wonder if they were ever going to get out of there, much less in time to stop Seavers.

He used Seavers's severed finger to open the door and walked into a round conference room dominated by a circular stone table and thirteen white marble busts in alcoves evenly spaced along the wall. In the center of the table was the terrestrial globe.

"The lair of the Alignment," Serena said. "These busts look to be the work of Houdon."

"Who?" Conrad asked, his eyes searching for another way out, but he couldn't find one.

"Houdon," Serena repeated. "A French sculptor during the Enlightenment who made famous busts of Washington and the Founding Fathers. I've seen his work on exhibit at both the Louvre in Paris and at the Getty in Los Angeles. Only these aren't America's Founding Fathers. These faces belong to the other founders, to the Alignment."

Something about the dimensions of the room struck Conrad as familiar and he felt drawn to an empty section of wall between two of the busts. As he stood there, his eyes adjusted enough to make out the faintest outline of a doorway. He pushed it with his hand and the previously invisible door slid open.

"I'll be damned," he said. "This is just like the shafts in the sublevels of P4 and the Great Pyramid."

"The Great Pyramid?" she repeated.

"When I was under the Library of Congress, I saw a monument the Masons proposed in the same chamber that held the celestial globe," he said. "Some kind of American Memorial, like they feared the worst and wanted to preserve their memory—and America's—through a monument that would stand as long as the pyramids. This is where I think both they and the Alignment knew it would be, wherever we are. So the Alignment basically graded the site. All it's waiting for is the pyramid on the surface."

"And it's going to go up as soon as America falls," Serena said.

"We've got to hurry," he said. "If this is like P4, then I know the way out."

He started for the door but Serena didn't budge.

"I told you, Conrad. I can't go with you. I can't risk spreading bird flu contagion on the surface and doing the Alignment's dirty work."

He stared at her. "But I gave you my homegrown vaccine, Serena. If it didn't work, you'd be showing symptoms by now."

"We don't know that for sure, Conrad. And I can't take that risk. You're going to have to stop Seavers yourself."

"And what are you going to do in the meantime?" he demanded.

"I'm going to stay here and wait for you and the cavalry to come back." She walked up to him, tears streaming down her face, and kissed him. "But if we get out of this alive, I'm going to walk out of here with you and walk away from my life as a nun. If you still want it, we're going to start a new life together."

He looked into her wet eyes. "What about the Church?"

She wiped her eyes. "I was supposed to betray you, Conrad, to use you to find the globes and take them from you. Please forgive me," she begged. "You have to believe I'm sorry."

Conrad could see she was. "But you always told me you believed that the Church is the hope of the world."

She shook her head. "Jesus is the hope of the world, Conrad. And the hope of the Church. We are called to be the Church and serve people in His name. I don't have to be a nun to do that. And I don't want to go on without you. I told you. I knew it the moment Max took me to your room and I expected to see your body instead of Brooke's."

"You swear to God?" he said.

"You know I don't like those kinds of oaths, Conrad. But, yes, I swear before God." She then threw her arms around him and hugged him tight. "Conrad, go."

He hesitated, then gave her a pistol and swipe card. "In case you change your mind," he said, and shut the door, leaving her alone with the globe and the faces of thirteen dead white men.

Serena stared at the faces of the thirteen marble Houdon busts. The founding fathers of the Alignment in America. They were so lifelike that she half-expected them to speak to her in the shadowy chamber.

And then one of them did.

It was the second to her right, a face oddly strange and familiar.

When she leaned forward to study the face, she suddenly recognized it.

She gasped. "Oh, my God."

Remembering the names from the Newburgh Charter that she had memorized, she now knew why Cardinal Tucci wanted the globe at the Vatican.

Dear Lord, my promise to Conrad.

She paced before the globe and her jury of the deceased, praying to God for some answer. The shot that Conrad had given her was clearly kicking in, and she was feeling stronger, more alert. So alert that it frightened her.

The Americans already had the celestial globe that the Masons had buried beneath the Library of Congress. If Conrad succeeded in stopping Seavers, as she prayed he would, then the Americans would have both globes. But if he failed, she now realized that the Alignment would control not only America but also the Church.

With a heavy heart she knew what she had to do.

Conrad, forgive me.

* * *

Conrad ran through a maze of corridors until he reached a door without a biometric keypad that would require the finger from Max Seavers. That suggested he was reaching the outer, less secure perimeter. He only needed to use one of the Marine's swipe cards to unlock it. He cracked the door open and sighed at what he saw: another dark corridor. When he was sure it was clear, he made his way out.

This corridor was different, and he immediately sensed it was some kind of neutral bridge between the Alignment's secret bunker and the larger world. At the end of it was a pinprick of light and a dull roar. He edged cautiously toward the door that emerged in the light when suddenly it was flung open. A Metro engineer stepped in and froze when he saw Conrad.

"Shit, you military people always scare me," the engineer said, "skulking around down here like shadows."

"And because of us you get to celebrate Independence Day," Conrad said and kept walking, without looking back.

Conrad emerged from a utility door onto a lower platform of the L'Enfant Plaza Metro Station. With no less than three Metro lines intersecting here, it now made complete sense why the Alignment chose the bunker below as their place to meet. But he was spotted across the platform by a D.C. police officer instantly, whose hand went to his mouth as he radioed in.

Conrad ran up the escalators to a food court tunnel, where four more policemen were coming toward him.

The underground food court connected him to the Loews L'Enfant Plaza Hotel, and when he cut across the lobby he emerged into the bright light of day and blinked.

There must have been several thousand motorcycles and leather-clad bikers revving their engines in front of him. Their black leather jackets said Rolling Thunder, and the backs of their bikes boasted American flags.

Conrad caught up to the rear of the group and scanned the nearest tattooed and bearded bikers prepping their machines. He found an old-timer in his sixties with a handlebar mustache and beer gut wearing a black "Ancient Riddles" T-shirt. He was wiping the chrome fork of his BMW chopper.

Conrad stole a helmet on the ground and brazenly walked up to the man. “Hey, partner, my bike’s busted and I could use a lift,” he said as he offered his hand. “I’m Conrad Yeats.”

The rider rose to his surprisingly tall six-foot-four-inch height and looked down at him. “Anything for the Griffter’s kid. My name’s Marty. Hop on.”

Conrad jumped on the chopper as Marty hit the accelerator and they rode off to join the others in the parade.

49

THROUGH THE SIGHT of her sniper rifle atop the National Archives, Sergeant Wanda Randolph watched the tail end of the Independence Day parade march down Constitution Avenue. She scanned the crowds for any sign of Conrad Yeats. America's most wanted criminal was presumably still on the loose after yesterday's Presidential Prayer Breakfast.

More than 22 government agencies, including the U.S. Capitol Police, U.S. Park Police, and Washington Metropolitan Police Department, were coordinating security: There were jets overhead, chemical sensors in the subways, Coast Guard boats on the Potomac, and more than 6,000 cops and troops on the streets.

Members of the 49th Virginia Infantry Regiment Civil War reenactment group now marched below to the cheers of onlookers, from babies to grandparents. It had been a morning of high school and military bands, and the Civil War types prompted as many smiles as the group that usually followed them.

Wanda could hear them now—the roar of thousands of Harley Davidsons revving down Constitution, their riders in jeans and leather jackets. Rolling Thunder was a motorcycling group that supported veterans. Today they had come out in full force, headlights blazing and American flags extending from the back of their bikes.

Her eyes followed them down Pennsylvania as they turned onto Constitution, one oddball biker in sunglasses after another. Several times she had to look away from the glare of the setting sun bouncing off the medals on their vests and the chrome on their bikes.

One neon yellow-and-chrome chopper with two riders caught her eye, and she followed it to the turn when another glare off the chrome blinded her for a split second. When she caught up with the chopper again on Constitution, it had only one rider.

What happened? Where'd he go?

She jerked her rifle back to the parade turn at Pennsylvania and Constitution and scoped the crowds. Nothing. And then she saw the small pump station building behind the crowd.

Dang, it was him, she thought. *It had to be. Conrad Yeats.*

She wanted to believe that Yeats was one of the good guys, but regardless of which hat he wore—white or black—he was about to get himself picked off by her or another sniper unless she could bring him in safely.

"Code red," she yelled into her radio. "Pump station."

She scrambled off the roof and out the National Archives, ran a block to the station and burst inside. Two Metro cops were down, knocked out, and a hatch to the sewer was open. Six FBI agents, plainclothes types from the crowd, swarmed in as she pulled out a map.

"The SEAL will pick him up in the sewer," one of the agents said.

But the SEAL swimming up and down beneath Constitution reported nothing. "He may have gone deeper," crackled the radio, the voice of a SEAL breaking up. "Shit, he's in the Tiber."

Long after the hill beneath the U.S. Capitol had ceased to be called Rome, the river upon which ships ferried marble from the White House to the Capitol retained the name Tiber Creek. And to this day the Tiber still runs beneath Constitution Avenue along the northern edge of the National Mall.

Conrad sloshed through knee-high water in the ancient sewer built of brick masonry. About 30 feet wide and ten feet high, the old sewer ran along the upper portion of the bed of the old Tiber Creek. Conrad could feel its rotting floor planks give way under his shoes and prayed he wouldn't step into a hole and get sucked into the bog, never to return to the surface.

He remembered the Tiber from a consulting gig when the feds asked him how to preserve downtown D.C. as the ancient Egyptians had preserved the pyramids. The Tiber, like the Nile, ran in front of the Capitol and through the Smithsonian.

The whole Mall, in fact, was one giant flood plain. The east wing of the Natural History museum, Conrad had discovered, was already sinking and pulling away from the main building because the Tiber still coursed beneath the Mall. Only a carefully built and even more carefully camouflaged levee kept the Mall from being under water. The feds did a great job planting trees on it to hide it. Only by lying down on the steps of the Lincoln Memorial and looking out toward Constitution Avenue could you see the levee with the naked eye.

Inside the old Tiber Creek sewer, however, there was very little to see. Conrad looked around the battered side walls and the stone arch ceiling over the river channel, which had seen better days. The brick was crumbling, and refuse from the more modern sewer line—cut in the 1930s—was raining down on him.

The sewer emptied out near the Washington Monument, where the east branch of the Potomac used to be before the feds filled it in. It was here Conrad started his search for a planned tunnel that may or may not have ever been built to the monument.

The "Capitol Fourth" concert was just getting under way on the National Mall when Max Seavers arrived at the Washington Monument, which was closed to the public today due to security concerns as well as a very special "private function"—a White House reception for Chinese Olympic officials.

Seavers checked his cell phone GPS, which confirmed that the aerosol canister containing his bird flu was in place and activated. Once everybody was inside the elevator, he'd speed dial the silent detonator and the revolution would be over before anybody even suspected it had started. The very thought that he could kill billions with the push of a button gave him a special kind of thrill, but not nearly as much as the knowledge that his vaccine would make him a savior to the rest of the surviving world.

He slipped the phone back in his pocket, next to the folded Newburgh Treaty.

"Dr. Seavers!"

Seavers turned to see the enthusiastic head of the Olympic delegation, Dr. Ling, walk up with a smile. "I saw you yesterday at the president's prayer breakfast. Very moving."

Seavers smiled, assuming Dr. Ling was being polite and that the Chinese had learned from the mistakes of the former Soviet Union when its leaders allowed a Polish pope and a cowboy American president to undermine their entire empire and bring it to collapse. The only reason he didn't release the virus at the prayer breakfast—his first choice—was that it was too easy to trace back to him as "ground zero." This plan was much simpler: The Chinese Olympic delegation would go up to the observation deck to enjoy the fireworks and by the time they came back down they'd be infected with the weaponized bird flu virus. The virus would incubate for 28 days until it made its day-and-date world premiere at the opening ceremonies of the Olympic Games in Beijing. From there it would fan across the world. And everybody would blame the Chinese.

Genius, he thought.

"Well, if you liked the breakfast, Dr. Ling, just wait until you see the fireworks! The National Symphony Orchestra plays Tchaikovsky's '1812 Overture' for the finale. The piece is accompanied by live cannons—four 105mm Howitzers set off by the U.S. Army Presidential Salute Battery."

Seavers led a delighted Ling and the small line of Olympic officials to the monument's new elevator. The glass cab held 25 passengers, and would take 70 seconds to go up to the observation deck at the 500-foot level. Special panels in the doors were timed to turn from opaque to clear at the 180-, 170-, 140-, and 130-foot levels, allowing passengers to view the 193 commemorative Masonic stones that lined the interior of the monument. Seavers, however, knew from a secret DARPA report filed during the Griffin Yeats regime that there were really 194 stones. He had yet to figure out which stone was omitted from the official count, let alone unlock its significance. But at this point, he concluded none of that Masonic nonsense mattered anymore.

As the group stepped inside the glass elevator, Dr. Ling shook his head. "My wife is never going to believe this."

"Don't worry, I'll take your picture," Seavers said, holding up his cell phone camera as the doors closed and the elevator began its ascent.

50

Few of the Capitol Fourth concert-goers who sat on the white marble benches and low, curving granite walls ringing the Washington Monument knew that these amenities were actually part of a multimillion-dollar security upgrade in the wake of the attacks of Sept. 11, 2001.

The decorative walls, for example, were augmented by retractable posts that could spring up in an instant to stop any charging vehicle packed with explosives from ever reaching the monument itself. And fifty feet below the marble benches was a secret 17-foot-wide, 400-foot-long tunnel connecting the monument, which was closed to the public today, with an off-site screening facility near 15th Street.

But Conrad knew.

Soaked with scum he didn't want to think about, he emerged from the ruins of the Tiber Creek sewer into the tunnel he had been searching for—the only piece of an official underground visitors center for the Washington Monument that the National Planning Commission could never get approved but built anyway. The feds wanted any acts of terror to occur at the base of the site rather than in the upper level of the monument itself, where the walls weren't as thick and where a blast would cause the sides to peel away and the entire structure to collapse.

Unfortunately, Conrad realized, Max Seavers was in that most vulnerable part of the monument right now—more than 500 feet above him.

* * *

On the observation deck, Max Seavers hurriedly herded the Chinese delegation back into the glass elevator. The fireworks on the Mall were almost over, save for the grand finale, and some of the Chinese had started talking about walking down the stairwell to view the Masonic commemorative stones after the show. Seavers couldn't allow it.

"The ride down is two minutes and eighteen seconds," he said. "So you'll have plenty of time to view 45 of the 193 then. Plus, you'll get to see the grand finale over the Capitol dome from our special private viewing area for you on the east side of the monument."

"Thank you so much, Dr. Seavers," said Dr. Ling as the doors began to close. "This has been fantastic. My wife will be . . ."

The doors shut and the elevator began its descent.

Seavers pulled out his cell phone, pressed the number 3 key twice and walked across the observation deck to the east window. He looked outside in wonder at the New World Order.

It is done, he thought.

The aerosol canister he had placed above the elevator cab's overhead compartment was slowly releasing its fine, imperceptible mist on the longer descent. He couldn't do it on the way up because of the shorter trip; his bird flu took a good two minutes of inhalation to guarantee infection.

By the time the Chinese walked outside and gawked at the last orgasmic gasp of Independence Day in the United States, they would be dead and they wouldn't even know it. Same for the republic.

His phone rang and he looked at the screen. It was a private number.

"Seavers," he answered.

"It's Yeats, you sick bastard. Your star-crossed plan failed. The Chinese aren't going to be spreading your germs after all."

The shock took a moment for Seavers to shake. *How did he escape?* Then a pit in his stomach formed. "How in hell did you get this number?"

The voice on the other end said: "I just ripped off the cell phone from your aerosol canister inside the elevator cab and returned the last call. By the way, I'm coming up for you right now."

Seavers shut the phone and frantically looked around the observation deck. He wasn't about to wait for the elevator doors to open and let Yeats take a shot at him. He was going to have to shoot first, and he knew he had less than a minute before the elevator reached the observation deck.

He ran past the gift shop a half-level below the observation deck and then bounded down the stone stairwell that lined the interior of the monument, several steps at a time. He had only made it to the 400-foot level before he saw the elevator coming up and positioned himself, bending down on one knee and aiming his Glock at the open air shaft.

The glass cab was coming up fast, its panel windows opaque. Seavers aimed carefully, his finger on the trigger as the glass began to clear.

But the elevator was empty.

Seavers's hands holding the gun wavered as he stared. Too late he saw Yeats hanging on to the bottom of the ascending cab with one arm, the other swinging up with a gun, firing.

The first bullet caught Seavers in the leg, spinning him back against the Masonic stone. He crouched in pain as he looked up and saw Yeats approaching the observation deck. He could hear shouts hundreds of feet below. Police would soon be swarming up the monument.

He fired twice at Yeats. A bullet bounced off the bottom of the elevator with a spark, and Yeats let go, falling into the darkness below. He heard a loud shout.

Seavers peered down and saw nothing. Then a bullet whizzed past his ear. Yeats had landed somewhere, hurt but alive and coming back up.

Seavers knew he had no choice now but to release the virus outside on the crowds below. And he wouldn't be walking out the front door of the monument now. He willed himself to stand and marched up the steps in the darkness, each footfall exploding in searing agony. He looked into the shattered cab at the top with caution and the empty observation deck. But he could hear footsteps coming up the stairwell.

"Game over, sport," he shouted. "You lose."

He unfastened the canister from the overhead compartment of the elevator. Thankfully, Yeats had removed only the remote detonator mechanism. The canister was still intact and full of the deadly virus.

If conditions were even remotely optimal outside, the virus could survive 24 hours after being sprayed like a small cloud into the air. Just one tiny droplet inhaled by one person on the Mall hundreds of feet below would start a time-delayed virulent chain reaction.

Seavers smashed the butt of his gun against one of the large reinforced observation windows, but the window wouldn't break. He would have to find some other means to release the virus outside.

He looked up at the ceiling above the observation deck and pulled a hidden latch to open a secret hatch door. A metal ladder like a fire escape telescoped down.

Seavers climbed up the ladder into the 55-foot-tall structure above the shaft called the "pyramidion," because of the way its four walls converged to form the point of the 555-foot-tall monument. It was packed with several banks of electrical machinery and classified surveillance equipment, but for the most part was as empty inside as a church steeple.

Slowly he began his ascent in the dark toward the capstone at the top of the pyramidion as he listened to the strains of the Capitol Fourth concert outside.

When Conrad reached the observation deck, it was empty. So was the elevator cab. Seavers had taken the canister with the virus. Conrad looked out the west window. A remote network television camera was stationed there, pointed out to capture the fireworks. From the east window he could hear the National Symphony Orchestra on the Mall reaching a crescendo.

He felt a stab of pain in the back, pushing him to the glass, blood smearing across it. The bullet passed right through his shoulder. Conrad heard two hollow clicks and looked up to see Seavers disappear through a hatch in the ceiling above the elevator shaft. He was out of ammo and had climbed up into the monument's pyramidion.

He's got the canister. The son of a bitch is going to release the virus.

Conrad knew the pyramidion was about 55 feet in height. So Seavers had another 40 feet to go to reach the capstone.

Forcing himself to stand up, Conrad put a hand to his shoulder, applying pressure on the gunshot wound. It felt like a heavy power drill, boring into him full blast. But he reached up, grabbed the ladder and pulled himself up with a gasp of pain.

"You've nothing to gain and everything to lose by stopping me," Seavers's voice called down from the dark. "Think about it. A new world order. No China. No religion . . ."

Conrad pointed his gun toward the sound of the voice. "You mean no Serena, you bastard."

Conrad paused. A thunderous boom outside from the cannons from the "1812 Overture" sounded.

At that moment Seavers swung down from the dark feet first and struck Conrad in the shoulder full force, knocking the gun out of his hand. Conrad watched it clink against the wall and fall fifty feet to the floor of the observation deck.

Conrad was now clinging by his shot arm to a metal lightning rod that ran along the masonry wall, which was lined with tiny cracks.

He looked up at a square of starlight. Somehow Seavers had popped open the aluminum capstone at the top in order to release the aerosol form of the bird flu into the air. The square aperture framed the constellation Virgo, its alpha star Spica directly overhead, shimmering between bursts of fireworks and smoke.

The alignment, he thought. *It's happening right now. Seavers is actually going to release his global plague at the exact moment the Washington Monument locks with Virgo.*

Conrad climbed up the lightning rod toward Seavers, who was trying to raise the canister through the opening, but the base of the capstone was too small.

"Don't do it, Seavers!" Conrad shouted. "Think of all the people."

"This isn't a democracy, Yeats," Seavers shouted as he tried to force the aerosol canister through the aperture. "Your vote doesn't count. It never did. This is a republic. It was built to be run by elite overlords."

"Like the Alignment?" Conrad reached behind his back and pulled out the Masonic dagger that Seavers had lifted from old Herc before he killed him.

"Do you want to know why George Washington and the Founding Fathers wanted a representative government? Because they were the representatives!" Seavers shouted, finally forcing the canister through the aperture and lifting his finger to push the button. "They're the real Alignment. I'm the cure."

"Got a cure for this?" Conrad said, and hurled the dagger across the air into Seavers's neck.

Seavers screamed and released his grip on the canister, which clanked down the pyramidion and disappeared into the darkness. Seavers himself began to lose his balance as he pulled the dagger from his neck and stared in fascination at the blade's Masonic markings coated with his own blood.

"Von Berg," he wheezed, gurgling up blood.

"What?" Conrad demanded. "Who?"

But Seavers's eyes rolled back into his head, his unconscious body wavering for a few seconds before it fell fifty feet to the observation deck below, killing him instantly.

Conrad reached up to the aluminum capstone, popped on its side like a hinge. It had been set atop the monument by Colonel Thomas Lincoln Casey, the same Mason responsible for the construction of the Library of Congress.

So close was Conrad that he could read the Latin letters engraved across the east face of the capstone, by design visible only to the heavens:

LAUS DEO

In Praise of God, Conrad repeated in English, and pulled it shut.

He climbed down the ladder and dropped down onto the floor of the observation deck. He leaned over Seavers's corpse and saw the twisted smile on his face. He then reached inside Seavers's jacket, removed the Newburgh Treaty, and pocketed it. He was about to pick up the canister of lethal virus when the thunder of boots rumbled up the stairwell and Sergeant Randolph in her flak jacket reached the observation deck.

"Drop the gun!" she shouted. "Hands in the air!"

Behind her popped up two more CPs with M-4s. A dozen more NPS officers clambered up behind them and surrounded him.

Conrad slowly laid the Glock on the floor and put his hands up. His left shoulder blazed with pain.

Sergeant Randolph kicked the gun away.

"Dang, Yeats," she said. "You killed Max Seavers."

"Before he was about to kill millions. That's a canister of bird flu on the floor. He was about to release it over the Mall. You're going to need a Haz-Mat team."

"You're going to need a doctor," she said, looking at his blood-soaked shoulder.

Conrad shook his head. "No time," he said. "Serena. You've got to get me back to her."

"Sister Serghetti?" Sergeant Randolph said. "Don't tell me you dragged her into this, too?"

Minutes later, while fireworks and cannons exploded over the Mall, Conrad and Randolph's R.A.T.S. burst into the secret underground laboratories beneath L'Enfant Plaza and found the Alignment boardroom empty.

Serena was gone.

And so was the terrestrial globe.

The shock of her betrayal stabbed Conrad like a dagger through the heart.

51

THE WHITE HOUSE

JULY 5, 2008

It was just before nine the following evening when Conrad, his arm in a sling, was admitted in the Oval Office. The president was sitting on a sofa, sipping some Scotch, staring into the empty fireplace as a gentle rain drummed the windows behind him. To the right of the fireplace stood the celestial globe.

"You have the Newburgh Treaty, Dr. Yeats?"

"Yes, Mr. President."

Conrad sat down on the opposite sofa, eyes fixed on the globe, thinking of Serena, and wondering where she had gone. Above the fireplace mantel was a portrait of George Washington. Conrad almost felt like Washington was studying him as closely as the current president was. He wondered if the president knew that the East Wing of the White House was designed by architect I.M. Pei as a triangle to mirror the federal triangle, based on the slope of Pennsylvania Avenue as it intersects with Constitution Avenue and 16th Street. But now was not the time to bring it up.

"I suppose the other globe is safe inside the Vatican by now," the president said. "Somewhere even we can't touch it. But these globes are meant to go together."

"I wanted to talk to you about that, Mr. President," Conrad said. "Sister Serghetti has already seen the signatures on the Treaty. The damage is done. I think we could make an exchange: the Treaty for the terrestrial globe."

The president looked him in the eye. "How about the Treaty for your freedom, Yeats, so I don't throw you in military lockup?"

Conrad handed it over.

The president calmly unfolded it and then pulled out a pair of reading glasses. For a crazy second Conrad wondered if the president would repeat Washington's famous line from Newburgh:

"Gentlemen, you will permit me to put on my spectacles, for I have not only grown gray but almost blind in the service of my country."

But the president simply looked over the Newburgh Treaty once, and then again. Finally, he sat back and stared at Conrad over his reading glasses. "Some of the signatures on this Treaty . . . it's beyond shocking."

"Like your ancestor John Marshall, Mr. President?" Conrad said. "It's the sixth name down if you need help finding it."

"I see it, thank you," the president said tersely. "And no, Dr. Yeats, like you I had no idea of the extent of my family's dealings with the Alignment. But as you discovered, when your roots go that far back in American history, it's probably unavoidable. Some of these names will turn up modern-day Alignment figures. Some won't. It will be a tricky but necessary ordeal to ferret them out. But we will."

"Like Senator Scarborough?"

Conrad knew the FBI had raided Scarborough's home in Virginia that morning. News reports said a federal grand jury was looking into his ties to a defense contractor—biotech billionaire Max Seavers.

"It appears Seavers funneled money to the senator," the president said, sounding genuinely shocked. "Scarborough's position in Congress, where he sits on the Armed Services Committee that controls the Pentagon budget, could have allowed him to influence the flow of contracts to Seavers's company, or even Seavers's appointment to DARPA."

So that's how it's going down, Conrad thought. "So the only reason you wanted the Newburgh Treaty was to take names?"

"Hell no, Yeats," the president said. "This is America. Nobody gives a damn what your ancestors did. Or shouldn't. We're judged by our fruits, not our roots. The sins of the fathers should not be visited on their sons. I should think you would appreciate that more than anybody else."

Conrad sighed at this none-too-subtle reminder of Antarctica and his father General Yeats.

"It's what the Newburgh Treaty and the Alignment represent that threatens our security," the president went on. "Science and technology have advanced more rapidly than the ability of politicians and generals to grasp their implications. That's what Plato implied was the real problem with Atlantis. Not the cataclysm that supposedly destroyed it. If we don't do any better in America, which Sir Francis Bacon prophesized to be the New Atlantis, we'll suffer the same fate. Hell, just a few years back I used to sweat over mass extinction from some terrorist biotoxin. Max Seavers was on the brink of bottling it as a vaccine with the label 'Made in the USA.' Thank God you stopped him."

"God?" Conrad repeated, wondering if the president really believed in America as "one nation under God" or was simply posing for Middle America at his prayer breakfast the other day.

The president gazed up at Washington over the fireplace.

"Washington's greatness lay in his readiness to surrender power and embrace his faith," the president said, a faraway look in his eyes. "He understood that true political freedom cannot exist without religious freedom. Sure, he bent over backwards not to favor any particular religion. But he instinctively grasped that Americans of religious faith are the true protectors of American liberty."

"He also gave his spies bags of gold, Mr. President."

The president paused for a moment, then pursed his lips and smiled at Yeats in a way that almost resembled a smirk. "You've done your part, Dr. Yeats, and America is grateful," he said. "Big-time."

The president put the Treaty down on the table beside him and picked up a box. "There's more, don't worry," he said, holding the box out to him. "This is the Presidential Medal of Honor with Military Distinction. The incredible truth is that you successfully carried out the orders of the commander-in-chief."

Conrad wasn't sure if the president was referring to himself or George Washington. But he felt an honest-to-goodness surge of pride as he opened the box and looked at the medal. It was a golden disc with a great white star on top of a red enamel pentagon. In the center of the star was a gold circle with blue enamel bearing thirteen gold stars. The medal hung from a blue ribbon with white edge stripes, white stars, and a golden American eagle with spread wings.

The president said, "Secretary Packard insisted you deserved no less and wanted me to tell you that he wants you back at DARPA."

"It's Danny Z and old Herc who deserve this," Conrad said, and closed the box. "Along with that poor soul you buried in my father's tomb."

The president only said, "Take a lesson from Sister Serghetti, son, and stop mourning for those you're sure to follow shortly."

"None of this changes the fact that we have one globe and the Vatican has the other," Conrad pressed. "Or that you and Sister Serghetti and I saw the names on the Treaty with our own eyes."

"That girl is going to do what she's going to do," the president said. "I have to do what I have to do."

The president rose to his feet, picked up the Newburgh Treaty and stepped to the fireplace. He touched a lighter to the corner of the Treaty and placed the Treaty in the fireplace.

Conrad looked on as a corner curled into black and then burst into flame beneath the watchful eyes of George Washington. Within seconds more black holes like growing welts appeared all over the Treaty until it went up in smoke.

52

VATICAN CITY

STILL TORMENTED OVER HER sudden abandonment and betrayal of Conrad, a resolute Serena marched into the office of Cardinal Tucci in the Governorate with the terrestrial globe and a plainclothes security detail of six Swiss Guards. Much like the American president's Secret Service, the centuries-old guards protected the pope both at home and abroad. Whether they would do the same for her now, well, she was about to find out.

Cardinal Tucci was seated in practically the same position she had last seen him days earlier, deep in his leather chair between two Bleau globes, echoes of the globes that Conrad had uncovered. Tucci held a glass of red wine in his hand. The silver Roman coin around his neck caught the morning light from the window beside him, warning her that he was the head of *Dominus Dei.*

She said, "A bit early in the morning for that, Your Eminence."

"Sister Serghetti, I see you brought me the globe," Tucci replied, "along with an entourage."

Serena turned to the captain of the guards and said, "I'd like a private audience with His Eminence for a moment. Wait outside."

As the guards withdrew and closed the door behind them, Tucci took another sip of his wine. "I take it you disobeyed my direct orders and opened the globe?"

"I did, Your Eminence. Both of them."

"I see."

"So do I," Serena said. "And I see your mother's family in Boston among the names at the bottom of the Newburgh Treaty. You're Osiris. And *Dominus Dei* is the Alignment's cell within the Church. It always has been. Long before the Knights Templar. It's the Church that's in danger, not just America."

"Is that what you told Dr. Yeats?" Tucci said dismissively. "I'm sure he appreciated your sentiments. Tell me, did you sleep with him on your adventure?"

Serena pointed her finger at him. "You are the wolf in sheep's clothing, Tucci! You don't love the Church. You've never loved the Church. You and your kind have only used the Church for yourselves, to build a worldly empire for the Alignment."

"Well, if you bother to look around, Sister Serghetti, you'll find that there are plenty of others like me. Where God builds a church, the Devil builds a chapel, you know. I take it by the guards that you've told the Holy See?"

"I have, Your Eminence, and this is one chapel I'm closing."

"Only to build the Antichrist's cathedral." Tucci finished his wine. "Indeed, the federal city of the future, the world's capital city, is going up soon. Something to make Washington and the new Beijing pale in comparison."

"What are you getting at?" she demanded.

"America is inconsequential in the sweep of history—it doesn't even merit a mention in the Book of Revelation," Tucci said. "It was the globes all along and not the Newburgh Treaty that the international Alignment was interested in."

"The globes?"

"They're necessary to begin the construction of the Third Temple," Tucci said in triumph. "By uncovering the globes you have now ensured the rise of the last master civilization."

"You're insane," she said.

"Soon you'll be, too." He placed his empty wineglass down and nodded toward the door. "Shall we call your guards?"

Serena took a step toward the door and caught a blur of movement in the corner of her eye. She whirled around in time to see Tucci rush toward the window and hurl himself through the glass with a thunderous crash. She heard a scream outside, ran to the sill and looked down to see Tucci sprawled on the pavement below, two uniformed Swiss Guards pointing up at her in the window.

"No!" she gasped.

She heard the door behind her fling open as the guards burst in. She turned from the window to see the captain staring. But not at the broken window and terrible scene outside. He was staring at the *Dominus Dei* pendant on the floor. She stared at it, too. The chain was unbroken, as if Tucci had removed it first before he had leapt to his death.

"Is everything all right, Sister Serghetti?" he asked her.

"Cardinal Tucci is dead, Captain. Obviously everything is not all right."

Her heart was pounding as she watched the captain pick up the medallion off the floor with great reverence and hand it to her. He was practically genuflecting, as if he now answered to her.

Somehow he has it in his head that I'm the new head of the Dei.

She took the chain and stared at the ancient Roman coin. Only the pope could nominate the head of the Dei, she knew. But then she recalled the jokes of conspiracy buffs in the College of the Cardinals who said that it was Dei all these centuries who picked the popes.

"Cardinal Tucci was not well," the captain said suddenly, as if forming his story for the Vatican's press release about the incident. He clearly knew more than he was letting on. "Arrhythmia, you know. It is a shame his heart should fail while looking out the window."

"Thank you, Captain. You are dismissed."

"Very well," he said and knelt to kiss the medallion now wrapped around her fingers. "I will post guards outside your door and leave you to your privacy."

She watched him close the door behind him and sat down in Tucci's chair, suddenly feeling like a prisoner in a cell full of secrets.

She stared at the medallion in her hands, realizing that it was her only way out now. To protect the Church she would have to root out the Alignment, even if it meant joining the Dei. She mourned for Conrad, but knew in her heart that she couldn't abandon the Church to these predators. She had to find out what the Dei was up to.

I do those things I don't want to do, and don't do those things I want to do, she thought, paraphrasing St. Paul. *What a wretched woman I am.*

Slowly she put the chain with the Dominus Dei medallion around her neck, feeling the silver Roman coin press heavily on her heart.

EPILOGUE

THE DAY AFTER

ARLINGTON CEMETERY

THE RAIN CAME DOWN even harder as Conrad approached his father's tombstone in the dark of night, consumed by an obsession for the truth that the burning of the Newburgh Treaty had only inflamed.

He shined a light on the three-foot-tall obelisk and again read the inscription beneath the engraved cross:

GRIFFIN W. YEATS
BRIG GEN
US AIR FORCE
BORN
MAY 4 1945
KILLED IN ACTION
EAST ANTARCTICA
SEPT 21 2004

He could feel it all coming up now inside him: the anger, the betrayal, the loss—first his father, and now Serena, all over again.

He stared at the numerical strings on one side of the obelisk that had led him to the Stargazer text and the three constellations engraved on the other side that had revealed the secret alignment of America's key monuments.

For some reason he couldn't shake the same uneasy feeling creeping up his spine that he experienced the first time.

There must be more.

Conrad felt a surge of anger and frustration as he leaned back and gave the obelisk a hard kick.

The heavy tombstone barely budged.

Conrad gave it another kick, with feeling.

This time the obelisk, its base loosened from the rain, moved about an inch before it settled back into the muck.

"You goddamn bastard!" he shouted as he kicked it again.

At last the gravestone toppled over on its side in the wet grass.

Conrad stared.

There it was, inscribed in the bottom of the obelisk, now facing him like a picture in stone as the rain washed away the dirt:

A Crusader's cross.

It was an emblem of the Templar Crusaders, a single cross made up of four smaller crosses.

It was also a symbol of Jerusalem.

The cross's four arms were of equal length, symbolizing the four directions and the belief that Jerusalem was the spiritual center of the earth.

He remembered the two columns in the Savage portrait of Mount Vernon, along with the two pillars to the entrance of King Solomon's Temple in that Masonic mural under the Library of Congress. Then he recalled what sat on top of those two pillars—globes with terrestrial and celestial maps.

The globes belonged in Solomon's Temple. Not just the original Temple. But the next Temple. And if each globe was reputed to have originally contained the secrets of Genesis or "First Time," then it stood to reason that together the globes worked to reveal the secret of . . . the end of time.

He stared at the cross, the last secret symbol that his father had left him.

Did Serena know about it? Conrad wondered. She must.

Now he knew, too.

"See you there, Serena," he said to the pounding rain, and walked away into the night.

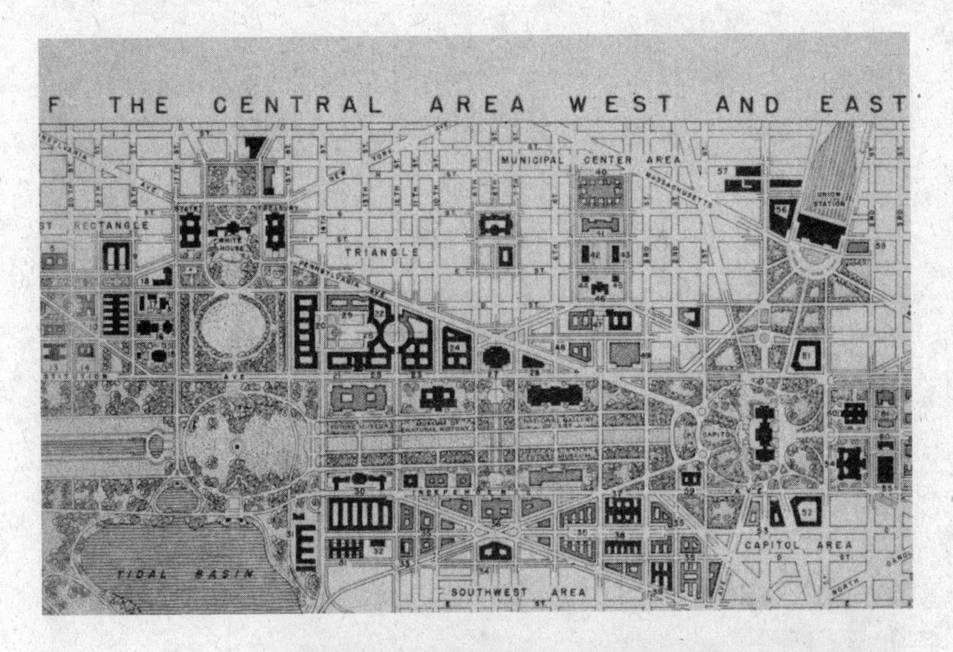
F THE CENTRAL AREA WEST AND EAST
MUNICIPAL CENTER AREA
UNION STATION
RECTANGLE
TRIANGLE
CAPITOL
CAPITOL AREA
TIDAL BASIN
SOUTHWEST AREA

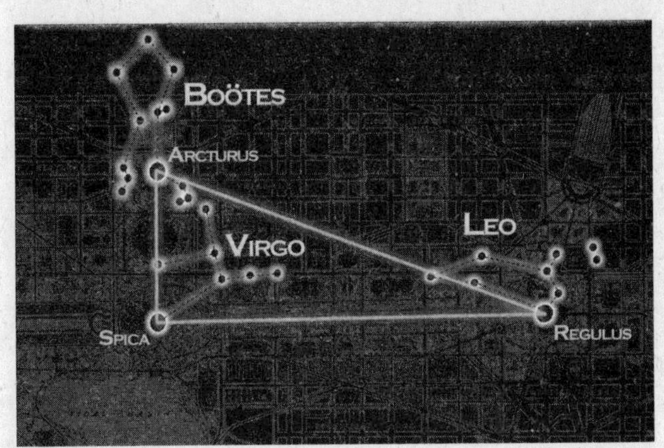
BOÖTES
ARCTURUS
VIRGO
LEO
SPICA
REGULUS

Atria Books
Proudly Presents

THE ATLANTIS REVELATION

THOMAS GREANIAS

Available from Atria Books in hardcover

Turn the page for a preview of

The Atlantis Revelation. . . .

1

THE CALYPSO DEEP

IONIAN SEA

Conrad Yeats started having second thoughts as soon as they anchored the fishing boat *Katrina* over the discovery.

It wasn't just that he hated the water. Or that it was three miles to the bottom, at the deepest part of the Mediterranean. Or that his Greek crew believed these waters were cursed. It was the words of a former U.S. secretary of defense warning that what Conrad sought didn't exist, but if it did, he was not to disturb it, or else. *Maybe it's time you gave it a rest, son, and let the damned past rust in peace.*

But he had come too far on his journey to recover a real-world relic from the mythological lost continent of Atlantis to turn back now. And he would never rest until he found out exactly what kind of damned past everyone would just as soon bury simply because it threatened their own vision of the future.

Conrad pulled the black neoprene wet suit over his shoulders and looked at Stavros, his diving attendant. The big, strapping Greek had hauled up the sonar towfish that a team of sidescan sonar experts from the exploration ship had used to get a fix on the target only hours ago. Now he was fiddling with Conrad's air compressor.

"You finally fix that thing?" Conrad asked.

Stavros grunted. "Think so."

Conrad glanced up at Polaris, the brightest star in the constellation Ursa Major, and then at the silvery waters. This location wasn't on any charts. He'd found it by using ancient poems, ship's logs, and astronomical data that only an astro-archaeologist like himself would take seriously.

Yet he wasn't alone.

The black cutout of a megayacht loomed on the dark horizon. For a pleasure palace cruising the Ionian islands on an Easter holiday vacation, the six-hundred-foot vessel boasted an impressive communications array, a helicopter, and for all Conrad knew, even a couple of submersibles. It was probably all for show, but Conrad still didn't like someone else with that kind of firepower near his find.

He planned to be long gone before the sun came up. "I need forty minutes of air to the bottom and back," he told Stavros.

Stavros threw out a small buoy tied to two hundred meters of line. "If she's still sitting on the edge of the trench, like the robotic camera showed, you'll be lucky to get twenty minutes bottom time," Stavros said. "If she's slipped into the Calypso, then it doesn't matter. The Baron of the Black Order himself will grab you by the leg and drag you down to hell." He shivered and made the sign of the cross over his heart.

Conrad could do without a Greek chorus to remind him that tragedy haunted these waters. In the light of day, the surface of the Ionian was among the most serene for sailing in Greece, surrounded by easy anchorage and safe bays for cruise ships and private yachts alike. But in the darkness of its depths was one of the most seismic areas in the world.

There, three miles down at the bottom of the Hellenic Trench, lay the vast Calypso Deep. It was the point where the African tectonic plate subducted the Eurasian plate, pulling anything too close under the plates and into the earth's magma. Even, some had argued, something as big as a continent.

"You worry about my oxygen, Stavros. I'll worry about the curse of the Calypso." Conrad slipped on his full-face dive mask and stepped off the bow, fins first, into the sea.

The cool Ionian water enveloped him as he followed the anchored buoy line to the bottom. His high-powered Newtlite head lantern illuminated the way through the darkness. Halfway down he met a school of bottle-nosed dolphins. They parted like a curtain to reveal the startling sight of the legendary *Nausicaa* rising out of the depths, her 37mm antiaircraft guns pointing straight at him.

The German submarine was imposing enough, which Conrad had expected. After all, it had belonged to SS General Ludwig von Berg—the Baron of the Black Order, as he was known to his friends in the Third Reich. Among other things, the baron was head of Hitler's Ahnenerbe, an organization of academics, philosophers, and military warriors sent to scour the earth to prove the Aryans were the descendants of Atlantis.

That mission had taken Baron von Berg as far away as Antarctica, where decades later, Conrad's father, USAF General Griffin Yeats, had uncovered a secret Nazi base and ancient ruins two miles beneath the ice. But any evidence of that lost civilization—Atlantis—was wiped away in a seismic event that killed Griffin, sank an ice shelf the size of California, and may well have caused the Indian Ocean tsunami of 2004 that killed thousands in Indonesia.

Ever since, Conrad had been trying to find some proof that what he had found under Antarctica wasn't a dream. Clues left by his father on his tombstone at Arlington Cemetery had told Conrad as much, and more. Soon he had discovered that his father's successor as head of the Pentagon's DARPA research and development agency, Max Seavers, had developed a weaponized flu virus from the infected lung tissue of dead Nazis found frozen in Antarctica.

Those discoveries ultimately led Conrad to the mysterious Baron von Berg. Classified American, British, and German intelligence files from World War II recorded that the SS general's U-boat, *Nausicaa,* was returning from its secret base in Antarctica when it was sunk by the British Royal Navy in 1943.

Conrad's hope was that he would find on board a relic from Atlantis.

He kicked through the water toward the sunken submarine. The *Nausicaa* lay like a gutted whale along the cusp of the Calypso Deep with her tail broken off and her forward section jutting out over the abyss like a metal coffin.

Conrad swam to the mouth of the broken fuselage and studied its teeth. The British torpedo that had sunk the *Nausicaa* had taken out the entire electric motor room. But it wasn't a clean break. One little nick of his air hose would cut off his oxygen. He spoke into his dive helmet's integrated radio. "Stavros."

"Right here, boss," the Greek's voice crackled in his earpiece.

"How's the compressor?"

"Still ticking, boss."

Conrad swam into the abandoned control room of the forward section, keeping his eyes peeled for floating skeletons. He found none. No diving officers, helmsmen, or planesmen. Not even in the conning tower. Just an empty compartment with unmanned banks of instruments to his port and starboard sides. Had all hands managed to abandon ship before she went down?

The captain's quarters were empty, too. There was only a phonograph with a warped album. Conrad could still read the peeling label on the album: *Die Walküre.* Von Berg had been playing Wagner's "Ride of the Valkyries" over the loudspeakers when the sub went down.

But no sign of Baron von Berg himself. Nor a metallic Kriegsmarine briefcase. Maybe the legend was true, and von Berg never carried secret papers with him, telling everyone instead: "It's all in my head."

Conrad's hopes of finding anything were sinking fast.

He swam up the cramped fore-and-aft passageway through the galley and officers' quarters. A creeping claustrophobia came over him as he slipped through the open hatch into the forward torpedo bay.

At one end were four circular hatches—the torpedo tubes. The atmospheric pressure gauges, frozen in time, told him the *Nausicaa* had fired off at least three torpedos and drained her tubes to fire more when the Brits sank her. Only the No. 4 tube was flooded.

The Baron of the Black Order obviously didn't go down without a fight.

Conrad turned to the bomb racks and found a large protrusion. He fanned away the accumulated silt. An object took form, and he realized he was staring at a human skull with black holes for eyes.

The bared teeth seemed to grin at him in the eerie deep. The skull had a silver plate screwed into one side—the legacy of a bullet to the head in Crete, Conrad had learned in his research.

SS General Ludwig von Berg. The Baron of the Black Order. The rightful king of Bavaria. That was what the old top-secret OSS report Conrad had stolen had said.

Conrad felt a shock wave in the water, and the *Nausicaa* seemed to lurch.

"Stavros!" he called into his radio, but there was no response.

Suddenly, the black holes in the baron's skull glowed a bright red and his skeletal arm floated up as if to grab Conrad.

Conrad backed away from the skeleton, figuring that the water was playing tricks on him. Then he noticed that the glow actually came from something behind the skull. Indeed, the Baron of the Black Order seemed to be guarding something.

Conrad's heart pounded as he brushed away more silt, revealing an odd hammerhead-shaped warhead. He shined a light on it and ran his hands across the torpedo's slick casing.

It had no markings save for a code name stamped across the warhead's access panel: *Flammenschwert.* Conrad's rudimentary grasp of German translated it to mean "Flaming Sword" or "Sword of Fire."

He recalled from his research that von Berg claimed to have developed a weapon that the Nazis were convinced could win them the war: an incendiary technology that allegedly was Atlantean in origin and could turn water into fire and even melt the ice caps.

Could this be the relic he was searching for that would prove Antarctica was Atlantis?

The mysterious glow was coming from inside the hammerhead cone of the torpedo, outlining the square access panel like a neon light. But this was no mere illumination. The light seemed to be consuming the water around the warhead like a fire consumes oxygen.

Conrad's dosimeter gauge registered no radiation, so he put the fingertip of his glove to the glowing seam of the access panel. It didn't burn his glove, but he could feel an unmistakable pull. The warhead was sucking in the water around it like a black hole.

He sensed another shock wave through the water and turned to see four shadowy figures with harpoon guns enter the torpedo bay.

They must be after the *Flammenschwert*! he thought. He'd rather sink the sub than let this weapon fall into anybody's hands.

He reached up for the blow valves above the four torpedo tubes and twisted the wheels, flooding three of them. The sub tilted forward toward the Calypso Deep, throwing the others back. The rumbling was deafening. Breathing hard in his mask, heaving as he kicked, he was swimming madly to escape the torpedo bay when a harpoon dart stabbed his thigh.

Grimacing in pain, Conrad grabbed his leg as three of the divers swarmed around him. He broke off the harpoon dart and stabbed in the gut the diver who had shot him. The diver doubled over as a cloud of blood billowed out of his wet suit. The other two had grabbed him, however, and before Conrad could tear away, their leader swam over, drew a dagger, and sliced through Conrad's lifeline.

Conrad watched in shock as silver bubbles rose up before his eyes like a Roman candle, literally taking his breath away.

Then he saw the dagger again, this time its butt smashing the glass of his mask. Water began filling the mask, and he inhaled some against his will. His life flashed by in a blur—his father, the Griffter, his childhood in Washington, D.C., his digs around the world searching for Earth's lost "mother culture," meeting Serena in South America, then Antarctica . . .

Serena.

His lips tried to repeat the prayer that Serena had taught him, the last prayer of Jesus: "Into Thy hands I commit my spirit." But the words refused to come. He could only see her face, now fading away. Then darkness.

When Conrad opened his eyes again, the phantom divers were gone. He wasn't breathing, but his lungs weren't filled with water either—laryngospasm had sealed his airway. He would suffocate instead of drowning if he didn't surface immediately.

He looked out through his shattered dive mask to see the skull of SS General Ludwig von Berg smiling at him. The fire had gone out of the baron's eyes. Also gone was the *Flammenschwert* warhead, along with the shadow divers. But the divers had left behind something for him: a brick of C4 explosive with a digital display slapped next to the torpedo's open casing.

The numbers read: 2:43 . . . 2:42 . . . 2:41 . . .

On top of the C4 was a metal ball bearing that glowed like a burning ember from hell. It must have been extracted from the *Flammenschwert,* which probably contained thousands of these copperlike pellets inside its core. The bastards were going to verify the design by detonating just one tiny pellet, simulating on a small scale the device's explosive power. In the process, they were going to destroy him and the *Nausicaa*.

Conrad mustered the last of his strength and tried to swim out, but his leg caught on something—the skeletal hand of SS General Ludwig von Berg. The baron, it seemed, wanted to drag him down to hell.

Conrad couldn't break free. The clock was down to 1:33.

Thinking quickly, he grabbed the baron's steel-plated skull with both hands and broke it off the skeleton. Slipping his fingers into the eyeholes as if the skull were a bowling ball, he brought it down on the finger bones clasping his injured leg and smashed them to pieces.

He was free, but his fingers were now stuck like a claw through the skull as another shock wave hit the *Nausicaa*.

The entire forward torpedo bay dropped like a broken table—silt and debris sliding past him to the front, further tipping the submarine over the edge of the Calypso Deep. Conrad's back slammed against the bomb rack, and he saw the compartment hatch and entire fore-aft passageway beyond rising like a great elevator shaft above him.

The *Nausicaa* was about to go down nose-first into the Calypso. Conrad had only seconds left. He positioned himself under the hatch, forcing himself to resist the temptation to panic. He held his body ramrod-straight, like a torpedo, his hands arched together with the skull over his head. Then he closed his eyes as everything collapsed around him.

For a moment he felt like a missile shooting up out of its silo, although he knew it was the silo that was sinking. Then he was clear. He looked down into the Calypso Deep as it swallowed the *Nausicaa* with the tiny pellet from the *Flammenschwert* still inside its belly.

The powerful wake of the plunging sub began to pull him down like a vertical riptide. He knew if he fought it, he'd go down with it. Instead, he made long scissor kicks across the wake and over the rim of the crater, putting as much distance between him and the abyss as possible. There was a flash of light behind him, and the water suddenly heated up.

Conrad looked back over his shoulder in time to see a giant pillar of fire shoot straight up from the depths of the Calypso. The sound of thunder rippled across the deep. Suddenly the flames fanned out and seemed to assume the form of a dragon flying through the water toward him. Conrad started swimming as fast as he could.

He surfaced a minute later into the dim predawn light of day, gasping for breath. Finally, when he was on the verge of passing out again forever, his larynx opened, and he coughed up a little water from his stomach as he desperately inhaled the salty air.

His groan sounded like jet engines in his own ears. He was sure he was experiencing some kind of pulmonary embolism from coming up so fast. Several deep gulps of air cleared his head enough for him to scan the horizon for his boat. But it wasn't there. In the distance loomed the silhouette of a megayacht, its decks stacked like gold bullion in the glint of the rising sun, turning away.

Debris floated around him—the remains of his boat. Poor Stavros, he thought. He swam toward a broken wooden plank to use for flotation. But when he got there, he realized it wasn't wood at all. It was the charred carcass of a bottle-nosed dolphin, burned to a crisp.

The horrific nature of the *Flammenschwert* sank in.

It works. It really turns water to fire.

Conrad stared at the dolphin's blackened rostrum and teeth. He felt some stomach acid rising at the back of his own throat and looked away. All around him were incinerated bottle-nosed dolphins, floating like driftwood across a sea of death.

2

SVALBARD GLOBAL SEED VAULT

SPITSBERGEN ISLAND

ARCTIC CIRCLE

Sister Serena Serghetti clutched the metal box containing African rice seeds to her chest as she walked down a long tunnel blasted out of the arctic mountain. High above her, fluorescent lights flashed on and off as she passed embedded motion detectors. Close behind, a choir of Norwegian schoolchildren held candles in the flickering darkness and sang "Sleep Little Seedling."

Their heavenly voices felt heavy in the freezing air, Serena thought, weighed perhaps by the tunnel's meter-thick walls of reinforced concrete. Or maybe it was her heart that felt so heavy.

The Doomsday Vault, as it was called when it opened in 2008, already housed more than two million seeds representing every variety of the earth's crops. In time it would house a collection of 100 million seeds from more than 140 countries here on this remote island near the North Pole. It had been built to protect the world's food supply against nuclear war, climate change, terrorism, rising sea levels, earthquakes, and the ensuing collapse of power supplies. If worse came to worst, the vault would allow the world to reconstruct agriculture on the planet.

But now the vault itself was in danger. Thanks to global warming, the shrinking ice caps had spurred a new race for oil in the Arctic. It was the next Saudi Arabia, if someone could figure out a way to extract and transport all that oil through a sea of ice. A few years earlier, the Russians had even planted a flag two and a half miles below the ice at the North Pole to claim its oil reserves. Now Serena feared they were preparing to start mining.

She passed through two separate air locks and into the vault itself, blinking into the glare of the TV lights. The Norwegian prime minister was in there somewhere, along with a delegation from the United Nations.

Serena knelt before the TV cameras and prayed silently for the people of the earth. But she was aware of shutters clicking and photographers' boots shuffling for better shots of her.

Whatever happened to finding a secret place to pray, like Jesus taught? she wondered, unable to shake a guilty feeling. Did the world really need to see Mother Earth arrayed in high-definition piety 24/7? As if the prayers of the Vatican's top linguist and environmental czar counted more than those of the anonymous humble field laborer whose hands culled the seeds she now held.

But this was a cause greater than herself and her tormented thirty-three-year-old soul, she reminded herself. And her official purpose here today was to focus the world's attention on its future.

As she knelt, tightly gripping the box of seeds, a feeling of dread came over her. What the vault meant, what it was built for: the time of the end, which the Bible had prophesied would come soon. The words of the prophet Isaiah whispered in her ear: God is the only God. He will draw all people to Himself to see His glory. He will end this world. And he will judge those who reject Him.

Not something TV audiences wanted to hear.

She felt a nagging sense of hypocrisy about her performance. A disturbing thought began to bubble up, a thought she couldn't quite formulate. Her dread began to take shape in the words of Jesus: "If therefore you are offering your gift at the altar, and there remember that your brother has anything against you, leave your gift there before the altar, and go your way. First be reconciled to your brother, and then come and offer your gift."

She didn't understand. She had plenty of people angry with her at the Vatican—for being a woman, for being beautiful, for drawing cameras wherever she went—and that was just within the Church.

Outside, there were the oil and gas companies she chided, and diamond merchants, and the exploiters of children.

But that wasn't what this word from God was about.

Conrad Yeats.

She fought to push his face out of her mind and felt the slightest tremor as her knees pressed against the concrete floor.

That rogue? That liar, cheat, and thief? What could he possibly have against me? Other than I wouldn't sleep with him?

But she couldn't get his face—his handsome unshaved face—out of her mind. Nor could she forget how she had left things in Washington, D.C., a few years back, after he had saved her life. She had promised to leave the Church and be with him forever. Instead she had stolen something priceless out from under him and the U.S. government, leaving him with nothing.

But, Lord, You know it was for Conrad's own good and the greater good.

When she opened her eyes and rose to her feet, she surrendered the box of African rice seeds to the Norwegian prime minister. With solemn fanfare, he opened the box for the cameras, revealing sealed silver packets, each labeled with a special bar code. Then he resealed the box and slid it onto its designated shelf in the vault.

After the ceremony, she went into the main tunnel and found her driver and bodyguard, Benito, waiting for her with her parka. She slipped it on, and they started walking toward the main entrance to the facility.

"Just as you suspected, *signorina*," he told her, handing her a small blue device. "Our divers found it at the bottom of the arctic seabed."

It was a geophone. Oil companies used them to take seismic surveys of the earth's subsurface in search of oil, in this case the earth two miles beneath the ice and water of the North Pole. Her visit to the Doomsday Vault had been a cover for her to meet with divers who could investigate for signs of drilling.

"So someone is planning to mine the bottom of the Arctic," she said, watching her breath freeze as they stood before the facility's dual blastproof doors. Slowly and heavily, the doors opened.

The arctic air slapped Serena in the face as she stepped outside, where a van with tanklike treads was waiting to take her to the island's airport, the northernmost in the world with regular flights. Behind her, the exterior of the Doomsday Vault looked like something out of a science fiction movie, a giant granite wedge protruding from the ice.

The Norwegian island of Spitsbergen had been chosen as the location for the seed vault because it was a remote region with low tectonic activity and an arctic environment that was ideal for preservation. Now oil exploration posed a direct threat to this environment. It would also accelerate global warming's melting of the ice cap, threatening coastal cities around the world.

So why was she thinking of Conrad Yeats?

Something is terribly wrong, she thought. *He's in danger.*

But she couldn't put her finger on why and blamed her gloomy thoughts on the sweeping vista of endless ice and water spread out before her. It brought back memories of her adventure with Conrad in Antarctica years ago.

Benito said, "Our divers say there are thousands of them, maybe even tens of thousands, below us."

Serena realized he was talking about the geophone in her hand. "It will take them at least six months to map all the underground formations," she said. "So we still have some time before they decide where to start drilling. That might give us a chance to stop them."

"The Russians?" Benito asked.

"Maybe." She flipped the geophone over and saw the manufacturer's name: Midas Minerals & Mining LTD. "But I know who can tell us."